THE SHEARINGS

PUBLISHED BY: Federico Iwan

Acknowledgements

I would like to thank my wife, Dr. Cara S. Iwan, for her invaluable assistance with the initial drafts of this book, including her reading, feedback, and editing. I also extend my gratitude to Michael McConnell for his insightful feedback, copy editing, and developmental editing.

To my beloved wife, whose unwavering support and love inspire me every day.

To my parents, whose guidance, values, and sacrifices have shaped me into the person I am today.

And to my grandparents, whose wisdom and values continue to light my path.

Thank you all for your endless encouragement and belief in me. This book is for you.

CHAPTER I

At the foot of the Blue Ridge Mountains, Charlotte and Mari Jones set up camp in their favorite spot, a secluded, quiet place by the lake that seemed like a hidden paradise created just for them. The tall, ancient oaks and hickories formed a lush canopy, their leaves whispering in the gentle breeze, while the soothing sound of nearby creeks and rivers created a serene ambiance. The crystal-clear lake gleamed under the sun, reflecting the vibrant hues of the surrounding landscape, making it an idyllic retreat for the sisters.

They often spent their days exploring the shoreline, their laughter blending with the calls of birds and the rustling of leaves. Mari, curious and smart, was always the first to suggest new adventures, her playful spirit bringing joy to every outing. Her contagious laugh could light up even the darkest moments, and her sweet nature made her the kind of sister that Charlotte felt lucky to have. But today was different. An unsettling feeling tugged at Charlotte. A whisper of unease that she could not ignore.

The air was unusually crisp for a July afternoon, even in the mountains, and fragrant with the scent of pine and wildflowers. The area's rich biodiversity invited adventure, while the lake's calm waters were perfect for casting lines and reeling in the day's catch. This picturesque setting was more than just a camping site; it was a cherished haven where Charlotte and Mari forged unforgettable memories, deepening their bond with each visit. But with Charlotte preparing to embark on an exciting new chapter of her life—heading off to college and pursuing law school—hers was a bittersweet excitement.

"Do you think everything will change when I leave?" Charlotte asked, breaking the comfortable silence surrounding them. Her gaze drifted to the horizon, where the sun dipped low, painting the sky in shades of pink and orange.

Mari, fourteen, looked up from the stones she was skipping across the water. Her bright green eyes sparkled with innocence as she shrugged. "I hope not! But I guess things will be different. You'll be busy with school and new friends."

Charlotte felt a pang in her chest at the thought of leaving her sister behind. She recalled the vibrant campus at Virginia Tech, the sprawling lawns and stately buildings, where students bustled between classes, their laughter and chatter filling the air. It was a world she longed to be a part of, yet the thought of stepping into it alone filled her with a quiet dread.

"I'll always come back, Mari. You know that, right?" she said, forcing a smile despite the tightness in her throat. The decision to attend Virginia Tech had been a difficult one. Still, the visit had solidified her choice—its blend of tradition and innovation resonated with her, offering a sense of belonging she hadn't expected.

"Yeah, I know," Mari replied. But Charlotte could sense the gravity of their unspoken fears. They were both acutely aware of the impending change closing in on them, and the air around them felt heavy with the knowledge that this trip was a farewell to their carefree childhood.

After the last traces of sunlight faded, the moon hung high in the sky, casting a silvery glow over the tranquil lake. Its surface shimmered like glass in the quiet night. The only sounds were the gentle lapping of water against the shore and the distant rustle of leaves in the cool breeze. Yet, a disquieting silence lingered. Charlotte and her younger sister sat by the campfire as the flames flickered, creating a warm halo in the chill air around them. They had spent the evening grilling a few rainbow trout they had caught earlier that day and sharing stories by the fire. The night felt perfect—a peaceful escape from the world, but deep down, Charlotte couldn't shake the feeling that something was lurking just beyond the tree line.

As the fire dwindled to glowing embers, a low, almost imperceptible sound echoed from the woods, a subtle crack that made Charlotte's heart skip a beat. She wrapped her arm around Mari, pulling her close. "Ready to head to the tent?" she asked, glancing at the dark outline of the forest surrounding them, shadows stretching ominously in the flickering light.

"Just a few more minutes!" Mari replied. "I want to hear more about the Virginia Tech campus and your trip to Blacksburg!"

Charlotte smiled, grateful for the opportunity to share her experiences. "It's beautiful, Mari. The campus is like a small city, with students everywhere and many different buildings and places to explore. There's this amazing library, and the sports fields are incredible. I think you'd love the energy there."

"That sounds amazing!" Mari exclaimed. "I can't wait to visit! I've been thinking about what I want to do when I grow up. I really like my biology class, so maybe I could study something related to that? I thought about marine biology, but I don't want to move away from the mountains. Do you think I could use that to protect the lake and places like this? She gestured toward the lake and the trees surrounding them, her passion evident in her voice.

Charlotte smiled, warmed by her sister's enthusiasm. "You'd be great at that, Mari. I can picture you working in the mountains, studying plants and animals, maybe even writing about them." Her voice was low and soothing, but an unsettling feeling crept into her gut. The night was too quiet, the air too still—almost as if the world around them was holding its breath. The silence stretched, heavy and oppressive, and just as she was about to dismiss her instincts, a sudden rustle from the trees shattered the calm.

Charlotte's senses spiked. "What was that?" she whispered, eyes darting toward the trees. Mari leaned closer, her fear evident in her wide eyes.

"I don't know," Mari whispered, her small fingers clutching Charlotte's sleeve. "Maybe it's just an animal … or maybe it's Jack Henry?" Jack Henry, Charlotte's boyfriend, had promised to visit their campsite that day but never showed up, casting a shadow of worry over the night.

Charlotte nodded, forcing a smile to reassure her sister, but the unease settled deeper. "Let's pack up and head to the tent," she suggested, trying to maintain a brave facade. They began to gather their things, but the rustling grew louder and more pronounced as if something—or someone—was approaching.

Before Charlotte could react, a shadowy figure, stark against the backdrop of the night, emerged from the tree line. The flickering firelight revealed his menacing form, and Charlotte's heart dropped. "Run!" she shouted, grabbing Mari's hand. They bolted toward the path leading to the tent, adrenaline fueling their escape as the figure closed in behind them. Their footsteps pounded like thunder in the stillness of the night.

"Charlotte, I can't!" Mari cried, her short legs struggling to keep up. Charlotte glanced back, panic rising in her chest. She could see the figure gaining on them, his intentions clear in the cold glint of his eyes. In a moment of desperation, they sprinted toward a steep hill that led down to the lake's edge. "This way!" Charlotte urged. But as they rushed down the slope, the ground beneath them gave way, and they tumbled uncontrollably down the hill, the world spinning in a blur of darkness and fear. Charlotte reached out for Mari, but the momentum pulled them apart. She could hear Mari's terrified cries fading into the distance as they rolled down the hill, finally coming to a jarring stop at the bottom, surrounded by shadows. The world faded to black.

CHAPTER II

When Charlotte came to, the world felt different—darker, filled with shadows and uncertainty. Dazed and disoriented, Charlotte blinked against the darkness, trying to gather her thoughts. "Mari?" she called out with a trembling voice. But there was no response, only the echo of her own voice in the stillness. As she slowly pushed herself up, she felt nauseous. *How long have I been unconscious? Was I drugged? I don't feel very good,* she thought. The last thing she remembered was the rush of the hill and the fear coursing through her veins. Now, as she looked around, she realized she was in a dimly lit space that felt damp and humid. Panic gripped her heart as she searched for Mari, her eyes beginning to adjust to the shadows around her. She was in a cave. The air was heavy with moisture and an unsettling chill. The only light came from a small crack in the cave wall, casting eerie shadows that danced across the rocky surface.

"Mari!" Charlotte shouted. Her voice echoed in the confined space, and all she heard was the silence that enveloped her. Dread sunk in. They were no longer by the lake, no longer safe. They were trapped, held captive in an unknown place. Charlotte's mind raced as she tried to make sense of what had happened. She took a deep breath, forcing herself to stay calm. She had to find Mari. Driven by determination, Charlotte began to explore the cave. Her heart raced as she ventured deeper into the darkness. She called out for Mari again and again, but no one responded.

As she moved farther into the cave, Charlotte stumbled upon a narrow passageway. The walls were rocky but slick with moisture. She hesitated for a moment before pushing forward. The air grew colder. Then, she heard a faint whimper, a sound so small yet so heart-wrenching. "Mari?" Charlotte called out, her voice trembling. She followed the sound as her heart increasingly pounded in her chest. Emerging into a small alcove, Charlotte's breath caught in her throat. There, huddled against the wall, was Mari. Her sister's face was streaked with dirt, and her clothes were torn, revealing bruises that marred her delicate skin. The sight of her sister, so vulnerable and afraid, shattered Charlotte's heart.

"Mari!" Charlotte rushed forward, embracing her sister in a protective hug. "I'm so sorry. I'm here. You're safe now."

Mari looked up at her sister with tears glistening in her eyes. "Charlotte, he hurt me," she whispered.

The weight of those words sent a wave of rage and sorrow crashing over Charlotte as she held Mari tightly, vowing to protect her from any further harm. As Charlotte cradled her sister, the reality of their situation settled in. They were in captivity, trapped in the darkness of the cave. *We have to get out of here!* Charlotte thought to herself. But before Charlotte could formulate a plan, the sound of footsteps echoed through the cave, sending a chill of fear through both sisters.

A figure emerged from the shadows. A man had spotted the two girls huddled together and was advancing toward them. Charlotte's heart raced as she instinctively pulled Mari closer. "Get away from us!" Charlotte shouted. The captor lunged forward, and chaos erupted as Charlotte shoved Mari behind her, ready to fight. The struggle was intense; Charlotte fought with every ounce of strength, grappling with the captor as Mari scrambled to her feet. In the chaos, Charlotte felt the captor's grip tighten around her wrist, but with a surge of adrenaline, she managed to break free, pushing the figure back. "Run, Mari! Now!" Charlotte shouted. Mari hesitated, but the sound of the captor recovering from the shove propelled her into action. The sisters dashed past the captor, their hearts pounding as they raced down the dark passageway. The sound of their pursuer's angry shouts echoed behind them, driving them forward. They didn't look back until they finally burst out into the open air.

The moonlight flooded over them as they stumbled onto the rocky shore of the river. The water was rushing nearby like a lifeline, a single curtain of overgrown branches and vegetation separating the cavern from the riverbank.

"Keep going!" Charlotte urged, grabbing Mari's hand as they sprinted along the riverbank, the sound of their pursuer's footsteps pounding behind them.

"Charlotte, where do we go?" Mari panted.

"We'll find a place to hide!" Charlotte replied, scanning the area for a hiding place.

As they stood at the river's edge, dread pooled in Charlotte's stomach. The icy water lapped at their feet, sending shivers through their bodies. The current swirled ominously, dark and turbulent, a reminder of the peril they faced. "We can't go back!" she insisted, her voice steady despite the turmoil inside her. "We have to cross!"

In a moment of courage, they leaped into the frigid embrace of the river together. The shock of the cold hit them like a wall, and the world around them transformed into a swirling storm. They fought against the current, the water tugging them in every direction. Charlotte could feel the icy fingers of the river gripping her, pulling her under. "Hold on, Mari!" she yelled, her voice barely rising above the roar of the water. But the river was merciless, and Mari's small frame was quickly overwhelmed by the deep, churning waters.

"Charlotte!" Mari cried, her voice filled with panic as the current swept her farther away.

Desperation surged within Charlotte as she swam with all her might, but the water was a relentless force, dragging Mari farther from her reach. "Swim to me!" Charlotte shouted, but the words felt futile against the chaos surrounding them.

As Mari struggled, Charlotte's heart shattered. She could see her sister's terrified face, and with each heartbeat, the distance between them grew. "No! Mari!" Charlotte screamed, fighting with every ounce of strength to reach her. The river roared, and with a final, haunting scream, Mari was swallowed by the swirling depths, disappearing beneath the surface.

Charlotte's world imploded. Gasping for air, she emerged alone on the riverbank, the moonlight casting an eerie glow on the water. "Mari!" she cried out, her voice cracking, echoing into the void. But there was no answer, only the haunting whisper of the water, a chilling reminder of the bond that had just been torn apart.

CHAPTER III

In the years that followed that fateful night, the echoes of Mari's screams would linger in Charlotte's mind, a darkness that would shape her path forward. As the sun dipped low in the sky, casting a warm golden glow over the expansive fields, Charlotte rode her mustang, Blaze, along the familiar trails that wound through her family's land. With each rhythmic thud of hooves on the earth, she sought solace from the chaos of her thoughts.

Twenty-two years had passed since that fateful night, yet the memories still haunted her like a shadow. Charlotte often found herself replaying the events in her mind, the terror of that moment forever etched in her heart. As a successful lawyer, she had dedicated her life to seeking justice for others, but the specter of her sister's kidnapping and death loomed larger than any case she had ever encountered.

Though she had spent countless hours in the courtroom, fighting for victims, the relentless pursuit of her sister's kidnapper consumed her. She had gathered evidence, interviewed witnesses, and followed leads that often went cold, yet the pain of loss remained a constant companion. Today, however, she needed to clear her mind. The pressure of an upcoming trial weighed heavily on her, and the thought of her sister's unresolved fate gnawed at her heart. With the wind whipping through her hair, Charlotte urged Blaze to pick up speed, hoping the rush of the ride would drown out the noise of her worries.

As they galloped along the trails, memories of Mari flashed before her eyes—laughter in the summer sun, whispered secrets at night, and the bond that had been torn apart too soon. Charlotte felt the familiar ache of grief swell within her, but she pushed it aside, focusing on the rhythm of Blaze's movement beneath her.

Blaze was a striking mustang, a living embodiment of the wild spirit that had run through Charlotte's family for generations. With a chestnut coat that glimmered in the fading light and a flowing mane that danced in the wind, he was more than just a horse; he was a connection to her ancestry. His lineage traced back to a wild mustang traded with her family in the late sixteen hundreds, a reminder of the bravery and resilience that had defined their heritage.

Charlotte often recalled the countless hours her grandfather, Louis Jones, had spent training Blaze, patiently earning his trust with gentle words and soft gestures. This bond of trust mirrored the lessons Louis had imparted—strength lies not only in might but in kindness and patience. He had been a guiding light in her life, teaching Charlotte and Mari to ride horses, fish, and hunt. He had shown her how to plant seeds and nurture them into something beautiful, emphasizing that strength came not just from physical prowess but from determination and kindness.

As Charlotte reminisced about Mari, a flood of memories swirled in her mind. She was thinking about Mari, but she also reflected on who she was and who she had become. Growing up in Floyd, Virginia, between the fifties and sixties, Charlotte's family faced challenges, yet they managed to carve out a comfortable life. She learned to appreciate the small joys in life from a very young age. However, as she grew older, she was drawn to the elegance of class and fashion, influenced by her mother and grandmother.

Initially, Charlotte resented Mari's arrival, fearing the loss of attention. However, it wasn't long before they became inseparable, sharing a love for the outdoors, horseback riding, and fly fishing. She often accompanied her father, William Jones, to his jobs, where he let her play with the farm caretakers' children. Her father instilled in her a deep sense of humility and respect for others regardless of their background, values that shaped her interactions with everyone she met.

Charlotte and Mari shared a special bond with their cousins. Her father's side of the family lived in Virginia, while her mother's side lived in New York. Their relationships were more akin to those of siblings or best friends. Together, they embarked on countless adventures, from hiking and fishing to playing hide and seek among the hay bales, much to the dismay of their father and grandfather when their games resulted in mischief.

Spring was Charlotte's favorite season, not only because it marked her birthday but also because it coincided with sheep shearing and tagging season. Her family and most other farms in the area bred sheep to produce and sell wool. Breeding sheep was not an easy endeavor. It required constant care and attention. Sheep need shearing not only to sell the wool but also to prevent the sheep from becoming sick or even dying. Overgrown wool often leads to overheating, mobility issues, and an increased risk of parasitic infections. Shearing each spring helps maintain their overall hygiene and well-being.

Shearing hundreds of sheep at a time was not a small undertaking. It required coordination and manpower to herd them all and lead them into the sheep yard. Once in the sheep yard, farmers made the most of it and performed other tasks also necessary to breed and commercialize wool or sheep in general. Following shearing, which typically occurs in early spring, tagging, castration, tail docking, and vaccinations were common practices.

Castration on the male lambs helps manage their behavior and reduces aggression. It also improves the quality of the meat. Vaccinations and parasite control prevent common diseases and improve productivity. Tail docking or tail removal also helps with the general well-being of the sheep because it reduces the risk of flystrike or maggot infestations.

The farm buzzed with activity as shearing crews arrived from across the state, transforming the farm into a hub of celebration and camaraderie. Charlotte relished the feeling of being the center of attention, as her birthday often marked the grand finale of the shearing activities. The last day of shearing involved a large gathering where farmers and shearing crews got together in celebration. Meats were cooked in open fire, and after tagging, even the lamb tails were cooked directly in the blistering charcoal. Roasted lamb tails were always the children's favorite treat.

Despite the challenges she faced, Charlotte never saw herself as a victim. She understood that hardship was an integral part of life, a lesson she learned from her father. He encouraged her to defend herself when necessary but always to seek peaceful resolutions where possible. Her mother, Victoria, instilled in her the importance of faith, guiding her with Bible teachings and the principles of compassion. These teachings helped Charlotte to navigate life's trials, reminding her to approach each situation with understanding and grace.

Mari's untimely death left an indelible mark on Charlotte, deepening her resolve to live a life of purpose and strength. While others urged her to take time off to grieve, Charlotte chose to forge ahead, believing that Mari would want her to pursue her dreams. She enrolled at Virginia Tech, majoring in biological sciences, with aspirations of becoming a patent attorney. Her dedication and work ethic carried her through, balancing academics with volunteering and part-time jobs to support herself.

Her journey continued at William & Mary Law School, where she faced whispers of privilege and wealth due to her refined appearance. However, few knew the hard work that had brought her to where she was. Her parents had saved diligently for her education, instilling in her the belief that everything worth having must be earned through effort and dedication. Their expectation was for her to return the loan, which she started paying back after she graduated.

Ironically, the class she initially disliked, criminal law, became a passion, thanks to the guidance of her professor, Mr. Byrd. His rigorous teaching challenged her, ultimately leading to her excelling in the subject and finding her true calling in the United States Attorney's office. Her experiences shaped her into a dedicated attorney, driven by a desire for justice, further fueled by the memory of Mari.

Charlotte's life was a testament to the values her family instilled in her: hard work, respect, and resilience. Her journey from Floyd to law school and beyond was marked by growth and the unwavering support of her loved ones. She understood that everyone has a story deserving of respect and that life's worth is measured by the challenges one overcomes.

The path led to a secluded clearing, a place where Louis used to bring Charlotte and Mari as children. Dismounting, she tied Blaze to a nearby tree to graze and took a deep breath, allowing the memories to wash over her. As she stood there, Charlotte's thoughts turned to her grandpa, who had been a guiding light in her life. Among the many lessons he'd imparted, one stood out vividly in her memory. On her eighteenth birthday, in that same secluded clearing, Louis had gifted her a beautifully designed rifle, its wood polished to a rich sheen and adorned with intricate engravings. "This isn't just a tool, Charlotte," he had said, placing it in her hands. "It's a symbol of your strength and your responsibility. Use it wisely." His patience had guided her as she learned to aim and fire, a skill that filled her with a sense of empowerment. In her mind, she could see him standing tall, his weathered hands demonstrating how to wield the rifle, his voice gentle yet firm as he encouraged her to embrace challenges. "You have the strength within you, Charlotte," he would say, his eyes twinkling with pride. "Remember, it's not about how many times you fall; it's about how many times you get back up."

Charlotte and Mari's grandfather was a tall, broad-shouldered man with a commanding presence. His tousled blond hair, streaked with silver, framed a face marked by deep blue eyes that sparkled with wisdom and warmth. He was a man of few words, but when he spoke, his voice carried a calming authority. Smart and hardworking, he dedicated his life to the family farm, where he raised cattle, sheep, and horses. His hands, worn and calloused from years of toil, told the story of a humble man who found joy in the earth and its creatures.

Alongside his beloved wife Ann, their grandmother, he had raised Charlotte's and Mari's father, William, along with three other children. He treated Charlotte and Mari as if they were his own daughters, stepping into a nurturing role while their dad was busy with work. He was sometimes hard on them but always fair, believing in the value of hard work and instilling this belief in the girls from a young age. They helped with chores around the farm, learning the importance of responsibility and teamwork. Mornings were spent feeding the animals, while afternoons found them in the garden, assisting their grandmother with the vibrant flowers and vegetables that thrived under her care. In the kitchen, their grandfather would share his culinary secrets, teaching them how to prepare hearty meals that celebrated the fruits of their labor. His stews, made with carefully cubed beef, delicious seasoning, and rice cooked to perfection, were a staple at the farm.

Beyond the farm, their grandfather held a PhD in agricultural engineering. His academic accomplishments led him to travel the world, teaching at prestigious universities in England, Wales, and Australia. He had a keen mind and a passion for sustainable farming practices, which he shared with students eager to learn. Yet no matter where he roamed, his heart remained in Virginia. He returned to the farm every time, bringing with him stories of distant lands and new ideas. Through it all, he remained grounded, teaching Charlotte and Mari not just about farming but about life, honesty, and humility. He was the backbone of their family, a guiding force who shaped their values and inspired their dreams.

As Charlotte stood in the clearing, the echoes of her grandfather's teachings lingered in the air, a comforting presence amidst her swirling thoughts. But then, suddenly, the sound of a breaking branch snapped her back to reality. Charlotte scanned the area, instinctively reaching for her rifle. It was a small fawn with its mother, slowly making their way through the bushes. She watched them walk by, her heart still pounding hard, as she thought of her dual life—one as a lawyer, tirelessly pursuing justice, and the other as a sister, forever seeking closure.

Sitting on a fallen log, Charlotte pulled out her notebook, filled with her thoughts and leads. She began to jot down notes, her focus sharpening as she considered new angles to explore. The clearing, once a place of joy, now served as a sanctuary for her resolve. It was here, among the trees and the whispers of the wind, that she reaffirmed her commitment to finding her sister's kidnapper. Charlotte was not just a lawyer; she was a warrior fighting for the truth. The teachings of her grandpa echoed in her mind, reminding her that strength was not just about physicality but about the courage to face her fears and humbleness to accept her mistakes.

The ride had cleared her mind, allowing her to see the path ahead. She would continue to dig deeper, to follow every lead, and to ensure that Mari's story would not remain shrouded in silence.

CHAPTER IV

As the sun began to set, casting long shadows across the clearing, Charlotte mounted Blaze once more. She rode back toward the horizon with her heart filled with renewed purpose. The journey ahead would be challenging, but she was ready to face it head-on, fueled by love, loss, and an unyielding desire for justice—a legacy passed down from her grandpa intertwined with her sister's memory.

As Charlotte rode back to the barn, the cool November air brushed against her cheeks, a crisp reminder that night had already fallen by five p.m. She dismounted Blaze with practiced grace, feeling the familiar sense of completion that came with a satisfying ride. Leading him inside, she took a moment to appreciate the tranquility of the barn—the earthy scent of hay mingled with the faint musk of horses, creating a comforting atmosphere that welcomed her home.

After securing Blaze in his stall, Charlotte began the ritual of removing the saddle. The saddle was a beautiful piece, its rich brown leather gleaming softly in the dim light of the barn. The supple leather was intricately tooled with floral designs, a testament to the craftsmanship that went into creating it. The stirrups, crafted from sturdy metal, hung gracefully at the sides, while the cinch straps were thick and robust, ensuring a secure fit against Blaze's powerful body. Charlotte carefully removed the saddle blanket, noting how the fabric was patterned with vibrant colors that reflected her family's history. Each piece of riding equipment was meticulously cared for, a habit instilled in her by her grandfather's unwavering attention to detail.

Charlotte led a freshly brushed Blaze out to the paddock, reflecting on the lessons her grandpa had instilled in her. He had taught her the importance of properly saddling up the horse, ensuring that every strap was secured and every inch was polished. He also emphasized putting everything away neatly after each ride, never leaving without feeding the horses, and ensuring they always had water. A lesson that had become second nature to Charlotte. As she arranged the saddle and its accessories alongside the others, she felt a swell of gratitude for the time they had spent together, learning the nuances of horse care and riding.

Just as she finished tidying up, Charlotte heard her grandma, Ann, calling her name from the house. "Charlotte, is that you? Come have your tea!" The invitation drifted through the barn, wrapped in the inviting aroma of freshly baked bread.

With a smile, Charlotte made her way to the house, crossing the threshold into the warm embrace of the kitchen. The house was primarily constructed of wood, its rustic charm evident in the old floors that creaked softly underfoot with each step. The walls were adorned with decorations, souvenirs from her grandpa's travels, and hung diplomas that spoke to his accomplishments. Built-in bookcases lined several walls, filled with hundreds of books, their spines offering a glimpse into countless stories and histories.

The living room was anchored by a beautiful fireplace, its mantel adorned with family photographs—some old, some newer—capturing moments of joy and togetherness. The fireplace radiated warmth and added to the coziness of the house, making it an inviting family home. Accent tables and chests were sprinkled throughout the room, each topped with treasured pictures of uncles, aunts, and cousins, further enriching the sense of family that permeated the space.

The tea table also used for family dinners, was strategically placed next to oversized windows that overlooked the serene lake and the majestic mountains beyond. The view was breathtaking, especially at sunset when the colors danced across the water.

Charlotte felt a swell of affection as she took in the surroundings. The house wasn't fancy, but it was beautiful and comfortable for family and guests, embodying the warmth of their shared history.

As she stepped farther into the kitchen, the table was beautifully set for tea, a cherished custom of their Welsh heritage. Grandma believed that teatime was sacred, and she was determined to make sure Charlotte was well-fed. The polished oak table gleamed under the soft glow of the hanging lamp. Delicate china with floral motifs adorned the table, each piece carefully arranged. The teapot, with its colorful hood, stood proudly at the center, a vibrant contrast to the elegant white and blue patterns of the dishes that surrounded it.

Charlotte's stomach grumbled at the sight of freshly made scones, golden and flaky, waiting to be slathered with homemade butter and elderberry jam. Nearby, a juicy raspberry pie sat temptingly, its crust perfectly baked to a warm golden brown. But it was the sight of the freshly baked German beer bread that made her heart swell with nostalgia. Her grandma had learned the recipe from her friend Irma, a fellow widow who lived on the neighboring farm. Irma spent her days baking pies and loaves of bread to sell at the local market, and her German beer bread had become a staple in their household. Charlotte had adored the soft, hearty texture of the bread since she was little, and Mari had shared that affection.

The family had a tradition of having tea around five p.m. and a late dinner, a habit rooted in their farming lifestyle. During the summer, they made the most of the sunlight, working the fields until dusk. When the sun finally set, they gathered for dinner, embracing the warmth of family after a long day.

Charlotte's grandma, Ann, was a remarkable woman, standing at just four feet eight inches but possessing a strong build that commanded respect. Her Spanish descent was evident in her darker skin tone, warm brown eyes, and dark hair that she often wore pulled back in a neat bun. She always donned nice, warm sweaters, frequently topped with an apron, ready for the bountiful meals she prepared. To keep her feet warm inside the house, she wore fluffy slippers made from sheep's wool, a small comfort that added to the cozy atmosphere.

Though tough and often intimidating—even to men— Grandma was also a pillar of sweetness. There was an undeniable strength in her demeanor, and Charlotte often thought that maybe even Grandpa was secretly scared of her. Firm with her rules and strict with the grandchildren, including Charlotte and Mari, Grandma had also been strict with her own children, although William, Charlotte's father, would often jest that she was not as hard on Charlotte and Mari. "That's because you were wild little devils when you were kids!" Grandma would respond with a twinkle in her eye, her tone both teasing and affectionate—but also with some truth to it.

The third spot at the table was set for Grandma's friend Irma, who frequently joined them for tea. Irma was just as warm and welcoming, often adding a touch of humor to their gatherings. Grandma was very well-mannered, ensuring that everyone at the table upheld good table manners, but she was also funny, known for her sarcastic remarks that kept everyone entertained. Charlotte felt a warm sense of belonging swell within her as she took her seat, surrounded by the love and care that infused every moment spent in her grandmother's home.

As Charlotte settled into her chair at the table, she felt the warmth of the fireplace wrapping around her like a comforting blanket. The aroma of freshly baked treats filled the air, and she couldn't help but smile at the sight of her grandma bustling around, pouring steaming tea into delicate china cups. The soft clinking of the cups against their saucers was a soothing melody, mingling with the crackling of the fire.

"Here you go, dear," Grandma Ann said warmly, placing a cup in front of Charlotte with a flourish. "The milk is over there if you'd like any. Would you like any sugar?"

Charlotte shook her head with a smile. "No, thank you, Grandma. I don't need any sugar. Milk is enough for me."

Grandma Ann nodded approvingly. "Of course. You don't want to ruin that figure of yours," she teased gently.

Charlotte chuckled softly. "Of course, Grandma. You know me too well."

Irma, seated across from them, raised an eyebrow. "I don't care about that. Pass the sugar. The more, the better!"

"Exactly!" Grandma Ann laughed. "At our age, we only care about the taste. The sweeter, the better!"

As they settled into the comforting routine of teatime, Grandma's expression shifted slightly. "You know, I heard that Jack Henry has moved back to town," she said, her voice casual but probing.

Charlotte's heart skipped a beat at the mention of his name. "Jack Henry?" she echoed, trying to keep her tone neutral.

"Yes, dear. You remember him, don't you? Your boyfriend back when... well, you know." Grandma's gaze softened.

Irma leaned in, curious. "Who is this Jack Henry?"

"He was Charlotte's boyfriend around the time of Mari's kidnapping," Grandma explained. "They were quite close, and he was supposed to visit the girls at the campsite that night."

Charlotte felt a lump form in her throat. "He never came," she said quietly. "And then he became a suspect. The police interrogated him for days."

Irma frowned. "That sounds awful. What happened between you two?"

Charlotte took a deep breath, memories flooding back. "After everything… we started to drift apart. I couldn't handle the weight of it all. The thought of Jack Henry potentially being the one responsible for what happened to Mari—I just didn't know what to think of him anymore. He was cleared as a suspect, but I could not look at him the same way anymore. It ended in a breakup and a falling out. We haven't spoken since."

Grandma reached out, placing a comforting hand over Charlotte's. "I know that was hard for you, dear. But I heard that Jack Henry's wife has left him, and that's why he's moved back. Perhaps this is an opportunity to reconnect?"

Charlotte shook her head firmly. "I have no interest in that, Grandma. The truth is, I'm still investigating Mari's kidnapping, and in my eyes, he's still a suspect. I think he was somehow involved."

Irma looked between the two, sensing the weight of the conversation. "You really think he's still a suspect? Do you think he knows more than he let on?"

Charlotte nodded. "That's what worries me. I can't shake the feeling that he might be the right suspect who just got away. Or at least one suspect. I mean, he was supposed to be there, and then he wasn't. He never had a good explanation for it."

Grandma squeezed her hand gently. "He was thoroughly investigated, Charlotte. He didn't do it. You need to let that one go. Besides, remember that life has a way of bringing people back together when they need it most."

Charlotte sighed. "Perhaps. But I live in D.C. now. I've built a career from this pain, but the investigation weighs on me. I need to find answers, and I don't think talking to him would help that process."

The room fell quiet for a moment, the only sounds being the crackling of the fire and the gentle rustle of the trees in the wind. Charlotte's mind raced with thoughts of Jack Henry— his warm smile, the laughter they shared, and the way he had once made her feel safe. But the shadows of the past loomed large, reminding her of the heartache that followed. *Could he really be innocent? Or was it just easier to think of him that way?* The memories felt like a double-edged sword, cutting deep with both nostalgia and pain.

Irma, trying to lighten the mood, broke the silence. "Well, whether you reach out or not, at least you have our lovely tea to enjoy! And these delicious scones! You're missing out if you don't dig in."

Charlotte managed a small smile, grateful for Irma's attempt to shift the atmosphere. "You're right. I should focus on the present."

As they continued their tea, Charlotte felt the warmth of family and friendship enveloping her. Despite the unresolved questions about Jack Henry, she knew that her grandma and Irma would be there to support her, no matter what path she chose. Yet, the thought of Jack Henry lingered, a constant reminder that closure was still just out of reach.

After finishing her tea and savoring the last bite of a scone, Charlotte glanced at the clock on the wall. Time had slipped away more quickly than she realized, and she needed to start preparing for her drive back home. The thought of the two-and-a-half-hour journey loomed in her mind, especially with court scheduled for Monday morning. She stood up, ready to gather her things, but Grandma Ann looked at her with a knowing smile. "Why don't you stay the night, dear? It's getting late, and you'll be much safer driving in the morning light. We can have breakfast together!"

The warmth in her grandma's brown eyes was hard to resist, and after a moment's hesitation, Charlotte felt the tension in her shoulders ease. "All right, Grandma," she replied, a smile creeping onto her face. "I'll stay the night." The decision brought her a sense of comfort, knowing she could enjoy more time in the cozy embrace of her grandmother's home before facing the challenges of the week ahead.

CHAPTER V

After the warmth of teatime at Ann's house, where Irma's presence added a sprinkle of humor and camaraderie, it was easy to see why she was cherished by those around her. Her laughter filled the room, and her stories painted vivid pictures of a life marked by resilience and love. As Charlotte watched Irma interact with Grandma Ann, she found herself reflecting on the remarkable woman who had become such an integral part of their family's tapestry.

Irma was more than just a neighbor; she was a beacon of warmth and resilience, a woman whose presence brought comfort and joy to those around her. Her life had been touched by both love and loss, yet she carried herself with grace and a quiet strength that inspired those who knew her. Widowed during World War II, she had raised her son, David, with unwavering dedication, instilling in him the values of kindness and perseverance.

Much like Charlotte's grandparents, Irma's farm was a testament to her hard work and love for the land. The farmhouse was a charming structure. Its wooden facade was painted a soft yellow that stood out against the rolling green hills. A wrap-around porch offered a welcoming space to sit and enjoy the view, adorned with hanging baskets of vibrant flowers that Irma tended with care. The barn, a sturdy red building nestled in the back, housed her beloved horses, their gentle whinnies a familiar melody that resonated around the farm.

Irma's son David lived on an adjoining piece of land, a farm he had inherited from his father. Physically, he bore the hallmarks of his German ancestry—tall and broad-shouldered, with a strong jawline and deep-set, thoughtful eyes. His demeanor was gentle yet commanding, a reflection of his mother's nurturing influence. David and his wife, Aiyana, had tried for years to have children, but instead, they found joy in their thirteen dogs, each one a cherished member of their family. The dogs were a lively bunch, their antics bringing laughter and companionship to the farm. They ranged in breed and size—from a playful Golden Retriever to a dignified German Shepherd—and were known for their loyalty and intelligence, often accompanying David and Aiyana as they worked the land.

Irma and Ann, Charlotte's grandmother, shared a bond that had deepened over the years, particularly after the passing of their respective husbands. They were kindred spirits, united by their love for fresh produce and the art of baking. Irma's kitchen was a haven of delicious aromas, her famous German beer bread and pies a staple at the local market. The kitchen was a cozy space, filled with the warmth of a crackling fire and the clatter of baking tins, each surface adorned with jars of homemade preserves and neatly stacked cookbooks.

Despite the years that had passed, Irma remained strong and active, her days filled with the tasks of farm life. She rode her tractor with pride, tended to her chickens with care, and collected eggs daily, each task a testament to her enduring spirit. Her connection to the land was profound, and she found solace in its rhythms, each season bringing new challenges and rewards.

David visited Irma daily, ensuring she was well and lending a hand when needed. His love for his mother was evident in the way he spoke of her, his admiration and respect unwavering. Aiyana, too, shared a close relationship with Irma, though it was different from the bond between Ann and Victoria. Irma had always admired Victoria, particularly the way she and Ann shared a unique connection—a friendship that transcended the traditional mother-in-law and daughter-in-law dynamic. Irma strived to replicate that bond with Aiyana, and while their relationship was filled with warmth and mutual respect, it lacked the same depth.

Irma's connection to Charlotte's family extended beyond friendship; she had been a source of support during the darkest times. After Mari's tragic death, Irma had been a constant presence, offering comfort and understanding. Her bond with Mari had been special, the two often spending Sunday afternoons baking together in Ann's kitchen, their laughter echoing through the house. Irma cherished those memories, holding them close to her heart as a reminder of the love and joy Mari had brought into their lives.

Irma was short but strong, her frame hinting at the resilience that defined her. She often joked that she was a quarter of an inch taller than Ann, a playful rivalry that never failed to elicit laughter. Her German heritage was evident in her cooking, each dish a celebration of tradition and flavor, from hearty stews to delicate pastries.

Irma's life was a tapestry woven with love, friendship, and resilience. Her presence was a balm to those around her, a reminder that even in the face of adversity, one could find strength and joy. Her farm was a sanctuary, a place where the past and present intertwined, and where the bonds of family and friendship were nurtured and celebrated.

In moments of reflection, Irma often thought of how fate had intertwined her life with those around her. She remembered the early days when David had harbored a crush on Victoria, a secret she had kept with a knowing smile. Though David had found his own true love in Aiyana, the memory of those youthful feelings brought warmth to Irma's heart, a reminder of the enduring connections that life wove.

CHAPTER VI

Charlotte stood alone in her office, looking out the window of her elegant apartment in Washington, D.C., characterized by its French architectural design. The high ceilings, ornate moldings, and tall windows created an airy atmosphere, allowing the morning light to flood the space. Elegant furniture, upholstered in soft fabrics and rich colors, complemented the architecture beautifully, while carefully curated artwork adorned the walls, each piece a reflection of her refined taste. Her apartment was in the center of the historic district of Georgetown, a neighborhood in Washington, D.C., renowned for its rich history and charming architecture. In the 1980s, Georgetown was a vibrant blend of old-world charm and modern vitality. The streets were lined with Federal-style townhouses, their brick facades and elegant columns harking back to the early days of the nation's capital. These buildings bore witness to the city's evolution, with some dating back to the eighteenth century. The neighborhood was a tapestry of cobblestone streets and tree-lined avenues, where history whispered from every corner. High-end boutiques, quaint cafés, and bustling markets infused the area with a lively energy. The C&O Canal, a remnant of the city's industrial past, added a serene touch to the bustling urban landscape. Living in Georgetown, Charlotte was surrounded by a community that cherished its history while embracing the modern pace of city life. This unique blend of past and present resonated with her own journey, serving as a constant reminder of the legacy she was building in her legal career.

Today was a pivotal day—a significant trial that could define her career as a United States attorney—and she felt the familiar surge of anticipation mixed with nerves. Her heart raced as she thought about the lives at stake, particularly the family of the little girl she was fighting for.

As she moved to her bedroom, she took a moment to admire her reflection in the full-length mirror. Charlotte was a vision of elegance and poise. Her blonde hair fell in soft waves past her shoulders, framing her striking blue eyes that sparkled with determination. At forty years old, she looked just as vibrant as she had at eighteen, with only a few laugh lines around her eyes to mark the passage of time, each a testament to the joy she had experienced.

She slipped out of her comfortable loungewear and began to prepare for the day ahead. First, she chose a tailored navy-blue blazer that fit snugly at the waist, accentuating her figure while providing a polished look. The fabric was high-quality wool, lending an air of sophistication to her ensemble. Underneath, she wore a crisp white blouse with delicate lace detailing at the collar, adding a touch of femininity without being overly distracting.

Charlotte paired the blazer with tailored trousers that matched perfectly, creating a streamlined silhouette that exuded confidence. Now in the eighties, it was relatively uncommon for women to wear trousers to court, but Charlotte was not afraid to break the norm. The fabric flowed gracefully as she moved, and the color highlighted her complexion beautifully, enhancing her long legs. She completed the outfit with classic black pumps that added just the right amount of height, making her feel powerful and poised.

As she adorned herself with jewelry, Charlotte chose simplicity and elegance. A pair of pearl stud earrings glimmered softly against her skin, while a delicate silver bracelet adorned her wrist—both pieces understated yet undeniably classy. She avoided anything too flashy or extravagant; after all, she was in court, where professionalism reigned supreme.

Looking at herself in the mirror, she admired how her mother's influence shaped her sense of style. Growing up, her mother had been a paragon of grace and sophistication, having spent her formative years in the city. Even after moving to a small town in the country, she never lost her flair for fashion, teaching Charlotte the importance of dressing well and carrying oneself with dignity. Those lessons had woven themselves into the fabric of Charlotte's identity, shaping her into the woman she had become.

Thoughts of the family she was representing filled her mind, their hope resting on her shoulders. She felt ready. She felt powerful. She was determined to make her mark in the courtroom, just as her mother had instilled in her all those years ago. Today, she would not only represent the law but also honor the legacy of elegance and strength that her mother had passed down to her.

Her thoughts drifted back to the moment she first laid eyes on this bright, airy apartment—a bright, airy space with French architectural charm, high ceilings, and tall windows that invited the city's energy inside. She had felt an immediate connection, knowing it was meant to be her sanctuary amidst the chaos of her work as a United States attorney.

The opportunity to own such a beautiful place came unexpectedly, a stroke of luck intertwined with years of hard work. Charlotte recalled the invention she had developed with her college friend—a groundbreaking artificial insemination technique for sheep. It had been a passion project rooted in her family's farming background, and they had utilized it on her grandparents' farm with great success. Eventually, the invention's intellectual property rights were sold, providing

Charlotte with the financial means to purchase her dream apartment. She had opted to sell her share to her business partner in exchange for royalties, allowing her to focus on her burgeoning legal career.

When she first visited the building, she met Alfred, the concierge. A kind, protective figure, Alfred reminded her of a paternal presence she had missed since her grandfather's passing. At sixty-eight, he was meticulous in his duties, ensuring the marble floors gleamed and the windows sparkled. But it was his genuine care for the residents that endeared him to Charlotte. He always greeted her with a warm smile, ready with coffee on mornings when she had court, and took meticulous care of her mail and packages.

Charlotte cherished their morning exchanges. Even if she was running late, she would always take a moment to inquire about Alfred's family or listen to his stories about his wife. Their friendship was genuine, a comforting constant in her life. On holidays, Charlotte made it a point to show her appreciation, gifting Alfred and his wife Christmas cards, baskets, and other presents. She often helped him decorate the building, finding solace in the simple act of hanging garlands and adorning the lobby with festive cheer.

Alfred had a soft spot for the building's children. He was always ready with candy or chocolates that brought smiles to their faces. His kindness extended to all, but Charlotte knew she held a special place in his heart. He had been a quiet source of support, aware of her sister Mari's story, offering comfort in subtle ways only someone who truly cared could.

Sitting in her apartment now, Charlotte felt a profound sense of gratitude for the community that surrounded her, grounded by the connections she had fostered and the memories she continued to create within these walls.

As she admired her reflection, a man's voice behind her broke the moment. "You are going to do great."

Charlotte turned slightly, catching his reflection in the mirror. With a confident and snarky smile, she replied, "I know."

"Don't forget to lock the door on your way out," she added, a playful glint in her eye.

With that, she grabbed her coat and her briefcase and made her way to the door, casting one last glance at her reflection. She was proud of the woman she had become—graceful like her mother, but fiercely her own. Today was just one more step in her journey, and she intended to make it count.

As she stepped out into the hall, she was greeted by Alfred, being as attentive as always. His eyes twinkled with a knowing amusement as he handed her a freshly brewed cup of coffee. "Running late again, Miss Charlotte?" he teased.

Charlotte chuckled, accepting the coffee gratefully. "You know me too well, Alfred," she replied, taking a sip of the rich brew.

Alfred leaned in, a conspiratorial smile on his lips. "And tell your friend to be careful with that door. It's tricky," he said with a wink.

Charlotte laughed, shaking her head. "I'll pass along the message," she promised. As she walked toward the main entrance, she considered the challenges that lay ahead. With each step, the reality of the trial grew more prominent, reminding her that today was not going to be easy. With that thought in mind, she stepped out into the bustling streets of D.C., the early morning air was crisp, and the sun had just begun to peek over the horizon. The courtroom awaited her, quiet and peaceful, a stark contrast to the energy of the city outside.

CHAPTER VII

Inside, the rich, dark wood of the paneling exuded a sense of history and gravitas. The polished floors gleamed under the soft light filtering through the tall windows, casting gentle shadows that danced across the room. The high ceilings, adorned with intricate moldings, seemed to lift her spirits, while the soft scent of old books and polished wood filled the air, mingling with a hint of fresh coffee from the nearby café. The walls were lined with portraits of esteemed judges and legal figures, their solemn expressions watching over the space as if to remind her of the weight of justice that rested upon her shoulders. The deep burgundy and gold accents of the decor added a touch of elegance, and the large, arched windows offered a view of the awakening city, where the promise of a new day awaited.

Charlotte took a moment to absorb the atmosphere. Each step deeper into the courtroom reminded her of the responsibility she bore for those who had suffered. With a confident stride, she moved farther down the aisle, ready to face the challenges that awaited her.

As she approached her desk, the weight of the case she had spent months preparing settled over her. This wasn't just any trial; it was a case that had captivated the nation, stirring outrage and sorrow across the country. It all began with the tragic disappearance of a young girl named Kaya, who had been taken from her own home's backyard in broad daylight. Despite the frantic search efforts by local authorities and her devastated family, Kaya's fate had ended in heart-wrenching tragedy—she had been kidnapped, molested, and ultimately killed.

The news of her abduction had sent shockwaves through the community, igniting a wave of fear among parents and sparking a widespread outcry for justice. Kaya's family was devastated. For Charlotte, this case had become personal. Over the past several months, she had immersed herself in the details, collecting evidence, interviewing witnesses, and meeting with Kaya's family to offer them support during this harrowing time.

As she prepared for trial, Charlotte learned that Kaya was not the only child to go missing in the area. A series of disappearances had haunted the community, with several families left in anguish as their children were taken without a trace. However, Kaya was the only victim whose remains had been found, and her case had become a focal point for all the families who had suffered similar losses. They looked to Charlotte not just as a United States attorney but as a beacon of hope, believing that if anyone could bring justice, it was her.

The primary suspect in the case was a man named Mark Reynolds, a local resident with a troubling history. He had been linked to multiple unsolved cases of child abductions, but the evidence against him had always been circumstantial—until now. Charlotte had worked tirelessly to build a case against him, knowing that the only solid evidence she had was tied to Kaya's murder. To secure a conviction, she needed definitive proof, such as DNA evidence, eyewitness testimonies, and a clear timeline of Reynolds's whereabouts on the day Kaya disappeared. These elements were crucial, as the burden of proof rested on the prosecution to establish beyond a reasonable doubt that he was responsible for Kaya's death.

However, the challenges were significant. Many of the witnesses were hesitant to come forward, fearing retaliation or simply overwhelmed by their trauma. Additionally, the forensic evidence, while compelling, was complex and required expert testimony to interpret. Charlotte knew that each piece of evidence had to be meticulously presented to create a compelling narrative for the jury, as any gaps or inconsistencies could lead to reasonable doubt. It was a challenging position, as many believed Reynolds was responsible for the other disappearances as well, but the court needed definitive proof to convict him for Kaya's death.

In the weeks leading up to the trial, Charlotte had poured over every detail, piecing together a timeline of events and gathering testimonies from anyone who had encountered Reynolds during the critical time of Kaya's disappearance. Each interview was a reminder of the pain endured by the families affected by these tragedies. She had met with Kaya's parents, had seen their anguish etched into their faces, and had vowed to do everything in her power to seek justice for their daughter.

As the trial date approached, the media frenzy intensified, with news outlets covering every development. The public's outcry for justice had reached a fever pitch, and Charlotte felt the pressure mounting. She knew that this case was not just about Kaya; it represented a struggle for all the families who had lost their children, a chance for closure, and a fight against the darkness that had cast a shadow over their lives. The stakes were high, and she knew that the eyes of the nation were upon her. But she was ready.

With the judge taking his seat and the courtroom settling into a hush, Charlotte was ready to begin her opening statement. She was prepared to lay bare the truth, to honor Kaya's memory, and to fight for the justice that the families so desperately needed.

"Ladies and gentlemen of the jury, today, we gather in this courtroom to confront a tragedy that has shaken our community to its core. We are here to seek justice for a young girl named Kaya, whose laughter was silenced far too soon and whose dreams were stolen in broad daylight. Kaya was only eight years old—a daughter, a sister, a friend—full of life and hope. She was a child who deserved the safety and love of her family, yet instead, she became a victim of a horrific crime that no parent should ever have to endure."

"Kaya was a radiant child, her beauty a reflection of her vibrant spirit. Her skin glowed with a warm, rich hue that seemed to capture the light of the sun. Her large, expressive brown eyes sparkled with curiosity and joy, revealing a depth of emotion that could instantly draw you in. Kaya's long, flowing black hair cascaded like a waterfall down her back, often adorned with colorful clips that showcased her playful personality. She had a smile that could brighten the darkest of days, and her laughter was a melody that echoed through the hearts of those who loved her."

"On that fateful day, Kaya was playing in her own backyard, a place filled with the laughter of children and the beauty of nature. The sun shone brightly, the birds chirped cheerfully, and the trees formed a comforting embrace around her as she played among the shadows. But in an instant, that safety was shattered. In a place where she should have felt secure, Kaya was taken, her innocence stolen from her, her family, and her community." Charlotte paused to take a drink of water.

"Imagine, for a moment, the unimaginable pain of losing a child. Picture the heartache of a mother whose arms ache to hold her little girl again, to hear her voice, to share in her laughter. This is the reality that Kaya's family faces every day. They are not just grieving a loss; they are living with the torment of unanswered questions and a profound sense of injustice."

"As we navigate through this trial, I ask you to remember that Kaya is not just a name on a case file. She is a child whose life was cut short, whose story deserves to be heard, and whose family deserves closure."

"You will hear evidence that clearly connects the defendant, Mark Reynolds, to Kaya's tragic fate. You will hear testimony from witnesses who saw him lurking near her home on that day, each account piecing together a timeline that cannot be ignored. You will learn about the forensic evidence that links him to this crime, the physical traces that tell a story of violence and sick propensities."

"The evidence may be difficult to hear, but it is essential. It paints a picture of a man who has repeatedly crossed the line, a man who has preyed upon the innocence of children in our community. The evidence will show that Kaya's disappearance was not an isolated incident but part of a disturbing pattern, one that has left many families in anguish, searching for answers."

"Today, we stand not only for Kaya but for all the children who have gone missing, for the families who have lived in fear, and for a community that has demanded justice. The evidence will demonstrate that the defendant is responsible for this heart-wrenching crime, and it is your duty to ensure that accountability is upheld."

"As you listen to the testimony and examine the evidence, I urge you to remember the real impact of this tragedy. The weight of your decision carries the hopes of a grieving family. A family that will never again see Kaya's beautiful, expressive brown eyes. A family that will never again see Kaya's smile or hear her infectious laughter—a family forever marked by the loss of a bright and innocent spirit."

"Together, we can honor Kaya's memory and ensure that her story does not end here. I ask you to return a guilty verdict, to deliver the justice that she and her family so desperately need. Thank you."

As Charlotte finished her opening statement, a heavy silence surrounded the courtroom. She turned to make her way back to her seat, her heart pounding. As she glanced toward the audience, her eyes fell upon Kaya's family. In the front row, Kaya's mother sat with her hands clasped tightly in her lap, her expression a fragile blend of hope and despair. Despite the pain etched across her features, there was a spark in her eyes—a glimmer of belief that justice could be served, that her daughter's memory could be honored through this trial.

Charlotte felt a swell of empathy as she met the mother's gaze. In that brief moment, an unspoken connection formed between them, a shared understanding of the heartache that had brought them to this point. Charlotte nodded subtly, conveying her commitment to seeking justice for little Kaya. With that silent promise lingering in the air, Charlotte took her seat, steeling herself for the journey ahead.

CHAPTER VIII

Set on a two-acre plot of land within the city limits of Washington D.C., Kaya's home was part of a unique enclave—a preserved community space cherished by her family and two other families, all descendants of the Monacan tribe. The land breathed history and strength, with towering trees providing shade and a sense of comfort that wrapped around the children as they played. The home itself was humble yet inviting, filled with cozy rooms that resonated with laughter and warmth, where the scent of home-cooked meals danced through the air.

Kaya was the second-to-youngest of five siblings. She was a vibrant spirit who brought joy to her family with her infectious laughter and boundless energy. The house buzzed with the antics of two boys and three girls, each with their own unique personality yet all bound by a deep and unbreakable bond. Kaya, as the youngest daughter, was often regarded as the princess of the household. Her siblings adored her, and while they had their occasional squabbles, their love for one another always shone through any disagreements.

Curiosity defined Kaya. Whether she was playing with her siblings or the other children from nearby families, she had an insatiable desire to explore the world around her. Yet even amidst the laughter and games, she cherished moments of solitude. Kaya often wandered off on her own, her imagination guiding her as she chased after fluttering butterflies or marveled at the delicate petals of wildflowers swaying in the breeze. The vast expanse of their land was her playground, and she found joy in the simplest of things—like the soft rustle of leaves or the sight of a tiny rabbit darting through the underbrush.

Her adventurous spirit led her to hidden nooks and crannies, where she would discover the treasures of nature—a smooth, shiny stone, a feather caught in the grass, or a cluster of bright mushrooms. Kaya would lose track of time, captivated by the little wonders of the world, often returning home with her pockets filled with her finds, eager to share her discoveries with her family.

Their mother, Mrs. Adkins, a devoted homemaker, ensured that their home was filled with love and laughter. She was a nurturing presence, her gentle hands crafting delicious meals and her warm voice soothing any troubles that arose.

With her five children often running in and out of the house, the air was filled with vibrant chaos—echoes of playful shouts, the pitter-patter of small feet, and the soft barks of their beloved family dog, a beautiful border collie named Scout. Scout had been a serendipitous find, discovered wandering the countryside one day by one of the kids. The family quickly adopted her, and she became an integral part of their lives, always ready for a game of fetch or a comforting nuzzle.

Kaya and her siblings often played with the children from the other families living nearby, forging friendships that blossomed under the expansive sky. Together, they would explore the woods, build forts from fallen branches, and share secrets whispered under the shade of the trees. The laughter of children filled the air, creating a symphony of joy that resonated throughout the land.

In the evenings, the adults would gather around, sharing stories not only about their daily lives but also about their ancestors—their rich heritage as members of the Monacan tribe. They spoke of the tribe's history, recounting tales of resilience and strength that had carried their people through generations. The Monacan tribe, once known for their connection to the land and their deep-rooted traditions, continued to honor many of those customs even in modern times. They practiced traditional crafts, celebrated seasonal festivals, and maintained a close-knit community that valued respect for nature and one another.

Kaya's father, Mr. Adkins, worked hard at a farm two hours away, tending to the horses and ensuring the farm ran smoothly. Though his job often kept him away from home, he made sure to carve out precious moments with his family whenever he could. The kids looked forward to his return, cherishing the time they spent together. He was a good dad, a man of integrity who taught his children the values of hard work, honesty, and respect for others. When he was home, he would share stories of the farm, teaching them about the horses he cared for and the importance of treating animals with kindness and patience.

Despite the challenges of long hours and occasional hardships, the family thrived on love and support. They faced tough times, of course—moments when finances were tight or when the weight of the world felt heavy—but they navigated those challenges together, drawing strength from one another. Kaya and her siblings learned resilience from their parents, understanding that hard work and determination were necessary to overcome obstacles.

Today, however, the vibrant laughter that once filled the air has been replaced by an eerie silence. The two-acre sanctuary that was once alive with joy now feels heavy with grief. Kaya's absence has cast a long shadow over the family, transforming the once-thriving household into a shell of what it used to be. The house, once a hub of activity, feels empty and still, as if the walls themselves mourn the loss of the little girl who loved to explore.

Kaya's siblings, once full of spirited energy, now seem subdued. The boys hardly venture outside anymore, preferring to sit quietly on the porch, staring off into the distance, while the girls sit together, their conversations lacking the laughter and lightness they once shared. The playful banter that used to fill the home has been replaced by a heavy silence, each sibling grappling with their grief in their own way. They miss their sister fiercely, and the void left by her absence is evident.

Their mother, who had always been the heart of the household, now carries an air of exhaustion. Her nurturing spirit seems dimmed, and her laughter is a mere echo of what it once was. She moves through the house like a ghost, preparing meals that go mostly uneaten, her mind often drifting to memories of Kaya—her curious nature, her infectious laughter, and the way she would bring her siblings together. The warmth of her presence has been replaced by a quiet sadness, and the vibrancy of their home has faded.

Kaya's father, once a figure of strength, now bears the weight of despair. The long hours at the farm feel even longer, as he struggles to find meaning in his work without the joyous return home to his children. The stories he used to share about the ranch now feel hollow, as he wrestles with the reality that there will be no new tales to tell about Kaya's adventures. His laughter is a distant memory, replaced by a solemnity that permeates his every action. The man who taught his children the importance of honesty and respect now grapples with his own feelings of helplessness and loss.

Life, once a beautiful tapestry woven with love, laughter, and the occasional thread of hardship, now feels frayed and tattered. The family's spirit of togetherness has been shattered, rooted in heartache rather than heritage. In the absence of their beloved Kaya, they find themselves navigating an uncharted territory of grief, struggling to hold onto the memories that once brought them joy, while trying to find a way to move forward in a world that feels impossibly dim without her light.

As she sat in the courtroom, Kaya's mom, Mrs. Adkins, felt a wave of memories wash over her. She could almost see Kaya's bright smile and hear her laughter echoing in the air. The weight of her grief hung heavily on her heart, a reminder of the joy that had been so cruelly taken from her. Just then, she heard her name being called.

"I call my next witness to the stand," Charlotte said, as she looked over her shoulder, searching for her witness. "Mrs. Isabelle Adkins, would you please come over."

"Mrs. Adkins?" The judge repeated, calling for her attention. "Would you please come up to the stand?"

With a trembling heart, Mrs. Adkins rose from her seat, her legs feeling heavy as she made her way to the witness stand. She took a moment to collect herself, wiping away a tear that had slipped down her cheek. The judge, an older man with a longstanding reputation for kindness and fairness, watched her with understanding. His skinny frame was complemented by a neatly trimmed white beard, and his green eyes, framed by thin glasses, held a warmth that seemed to embrace those in his courtroom. He had practiced law for twenty years before becoming a judge in D.C., and his kind demeanor reassured many who appeared before him.

"Thank you for being here, Mrs. Adkins," Charlotte said softly. "I know this is difficult for you. Can you please tell the jury about the day of Kaya's disappearance? What were you and the children doing?"

Mrs. Adkins took a deep breath, her voice quivering slightly as she began. "It was a warm morning. The kids were outside playing on our property, which is quite large."

"Would you please briefly describe your property? Are you close to the road?" Charlotte asked gently.

"We live on the edge of the woods. There isn't much around our house other than the two other houses on our property and a big barn that we all share. We have a garden on the side of the house, and there is a small creek that runs beside it. There aren't many roads around there—just one, which you can see from our front porch. The road circles around the back of our home and through the woods. There aren't any fences or anything. It is a quiet area; not many vehicles pass by, so when they do, they stand out."

"Where were you while the kids were playing outside?" Charlotte asked.

"I was working in the garden, collecting some vegetables to get lunch ready," said Mrs. Adkins.

"Did you see anyone or hear anything unusual that day?" Charlotte continued, her tone sensitive as she guided Mrs. Adkins through her memories. "Any vehicles that caught your attention?"

Mrs. Adkins paused, her eyes welling with tears. "I remember hearing a loud pickup truck passing by. It didn't seem to be working properly. The exhaust kept making these sounds... like it was about to die. Vehicles aren't frequent in our area, so those sounds were loud and clear. I thought it was a bit strange, but I didn't think much of it at the time."

"What color was the pickup truck?"

"It was white," said Mrs. Adkins with certainty in her voice.

"Did you see the pickup truck stop at all?" Charlotte continued with the line of questioning.

"I did not. But I did stop hearing the loud sounds it was making. I don't know if it had stopped or, you know... maybe it got fixed on its own. Like I said, I wasn't paying much attention at the time."

At that moment, Mrs. Adkins broke down in tears. *I wish I had paid more attention. Maybe if I had, I could have protected Kaya*, she thought.

"Take your time, Mrs. Adkins," Charlotte said softly. "There is no rush."

The judge nodded, providing a supportive presence as he leaned slightly forward, encouraging her to continue when she felt ready. "You're doing well, Mrs. Adkins," he said, his voice gentle.

After a moment, Mrs. Adkins continued. "I continued collecting my vegetables, and then I went inside to get lunch ready. Once everything was prepared, I called the kids in, and that's when I noticed Kaya wasn't there. I thought she might be exploring a little farther, but she never strayed far from the house. I started to panic when I couldn't find her. It wasn't like her to go missing."

"Can you tell us more about the kids? Were they playing together that day? Did they notice anything unusual?" Charlotte pressed gently, sensing the weight of the moment.

"They were all playing in the forts their father had built for them," Mrs. Adkins replied. "They were laughing, and I can still hear their shouts in my mind. But when I asked them about Kaya, they said they hadn't seen her for a little while. I thought she might just be hiding, playing a game."

"Did you hear anything at all that seemed out of the ordinary? Anything else?" Charlotte pressed further, conscious of how difficult it was for Mrs. Adkins to discuss such a painful topic.

"No, nothing else," Mrs. Adkins whispered, tears streaming down her cheeks. "It all felt so normal... until it wasn't. I just... I just wish I had paid more attention."

"Mrs. Adkins," Charlotte continued gently, "had you seen that pickup truck going by before that day?"

"Yes," Mrs. Adkins replied. "I had seen it twice before that week. It made similar noises then, too. I didn't think much of it at that time, either."

"Thank you, Mrs. Adkins. That is very helpful," Charlotte said, nodding as she took a moment to gather her thoughts. "Now, I'd like to direct your attention to something else."

"Does your family have a dog?" Charlotte asked.

"Yes, we have a dog," Mrs. Adkins said. "Her name is Scout. She's a beautiful border collie, full of energy and always eager to play. Kaya loved her more than anything."

"Did you notice Scout that morning at all?"

"I did see her earlier that day. She was with me while I was in the garden," Mrs. Adkins replied. "But after I went inside to get lunch ready, I didn't see her anymore."

"Did you see her at all when you called the kids inside?"

"No, I didn't," Mrs. Adkins admitted.

Charlotte paused, carefully framing her next question. "Have you seen Scout at all after that day?"

Mrs. Adkins hesitated. "After we noticed Kaya was gone, we all started looking for her in the woods. We were calling her name. Our hearts were pounding with fear. And that's when we found Scout... laying there."

A shiver ran through the courtroom as Mrs. Adkins continued. "She wasn't responding. We didn't know why she was lying there, so still and quiet. It was terrifying."

Charlotte leaned in. "What happened next?"

Mrs. Adkins swallowed hard. "I wasn't sure what to do. My husband wasn't there, and the kids were all too young to drive. And Kaya was missing! Luckily, one of our neighbors saw us panicking and offered to take Scout to the vet while our search continued."

Relief washed over her as she remembered that neighbor's kindness, but her fear for Kaya still loomed large in her heart.

Charlotte moved in closer. "Was the vet able to help at all?"

"Yes, she did. And that's when we found out... she had been poisoned," Mrs. Adkins said, her voice breaking.

The room fell silent. The jury exchanged glances. Then Mrs. Adkins continued. "Thanks to my neighbor, the vet was able to save her. She came back home after a few days."

"Thank you, Mrs. Adkins," Charlotte said softly. "I have no further questions at this time."

As Mrs. Adkins stepped down from the stand, the judge offered a kind smile, understanding the emotional toll the testimony had taken on her. His presence reminded her that justice could be pursued with compassion, even in the face of such profound loss.

The courtroom shifted its focus as the next witness was called. "I'd like to call Mr. Brian Rowlands to the stand," Charlotte announced.

Mr. Rowlands approached, a sturdy man with grease-stained hands and a friendly demeanor. After establishing his credentials as an experienced mechanic, Charlotte leaned in. "Do you know the defendant, Mark Reynolds?" she asked.

"Yes, I do," he replied, nodding.

"And how do you know him?"

"He brought his pickup truck to me a few times in the past," Mr. Rowlands explained.

"What color was the defendant's pickup truck?"

"It was white," he said, his voice clear and confident.

"Can you tell us what the issue was with the pickup truck?"

Mr. Rowlands leaned forward. "The truck had a few mechanical issues that caused it to make loud noises as if it were about to die. Specifically, there were problems with the exhaust system and the ignition timing. It was making a rattling sound, and the engine was misfiring."

A murmur rippled through the courtroom as the audience absorbed his words.

Charlotte nodded, prompting him to continue. "Unfortunately, I couldn't fix the problem because I didn't have the parts we needed at the time. So, the defendant took the pickup truck back," he concluded.

"Do you remember the last time the defendant brought the pickup truck in?"

Mr. Rowlands scratched his chin, recalling the details. "Yes, it was exactly the week before the girl's disappearance."

"How can you be so sure?"

"Because I remember telling Mark that I was going to place the order for the part we needed and that it was going to take a week for it to arrive. So, we scheduled his appointment for the week after. I wrote the appointment on my calendar."

"Mr. Rowlands," Charlotte continued, holding a piece of paper up and walking closer to the witness stand. "Can you please tell me what this is?"

"It's a copy of the calendar."

Charlotte continued, "Can you please read to the jury what is written under April eighteenth, exactly six days after Kaya's disappearance?"

Mr. Rowlands put on his glasses and, leaning forward, said, "'Pickup truck. Mr. Reynolds.'"

A hush fell over the courtroom, the weight of the revelation settling heavily on everyone present.

"Thank you, Mr. Rowlands," Charlotte said, concluding her line of questioning and passing the copy of Mr. Rowlands's calendar to the jury. "I have no further questions, Your Honor."

The judge nodded. "Cross-examination?" he asked, looking at the defense table.

"Yes, Your Honor," said the defense attorney, standing up. He walked slowly toward the witness and leaned on the edge of the witness stand.

"Mr. Rowlands, you mentioned you know Mr. Reynolds because he took his truck to your shop many times. Correct?"

"Yes, that is correct."

"And that truck was white?"

"Correct."

"Can you tell us the year and model of the truck?"

"It was a nineteen seventy-five Ford F-150."

"Thank you, Mr. Rowlands. Now, can you tell the jury conclusively that the white pickup truck Mrs. Adkins heard on the afternoon in question was in fact Mr. Reynold's truck?"

Rowlands hesitated. "No, not conclusively. I just know that the noises she described were very similar to the ones Mr. Reynold's truck was making."

"Would you say that year and model truck is fairly popular in the area?"

"Yes, of course. It's a very common truck."

"And Ford probably made hundreds, if not thousands, of the same nineteen seventy-five F-150 in white?"

"Sure. Probably."

"And isn't it true that this particular model was known to have issues with the exhaust system and the ignition timing?"

"Yes. That's true. In fact, I've seen many other similar cases with this year and model."

"Then would it be possible that a different white pickup truck, same year and model, with the same problems with the exhaust system and the ignition timing, would produce identical noises?"

"It is possible –yes."

The defense attorney paused, letting Mr. Rowlands' answer settle with the jury. "In other words," he continued, "you can be sure about the problems with Mr. Reynolds' truck because you worked on it, but you cannot guarantee that the specific pickup truck Mrs. Adkins heard near her home was his. Correct?"

"Yes. That is correct," said Mr. Rowlands lowering his gaze.

"Thank you, Mr. Rowlands. No further questions, Your Honor."

Charlotte sprang to her feet, almost knocking her chair to the floor. "Re-direct, Your Honor?"

"Go ahead," the judge said.

Charlotte grabbed a plastic bag marked as *Exhibit D*, already entered into evidence, and walked to the witness stand.

"Mr. Rowlands, isn't it true that Mr. Reynolds' truck was taken to your shop after his arrest?"

"Yes, that is correct."

"Did you find anything inside the truck at that time?"

"Yes, I did."

Charlotte raised her arm, holding up the plastic bag. Inside was a small prescription bottle. "Is this what you found inside the truck?"

Rowlands looked at the bag and nodded. "Yes, that's it."

"What was in the prescription bottle, do you know?"

"It had some residue of a drug that's commonly used to put down dogs."

"How do you know?" Charlotte pressed.

"It's general knowledge ... and also, I know because I recently had to put my own dog down," Rowlands answered trying to hold back tears.

Charlotte turned to the jury and said in a clear voice, "Let the record reflect that this prescription bottle was also listed in the inventory prepared at the time of the arrest and that this inventory has been admitted into evidence and shared with the defense."

"Mr. Rowlands, one last question: you heard Mrs. Adkins' testimony a moment ago, didn't you?"

"Yes, I did."

"Then you also heard that her dog was drugged?"

"Objection, Your Honor! the defense attorney shouted from his seat.

"Withdrawn, Your Honor," Charlotte replied glancing at the defense attorney with a small grin. "I have no more questions."

Back in her seat, Charlotte looked at the defense attorney with a faintly mocking expression, making it clear she had regained control of the trial.

"The court will take a break for lunch," the judge announced, as the audience shifted in their seats.

As Charlotte stepped out of the courtroom, she felt a great feeling of accomplishment. It had been a good morning so far, but she knew there was still much more to do.

After the lunch break, the proceedings continued. Over the next two days, Charlotte called various witnesses to the stand. However, they were still waiting on some third-party forensic reports. Recognizing the need for more time, Charlotte requested a continuance until after Thanksgiving, which was approaching. Understanding the importance of the forensic reports to the prosecution's case, and the fact that the holidays were approaching, the judge granted the continuance, and a sense of gratitude settled over Charlotte.

As the courtroom emptied, the weight of the day settled heavily on Charlotte's shoulders. She stood alone for a moment, letting the magnitude of the trial's events settle. The echoes of witnesses' testimonies and the intense cross-examinations reverberated in her mind, each detail a reminder of the stakes involved.

Charlotte's gaze drifted to the now-empty jury box. She felt a mixture of relief and exhaustion, a testament to the emotional roller coaster she had ridden throughout the trial.

The pursuit of justice for Kaya and her family was all-consuming, leaving her both invigorated and drained.

As she gathered her belongings, Charlotte allowed herself a moment of introspection. She thought of Kaya's mother and the quiet strength in her eyes as she listened to the proceedings, and the courage it took to face such a harrowing ordeal. This case was more than just a professional challenge; it was a deeply personal mission to honor the memory of a child whose life was tragically cut short.

With a final glance around the courtroom, Charlotte steeled herself for the next step. The trial was far from over, but for now, she needed to recharge, to find solace in the company of her colleagues and the familiar ambiance of The Gavel. The bar was a place where she could momentarily set aside the burdens of her work, reconnect with the companionship of her peers, and perhaps find a moment of levity amidst the gravity of her responsibilities.

CHAPTER IX

As the stress from the courtroom began to dissipate, Charlotte found herself heading to The Gavel, a nearby bar, with her colleagues. It was a tradition—a way to unwind and revel in the camaraderie often elusive in the high-stakes world of law. The Gavel was tucked away just a few blocks from the courthouse, a cozy enclave where attorneys from nearby law firms frequently gathered.

The Gavel exuded charm, its ambiance a blend of rustic comfort and understated elegance. Exposed brick walls were adorned with vintage legal paraphernalia—old gavels, scales of justice, and framed newspaper clippings of landmark cases. The warm glow of pendant lights cast a soft, inviting light over the polished wooden bar, and patrons clustered around it. The air was filled with the rich aroma of aged whiskey and the faint scent of leather from the plush bar stools.

The bar had a storied history, established nearly a century ago by a retired judge who wanted to create a space for legal minds to gather and exchange ideas. Over the years, The Gavel had become a beloved institution frequented by attorneys, judges, and even politicians. It's rumored several landmark decisions were influenced by conversations held within its walls, and the place had seen its share of influential figures. Photos of well-known judges and politicians adorned the walls, capturing moments in history when the bar served as a backdrop to critical discussions.

Charlotte and her colleagues claimed their usual spot in a corner booth, a semi-circular enclave offering a perfect vantage point for observing the bar's lively atmosphere. The booth's leather seats were well-worn but comfortable, molding perfectly to the contours of weary bodies. The table was adorned with a small vase of fresh flowers, a touch of elegance amidst the otherwise rugged decor.

As they settled in, conversation flowed easily. Charlotte ordered a glass of champagne; her choice met with playful teasing from her colleagues, who knew her disdain for the bar's wine selection. "Always the champagne, never the wine," one quipped, raising a glass in her direction. Charlotte grinned, embracing the good-natured ribbing.

"Well, you know what they say," Charlotte began. "Champagne is always a safe choice. It's the drink of celebration, after all!" Her colleagues leaned in, eager to hear her explanation.

"True champagne," Charlotte continued with an enthusiastic tone, "can only come from the Champagne region of France. It's made using specific grape varieties—primarily chardonnay, pinot noir, and pinot meunier—through a process called *méthode champenoise*, or the traditional method. A secondary fermentation in the bottle, which is part of this method, is what gives champagne its unique bubbles."

Her colleagues nodded, some raising eyebrows in newfound appreciation. "So, it's not just sparkling wine?" one asked.

"Not exactly," Charlotte replied, a satisfied smile playing on her lips. "Only sparkling wine produced in that specific region and following those strict methods can be called champagne. It's several factors about the environment, the soil, the climate, and the meticulous process that make it so unique and delicious. Plus, there's something about those fine bubbles and the delicate balance of flavors—citrus, apple, and sometimes even notes of brioche—that just makes it irresistible."

"Sounds fancy," another colleague teased.

Charlotte chuckled, raising her glass in a mock toast. "Maybe a little, but that's why it's my preferred choice. It's more than just a drink; it's an experience. And honestly, I'm pleasantly surprised they even have champagne at The Gavel, especially considering their red wine selection leaves much to be desired. Champagne is my go-to here because it never disappoints."

The group laughed, fellowship deepening with each shared story and sip of their drinks. For Charlotte, the evening was a reminder of the simple joys of good company, lively conversation, and a well-chosen glass of champagne.

It wasn't long before the topic shifted to Charlotte's personal life, a subject of endless fascination and speculation among her peers. "So, Charlotte," began one colleague with a mischievous glint in her eye, "when are you going to introduce us to this mystery man we've all heard about?"

Charlotte feigned ignorance, a playful smile tugging at her lips. "A mystery man? I have no idea what you're talking about," she replied.

"Come on, Charlotte! We know there's someone," another colleague chimed in. "Is it true he's from the courthouse? Maybe someone we know?"

Charlotte shook her head in denial. "You all have such vivid imaginations," she teased, taking a sip of her champagne. "I assure you, there's no mystery man."

"Not even from the opposing table in your current case?" a third colleague ventured.

At this, Charlotte's thoughts flickered to her opposing counsel—a man she had met in law school, whose intelligence and charm always intrigued her. They shared many spirited debates and exchanged ideas that challenged her thinking. But she quickly dismissed the notion, smile unwavering. "Absolutely not," she said firmly, though her heart skipped a beat at the mere thought of him.

"Well, if there ever were a man to sweep Charlotte off her feet, it would have to be someone who can keep up with her in court," another remarked, earning a round of laughter from the group.

Charlotte rolled her eyes good-naturedly. "You all give me way too much credit," she said. "The only thing I'm focused on right now is this case."

The conversation meandered through various topics, chatter and laughter a comforting backdrop to the evening. As the night wore on, Charlotte found herself grateful for the companionship of her colleagues, their camaraderie a balm to the pressures of her work. The Gavel, with its inviting atmosphere and familiar faces, provided a temporary refuge from the weight of her responsibilities.

Eventually, the group began to disperse, each attorney and paralegal bidding farewells and making their way home. Charlotte lingered, savoring the last sip of her champagne, before rising to leave.

Walking back to her apartment, with the city's lights twinkling around her, Charlotte reflected on the evening and the unwavering support of her colleagues. She knew their teasing about a mystery man wasn't entirely unfounded, but she preferred to keep that part of her life private. At that moment, she felt a deep appreciation for the friendships that enriched her life. The path ahead was daunting, but she knew she wasn't facing it alone.

Her mind drifted to the journey she had to prepare for the next day—a trip to her grandparents' farm for Thanksgiving. The thought of the warm embrace of family, the familiar sights and sounds of the farm, filled her with comfort. It was a welcome respite from the whirlwind of her work, a chance to reconnect with her roots and find solace in the traditions that had shaped her.

As she entered her building, Alfred was there, offering a nod and a knowing smile. "A late night for you, Miss Charlotte?" he teased gently.

"Just a little," she replied with a soft laugh. "But it's always nice to unwind with friends. Have a happy Thanksgiving, Alfred. I am sure your wife has planned quite a spread."

"Yes, she has. Safe travels tomorrow," Alfred said warmly. "And give your family my regards."

"I will, Alfred," Charlotte promised, heart full as she made her way to her apartment. The city buzzed with life outside, but inside, she found peace.

CHAPTER X

As Charlotte navigated the winding roads toward her grandmother's farm, the tranquility of the autumn scenery enveloped her like a warm embrace. She settled into the supple leather seats of her dark blue Mercedes, the smooth engine humming softly as she pressed the accelerator. Memories of childhood summers spent here flooded her mind, mingling with the unease that had taken root since she received the latest report about Kaya's case.

The landscape unfolded in a tapestry of fall colors, trees ablaze in hues of crimson and gold. The road meandered through the foothills of the Blue Ridge Mountains, drawing her gaze to the breathtaking view that invited her to breathe deeply. She rolled down the window slightly, allowing the cool, crisp air to rush in, carrying with it the earthy scent of leaves and the faint aroma of woodsmoke from distant cabins.

The soft rustle of leaves overhead and the occasional call of a bird punctuated the serene environment, creating a symphony of autumn that contrasted sharply with the turmoil brewing in her heart.

Yet as Charlotte drove, her mind was a whirlwind of thoughts. The recent discovery in one of the reports provided by the investigators gnawed at her. A particular detail about Mark Reynolds's troubled upbringing had struck her, igniting a flicker of unease. Why did it feel like pieces of a puzzle were snapping into place, but the big picture was still just out of reach?

Mark Reynolds had grown up in Rutherford County, Tennessee, a place where shadows loomed long for a boy like him. Losing his father during the Second World War left a void in his life that his mother struggled to fill. Unable to cope with the grief and the responsibilities of raising two children alone, she eventually moved away, leaving Mark to live with his aunt in a modest, rundown house on the outskirts of town. The atmosphere there was a reflection of their hardships, thick with the smell of stale cigarettes and cheap whiskey.

Mark was always getting into trouble, a pattern that only continued as he grew older. With tousled dark hair and a rugged appearance, he stood at six feet tall, his athletic build the result of a rough-and-tumble childhood. His sharp jawline and deep-set, piercing blue eyes often held a brooding intensity, hinting at the turmoil within. By his late teens, a cigarette was perpetually dangling from his lips, casting a haze of smoke around him, a habit that only intensified as he turned to alcohol and late nights with rough company.

Once he reached adulthood, he struggled to keep a job, often working odd jobs around various farms in the area while frequently finding himself in and out of jail for public disturbances, stalking, vandalism, and crimes against property. In his late teens, he joined a group of sheep shearers traveling through Tennessee and Virginia during shearing season. It was during this time, in the late fifties, that he moved to Virginia, seeking shearing crews whenever he had the opportunity—and was sober enough to do the work. Despite his troubled past, he gained a reputation for his skill, shearing sheep with a deftness that impressed farmers desperate for good hands.

By the mid-sixties, Mark found a more permanent job on a farm near the Blue Ridge Mountains, working for the Evans family. Mr. Evans needed a caretaker to look after the farm while he traveled for business, living with his family closer to Washington, D.C. Mr. Evans decided to give Mark a chance, but that opportunity was short-lived. Accused of attempting to rape a bar patron outside a local tavern, Mark's life spiraled further into chaos, leading to his arrest and conviction.

After serving his time, Mark moved to the D.C. area in the late seventies, where he took the only job he could find after his release, working in a gritty warehouse on the outskirts of the city. He remained there until his arrest for Kaya's kidnapping and murder. The details of his life painted a troubling picture, and Charlotte couldn't dismiss the notion that connections were waiting to be uncovered.

As the mountains grew closer, the temperature dropped, and the air grew cooler and crisper. Charlotte wrapped her scarf tighter around her neck, letting the chill invigorate her senses. With each passing mile, the majestic forms of the mountains loomed larger against the pale blue sky, their beauty undeniable yet carrying an undercurrent of melancholy—a reminder of the fragility of happiness.

The farm came into view, a welcome sight nestled among the rolling hills. The familiar sight of the farmhouse, adorned with pumpkins and hay bales, brought a wave of nostalgia. Memories of Thanksgivings past flooded her mind—her grandmother's laughter, the aroma of roasted turkey, and the warmth of family gathered around the table. It was a sanctuary where love and connection flourished, a stark contrast to the heartache she faced in her professional life.

As she turned onto the gravel driveway, the crunch beneath her tires stirred a flood of memories. Charlotte was ready to immerse herself in the warmth of family, to share in the traditions that had always anchored her. But the weight of her responsibilities lingered, a reminder that while she could find solace in the company of loved ones, the fight for justice was far from over.

With the view of her family through the bay windows, Charlotte parked her Mercedes and took a moment to steady herself, grounding in the present. She was home, surrounded by the love that had shaped her. As she stepped out of the car, she vowed to honor both Kaya and Mari by continuing the fight against the darkness that threatened to overshadow their stories. Today, she would celebrate the bonds of family, but tomorrow, she would return to the pursuit of justice, carrying the memory of her sister and the hope for a brighter future.

As Charlotte walked toward the farmhouse, the first thing she noticed was her dad's pickup truck parked by the barn, its dusty exterior a testament to his hard work around the fields. The old but reliable Ford, with chipped paint and a bed filled with tools and hay bales, reflected the life he led as a farmer and consultant. It had seen better days, but it was well-loved, much like the family it served.

Stepping into the house, Charlotte was greeted by the warm aroma of freshly baked goods wafting through the air. She found her mom, dad, and Grandma gathered around the kitchen table, engaged in their usual ritual at five p.m.: enjoying tea, scones, and freshly baked German beer bread. The sight brought a smile to her face.

"Hey, everyone!" Charlotte called out. Her mom looked up, her eyes lighting with joy, while her dad raised his hand in a casual wave, and Grandma Ann beamed with pride.

"Come in, dear! Have some tea," Grandma said with a warm smile.

Charlotte accepted the offer, though she couldn't ignore the feeling of unease that settled in her chest. There was something on her mind, a nagging anxiety that made her feel restless. She sensed that Grandma was anxious to finish teatime, but she knew better than to act rude; that would upset Grandma and her dad. So, she patiently sipped her tea, nibbling on a scone, until she was able to politely pull her dad aside.

"Can you help me get my things from the car?" she asked, feigning a casual tone. He nodded, sensing her need for a moment alone, and together they stepped outside into the cool autumn air.

As they walked toward the barn, Charlotte took a moment to observe her dad. Standing at five feet ten inches, William Jones had broad shoulders and a strong frame that spoke of years spent working the land. His strong jawline and dark hair framed a face that bore the marks of wisdom and experience, while his warm brown eyes held a depth of kindness that reminded her of Grandma Ann. Some features resembled his mother, particularly his eyes, which sparkled with genuine interest in the world. But his strong build and sharp jawline echoed his father, Grandpa Louis.

Charlotte's dad was one of the most intelligent people she had ever known. His insatiable curiosity led him to constantly read, whether it was a novel, a history book, or an academic text. Like his father, William had become an agricultural engineer, dedicating his life to consulting services for farmers across multiple states. His expertise helped them maximize production while ensuring that the soil and environment were cared for, creating a sustainable cycle that allowed for continued growth. He understood that by nurturing the land and allowing it to recover when needed, he was not only enhancing the immediate yield but also setting the stage for long-term productivity. This holistic approach was vital for maintaining the health of the farms he worked with, ensuring they could thrive for generations to come.

Honesty was his hallmark; he was well-respected by his peers and everyone who worked with him. Yet beneath his tough exterior, he had a soft spot for Charlotte and his wife Victoria. He treated them like delicate flowers, with a gentle kindness that balanced his strictness. His protective nature often manifested in a way that made Charlotte feel both cherished and constrained, especially during her teenage years.

"Daddy," Charlotte began, her voice low as they reached the barn. "I've been thinking about some things related to my work, and I really need to talk to you about it to clear my head."

He looked at her with concern. "Of course, sweetheart. What's on your mind?"

"Do you keep records of everyone who has worked at our farm?" she asked.

"We do keep records," her dad replied. "Your mom has always helped make sure of that—she still does, now helping me, but before that, she helped your grandpa. Why do you ask?"

"I need to see those records."

Her dad paused, considering her request. "The records are at back at our house."

"Can we go tonight?" Charlotte demanded.

"That is twenty minutes there and twenty more back. We should stay to help your grandmother with dinner. What is so important that cannot wait until the morning?" he asked.

"Do you remember that caretaker Grandpa Louis hired when I was a teenager? The one who was always staring at me and Mari? The one we later discovered had been stealing from Grandpa and was threatened with lawsuits once Grandpa fired him?"

Her dad nodded slowly. "I do remember. He was an odd guy and caused quite a headache for me and your grandpa back in the day. But what does that have to do with anything?"

"Do you remember his name?"

"I don't," her dad admitted. "You know I'm terrible with names, and that was more than twenty years ago. But your mom probably does."

"Was it Mark Reynolds?" Charlotte interrupted, hoping that would trigger her dad's memory.

"No, I don't think so. That name doesn't sound familiar."

"Let's go inside. I'm sure your mom will remember," he suggested.

As they stepped inside the house, the warmth of the kitchen enveloped Charlotte, but her mind was racing with questions. She turned to her grandma and mom, eager to bring them up to speed with her conversation outside.

"Mom, Grandma," she began, "I just spoke with Daddy about the records of everyone who has worked on the farm. I need your help. Do you remember that caretaker who worked at the farm when I was a teenager? The one that Grandpa had so many problems with?"

Her mom looked thoughtful. "I remember someone like that," she replied hesitantly. "But I can't quite recall his name."

After a pause, she added, "Yes! His name was Emmanuel. I don't remember his last name. I think it was some sort of Spanish last name."

Charlotte turned to Grandma Ann, who was listening intently. "Grandma, do you remember anything about him?"

Grandma shook her head slowly. "I don't remember his name either, but I do remember that particular character and especially the way he acted around you and Mari during that time. I didn't like that at all and asked Louis to replace him several times."

Charlotte's heart raced as she listened. "But he stayed, right?"

Her mom nodded. "Yes, Louis tried to get rid of him, but the guy's threats of suing him delayed the process. It was a difficult situation."

"We were finally able to get rid of him a couple of years after Mari's death," Grandma added.

After that conversation, Charlotte insisted on going to look for the records, but her dad explained that the caretaker was not who Charlotte was asking about. "It wasn't Mark Reynolds," he insisted. "Your mom said his name was Emmanuel."

"Why do you still need to see the records?" he asked.

"I need to take a look anyway. Maybe there's still something in there that can be helpful. I don't know. Maybe there's something else. Or someone else in there that can lead me in the right direction."

Seeing the intensity in her eyes, Grandma stepped in to ease the tension. "How about we focus on dinner for now? Open a bottle of wine, my dear," she suggested warmly. "Everyone is sleeping here this weekend."

With a nod, Charlotte let the idea of dinner wash over her. The comforting routine of family ground her as she moved to the kitchen, ready to help prepare a meal that would bring them all together once again. The mystery surrounding the records lingered in her mind, but for now, she embraced the love and warmth of her family.

As she stepped farther into the kitchen, the scene was bustling with activity. Charlotte's mom and Grandma Ann were already working together to set the table for dinner, and the air was filled with the delightful aromas of the meal that awaited them. The polished oak table gleamed under the soft glow of the hanging lamp, its surface meticulously cleaned and adorned with a crisp, white linen tablecloth that cascaded elegantly over the edges. Delicate lace trim added a touch of charm, reflecting the family's love for tradition.

Charlotte watched as her mom unfolded matching cloth napkins, each neatly pressed and placed beside the plates. The silverware sparkled in the light, a mix of stainless steel and a few cherished heirlooms that had belonged to Grandma's mother. Forks and knives were arranged with precision, while polished spoons glimmered in anticipation of the delicious dishes they would soon hold.

The centerpiece was a vibrant arrangement of seasonal flowers, their colors bright against the white tablecloth. Sunflowers, daisies, and wildflowers danced together in a glass vase, filling the air with a subtle, sweet fragrance that added to the warmth of the gathering.

As the table was set, Charlotte's mom carefully placed the dishes, each a piece of their heritage. A large, succulent turkey sat prominently in the middle, its golden-brown skin glistening with herbs and spices, surrounded by a fragrant stuffing studded with chestnuts and cranberries. Next to it, a juicy honey-glazed ham gleamed, the sweet aroma mingling with the savory scent of the turkey.

On one side of the table, a colorful salad was presented in a crystal bowl, vibrant greens topped with slices of avocado, fresh berries, and a drizzle of tangy vinaigrette. Nearby, a dish of creamy mashed potatoes waited, their surface dotted with melted butter and a sprinkle of fresh chives.

In keeping with their Welsh heritage, a traditional lamb stew simmered in a deep pot, its rich aroma wafting through the kitchen, bringing warmth and comfort. Next to it, a plate of freshly baked Welsh cakes, golden and lightly spiced, was set aside, ready to be enjoyed as a delightful treat after the meal.

Charlotte felt a deep sense of gratitude as she helped finish setting the table. The combination of family recipes and cherished traditions created a beautiful tapestry of flavors and memories, making her feel deeply connected to her roots.

"Everything looks wonderful!" Charlotte exclaimed, taking a step back to admire their work.

Grandma smiled with pride. "Just wait until you taste it, my dear. This meal is all about family, and having everyone together is a joy."

With the table beautifully set and the delicious aromas enveloping her, Charlotte felt a sense of anticipation for the evening ahead. The mystery of the records still lingered in her mind, but as she stood surrounded by her family, she felt a flicker of hope that even in the darkest of times, love and connection could light the way forward.

***

The following day, Charlotte woke up with the sun streaming through the window, casting warm rays across the room. The memories of the previous night—a table filled with family, laughter, and the comforting embrace of tradition—lingered in her mind. Yet one thought overshadowed her morning reverie: the farm records. She felt a bubbling urgency to delve into the past, to uncover any hidden truths that might connect to Kaya's case. However, as she swung her legs over the side of the bed, Charlotte realized she needed to reorient herself. The remnants of the wine from the night before dulled her senses, making it a challenge to awaken fully. With a sigh, she pushed herself up and headed to the bathroom to splash cold water on her face, hoping to shake off the lingering fog.

As she made her way down the hallway, the delightful aroma of toast, fresh coffee, and brewed tea wafted through the air, beckoning her toward the kitchen. The familiar sounds of her family filled the space—soft laughter, the clinking of dishes, and the rustling of newspaper pages turning.

Stepping into the kitchen, Charlotte was greeted by a scene that felt both comforting and casual. The kitchen table was set for breakfast, a simple but welcoming display. A cheerful yellow tablecloth adorned the surface, and mismatched plates were arranged in a haphazard yet charming way. Freshly toasted bread lay in a basket at the center, steam rising from its golden surface, while a pot of coffee brewed on the counter, filling the room with its rich aroma. Beside it, a teapot sat patiently, its floral design reminiscent of Grandma's favorite china.

Her mom, wearing a cozy sweater, was flipping pancakes on the griddle, their sweet scent mingling with the toast. Grandma Ann sat at the table, nursing a cup of tea and flipping through a magazine, her eyes sparkling with warmth as she caught sight of Charlotte.

"Good morning, my dear!" Grandma called, her voice as inviting as the aroma surrounding them. "Come and join us!"

"Morning, everyone," Charlotte replied, forcing a smile as she slid into a chair. She felt the warmth of family envelop her, but her mind was already drifting back to the records. She knew she had to spend this time with them to savor the moments that had shaped her childhood, but the thought of uncovering the past tugged at her insistently.

As they sat around the table, they engaged in light conversation, enjoying the cozy atmosphere. Charlotte poured herself a cup of coffee, the bitter warmth helping to clear her foggy mind. Her dad entered the kitchen just then with tousled hair and a sleepy smile, and Charlotte felt a pang of affection for her family.

"Sleep well?" he asked, taking a seat and reaching for the toast.

"Like a log," Charlotte replied, though she knew her mind had been racing even in her dreams.

They shared a pleasant breakfast, and laughter and stories flowed easily between them. Her mom recounted a funny mishap from the previous day, and Grandma chimed in with a memory from her own childhood, drawing chuckles from everyone. Amid the lightheartedness, the conversation turned to memories of Mari, Charlotte's sister, who had been kidnapped alongside her years ago.

"Remember the time we used to play in the backyard, and Mari insisted on being the princess?" Charlotte's mom said, her eyes misting with nostalgia. "She always loved to dress like a princess."

"Yes, and she would boss us all around," Charlotte's dad added with a fond smile. "But we loved it. She had such a big heart, always trying to keep everyone together."

As they reminisced about Mari's vibrant spirit, Charlotte felt a bittersweet ache in her chest. The warmth of their memories was tinged with the sorrow of loss, a reminder of the shadow that had hung over their family for so long. Yet amidst the laughter, there was also a sense of connection, a shared bond that kept her sister's memory alive.

As they neared the end of their breakfast, the conversation naturally shifted toward plans for the day. Charlotte saw her chance. "So, Dad, can we talk about the farm records?"

Her dad raised an eyebrow, a knowing smile creeping onto his face. "I figured you wouldn't let that go. You've had it on your mind since last night."

"I really need to see them," Charlotte pressed. "I have a feeling there's something important in there."

With a resigned chuckle, her dad nodded. "All right, I'll come with you to show you where they're kept. But let's finish breakfast first; I want to be sure you're fueled up for the digging we might have to do."

Charlotte felt a wave of relief. She was grateful for his support, knowing that together, they would uncover the truths hidden in the records. As they finished their breakfast, she felt the warmth of family surrounding her, a comforting reminder that they would face the challenges ahead, even amidst the turmoil.

Once Charlotte and her dad arrived at her parents' house, memories flooded back. The house stood proudly on the outskirts of a small town, slightly elevated compared with the other homes in the area, giving it a commanding view of the surrounding landscape. The exterior was a warm, inviting shade, with large window panels allowing sunlight to pour in and illuminate the space.

The property encompassed a sprawling one-acre lot, surrounded by a lush yard that felt like a sanctuary. Pine, spruce, and fir trees lined most of the perimeter, remnants of a time when they had been Christmas trees, their tall, slender forms swaying gently in the breeze. The scent of the coniferous trees mingled with the crisp autumn air, wrapping around Charlotte like a familiar embrace.

By the corner of the lot stood a sturdy barn, which had served multiple purposes throughout the years—acting as a garage, boat storage, and a woodwork station for her dad. The barn was a hub of activity, especially during family gatherings, where laughter and stories echoed off its walls. Attached to the back of the house was a large fireplace with a grill for roasting meats, a cherished tradition during weekends, birthdays, and other celebrations. She could almost hear the sizzling sounds of steaks being cooked, the aroma wafting through the air as family and friends gathered around, sharing meals and creating memories.

The house featured a beautiful wrap-around porch adorned with her mom's beloved potted plants and colorful flowers blooming in the sunlight. The second story boasted a stunning bay window with a small balcony, a perfect spot for sipping morning coffee and watching the world wake up. Surrounding the yard were various apple trees, their branches heavy with fruit, and a large elderberry tree beside the barn, a favorite climbing spot for Charlotte and Mari during their childhood.

As they walked through the front door, Charlotte's gaze swept over the familiar interior, but she noticed that most of the furniture had been moved around, giving the space a different feel. The living room, once arranged for cozy family gatherings, now had a more open layout. Plush sofas were positioned to encourage conversation, and a large coffee table was strewn with magazines and books, remnants of the last family gathering.

The dining room, usually set for formal dinners, now had a more casual vibe. The dining table was adorned with a simple cloth, and chairs were pushed in haphazardly as if they had just wrapped up a meal. The walls were lined with framed family pictures, capturing moments of joy and love, while beautiful rugs and animal skins added warmth and texture to the space.

Charlotte's eyes were drawn to the office studio, a room filled with built-in bookcases overflowing with books—some well-worn, others pristine. The cozy feel of the room was enhanced by various pieces of artwork hanging on the walls, each telling a story of its own. But amidst the memories, one portrait stood out—a striking image of Mari, captured on her thirteenth birthday. In the picture, Mari wore a beautiful dress that Charlotte had helped pick out, her radiant smile lighting up the room. The soft fabric of the dress flowed around her, perfectly framing her youthful glow. The memory of that day flooded Charlotte's mind, and she felt tears prick in her eyes. It had only been a few months since she last visited the house, but the emotional impact was always profound. Memories of Mari seemed to linger in every corner, filling the space with a bittersweet nostalgia.

Charlotte knew Mari's bedroom was at the end of a long hallway, past the kitchen, but she hesitated at the thought of going there today. The memories of her sister were etched into every fiber of that house, similar to the feeling she had at her grandparents' farm. Sometimes, she found the strength to venture into Mari's room, but today was not one of those days. Today, she needed to focus on the records of her grandparents' farm, hoping to uncover any slight clue that could help in solving her sister's case.

With that resolve in mind, she turned to her dad, who was patiently waiting nearby. "Can you show me where the records are?" she asked.

"Of course," he replied, leading her through the familiar halls and past the living room, his presence comforting. As they approached a large cabinet with drawers full of documents, Charlotte felt anxious, unsure of what they might find. Her dad opened the cabinet, revealing a treasure trove of memories and history, and then he stepped back, giving her the space she needed.

"Take your time, sweetheart. I'll be right here if you need me," he said softly, his reassuring tone grounding her as she prepared to dive into the past.

Charlotte opened the first drawer, knowing the answers she sought might lie within these pages.

The cabinets were neatly organized by year, topic, and alphabetical order—a trait Charlotte recognized as distinctly her mom's. She took a moment to appreciate the meticulousness of it all, a comforting reminder of the order her mother always sought to maintain amidst the chaos of life. Charlotte began her search, focusing on a particular time range that felt crucial. She was especially interested in the names of people who had worked at the farm between 1950 and 1965.

Mari's death during the summer of 1962, specifically on July 27, haunted her thoughts. Charlotte thought that looking for clues from a few years before and after that date could provide valuable insights. If there was any connection to Mark Reynolds, it must have happened during that timeframe. Her sources indicated that Reynolds had moved to the area in the early fifties and had been incarcerated from the mid-sixties to the late seventies. Charlotte was determined to prove her parents wrong, convinced that Reynolds had, in fact, been the caretaker she was asking about the previous night.

She scanned the neatly labeled folders, her heart racing with anticipation. But then there it was—the caretaker during the years 1960 to 1964 had been a man named Emmanuel Salazar. Her mom was right. Charlotte could hardly believe it! The certainty that had fueled her search began to wane, replaced by a feeling of defeat. She continued flipping through the pages, her interest dwindling as the weight of disappointment settled over her.

Just as she was about to close the drawer and abandon her search, she noticed another one of her mom's organizational traits. Next to the label for "Employees," there was a different label that read "Seasonal Workers." This sparked a flicker of renewed hope within her. She pulled the records for seasonal workers and began to flip through the pages with a sense of urgency.

As she scanned the list, her heart raced with each name. Then there it was—confirmation of her gut feeling and a flurry of what-ifs. Mark Reynolds was listed among the seasonal workers her grandfather had contracted to shear sheep from 1961 through 1964.

She had finally gotten a breakthrough—something that could potentially lead to answers. It was just a hunch, but now it had a name backed up with actual records she could use to prove her theory. The realization that Mark Reynolds had been connected to the farm during such a pivotal time in her family's history sent shivers down her spine.

This was the lead she had been searching for, a tangible connection to the past that could unlock the mystery surrounding her sister's kidnapping, resulting in a tragic loss. She knew that she needed to approach this carefully, to gather all the evidence before presenting it to her parents. But for now, the thrill of discovery ignited a fire within her, and she couldn't help but feel that she was one step closer to finding the truth.

As Charlotte flipped through the pages, another name struck her, giving her goose bumps. *Wait... what is this? "Mr. Adkins" ... Kaya's father?* During 1961 and '62, Mr. Adkins was listed as part of the same shearing crew Mr. Reynolds had been a part of. *But... could it be him? Did they know each other?* The implications rushed through her mind like a storm. She could feel her heart pounding. What if these connections ran more profound than she had thought? Questions flooded her thoughts, mingling with the unsettling sense of urgency that had brought her to this very moment.

This was no longer just a search for answers; it was a potential link to the heart of the mystery surrounding both, Kaya's and Mari's case.

As they drove back toward the grandparents' farm, silence enveloped the car, heavy with unspoken thoughts. Charlotte's dad, a man of few words, kept his hands firmly on the wheel, his brow slightly furrowed as he navigated the winding mountain roads. He had always been a man of action rather than conversation, preferring to let the quiet moments speak for themselves. This time, he sensed the weight of Charlotte's thoughts and chose not to interrupt the storm brewing in her mind.

Charlotte sat in the passenger seat, her fingers tapping nervously against her thigh as she gazed out the window. The world outside blurred past her—an impressionistic painting of vibrant autumn hues swirling together. Deep reds and burnt oranges danced among the evergreen trees, their leaves slowly surrendering to the breeze. Yet her mind was a tumult of possibilities, each one more tangled than the last, as she weighed her next steps in the investigation.

The sky darkened, and a light drizzle began to fall, creating a soothing rhythm against the windshield. The soft patter of raindrops starkly contrasted with the chaos inside her head. She felt overwhelmed, grappling with the implications of her findings. The connections she had uncovered felt almost too significant to comprehend. What did it mean for her family? What did it mean for Kaya's case? Questions swirled like the leaves outside, caught in the whirlpool of her thoughts.

The road narrowed as they climbed higher into the mountains, flanked by towering trees that seemed to close in around them. The mist rising from the forest created an ethereal atmosphere, making the world feel familiar and distant. Charlotte could see the outline of the Blue Ridge Mountains in the distance, their majestic peaks rising proudly against the slate-gray sky, a reminder of the sanctuary she had always sought in this place.

As they continued on the winding road, the landscape shifted. The trees thickened, their branches arching overhead like protective arms, casting dappled shadows on the asphalt beneath them. The scent of damp earth and pine filled the air, mingling with the crispness of the rain, grounding Charlotte in the present moment. She inhaled deeply, trying to calm her racing thoughts, but they lingered like the fog settling over the mountains.

Glancing over at her dad, Charlotte could see the deep lines of worry on his face. He was processing his own concerns, undoubtedly worried about her well-being and the weight of the investigation. They both understood the unspoken bond they shared, a connection forged in love, loss, and the shared journey of navigating the unknown. In silence, they drove on, each lost in their thoughts yet united in purpose.

The road twisted and turned, leading them deeper into the embrace of the mountains. Charlotte felt the familiar pull of nostalgia, the memories of childhood summers spent here flooding her mind once more. Yet this time, the joy was tinged with the uncertainty of what lay ahead. As they approached the familiar turn that led to the farm, she couldn't help but wonder if the haven she sought would offer the answers she so desperately needed.

As the rain began to fall steadily, Charlotte steeled herself for the conversations that awaited her. The journey back was not just a return to the farm; it was a step into the heart of the mystery that had haunted her for so long.

CHAPTER XI

"Those potatoes are not going to peel themselves, you know?" Victoria called out playfully, her warm smile brightening the kitchen as she glanced back at Charlotte. The laughter in her voice was light and teasing, but it held a gentle understanding that her daughter was lost in thought, staring absentmindedly at the countertop.

"Sorry, Mom," Charlotte replied, shaking off her reverie. "I'll help." She stepped forward to join her mother, reaching for the peeler and a few potatoes that lay waiting on the cutting board. The familiar task brought a sense of comfort—a reminder of all the times she and Mari had helped their mom in the kitchen two decades ago.

Peeling potatoes had always been Charlotte's designated duty, a chore she and Mari had often grumbled about as children. "It's like being in prison, forced to work in the kitchen!" she used to joke, laughing as she wielded the peeler with the precision of a seasoned inmate. Mari had her own set of responsibilities—drying the dishes, putting them away, and setting the table for every meal. The routine had been a staple of their family life, shifting from obligation to cherished ritual as they grew older.

Victoria moved gracefully around the kitchen, a picture of elegance and efficiency. She had a slim build, standing at five feet five inches, with long, blonde hair that fell in soft waves to her shoulders, framing a heart-shaped face. Her green eyes sparkled with warmth and intelligence, exuding kindness and an innate ability to make those around her feel at ease. Even in the bustling kitchen, she maintained a sense of approachable and genuine class.

Dressed in a fitted, pale blue blouse paired with well-tailored jeans and soft ballet flats, Victoria embodied a blend of sophistication and practicality. Her style reflected her upbringing—she was a German-Italian descendant, raised in New York City, where her father was a real estate lawyer, and her mother was a devoted stay-at-home mom. Growing up with four siblings, she learned the values of teamwork, sharing, and hard work.

Charlotte often marveled at how her mother seamlessly combined the best of both worlds. Victoria was the embodiment of strength, kindness, and resilience, carrying the family through challenges, including the heartache surrounding Mari's passing. Even when life became overwhelming, Victoria remained a beacon of hope.

As Charlotte peeled the potatoes, the rhythmic motion brought her a sense of calm. She could almost hear her grandmother's voice in her head, reminding her of the importance of family values and hard work. The kitchen buzzed with warmth, filling the air with the aroma of herbs and spices as Victoria prepared for their late lunch gathering that afternoon.

"Do you remember that time you woke up early to make breakfast for everyone?" Victoria asked, a playful smile crossing her lips as she glanced over at Charlotte. "You were attempting to fry a few eggs, but instead of adding a few drops of oil, you submerged the eggs in it! The kitchen was so filled with a thick black smoke, your dad had to open all the windows in the house!"

Charlotte chuckled, a flush of embarrassment warming her cheeks. "I just wanted to be helpful! I thought it would be a nice treat, but I had no idea I could cause such a disaster!"

Victoria laughed, shaking her head. "You nearly asphyxiated us! But it's one of my favorite memories. It showed your determination—and your complete lack of knowledge about cooking at the time! It's a good thing you quickly learned how to cook properly after that!"

Charlotte smiled, appreciating her mother's encouragement. "Thanks, Mom. I guess I've come a long way since then!"

"What are you making with the potatoes?" Charlotte asked, curious about the dish Victoria was preparing.

"Keeping it simple today," Victoria replied, stirring a pot on the stove. "But I'm making one of your favorites: schnitzel with mashed potatoes!"

Charlotte's eyes lit up. "Schnitzel! I can't wait! You always make it so perfectly crispy. I can't ever eat enough of them!"

Just then, the door swung open, and Grandma Ann shuffled into the kitchen, followed closely by Charlotte's dad. "It smells wonderful in here!" Grandma exclaimed. "I could smell it from the porch!"

"Everything is ready to set the table," Victoria said, wiping her hands on a towel. "Can you help me, Charlotte?"

"Of course!" Charlotte replied. She and Grandma Ann moved to the dining room to gather the plates and utensils.

As they set the table together, Charlotte noticed the warmth in Grandma's eyes. "I hope you managed to catch a little nap, Grandma," she said. "You looked like you needed it after last night."

"Oh, I did! A short one, but it helped," Grandma Ann replied with a smile. "I'm glad things got a little delayed today; it gave me a chance to rest."

Charlotte and Grandma finished setting the table and arranging everything just right. Soon, they all gathered around, taking their seats. The late lunch felt like a celebration of family despite the hectic morning they had endured.

As they began to serve the schnitzel and mashed potatoes, Charlotte glanced around the table, her heart swelling with gratitude. It was moments like these that reminded her of the strength they shared as a family.

As they settled into their meal, the rain outside intensified, tapping insistently against the windows. At first, it was a gentle patter, a soothing backdrop to their conversation. But soon, the sound transformed into a steady rhythm, the droplets striking the glass with increasing force, creating a symphony of nature that filled the cozy kitchen. The skies darkened, and the occasional rumble of thunder echoed in the distance.

Charlotte glanced outside, watching as the rain blurred the landscape, turning the familiar view into a watercolor painting of muted grays and browns. Mostly bare now, the trees stood tall and sad, their branches swaying lightly in the wind. Some stubborn leaves clung to the branches, a few remaining golden and rust-colored remnants of autumn, while others spiraled down in graceful arcs to the ground below, forming a damp carpet of color.

The garden, once vibrant with pumpkins and late-season flowers, now drooped under the weight of the downpour, its colors muted by the relentless rain. The mountains in the distance were shrouded in mist, lending an ethereal quality to the scenery as if the world outside had been pulled into a dream. Inside, the kitchen's warmth contrasted beautifully with the storm outside, the smell of schnitzel and mashed potatoes wrapping around them like a comforting blanket.

"Charlotte," Grandma Ann began, her voice breaking through the sound of the rain. "Your dad mentioned that you found information about Kaya's father working at our farm in the sixties. What do you think about that?"

Charlotte paused, her fork hovering over her plate. "Honestly, I don't know what to think about that yet," she admitted. "I'm puzzled. I can't understand why Kaya's dad wouldn't say anything about knowing Reynolds. It feels like there is something more there that we're not seeing."

She paused briefly, recalling her brief encounter with Mr. Adkins. "I met Mr. Adkins, and he seemed like a nice guy. He really cares about his family and works hard. It just doesn't fit, you know? How does he connect to all of this?"

Grandma nodded thoughtfully. "Didn't you mention they were from the Monacan community?"

"Yes," Charlotte replied. "But what does that have to do with anything?"

"I wonder if they have anything to do with the issues we faced with several neighboring farms back in the fifties and sixties," Grandma said. "There were some Native American activists at the time who were quite vocal about the way the Welsh had treated them centuries ago."

Charlotte leaned in, intrigued. "What happened?"

"Well," Grandma began, "the Welsh settlers and the Monacans had a complicated relationship. When the Welsh arrived back in the seventeenth century, they often relied on the Monacans to teach them how to work the land. At first, the Monacans did not want anything to do with them. In their eyes, English and Welsh were just the same—and they hated the English. That's why many Monacans moved to the west of the state and settled close to the mountains—in Amherst County. They wanted to distance themselves from the English. In fact, many Monacans ended up moving into Pennsylvania and even Canada. But after a while, some Monacans understood they were not the same and became friendly with the Welsh. Monacans and Welsh eventually settled around the James River, close to what's now Lynchburg, and lived there for at least a couple hundred years. Monacans showed the Welsh how to cultivate crops and care for the animals they used for farming. They even taught them how to grow tobacco, contributing to what later became one of the largest markets in the world. It was a mutually beneficial relationship for a time. However, other tribes in the region didn't see eye to eye with the Monacans. The Powhatans, for example, were one of them. Those tribes would often steal from the Monacans or even burn their homes."

Grandma's gaze turned distant as she recalled the stories passed down through generations. "There were moments when everything got muddled—Welsh settlers mistaking the Monacans for other tribes and treating them poorly out of confusion. Despite their friendship, some settlers did commit acts of violence against the Monacans, further complicating their interactions."

"Wow. I had no idea," Charlotte murmured.

"They didn't just grow crops and tobacco. They also grew a great variety of other foods, including fruits, and mined copper, which they used to make necklaces and other jewelry. Over the years, the Monacan tribe and the Welsh settlers developed a long history of trading horses and other livestock. However, as time went on, there were activists among the Native Americans who sought revenge for the injustices of the past. They began stealing horses from local Welsh farmers, and in some cases, even cattle and sheep."

Charlotte's eyes widened. "So, you think that maybe Mr. Adkins could be connected to all of this?"

Grandma sighed. "It's possible. Mr. Adkins was working at the farm in the sixties, but that doesn't mean his family didn't have ties to the Welsh settlers from earlier. If there were tensions brewing between the tribes and the settlers back then, it could explain some of the complexities we're facing now. Maybe Kaya's family has a deeper rooted history than we realize, one that intertwines with the struggles of our ancestors."

Charlotte leaned back in her chair, her mind racing with the new information. The rain continued to fall outside, a steady reminder of the storm brewing not just in the skies but also in their lives. She glanced around the table at her family, feeling the weight of history pressing down on them, binding them together in a web of stories, struggles, and hope for understanding.

Charlotte furrowed her brow. "Okay, let's think this through," she said. "Mr. Reynolds was at the farm at the time of Mari's kidnapping, and now he's on trial for Kaya's kidnapping and murder." She took a moment, her heart pounding. "And then there's Kaya's dad—he was working at our farm around the same time too. But if anything, he might have had some animosity against our family, not Reynolds, right? So, why did Reynolds target Mr. Adkins's family?"

Her family exchanged glances, the weight of her words settling in like the storm outside. The rain pounded harder against the windows, and a flash of lightning momentarily illuminated the kitchen.

"Who else was at the farm during that period? Are there more connections we should consider?" Charlotte pressed.

"Well, there was also that other deplorable guy, Emmanuel Salazar," William chimed in, a hint of disdain creeping into his tone. "I never liked him. There was something off about him, and... well, you know how it ended. Always threatening your grandfather with a lawsuit if he was fired."

Charlotte nodded, remembering the way Emmanuel Salazar had always lingered uncomfortably in the background. "Your ex-boyfriend, Jack Henry, was also there at that time, remember?" Grandma added. "He was around the same age at the time. I don't know who exactly he hung out with, but Jack Henry enjoyed raising horses and would often help out with the crews working at the farm. He was there often, especially during the summers, helping with cattle and sheep."

"Right," Charlotte said. "So, we have Mark Reynolds, Kaya's father (Mr. Adkins), Emmanuel Salazar, and Jack Henry all overlapping during that time." She paused. "But what does it all mean? What are you going to suggest next? That it wasn't a coincidence that I was assigned to Kaya's case?" She tried to inject a note of incredulous humor into her voice, but it came out more strained than she intended.

Her family sat in contemplative silence, the rain outside continuing to drum steadily against the windows, mirroring the storm of thoughts swirling in their minds.

"Well, was it?" Grandma suggested.

Charlotte laughed nervously. "Grandma, I was assigned the case because I asked for it. You know how much I care about these cases involving children. They make me feel like I can help at least some of those kids. Even though I couldn't save Mari," Charlotte responded, conclusively dismissing the suggestion.

The rain continued to fall. Charlotte's heart ached at the weight of her words, the memories of Mari pressing against her like a heavy blanket, suffocating yet familiar.

As the kitchen's warmth surrounded her, Charlotte's mind drifted into quiet contemplation. Her family's laughter faded into the background, and thoughts churned in her head. She felt a growing urgency to act, to uncover the truth behind the memories that haunted her and the connections that seemed to intertwine in unexpected ways.

"How quickly can we get to Mr. Underwood's farm?" she suddenly asked, breaking her silence.

Her dad looked up, slightly taken aback by the abrupt question. "In the rain, it might be about a thirty- to forty-minute drive," he replied. "Why do you ask?"

"That's where Mr. Adkins works," Charlotte said, as she grabbed her coat from the back of a chair.

As she searched the entryway for her boots, Charlotte was wearing her grandma's wool-made slippers, thick and cozy, providing a sense of comfort amid her swirling thoughts. She carefully took off the slippers and began to put on her boots, but her fingers fumbled as she struggled to fit her feet in.

"Charlotte, it's getting dark, and it's still raining. You shouldn't go there tonight," her dad cautioned. The gentle tone of his voice reflected the love he held for her, but she could see the worry etched on his face.

However, Charlotte's resolve only strengthened. "I have to go," she insisted. "There's something I need to figure out. I can't let anything stop me. Please, I need to do this for Kaya and Mari."

Her dad sighed. After a moment of silence, he relented, his protective instincts battling against her fierce determination. "Fine... I'll drive, but bring your rifle. If Mr. Adkins has anything to do with Mark Reynolds or Emmanuel Salazar, we should be prepared," he said, a hint of resignation in his voice. "Mine are both already in my truck."

With a nod of acknowledgment, Charlotte felt a rush of gratitude for her father's understanding. She quickly grabbed her rifle, feeling its weight in her hands—a reminder of the legacy of strength that coursed through her family. The storm outside echoed her resolve as she prepared to face whatever truths awaited her at the Underwoods' farm, determined to uncover the truth that could lead her closer to justice for both Kaya and Mari.

As the rain continued to pour, casting a shroud of mist over the landscape, Charlotte found herself in the passenger seat of her father's truck. The rhythmic drumming of raindrops against the roof mirrored the persistence of her thoughts. The world outside was cloaked in shadows, and the headlights cut through the darkness as they navigated the winding roads toward the Underwoods' farm.

Inside the truck, the warmth of her father's presence was a comforting contrast to the storm raging outside. Charlotte clutched her rifle, its weight resting reassuringly across her lap. The journey ahead felt heavy and significant, each passing mile drawing her closer to the answers she sought.

Her mind drifted to the Underwoods, a family who had always welcomed her with open arms. Memories of their kindness and hospitality lingered in her heart, but the farm held a different purpose tonight. It was a potential key to unraveling the mysteries that had haunted her for years—a chance to confront the shadows of the past and seek the truth.

Charlotte's determination was unwavering, fueled by the recent revelations that had stirred long-buried questions about her sister Mari's disappearance. She knew the visit to the farm was not just a casual call but a necessary step in her journey toward understanding and justice. The rain-soaked landscape seemed to echo her resolve, a reminder of the storm she was willing to weather to find closure. With a final glance at her father, who offered a reassuring nod, Charlotte steeled herself for the encounter.

CHAPTER XII

The Underwoods had long been a fixture in the community, their farm a cornerstone of history and tradition. Though not directly related to Charlotte's family, their lives had intertwined over the years in ways that only time and shared experiences could weave.

Mr. Harold Underwood was a man of the land. His broad shoulders and weathered hands told the story of a life spent working the fields. With hair that had long since turned silver, he carried himself with a quiet dignity that commanded respect. His piercing blue eyes held a spark of wisdom from years of observing the world around him. Known for his meticulous nature, Harold took pride in the precision of his work, whether tending to the fields or repairing a piece of machinery.

Harold and Charlotte's dad, William, had developed a long-standing working relationship, one that began when William was just a young man. William often helped Harold with his land and sheep, advising on the best times to move the flocks to ensure the soil could renew and flourish. It was a collaboration built on mutual respect and love for the land. Many a day, William would bring Charlotte along for these work visits, promising her a chance to go fly fishing once the day's labor was done.

The Underwoods' farm extended over a vast area, rich with rivers and lakes that provided excellent spots for fishing. Though Charlotte sometimes found it hard to wait for her father to finish his work, she knew that the late hours of summer and early fall were prime times to catch fish. Unless they were camping by the water, she wasn't too keen on waking up early, so the evening fishing trips were well worth the wait.

While her father worked, Charlotte often spent time with Edna Underwood, listening to her stories and indulging in fresh cakes and pies. Edna was the heart of their home, slightly shorter than her husband, with a warmth that enveloped everyone she met. Her hair, once a rich auburn, was now a soft gray, pulled back into a neat bun that spoke to her practicality. Her deep brown eyes radiated kindness and a touch of mischief. Known for her culinary skills, Edna's pies and preserves were a staple at the local market, and her kitchen was a haven of delicious aromas.

As Charlotte grew older, she began visiting the Underwoods' farm by herself, riding her horse from her grandparents' adjoining land. She loved these solitary rides, stopping by the farmhouse to ask permission to continue to the river, even though the Underwoods always told her it wasn't necessary. Her father had instilled in her the importance of respect and manners, and she took this lesson to heart.

The Underwoods farm was not only an excellent spot for fishing but also home to several beautiful swimming areas. Large rocks by the river created natural pools where Charlotte, her friends, and often Mari would spend sun-drenched afternoons swimming. During the hot seasons or when fishing wasn't ideal, these pools provided the perfect retreat.

The Underwoods had a daughter who lived in D.C. Although she rarely visited, her children often spent summers with their grandparents. Charlotte and Mari had become close to the Underwoods' grandchildren, forming bonds that enriched their summers. Having been raised in the city, fishing wasn't their favorite pastime, but Charlotte didn't mind altering her plans to include swimming and hanging out by the natural pools, enjoying the company of her summer friends.

The Underwood family had seen the community through its ups and downs, offering a steady presence in times of change. They were pillars of wisdom and support, often sought out for advice or a listening ear. Their friendship with Louis and Ann Jones, Charlotte's grandparents, had deepened over the years, strengthened by shared history and mutual respect.

The Underwoods had been there for the Jones family during the darkest of times, offering solace and support after Mari's death. They had brought over casseroles and offered a quiet hand of comfort, their presence a balm to the grieving family. Their unwavering friendship had been a source of strength for Charlotte as she navigated her path, a reminder of the enduring bonds that tied the community together.

As Charlotte prepared to visit the Underwoods' farm, she reflected on their role in her life. Their wisdom and kindness had left an indelible mark on her, shaping her understanding of community and the power of connection. She knew that whatever mysteries lay ahead, the Underwoods would be there, steadfast and supportive, as they always had been.

With the rain tapping softly on the windows and the memory of her family's laughter still echoing in her mind, Charlotte felt a sense of gratitude for the Underwoods and the role they had played in her life.

CHAPTER XIII

As Charlotte and her dad drove along the long gravel driveway leading up to the Underwoods' house, the rain had slowed to a gentle drizzle, but the darkness of the early evening was stark. The fading light cast a muted gray hue over the landscape, rendering the surroundings more subdued than usual.

Tall, shadowy trees lined the driveway, their leaves whispering in the wind. To the right, the barn stood sturdy and weathered, its chipped paint hinting at years of use. On the left, the caretaker's house glowed warmly from within, inviting yet unassuming, with rocking chairs on the porch that swayed gently in the breeze.

Charlotte took in the Underwoods' home as they approached the main house. It was a modest, two-story dwelling, its exterior a soft cream with dark green shutters framing the windows. The porch was decorated with potted plants, their colors muted by the rain-soaked earth. The roof had a slight slope, and the chimney puffed a thin wisp of smoke, promising warmth within. Despite the dim light, the house exuded a sense of welcome and familiarity, reminiscent of her grandparents' home.

Suddenly, a tall figure emerged from the shadows of the porch—a man holding a rifle, cautious at the approach of unexpected visitors in the rainy evening. He stepped forward to see who had arrived, the outline of his form stark against the soft glow of the porch light. Recognizing him as Harold Underwood, Charlotte and her dad quickly exited the truck, leaving their rifles behind, their arms raised to signal they meant no harm.

"We're not looking for trouble, Mr. Underwood!" Charlotte called out. "We're sorry if we're interrupting dinner!"

"Charlotte! It's good to see you!" Mr. Underwood replied, lowering his rifle as he recognized them. "I know you and your family well. Come on in!"

He gestured for them to approach, and they stepped onto the porch, feeling the warmth emanating from inside. Mr.

Underwood set down his rifle, acknowledging that these were friendly visitors and no danger lurked.

Inside, the Underwoods' home felt cozy, much like Charlotte's grandparents' house but smaller. The walls were painted a warm beige and adorned with family photos that chronicled decades of memories. A large wooden table occupied the center of the living room, surrounded by matching chairs, and a small fireplace crackled softly in the corner. The scent of wood smoke mingled with the faint aroma of baked goods, creating an inviting atmosphere. Mr. and Mrs. Underwood, both in their early eighties, sat comfortably in their armchairs, their faces illuminated by the firelight.

"Not interrupting at all," Mrs. Underwood said with a warm smile. "We just finished dinner. Would you like some tea?"

Charlotte hesitated, eager to ask about Kaya's father, Mr. Adkins, but remembering her manners, she nodded. "Yes, please." Her dad echoed her response.

"Milk?" Mrs. Underwood offered, and they both replied in unison, "Yes, please."

Once everyone had filled their teacups, cradling the warm cups with their saucers, Mr. Underwood looked at them, curiosity evident in his eyes. "What brings you here so late on an awful rainy evening?"

Charlotte felt the weight of her thoughts, wanting to tread carefully. She didn't want to scare anyone, especially since she wasn't entirely sure what her recent discoveries about Mr. Adkins meant. "I'm the attorney responsible for Mr. Adkins's daughter's case," she started, gauging Mr. Underwood's reaction as he nodded. "I'm sure you've heard about the trial concerning Mr. Adkins's daughter, Kaya. I think Mr. Adkins might be able to help me understand some information I just received."

Anticipating that Mr. Underwood may still be wondering why she had come at such a late hour, she added, "I'm also following some other leads while I am in town related to my sister's kidnapping, so I couldn't really wait to talk to Mr. Adkins before heading back to D.C. tomorrow."

Mr. Underwood nodded in understanding. "Of course. He's in the caretaker's house. Just head that way," he said, pointing. "You may want to take this flashlight; some of the lights out there are not working."

Charlotte finished her tea and stood up, thanking Mr. Underwood as she walked toward the door, her dad following closely behind. They both felt a sense of relief that the situation wasn't dangerous. The caretaker's house was less than two hundred yards from the main house, and they knew Mr. Underwood was armed, which eased their tension.

As they walked past the barn, they noticed a dim light spilling from the cracks in the door, along with the sound of someone shuffling hay around. Pushing the door open, they saw Mr. Adkins was inside. He looked exhausted as if he hadn't slept or shaved in days. Surprised to see Charlotte, he paused, his voice barely above a whisper. "Ms. Jones?" After a moment, he added, "Mr. Jones?" his confusion evident. "What are you both doing here?"

His surprise only fueled Charlotte's growing frustration. "You don't know who my dad is? How could you not recognize him?" her voice sharper, tinged with accusation.

Mr. Adkins nodded slowly. "We are acquainted."

Without waiting for a response, he put down the spade fork and signaled them to follow him. He led them to his house by the barn, politely inviting them inside.

The small house was simple but functional, with one main room that combined the living area and kitchen. It had a rustic charm, with a wood-operated iron stove in the corner, some chopped wood piled neatly beside it, and an old, rusty pot resting on top. A small table with two mismatched chairs occupied the center of the room, and a worn tablecloth covered the stained and heavily worn surface. Everything was slightly tinged with a thick layer of dust and grime, but it all felt in its place.

Some people might have hesitated to sit on those chairs or touch that table, but not Charlotte. She had been raised visiting many different farms with her dad, who always taught her to treat everyone with respect and to accept whatever the caretakers offered. She remembered fondly when she was around eight years old, making friends with the daughter of one of the farm's caretakers, climbing hay bales, and hiding among the gathered sheep.

As Mr. Adkins offered them a seat, he pulled another chair from the small bedroom adjacent to the kitchen, settling into it while avoiding eye contact, his body language betraying his internal conflict.

After a moment of silence, Mr. Adkins finally looked up at Charlotte, his expression heavy with regret. "Ms. Jones," he began, "I knew this would come up someday. But I swear I have nothing to do with my daughter's murder... or with your sister's death."

Surprised by his words, Charlotte asked, "What do you mean?"

"Ms. Jones," he said, "I'm not stupid, and I know you aren't either. I was surprised you didn't recognize me when we first met to discuss Kaya's case, but I knew you'd make the connection sooner or later."

Mr. Adkins hesitated, shifting uncomfortably in his chair, his body language revealing the weight of his secrets. He stood up, walked to the counter, and poured water into two glasses. Returning, he offered them to Charlotte and her dad, his hands trembling slightly as he did so.

"And what connection is that?"

"The fact that I worked for your grandfather, and so did Mr. Reynolds, during the same time..." Mr. Adkins hesitated. "But you don't understand..."

"Understand what?"

"It was a long time ago. I was young and foolish..." Mr. Adkins began, his gaze distant. He explained how he had gotten involved with a group of activists who routinely stole horses from Welsh farmers. When the group planned to target Charlotte's grandfather, they intended not only to steal but also to burn the farm and take everything they could.

"Your grandfather had always been nice to me," Mr. Adkins continued. "I didn't want to participate in that. I thought I had stopped it, but some of the people in the group ended up taking some of your grandfather's horses. When Reynolds found out about my involvement, he used it against me. He threatened to tell your grandfather if I didn't keep quiet about everything I knew—his dealings with the activist group and how things were spiraling out of control." "But why would Reynolds care? What dealings?"

Mr. Adkins looked down. "I think he knew I heard things about his past. I had overheard conversations that hinted at his darker dealings. He was involved in things beyond just the farm—things that could ruin him if they came to light. I think he wanted to keep me silent, not just to protect himself but to safeguard whatever twisted arrangement he had with Emmanuel Salazar."

"Emmanuel?" Charlotte asked, recalling the name from earlier. "My grandfather's former farm caretaker? What role does he play in all of this?"

"Yes. The farm caretaker. Emmanuel Salazar was always eager to please Reynolds," Mr. Adkins replied. "Emmanuel wanted to be in his good graces, and I never trusted him. He had a reputation for being ruthless, and I suspected he knew more than he let on about Reynolds's activities. They were close, and I worried that if Reynolds was determined to silence me, Emmanuel could easily turn against me, too."

"So, you think Reynolds might have targeted Kaya to get back at you? To silence you?"

"I don't know," Mr. Adkins replied. "I hadn't seen or heard from Reynolds in about twenty years. But I can't ignore the idea that my past made Kaya a target. I've lived with that guilt ever since. If I hadn't been so afraid of Reynolds and Emmanuel Salazar, maybe I could have done something to protect her." As he spoke, tears welled up in his eyes, his emotions laid bare for the first time.

Charlotte's heart ached for Mr. Adkins. "But why didn't you tell me? Why didn't you mention any of this when I first interviewed you about Kaya's case?"

"I was too ashamed," he said, gaining some composure. "I have always been grateful for everything your grandfather has done for me." Mr. Adkins shook his head. "I didn't want you to see me any differently. I knew that if my past came to light, I could also have been made a suspect in my own daughter's murder! I just couldn't bring myself to tell you. I am sorry, Ms. Jones. I really am."

"Tell me more about Reynolds and Emmanuel Salazar," Charlotte urged, ignoring his apology. "I need to know everything you can tell me about their connection and what they might have been involved in."

Mr. Adkins hesitated, glancing at the door as if he expected someone to burst in at any moment. With a deep sigh, he began, "Reynolds always had a way of knowing things. He was manipulative, and he had his fingers in many pies. I overheard him talking about other girls who had gone missing in the area. I knew he was dangerous, but I was too afraid to act. Emmanuel Salazar was his right-hand man. They were involved in something... something dark."

"What do you mean by dark? What were they involved in?"

"I don't know all the details," Mr. Adkins confessed. "But I suspect they were trafficking girls. I heard whispers and saw things that made my blood run cold. I thought I could protect my peace and my family if I kept my head down and stayed quiet. But now... now I fear I put them all in danger."

Charlotte felt a chill creep down her spine and pulled her quilted-down jacket tighter around her. "Do you think they could have been involved in Mari's kidnapping too? That they could have been behind it?"

"I can't say for sure," Mr. Adkins replied, shaking his head. "But the timing... it all fits. Reynolds had a network, and I fear he wasn't acting alone."

His words heightened Charlotte's urgency to uncover the truth, underscoring the significance of their conversation. She also recognized the delicate balance of Mr. Adkins's emotions, especially considering how raw and honest he had just been. "I need to know everything you can tell me about Reynolds, about Emmanuel Salazar, and about what happened back then," she urged. "If I'm going to find justice for Kaya, I need every detail, no matter how small. No exceptions."

"I'll tell you what I know."

Charlotte nodded. "We have to move quickly. The trial is resuming in a few days, and if we can find a connection between Reynolds and what happened to Kaya and my sister, we might be able to secure a conviction and expose him for his past at the same time.

As Charlotte listened to Mr. Adkins, a nagging sense of unease began to creep into her mind. She knew that the possibility of Kaya's case intertwining with her sister's case could present significant challenges for her as a prosecutor. While she was free to investigate Mari's case—especially since there was no active suspect—she also understood the ethical implications of delving too deeply into a matter that could conflict with her role in the prosecution of Mr. Reynolds in the current trial. Prosecutors are expected to remain impartial and allow investigators to do their job; stepping outside those boundaries could lead to complications regarding attorney ethics and evidentiary rules. If Charlotte pursued leads in her sister's case while actively prosecuting Reynolds, she risked the integrity of her position. Any evidence she uncovered was at risk of being deemed inadmissible in court if it was perceived as biased or improperly obtained. Therefore, while she felt the urgency to find the truth, she also recognized the need to proceed with caution, ensuring that her actions would not jeopardize the very justice she sought to deliver for both Kaya and Mari.

Mr. Adkins leaned back. "Then let's start from the beginning. I'll tell you everything I can remember."

As Mr. Adkins settled back into his chair. "Ah, Emmanuel," he began, shaking his head slightly as if the memories were difficult to digest. "He was an odd man, small in stature—only about five feet four inches tall—with dark hair that seemed perpetually unkempt and skin that bore the sun's marks from long hours spent outdoors. He always wore a hat, even indoors, as if he were trying to shield himself from the world. I think it was his way of holding onto some semblance of control."

Mr. Adkins paused, recalling the details. "As you know, Emmanuel Salazar lived at the caretaker's house on your grandfather's farm with his wife and seven children. It was a crowded house, especially with the demands of a family that large. His eldest child had Down syndrome, and the middle daughters were always tasked with taking care of him. You probably met them. Their mother was stretched thin, responsible for the two youngest—both still under two years old. It was a tough life for them, and I could see the strain it put on the family."

He leaned forward. "I think that's where much of Emmanuel's jealousy stemmed from. Whenever he saw you and Mari playing without a single care around the farm, riding horses, or simply enjoying the outdoors, I could see the envy flickering in his eyes. He thought it was unfair that your dad and grandfather allowed you two to have such carefree experiences while his own children were stuck working on the farm, taking care of their older brother. He often voiced his resentment, making snide comments about how 'the rich get richer' while he was left with the burdens of his family."

Charlotte felt a surge of indignation at Mr. Adkins's words. "That's not fair!" she interjected. "Mari and I had to work just as much as Emmanuel's kids did. Our dad and grandfather made sure we pulled our weight around the farm. We spent countless hours doing chores, whether feeding animals, mucking out stalls, or helping with the garden. We weren't just playing all the time!"

Mr. Adkins, attempting to calm her, added a soothing tone to his voice. "I know, I know. But he didn't see it that way. To him, it was all about perception. He felt like you two had a freedom that his children didn't, and it ate away at him. He was a small-minded man."

Charlotte's frustration simmered just below the surface. "He was wrong. If he said things or acted like we were somehow privileged, then he clearly did not know we worked hard for everything we had. I can't believe he would take that out on us!"

Mr. Adkins's expression darkened. "Emmanuel Salazar had a problem with alcohol, too. He'd drink more than he should, making him even more bitter. He was vocal about his feelings toward your grandfather and your family. He'd complain about how he felt taken advantage of and wasn't given the same opportunities. It was hard to hear him speak that way about your family.

On top of that, he was known for stealing from your grandfather. He'd kill sheep and sell them on the side, pocketing the proceeds for himself. He even allowed strangers onto the farm to hunt or chop wood without your grandfather's permission. It was his own side business, in a way, at your grandfather's expense."

Charlotte frowned. "That's awful. I can't believe he would betray my grandfather's trust like that."

"It gets worse," Mr. Adkins continued. "He was lazy, always trying to avoid work whenever possible. If he were singled out for a specific task, he'd act offended, as if he were somehow above it. He was always looking for ways to cut corners, to take the easy route."

Charlotte's dad, who had been listening intently, nodded in agreement. "I remember that well. Emmanuel would sulk around the farm, often grumbling under his breath when he saw you and Mari enjoying your time. He was always on the lookout for opportunities to complain, and I think it made him resentful of me and your grandfather for giving you girls a life of privilege that his children didn't have."

Mr. Adkins sighed, rubbing his temples as if trying to ease the weight of the memories. "One time, he even bragged about a knife he had stolen from you, Charlotte. It was a beautiful piece—your dad had given it to you, with a handle made from wild boar tusk and German steel. I remember seeing it. It was beautiful. He acted like it was a trophy to show off to his friends. I remember him boasting about how easy it was to take it when you weren't looking. It was almost perverse to hear him boasting about stealing from a child."

Charlotte felt a mixture of anger and sadness wash over her. "I had no idea. It's infuriating to think that he was allowed to stay around the farm with that kind of behavior. What was my Grandpa thinking?"

"He was crafty, and your grandfather didn't want to deal with the hassle of firing him," Mr. Adkins explained. "But in hindsight, it was a mistake. Emmanuel Salazar had his own agenda, and I think he was always looking for ways to exploit the situation. I wouldn't be surprised if he had connections with Reynolds's dealings if those rumors were true. They both had a knack for manipulation and with their secrets, I fear they might have been more involved than anyone realized."

Charlotte's heart raced as she absorbed all of this information. Everything was starting to fall into place, setting her mind into motion. "So, you're saying they could have been working together?" she asked.

"It's a possibility," Mr. Adkins surmised. "If that's the case, we need to tread very carefully. Reynolds is dangerous, and I fear Emmanuel could be just as much of a threat. You have to be cautious, Ms. Jones."

As she considered Mr. Adkins's warning words, Charlotte felt an acute need for haste. The potential connections between the past and present loomed large, and she knew that she had to act swiftly to uncover the truth.

As the conversation wound down, Charlotte leaned forward. "Mr. Adkins, do you have any idea where I could find Emmanuel Salazar?"

"Last I heard, he moved his family into town. He was picking up odd jobs here and there but hasn't seemed to secure anything permanent. From what I gather, he's been struggling financially."

Charlotte nodded, taking in his words. There was a sense of finality in the way Mr. Adkins spoke, but she couldn't shake the feeling that there were still many things left unsaid. "Thank you for your time, Mr. Adkins," she said. "I appreciate your willingness to share all this with us."

"No problem. Just be careful, Ms. Jones."

As they stepped outside, the air felt charged with the gravity of the revelations they had just uncovered. Charlotte's dad turned to her. "Do you believe him?"

"I only believe what I can prove," she replied. "And right now, all I have is his side of the story... We'll see."

They walked around the barn, the night enveloping them in a quiet stillness. The rain had stopped, and the skies had cleared, revealing a canopy of stars twinkling overhead. The darkness was punctuated only by the soft glow of the moon, casting a silvery light across the landscape. The farm felt peaceful now, a stark contrast to the heaviness of their conversation with Mr. Adkins.

As they approached the truck, Charlotte realized they had lost track of time. The Underwoods' home was dark now, indicating that Mr. and Mrs. Underwood had likely gone to bed. With a sense of relief, they climbed into the truck; the familiar comfort of the worn leather seats invited them to settle in for the familiar ride back home.

"Hopefully, Grandma and Mom have prepared some dinner for us," Charlotte said, her stomach grumbling in agreement.

As her dad started the engine, Charlotte couldn't dismiss the feeling that this was just the beginning. The threads of the past were beginning to weave into a tapestry of truths and mysteries that she was determined to unravel, no matter where it led her.

With one last glance at the quiet farm, they drove away, the path ahead still shrouded in uncertainty but now illuminated by the faint glow of hope.

CHAPTER XIV

The sun streamed through Charlotte's office window, illuminating the stacks of case files piled high on her desk. She sat in front of her notepads, fingers toying with her blue pen. The trial for Kaya's case loomed large, a weight pressing on her shoulders. Charlotte felt the familiar tug between her role as a prosecutor and her personal quest for answers about Mari's kidnapping. She had made significant progress in piecing together the connections between the two cases, but the fear of jeopardizing Kaya's trial kept her grounded in the present.

Dressed in a tailored gray suit that accentuated her blue eyes and stunning curves, Charlotte felt a wave of confidence. The fabric hugged her toned form, and the crisp white blouse elegantly framed her neckline. Her glossy blonde hair was pulled back into a sleek bun, giving her a polished appearance that matched her determined mindset. Today, she needed to exude confidence and professionalism as she stepped into the courtroom, ready to present her case with clarity and conviction.

"Focus, Charlotte," she murmured to herself, glancing at the clock. Time was slipping away, and she had to prepare for the day ahead. The atmosphere in her office felt charged with anticipation—she was on the brink of something significant.

The courtroom was a familiar yet intimidating space, filled with the weight of expectation. As Charlotte walked in, she felt the eyes of the spectators on her. The wood-paneled walls and high ceilings loomed above, creating a solemn atmosphere that filled the air. The judge's bench stood at the front, an imposing presence that commanded respect. The jury sat to her right, their expressions a mix of curiosity and seriousness as they prepared to hear the details of the case.

Charlotte glanced across the room at the defense table, where Mark Reynolds sat, his demeanor calm but unsettling. Just then, Charlotte's gaze was drawn to a familiar figure entering the courtroom—Reynolds's attorney, Eric Carter. Charlotte and Eric had a long history, having met at William and Mary Law School, where they both studied. Their relationship had been forged in late-night study sessions at the law school library and spirited arguments during mock trials. Eric was in his early forties, tall, with dark hair and a confident stride that exuded charisma. His presence under the courtroom lights was commanding, and his piercing green eyes held an intensity that could cut through the tension. Today, he was impeccably dressed in a tailored navy suit that accentuated his broad shoulders, paired with a crisp white shirt, a silk burgundy tie, and a matching pocket square that added a touch of sophistication. His shoes and silver cufflinks were polished to a mirror shine, reflecting his commitment to professionalism.

As their eyes met for a brief moment, Charlotte couldn't help but recall the irregular and secret romantic encounters they had shared during those years in law school. Though their timing had never seemed right, and both had pursued short-lived relationships with others, there had always been tension between them - a spark that neither had fully extinguished. Now, standing on opposite sides of the courtroom, they were once again locked in a battle of wits, their past connection adding an undercurrent of complexity to their professional rivalry.

Charlotte felt a mix of respect and competitiveness. Eric had always been a formidable opponent, known for his sharp wit and unwavering dedication to his clients. During their time at law school, they had often exchanged ideas and engaged in spirited debates, each pushing the other to grow. Despite their competitive nature, there had always been an underlying mutual respect that colored their interactions—a trait that had been rare in their field.

"Charlotte," Eric said with a nod as he approached the prosecution table, a slight smirk on his lips. "Ready to dance in the courtroom today?" he quipped in his velvety yet slightly cocky tone.

"Always," she replied; she was determined not to let his assertiveness rattle her. "How's your client feeling about today?"

"Confident," he replied, his smirk widening. "And why wouldn't he be? The evidence is flimsy at best."

Charlotte felt a flicker of irritation at his dismissive tone, but she pushed it aside. "We'll see how confident he is once the expert witnesses take the stand," she said, pursing her full lips.

Eric raised an eyebrow. "Ah, I see. Let's hope they have their facts straight."

With that, the judge entered the courtroom, and the atmosphere immediately shifted. The gavel struck the wood, commanding attention as everyone rose to their feet. The judge, a seasoned figure with years of experience, surveyed the room with a keen gaze before settling into his seat.

"Good morning, everyone," the judge started. "We will continue with the case of the United States versus Mark Reynolds."

Charlotte felt the familiar rush of adrenaline as she prepared to present her case. The next few hours would be crucial, and every moment counted. She had called an expert witness to the stand—Dr. Emily Hartman, a forensic specialist renowned for her work in child abduction cases. Charlotte had spent weeks meticulously preparing her for testimony, laying the groundwork for a compelling argument that would connect Reynolds to Kaya's tragic fate.

Dr. Hartman took the stand. The woman was in her late thirties, tall and composed, with shoulder-length brown hair tied back in a neat bun. Her glasses hung from the front pocket of her tailored black suit, and her crisp white blouse exuded confidence. The jury's attention shifted to her as she prepared to share her insights.

"Dr. Hartman, can you please state your qualifications for the court?" Charlotte began.

"Certainly," Dr. Hartman replied. "I hold a PhD in forensic science from Johns Hopkins University, and I have over ten years of experience working in child abduction cases. I've collaborated with law enforcement agencies across the country to analyze evidence and assist in investigations related to abductions and homicides."

Charlotte nodded, affirming the expert's credentials. "Thank you, Dr. Hartman. Can you explain the forensic evidence you examined in relation to this case?"

"I analyzed all of the forensic evidence collected from Kaya's crime scene."

Charlotte leaned in, carefully guiding Dr. Hartman through her examination. "What did your analysis reveal?"

Dr. Hartman began to lay out the evidence confidently. "My analysis revealed the presence of DNA found by the Potomac River, where the victim was found, specifically a hair sample that matched the defendant's, as well as trace evidence of fibers consistent with the clothing he was known to be wearing the same day Kaya's disappearance was reported to the police."

"Thank you, Dr. Hartman. Was there any indication of anyone else being present where the body was found?" Charlotte asked, her eyes locked onto the witness, willing her to maintain her composure.

Dr. Hartman's brow furrowed slightly. "No, there wasn't. The DNA evidence is quite specific to the defendant and to the victim."

"Can you explain the significance of the DNA evidence in this case?" Charlotte pressed.

"The presence of the defendant's DNA at the crime scene is crucial. It provides a direct link between Mark Reynolds and the location where Kaya was found. This connection is an essential part of establishing his involvement in the crime."

Charlotte nodded, sensing the jury leaning in closer, captivated by the gravity of Dr. Hartman's words. "What can you tell us about the reliability of DNA evidence in general?"

"DNA evidence is considered one of the most reliable forms of forensic evidence available. It is highly specific and can often provide definitive links between an individual and a crime scene. However, it is important to consider the context and the circumstances surrounding its collection."

"Could you elaborate on what you mean by that? How might the context and circumstances surrounding its collection affect the interpretation of the evidence?"

"Yes, absolutely. The context and circumstances around how the DNA was collected are really important because they impact how reliable the evidence is. For example, knowing when and where the DNA was found helps determine whether it actually relates to the crime. If it was collected from a place the suspect could have been legitimately, like a public area or somewhere they were known to visit, then it might not mean as much. But if it was found somewhere they had no reason to be, that's different. That's why it's so important that DNA is collected and handled properly, according to strict protocols. To make sure it holds up in court and can be trusted."

Charlotte smiled. "Thank you, Dr. Hartman. I have no further questions at this time."

As Charlotte walked back to her desk, the atmosphere shifted. Eric Carter, the defense attorney, rose for cross-examination with calculated confidence. "Dr. Hartman," Eric began, "can you please explain how DNA samples are generally collected?"

"Certainly," Dr. Hartman replied. "The collection of DNA samples is a very precise process because any misstep can compromise the integrity of the evidence. There are a series of steps that must be followed carefully, which include securing the scene to prevent contamination and preserve the evidence. This may involve cordoning off the area and restricting access to authorized personnel only."

"After the area is secured, an initial assessment is performed, where investigators assess the scene to identify potential sources of DNA evidence, such as bodily fluids, hair, skin cells, or items that may have come into contact with the victim or the perpetrator. Once this is done, the scene is meticulously documented through photographs and videos to capture the overall context and specific details of the evidence found. Investigators create sketches and take notes about the location of the body, any potential evidence, and the environmental conditions present at the scene."

Dr. Hartman paused and took a sip of water. "During the examination of the body, medical examiners or forensic pathologists, conduct an examination of the deceased to find potential foreign DNA sources. This may include collecting swabs from areas such as the mouth, nose, and any visible wounds to gather biological material; collecting hair samples from the body or surrounding area, which can provide DNA; if there are signs of a struggle, nail clippings may be taken to look for traces of the assailant's skin or other biological material. Investigators use sterile swabs, gloves, and containers to prevent contamination. Each item needs to be properly labeled and sealed after collection."

"It is very important to maintain a chain of custody for all collected evidence. That is why documenting who collected the evidence, when and where it was collected, and how it was stored and transported is crucial. DNA evidence must be stored in appropriate conditions to prevent degradation. For example, biological samples may need to be refrigerated or frozen. Then the evidence needs to be transported to a forensic laboratory for analysis ensuring that the chain of custody is maintained throughout the process. In the lab, forensic scientists extract DNA from the collected samples using specialized techniques. The extracted DNA may be amplified using different techniques. For example, we use Polymerase Chain Reaction (PCR) to create enough material for analysis. The DNA is analyzed to create a genetic profile, and this can then be compared to known samples (e.g., from suspects or databases) to find potential matches. After that, the laboratory generates a report detailing the DNA analysis results, including the likelihood of a match and any conclusions drawn from the data."

"Thank you for such a detailed response," said Eric, a small smirk playing on his lips. "So, was that detailed process carefully followed in this particular case?"

"Yes," responded Dr. Hartman. "To my knowledge, yes, it was."

"Are you sure, Dr. Hartman? Remember, you are under oath."

"Yes, I am sure. Why wouldn't I be?"

Eric walked to the defense's desk behind him and grabbed a stack of papers. Walking back to the witness stand, he raised it up. "Your Honor, this is a copy of the forensics report that Dr. Hartman prepared for this case, which has already been admitted into evidence. I would like to use it to refresh Dr. Hartman's recollection of her own report."

"I'll allow it," said the judge.

"Dr. Hartman," Eric continued, "please go to page seventy-eight and read the sentence that is highlighted in yellow. Only that sentence, please."

Dr. Hartman put on her glasses and leaned down, reading with some hesitation, "'However, I must stress that there were some discrepancies in the collection process.'"

"Dr. Hartman, can you elaborate on those discrepancies?" Eric asked politely.

Dr. Hartman looked momentarily uncomfortable, her eyes darting to the jury before returning to Eric. "The collection of evidence may not have been conducted in a completely sterile environment, which could raise some questions about contamination. The body was found outdoors, by the river. This can, at times, present challenges in maintaining a sterile environment, but—"

Interrupting Dr. Hartman, Eric continued reading directly from the report: "Additionally, the timeline of the DNA testing process was unusually prolonged, which leaves room for potential errors in the results." Isn't that correct?

"Yes. That is correct," Dr. Hartman replied.

Eric continued. "While the match is compelling, the possibility of cross-contamination cannot be ruled out."

A heavy silence fell over the courtroom as the implications of Eric's words sank in. Charlotte felt a knot tighten in her stomach; Eric had capitalized upon this uncertainty, casting doubt on the prosecution's case.

"Dr. Hartman," Eric continued, "in your report, are you suggesting that the DNA evidence collected in this particular case could potentially be unreliable?"

"Yes," Dr. Hartman replied. "While the DNA does match, the circumstances surrounding its collection could undermine its reliability. In forensic science, we must account for all variables, and in this case, the potential for error exists, albeit small."

Eric pounced on her admission, his questions rapid-fire. "And isn't it true that without a controlled environment, any evidence collected would be deemed questionable? That this opens the door to various interpretations of the evidence?"

Dr. Hartman nodded, her confidence visibly shaken. "That is correct. The area was frequented by others, which could lead to alternative explanations for the presence of DNA in the vicinity."

Leaning in, Eric's voice took on a pointed, almost mocking tone. "So, while the evidence may link the defendant to the scene, it does not definitively prove his guilt, does it?"

"No, it does not," Dr. Hartman admitted with frustration.

Charlotte felt an uneasy weight settle in her chest. Eric's demeanor shifted to one of calculated confidence, a smirk playing on his lips as he paced in front of the witness stand.

"Let's explore another possibility, shall we?" Eric continued, his tone almost mocking. "Isn't it true that this particular sample of DNA could belong to someone else entirely? Perhaps even a family member or friend of the victim? Maybe her father?"

"Yes, but—" Dr. Hartman began, her voice faltering.

Eric cut her off, his intensity rising. "But nothing, Dr. Hartman. You see, the prosecution is painting a pretty picture, but what you're saying here is that this match—this hair sample—is not conclusive evidence of guilt. Isn't that correct?"

Dr. Hartman, now visibly rattled, struggled to maintain her composure. "While the evidence does suggest a connection, it's important to consider the context and the potential for error. The presence of DNA alone does not equate to guilt."

"Thank you, Dr. Hartman," Eric said with a smirk, turning to the jury. "Ladies and gentlemen, you've heard it directly from the expert. The evidence presented is not only circumstantial but is also marred by doubt. The prosecution wants you to believe that Mark Reynolds is guilty based on shaky evidence. I urge you to keep in mind the principle that a man is innocent until proven guilty, and today, the prosecution has failed to meet that burden."

The courtroom buzzed with murmurs as the jury processed the implications of the cross-examination. Charlotte felt her heart race as she sensed the jury's growing doubt. She watched with frustration as Eric leaned back, a triumphant smile on his face.

After a lengthy and intense exchange, Dr. Hartman stepped down from the stand. The atmosphere in the courtroom shifted, a cloud of uncertainty hanging heavy in the air. Everyone seemed to be grappling with the new doubts that had been sown.

As Eric returned to his seat, Charlotte felt a sense of defeat. The defense had successfully cast doubt on the forensic evidence, a crucial pillar of her case. She glanced at the jury, their expressions now clouded with uncertainty, and felt a surge of frustration. How could this have happened? All her hard work—her dedication to seeking justice—felt like it was slipping away.

The trial continued for the next few days, but the momentum had shifted. Despite Charlotte's unwavering resolve, the defense capitalized on the doubts raised during Dr. Hartman's testimony. Witnesses were called, including Kaya's father, whose responses cast additional doubt on whether Reynolds was the actual killer. His testimony hinted at possibilities that Mr. Adkins himself could have been involved, creating an unsettling atmosphere in the courtroom. The buzz of speculation filled the air as the jury processed the evidence presented.

Charlotte poured her heart into her arguments, but the shadow of doubt loomed larger with each passing day. And though Reynolds had been convicted in the past, the question of guilt now hung in the balance, leaving Charlotte grappling with the weight of uncertainty.

***

The rain had finally stopped, leaving behind a glistening landscape as Charlotte drove toward the courthouse for the final day of the trial. The sky was a soft blue, dotted with fluffy white clouds that seemed to mirror the lightness she hoped would accompany her presentation that day. The air was crisp and invigorating, filling her lungs with fresh hope as she walked up the stairs for closing arguments.

Today, she wore a striking black dress that hugged her figure perfectly, its tailored silhouette exuding confidence. A fitted blazer topped the ensemble, a stark white color that contrasted beautifully against her dark attire. She paired it with sleek black heels that clicked purposefully against the marble floor of the courthouse as she walked.

As she entered the courtroom, Charlotte felt the familiar tension that seemed to envelop the room. Knowing her dad was there, as he often was at her trials, provided an extra layer of support. The judge presided over the proceedings with an air of authority. The jury's expressions were serious, their faces a canvas of contemplation as they prepared for the final arguments that would determine the outcome of the trial.

"Good morning, ladies and gentlemen," the judge announced. "We will now proceed with closing arguments."

Charlotte collected herself, her heart racing as she prepared to deliver her final plea for justice. She stood before the jury, her gaze steady and confident. "Ladies and gentlemen, today we stand at a crossroads—a moment that will shape the course of justice for a little girl who can no longer speak for herself. Kaya Adkins was a vibrant, beautiful child whose life was cut tragically short. She was a daughter, a sister, and a friend. Her laughter filled the rooms of her home, and her absence leaves an indelible mark on the hearts of those who loved her."

As she spoke, Charlotte felt the jury's attention upon her, the importance of the moment settling in. "You have heard the evidence presented during this trial. You have listened to the testimony of witnesses who saw the defendant near the location Kaya was last seen, the forensic experts who analyzed DNA, and the people who knew Kaya and her family. Each piece of evidence is a thread, woven together to form a tapestry of truth that cannot be ignored."

She paused, allowing her words to resonate deeply in the room. "Mark Reynolds is not just your average defendant. He is a man with a history—a man whose actions have consequences. The forensic evidence linking him to this crime is compelling, but it is the circumstances surrounding Kaya's abduction that paint the most disturbing picture. This is a man who has evaded justice for far too long, and it is your duty to ensure that he does not slip through the cracks once again."

Charlotte's voice rose with fervor, fueled by the emotion swirling within her. "The defense may try to cast doubt, to confuse you with technicalities and plausible deniability. But I implore you to remember the impact of your decision—not just on the defendant, but on the family whose lives have been shattered by this tragedy. Kaya's mother and father deserve closure. They deserve to know that their daughter's life matters—that her story will not be forgotten."

With each word, Charlotte poured her heart into her argument, invoking the memory of Kaya and the love she had for her family. "Consider the evidence carefully. Yes, the DNA was collected outdoors, but this does not mean it is unreliable. It is also a crucial part of the case that cannot be dismissed. The timeline, the witness testimonies, and the connections we have uncovered all point to one undeniable truth: this defendant is responsible for Kaya's death."

In that moment, Charlotte paused again. She closed her eyes and pictured her sister, Mari—her bright smile, her laughter, her dreams of becoming a marine biologist. She recalled the warmth of her last hug at the campsite, Mari's aspirations to protect the lakes and forests of Virginia, to explore the world and make it a better place. But in an instant, those dreams were stolen away, leaving only a void.

Opening her eyes, Charlotte looked directly into the jury. "I want you to see me not just as a prosecutor, but as a sister. Look at me, and then look at Kaya's siblings in the audience.

Can you imagine their pain? Can you see the confusion in their eyes? The ache in their hearts as they process the loss of their youngest sister? The one who should have grown up with them, who should have laughed with them, dreamed with them? Can you feel that pain? The pain of losing one's own little sister?"

Thinking about her own sister, huddled against the wall in that cavern, face streaked with dirt, clothes torn, hurt, Charlotte paused for a moment. "This man ripped Kaya from the safety of her own home. He took her from her parents. He took her from her brothers and sisters. Mark Reynolds stole Kaya from her own backyard. He drugged her. He tied her up. He raped her... numerous times. And when he had no more use for her, he disposed of her in the river. Can you imagine? Kaya's small body tied up, beaten ... raped ... by a man *that* size?" She pointed at the defendant.

Charlotte's voice shook with emotion as she continued. "I know that pain. I had to confront the harsh reality that my sister would never grow up to fulfill her dreams. Every birthday, every milestone, every Christmas—those moments are forever gone. My sister didn't deserve that. *Kaya* didn't deserve that. And Kaya's siblings ... Kaya's siblings deserve to feel safe, to have their sister's memory honored—just as I wish every day for Mari's memory to be preserved."

She took a step forward, then paused. "You have the power to bring justice to this family, to give voice to a little girl who can no longer speak for herself. This is not just a verdict; it is a chance to affirm that the life of an innocent child holds weight in our society. I implore you to look beyond the noise and focus on the heart of this matter. Kaya deserves justice. Her brothers and sisters deserve justice. Her family deserves peace. And it is your solemn duty to deliver that justice."

With that, Charlotte stepped back, her heart pounding in her chest as she felt the weight of her words settle in the room. The silence that followed was deafening, filled with the echoes of her emotional plea—a plea that lingered in the air, waiting for the jury's response.

As the defense attorney rose to present his closing argument, Charlotte felt a mix of emotions. Eric Carter approached the jury with an air of confidence, his posture relaxed and his tone smooth. "Ladies and gentlemen of the jury, I understand the emotional weight of this case. But it is essential to remember that we are here to seek the truth, not to succumb to emotion."

Eric began to dismantle Charlotte's arguments, meticulously picking apart the details of the evidence. "You heard Dr. Hartman's testimony about the potential contamination of the DNA. The prosecution wants you to ignore the reasonable doubt that exists. Can you truly convict a man based on evidence that may be flawed? The answer is no."

Charlotte's heart sank as the defense attorney expertly cast doubt on the prosecution's case. "Mark Reynolds is not a monster. He is a man who has been wrongfully accused. The evidence presented is circumstantial at best, and the prosecution has failed to prove beyond a reasonable doubt that he is responsible for Kaya's tragic death."

The tension in the courtroom rose as Eric continued, his words weaving a narrative that sought to exonerate Reynolds. "We cannot allow emotions to cloud our judgment. We must be diligent in our duty to ensure that justice is served—not just for Kaya, but for Mark Reynolds as well. A conviction based on shaky evidence would not serve justice; it would be a miscarriage of justice."

Charlotte sat gripping her seat with white knuckles, her heart racing as she watched the jury's expressions shift, uncertainty creeping into their faces. She knew the stakes had never been higher, and the weight of doubt hung heavily over the courtroom.

Once Eric concluded his argument, the judge called for a brief recess. The courtroom buzzed with whispers as the audience processed the impact of the closing arguments. Charlotte felt the weight of the world on her shoulders, her thoughts racing as she considered the implications of Eric's arguments.

As the recess drew to a close, Charlotte took a moment to gather her thoughts. She knew that she had to remain focused, to believe in her case and the evidence she had presented. The jury was about to deliberate, and the outcome would determine not just the fate of Mark Reynolds, but also the future of Kaya's family and the search for justice that had consumed her.

When the judge returned to the bench, the courtroom fell silent once more. "Ladies and gentlemen of the jury, you have heard the evidence presented during this trial. It is now your duty to deliberate and reach a verdict."

Charlotte's heart raced as the jury filed out of the room, their expressions serious and contemplative. As the jury exited, Charlotte also left the courtroom and sat outside, seeking a moment of calm in the quiet hallway. Her dad sat on a bench in front of her. The moments stretched into hours as she waited. She exchanged a glance with her dad, who offered a reassuring nod, but she could see the worry etched on his face.

Time crawled by, each tick of the clock resonating in the silence of the courtroom. Charlotte had poured her heart and soul into this case, and now it was in the hands of the jury.

Finally, after what felt like an eternity, the jury returned, the foreperson holding a piece of paper in hand. The courtroom held its breath as the judge called for order.

"Have you reached a verdict?" the judge asked.

"Yes, Your Honor."

Charlotte's heart raced as she leaned forward, eager to hear the outcome.

"On the charge of murder on the first degree, we find the defendant—"

The world around Charlotte seemed to blur as the foreperson continued, their words echoing in her mind. "Guilty."

As the judge banged his gavel, signaling the end of the trial, surge of relief engulfed her, mingled with disbelief. The courtroom erupted in murmurs, a mixture of shock and satisfaction rippling through the audience. Tears filled Charlotte's eyes, and she felt the weight of the moment crash down on her like a tidal wave.

Kaya's family erupted in quiet sobs, their expressions a mixture of relief and grief. They had finally received justice for their daughter, a long-awaited acknowledgment of the tragedy that had shattered their lives.

Just as Charlotte was beginning to process the victory, the courtroom buzzed with activity as people started to rise and prepare to leave. She felt a sense of closure beginning to settle within her, but it was quickly interrupted as one of her junior associates burst into the courtroom, a look of urgency on her face, rushing toward her with a folded piece of paper in hand.

Charlotte took the note, her fingers trembling slightly, amidst the loud, chaotic courtroom. People were everywhere, trying to leave, their voices creating a cacophony as she unfolded the note and read it quickly: another victim had been found about twenty minutes west of the downtown area in Washington D.C. The body of a ten-year-old girl, with certain characteristics suggesting she had been in captivity for an extended period and sexually abused. The girl had been abducted in broad daylight from her parents' home just a few months ago. Striking similarities to Kaya's case and the patterns of other victims sent a chill through Charlotte.

"Oh my God," she breathed. A wave of nausea washed over her, and she pressed her palm to her forehead, trying to steady herself. The victory she had just savored felt overshadowed by the grim reality of another loss.

Seeing Charlotte's expression, Eric walked up to her and asked what was going on. Charlotte gave him the piece of paper she had just received, her hands shaking.

"Charlotte, is there anything I can do?" the associate asked.

Before Charlotte could respond, the atmosphere shifted dramatically.

"Your Honor," Eric began, quickly stepping forward as the judge had just started to walk back to his chambers, "in light of the recent discovery of another victim with striking similarities to this case, I move for a new trial." He knew it was a long shot, a far-fetched motion, but one that, under the circumstances, he was entitled to request. Under D.C. law, a motion for a new trial can be made if new evidence surfaces that could potentially alter the outcome of the original trial. However, such motions are typically considered far-fetched unless the new evidence is compelling and was not available during the original proceedings. The evidence must be significant enough to raise doubts about the verdict. In this case, while Eric had a legal basis to request a new trial due to the discovery of a new victim with striking similarities to the current case, the challenge lay in proving that this new evidence was directly relevant and could potentially exonerate Reynolds or lead to a different verdict.

A hush fell over the courtroom, as everyone awaited the judge's response. The judge regarded Eric thoughtfully. The room seemed to hold its breath as the judge considered the request, his gaze shifting from Eric to Charlotte and then back again.

After a few moments, the judge addressed the room. "We will take a twenty-minute recess," he announced, "to deliberate on this matter."

Taking a recess in such circumstances was certainly unusual, indicating the seriousness with which the judge was considering the motion. Typically, judges in D.C. might not immediately grant a recess for deliberation without thoroughly reviewing any supporting evidence first, but the gravity of the new information warranted it.

As the courtroom emptied slightly, a buzz of anticipation filled the air. The audience, sensing the significance of the situation, lingered in clusters, whispering among themselves rather than leaving. The judge instructed the jury to remain in the jury room during the recess, ensuring they were not influenced by the discussions happening outside. Charlotte sat at the prosecution table, her heart pounding in her chest, her mind racing with the implications of this new development.

When the break ended, the judge returned to his seat, the courtroom settling into a charged silence once more.

"After careful consideration of the motion for a new trial," the judge began, "I find that the evidence presented during the original trial was sufficient to support the conviction. The forensic evidence, while questioned, was corroborated by witness testimonies and other circumstantial evidence that collectively established the defendant's guilt beyond a reasonable doubt."

The judge paused, allowing his words to sink in. "Furthermore, the newly discovered evidence regarding another victim, while tragic, does not undermine the integrity of the original trial's findings. Therefore, the motion for a new trial is denied."

A collective breath was released in the courtroom as the judge's words echoed throughout the room. For Charlotte, it was a moment of vindication—a recognition of the meticulous work she had put into the case and the justice that had been served for Kaya's family.

As the courtroom emptied, Charlotte stood there, taking in the moment—a hard-fought victory for Kaya that felt tainted by the emergence of yet another tragic story.

CHAPTER XV

With the trial behind her, Charlotte found herself back at The Gavel with her colleagues, celebrating their hard-earned victory earlier that day. The bar, decked out in festive holiday decorations, exuded warmth and cheer. Twinkling lights adorned the windows, casting a soft glow over the room, while garlands of evergreen and holly draped along the walls filled the bar with the scent of pine.

Charlotte loved Christmas, and the bar's holiday-inspired cocktails were a delightful nod to the season. She savored a sparkling concoction made with champagne, infused with cranberry and a hint of cinnamon, the flavors dancing on her palate like a festive symphony. Yet, amid the celebrations, her mind drifted back to the trial—each moment replaying vividly, the faces of Kaya's family imprinted in her memory. The relief of the verdict felt bittersweet, a reminder of the lives forever altered by tragedy.

Amidst the celebration, Charlotte couldn't help but notice Eric Carter, her opposing counsel, entering the bar. His presence was commanding, drawing the attention of those around him with his confident stride. Dressed in a tailored suit and a festive tie, he exuded a charisma that was both captivating and unnerving, his olive skin contrasting sharply against the crisp white of his shirt.

As he approached their table, Charlotte felt a mix of excitement and caution. "Congratulations on the win, Charlotte," Eric said, his voice smooth and genuine, carrying a hint of something more beneath the surface.

"Thank you, Eric," she replied, her tone polite yet guarded, aware of the eyes watching them both. Memories of their secret encounters twinkled in her mind—those stolen moments that felt both exhilarating and forbidden.

Their banter was light, but an undercurrent of tension thrummed between them—an unspoken acknowledgment of their shared history and the rivalry that had defined their interactions. Eric's gaze lingered on Charlotte, his eyes glinting with an admiration that seemed to dance dangerously close to something more intimate.

"So, what's next for you?" Eric asked, his question loaded with a curiosity that seemed to delve deeper than mere professional courtesy. Charlotte felt a pang of vulnerability as she considered her uncertain future.

Charlotte shrugged, maintaining a neutral expression despite the warmth of his attention. "Just enjoying the holidays and preparing for the next case," she replied, unwilling to give away more than necessary.

Eric nodded, a faint smirk playing on his lips, as if savoring the challenge she presented. "You deserve a break after all that hard work," he remarked.

"Thanks, Eric."

"So, are you heading back home for the holidays?" Eric probed, searching for any hint of personal insight she might divulge.

"Yes, I'm visiting my family in Western Virginia," Charlotte confirmed simply, her eyes scanning the room, taking in the festive surroundings rather than focusing solely on him. She felt a flicker of connection, remembering how he had once shared stories of his own family during their late-night study sessions, a glimpse into his world that added layers to his character.

"It must be nice to get away from the hustle and bustle of the city for a bit," he continued, trying to draw her into a more personal conversation. Charlotte noticed the slight shift in his demeanor, a momentary vulnerability that made her feel seen.

"It is," Charlotte agreed, offering him a polite smile. "I always enjoy spending time with my family. What about you? What are you doing for the holidays?"

"I don't know yet. I always like to wait until the last minute. Keep all my options open, you know?" Changing the subject, Eric leaned in slightly, lowering his voice as if sharing a secret. "You know, I always thought you'd end up somewhere else—maybe a big law firm or even politics," he mused, his words tinged with admiration. "You've got that presence about you—the way you handle a room, your ability to stay composed under pressure—and your beauty. It's impressive. I could easily see you leading a campaign or making a difference on a larger stage."

Charlotte chuckled softly, shaking her head. "I am not interested in politics. I'm happy where I am. The work is fulfilling," she said, her tone implying that she had no intention of revealing more.

He paused, as if contemplating his next move. "Well, if you ever change your mind, I'm sure you'd make a great senator," he teased lightly, his eyes twinkling with a hint of flirtation. Charlotte felt her cheeks flush, the compliment stirring something deep within her—a reminder of their past connections.

"Thank you for the vote of confidence," Charlotte replied, her smile unwavering as she tried to ignore the color rising in her cheeks. "But I think I'll leave politics to someone else."

Eric laughed, a rich, warm sound that seemed to fill the space between them. "Fair enough. If you ever need a campaign manager, you know where to find me. I know an excellent one I could introduce you to."

Charlotte nodded, acknowledging his playful offer with a polite nod. "I'll keep that in mind," she said, her tone light yet definitive, signaling the end of that topic.

Undeterred, Eric leaned in once more. "So, any big plans for the New Year?" he ventured.

"Just spending time with friends and family," Charlotte replied, keeping her response intentionally vague.

"Well, I hope you have a wonderful holiday," Eric said, his voice softening slightly.

"Thank you, Eric. I hope you do as well," Charlotte replied, her tone cordial but not inviting further conversation.

Their interaction was interrupted by one of Charlotte's female colleagues, who pulled her aside. "Hey, just wanted to give you a heads-up," her colleague said in a hushed tone. "Be careful around Carter. He's married."

Charlotte felt a jolt of indignation at the implication, her pride bristling at the suggestion. "Why would you mention that? There's nothing going on between us," she replied firmly. "We went to law school together, and that's it. This is strictly professional."

Her colleague nodded, but the concern lingered in her eyes. "Just looking out for you, Charlotte. You know how people talk. There's been a lot of gossip about him lately," she said, lowering her voice conspiratorially. "Some say he's been quite the charmer with a few others at the firm."

Charlotte sighed, her frustration mounting. "I appreciate the warning, but I'm not interested in rumors. Eric and I are just old friends."

"I get it," her colleague continued, "but you know how these things can get blown out of proportion. Did you hear about that junior associate who recently left his firm suddenly? There were whispers that Eric might have been involved somehow. Not saying it's true, but you never know."

Charlotte frowned, the gossip unsettling her. "People love to speculate, don't they?" she said, her tone dismissive but inwardly troubled by the potential implications.

"Yeah, they do," her colleague agreed placing a hand on Charlotte's shoulder. "Just be careful, okay? I'd hate for you to get caught up in any unnecessary drama."

"Thanks for the heads-up," Charlotte replied, trying to keep her tone light despite the irritation simmering beneath the surface. She valued her reputation and the integrity of her professional relationships, and the last thing she needed was unfounded gossip complicating matters.

As she returned to the table, Charlotte couldn't ignore the sense of frustration that had settled in her mind. The suggestion that there was something more between her and Eric felt intrusive, a misunderstanding of the dynamic that had always existed between them. She valued their professional rapport, but the insinuation of impropriety cast a shadow over the evening's celebration. Determined to focus on the positive, she rejoined her colleagues, ready to enjoy the rest of the night despite the unwelcome distraction.

Still, as the evening wore on, Charlotte found herself reflecting on her past encounters with Eric. She remembered their mock trial competitions in law school, where he had beaten her once, only for her to claim victory in the next round.

Their rivalry had been spirited, each pushing the other to excel, and it had remained a constant thread in their professional lives. But there had been moments of warmth, too—those late-night study sessions where laughter turned to shared secrets, where the line between friendship and something more had blurred.

Now, with Kaya's case resolved, Charlotte felt a sense of closure, yet also a lingering awareness of the complexity of her relationship with Eric. The festive decorations around her—the twinkling lights, the cheerful garlands—seemed to echo the duality of the moment: joy and tension intertwined.

As she glanced around the festively decorated bar, she allowed herself to savor the moment—the camaraderie of her colleagues, the joy of the season, and the satisfaction of a job well done. The road ahead was uncertain, but Charlotte knew she would face it with the same determination and grace that had carried her through the trial.

As she nursed her holiday cocktail, she couldn't help but smile, ready to embrace whatever came next.

As the night drew to a close, Charlotte decided to walk back to her apartment, the crisp winter air invigorating her senses. The city was alive with the glow of holiday lights, each twinkle a reminder of the season's magic. Her mind wandered to the events of the past few weeks, the triumphs and challenges, the moments of doubt, and the ultimate victory.

As she approached her building, she saw Alfred, the building's concierge, standing by the entrance. "Another late night, Miss Charlotte?" he teased gently.

"You know me too well," she replied with a soft laugh. "You know what I say. It's always nice to unwind with friends."

"Safe travels tomorrow," Alfred said warmly. "And give your family my regards."

"I will, Alfred," Charlotte promised. As she started to make her way to her apartment, she paused and turned back. "Merry Christmas, Alfred."

"Merry Christmas, Ms. Charlotte" Alfred replied with a gentle smile as he headed to his own apartment.

The city buzzed with life outside, but inside, she found peace.

As she reached her apartment, Charlotte reconsidered. Knowing she was leaving the next day for her family's annual holiday gathering, she decided to share a moment of gratitude with Alfred and his wife. She went to the kitchen, grabbed a bottle of champagne and three glasses, and headed back downstairs. She knocked on Alfred's door, ready to toast with him and his wife, sharing a moment of connection and warmth in the midst of the bustling holiday season.

Alfred's apartment, tucked away in a cozy corner of the building, was a delightful surprise. As Charlotte stepped inside, she was greeted by a space that exuded warmth and character. The walls of the entryway were adorned with colorful photographs, capturing moments of joy and laughter shared with family and friends. A soft, inviting glow emanated from a series of lamps strategically placed throughout, casting a warm, golden light that enveloped her in comfort.

The living room was a blend of classic elegance and personal touches. A plush, overstuffed sofa sat against one wall, adorned with colorful throw pillows that added a pop of color to the space. A wooden coffee table, its surface polished to a shine, held a selection of well-thumbed books and magazines, hinting at Alfred's love for reading. The room was filled with the gentle hum of holiday music playing softly in the background, adding to the festive atmosphere which was made complete by a lovely Christmas tree adorned with twinkling lights and mismatched home-made ornaments.

Alfred's wife, Margaret, greeted Charlotte with a warm smile, her eyes crinkling with kindness. She was a petite woman with a gentle demeanor, her big silver hair styled neatly in a way that echoed the elegance of the eighties. She wore a cozy sweater that matched the warmth of her home. "Charlotte, what a lovely surprise!" she exclaimed. "Come in, make yourself at home."

Charlotte handed over the bottle of champagne and the glasses, feeling a sense of gratitude and connection. "I thought we could share a little toast before the holidays," she said, her heart full as she took in the cozy surroundings with a smile.

As they settled into the living room, Alfred expertly popped the champagne cork, the sound a cheerful punctuation to the evening. He poured the bubbly liquid into the glasses, the bubbles dancing merrily as they rose to the surface.

"To friendship and the joy of the season," Charlotte toasted, raising her glass with a wide smile.

"To family and cherished moments," Margaret added, clinking her glass gently against Charlotte's.

The three of them sipped their champagne, the warmth of the drink spreading through them, mirroring the warmth of the conversation that flowed easily between them. They spoke of holiday plans, shared memories, and the simple joys that filled their lives.

Charlotte's eyes wandered to a family photograph on the wall. "Is that your family?" she asked, intrigued by the smiling faces captured in a moment of happiness.

Margaret nodded, her eyes softening as she followed Charlotte's gaze. "Yes, that's our family. Our daughter, Emily, and our son, Joe, and their families. It's a bit of an older photo, but one of my favorites."

"Do they live nearby?" Charlotte inquired.

"Emily is in Boston, working as a nurse," Margaret explained, pride evident in her voice. "And Joe is in Seattle. He's an architect and loves it there. It's a bit far, but we make it work."

Alfred chimed in, his voice warm with affection. "They're both planning to visit for the holidays, so we'll have a full house soon. It's always a blessing to have everyone together, even if just for a little while."

Margaret smiled. "We can't wait to have the grandkids running around. It's the chaos we love."

Charlotte felt a deep sense of warmth listening to their stories. "It sounds wonderful," she said softly, imagining the lively scenes that would soon fill their home.

"It is," Margaret replied. "Family is everything to us, and these gatherings are what we cherish most."

In that moment, surrounded by Alfred and Margaret's warmth and hospitality, Charlotte felt a profound connection. Their stories about their family resonated with her, reminding her of the true spirit of the season. Together, they shared more laughter and stories, the evening stretching into a tapestry of cherished moments that would linger in Charlotte's heart long after she returned to her own quiet apartment.

CHAPTER XVI

The drive to her grandparents' farm early on Christmas Eve morning was a familiar journey for Charlotte, one that stirred a blend of nostalgia in her heart. The winding road carried her through the breathtaking landscape of the Blue Ridge Mountains, where the air was crisp and filled with the promise of snow. The still sun hung low in the sky, casting a golden hue over the already snow-covered peaks, while the trees lining the road stood tall, their branches adorned with a delicate dusting of frost that sparkled like diamonds in the early sunlight. The soft crunch of snow under her tires resonated with each turn, echoing the memories of past holidays spent here.

Arriving at her grandparents' farmhouse, Charlotte felt a rush of warmth as she parked her car in the driveway. The sight of the charming home, decorated for the holidays with vibrant wreaths on the doors and garlands draped over the porch, brought a smile to her face. Twinkling lights wrapped around the pillars and dotted the evergreen tree in the front yard, creating a magical ambiance that welcomed her back. The air was filled with the sweet scent of pine mingling with the earthy aroma of the snowy landscape, a reminder of the many Christmases spent here with her family, the laughter of her sister Mari ringing in her ears.

Stepping inside, Charlotte was enveloped by the warmth and vibrancy of the kitchen, where her mother and grandmother were already bustling about in preparation for the evening's festivities. The countertop was adorned with an array of colorful ingredients—vibrant red bell peppers, fresh herbs, and the golden shine of butter—while the rich aroma of spices filled the air, promising a feast to remember. The sounds of sizzling and chopping blended with the soft hum of holiday music playing in the background, creating a comforting symphony of holiday preparations.

Grandma Ann, dressed in a vintage green cardigan which brought out her warm brown eyes, moved gracefully around the kitchen. Her gray hair was pulled back into a neat bun, with a few wisps framing her face, the years of experience evident in her nimble movements. As Charlotte stepped farther into the kitchen, her heart swelled with gratitude for the traditions that bound them together. The warmth of the stove radiated around them, wrapping them in a cocoon of familial love, a stark contrast to the chill that lingered in her own heart.

"Charlotte! You made it!" Grandma exclaimed, her eyes sparkling with joy as she stirred a pot of savory gravy on the stove. The kitchen table, beautifully set with a festive red tablecloth and carefully arranged dishes, was a sight to behold. Grandma's meticulous touch was evident in the way the silver flatware gleamed, and the centerpieces of poinsettias and other seasonal flowers added a delightful pop of color.

"Everything looks wonderful!" Charlotte replied, taking in the scene around her as she shed her scarf and coat. Memories flooded her heart—decorating the tree with Mari, laughter echoing in the halls, and the warmth that filled their home during the holidays. Yet a wave of melancholy washed over her as she thought of Mari's absence, now a bittersweet reminder of the joy they once shared.

"Your mom started cooking early this morning, so we can enjoy the evening without rushing," Grandma continued. "We're having all of our favorites tonight, celebrating everyone's roots—Welsh, German and Italian—as we do every Christmas."

Charlotte moved to help her mom, who was busy preparing the potato salad, a cherished family recipe. This German dish consisted of tender boiled potatoes mixed with chopped boiled eggs and onions, seasoned simply with mayonnaise or with salt, pepper, olive oil, and vinegar. The creamy concoction always reminded Charlotte of her childhood, of the joy in helping her mom in the kitchen, their hands covered in flour as they baked together. Beside the potato salad sat a dish of vitello tonnato, a rich Italian creation of thinly sliced veal dressed in a creamy tuna sauce and capers—a cold dish that everyone looked forward to every Christmas. Just as she finished helping with the potato salad, Charlotte's stomach rumbled in anticipation of her favorite dish—deviled eggs made with actual deviled ham, a delightful twist that added flavor and richness to the classic appetizer. "I can't wait for the deviled eggs," she said, her eyes lighting up.

As they worked, chatting and laughing together, Charlotte's felt a deep sense of gratitude for the traditions that bound her and her mom. The kitchen was alive with the sounds of chopping vegetables and the gentle clinking of utensils, a comforting melody of holiday preparations.

Just then, the sound of laughter echoed through the house as the Adkins family arrived. Charlotte turned to see Kaya's siblings—two boys and two girls—bounding through the door, their faces flushed with excitement. Charlotte had invited the Adkins family to spend Christmas with them this year, a gesture of solidarity and support after the recent tragedy and the long agony the trial for Kaya's death had caused.

"Charlotte! Come play with us!" Kaya's younger brother called out. The children raced past her, their laughter and footsteps filling the air like music as they headed to the den, where a beautifully decorated Christmas tree stood proudly in the corner. It was adorned with colorful ornaments, twinkling lights, and handmade decorations that told stories of Christmases past, each ornament a cherished memory.

Charlotte turned to her mom, feeling a warmth that only her mother's presence could bring. "Did you remember to get presents for the Adkins kids?" she asked.

"Of course, dear!" her mom replied, smiling. "They're in the closet. We'll put them under the tree while they look for Santa outside at midnight." Their family tradition was a little different than most. Instead of going to bed early on Christmas Eve and waking up on Christmas morning to open presents, the parents encouraged the kids to go look for Santa outside right as the clock was about to strike midnight. While the kids were outside, the adults rushed to put the presents under the Christmas tree, which the children would find moments later, often swearing they had just seen a reindeer or a sleigh flying over the house. Charlotte felt a surge of happiness as she imagined the excitement on the Adkins children's faces when they discovered their gifts. It was a tradition they had continued after Mari's passing, honoring her memory by ensuring that the spirit of giving and joy remained alive within their family.

As evening approached, the family gathered their coats, scarves, and hats, ready to head to church. The temperature outside had dropped quickly, the air crisp with the promise of snow. Hand in hand, they walked through the soft crunch of snow, the lights from the farmhouse flickering in the distance like stars in the night sky. The church stood at the end of the road, its steeple rising high above the treetops, illuminated by soft, golden lights that adorned its entrance.

Inside, the warmth of the church enveloped them, a stark contrast to the cold outside. The scent of pine mingled with the scent of burning candles, filling the sanctuary with an inviting aroma. The congregation was gathered, their voices lifted in song, harmonizing beautifully as they welcomed the Christmas spirit. Charlotte scanned the faces in the crowd, recognizing familiar friends from the Monacan community— children she had grown up with, many of whom had come to share the evening with her family, just as they had done since Mari's passing. This tradition began as a gesture of support and solidarity, a way for the Monacan community to honor Mari's memory and provide comfort during a difficult time. Over the years, it had evolved into a cherished ritual, symbolizing the enduring bonds of friendship and reflecting their mutual curiosity and respect for each other's beliefs and traditions.

As the service unfolded, Charlotte found herself lost in memories of childhood. She remembered the many Christmases spent with her Monacan friends, their families joining hers in celebration. The connection between their communities had always been strong, a bond that transcended differences and created a sense of belonging. In a school where most kids had dark hair and dark skin, characteristics of the Monacan lineage, Charlotte often felt like an outsider with her almost white, blonde hair. She had faced bullying for being different, the taunts and jeers stinging her young heart. But her Monacan friends had stood up for her, defending her against the bullies and welcoming her into their circle.

The memories flooded back—days spent playing in the woods, climbing trees, and sharing stories of their heritage, the laughter ringing out like music in the cool air. Charlotte had developed a deep interest in the Monacan way of life, eager to learn about their history and rituals. The Monacan children, in turn, were just as curious about her Welsh roots. Together, they forged a friendship built on understanding and mutual respect. She recalled their vibrant corn harvest ceremonies, where families gathered to give thanks and celebrate the bounty of the land, and the spring planting rituals that blessed their crops, reflecting a profound respect for nature. They often asked her to share stories of St. David's Day celebrations, where her family would gather for feasts and festivities, and enjoy cultural performances featuring traditional Welsh songs, poetry readings, dancing, and recitations of famous Welsh literature.

With each hymn sung, Charlotte felt a wave of gratitude for those friendships, especially during this difficult time for the Monacan community. The recent trial weighed heavily on her mind, a reminder of their lingering pain and loss. The church service brought a sense of peace, a moment to reflect on the love that surrounded them and the strength that came from community. As the pastor spoke of hope and resilience, drawing parallels between the Christmas story of new beginnings and the enduring spirit of the Monacan people, Charlotte's heart swelled with a renewed sense of purpose. She felt the warmth of the season embracing them, a reminder that even in the face of adversity, the light of love and faith could guide them forward together.

After the service, the families mingled outside, laughter filling the air as they exchanged holiday greetings and warm hugs. Charlotte felt a comforting presence among her friends, their shared history illuminating the darkness within her heart.

As they made their way back to the farm, Charlotte's thoughts drifted to Mari—her sister who had always loved Christmas, delighting in the decorations, helping their mother in the kitchen, and crafting special gifts for everyone. Mari had always been bursting with excitement, her laughter ringing through the house as they hung ornaments on the tree and baked cookies in the warmth of their kitchen. They would often prepare Bara Brith, a traditional Welsh fruitcake that Charlotte's family had slightly modified into a rich, fruity cookie. They also enjoyed baking Welsh cakes, their sweet scent mingling with the festive atmosphere. Mari would eagerly suggest making snowballs, the coconut macaroons dusted with sugar, ready to be shared with friends and family.

Once they arrived to Grandma Ann's home at the farm, the atmosphere was electric, filled with the warmth of family and the excitement of Christmas. They gathered around the table, beautifully set and adorned with festive decorations, as they prepared to share a meal that would nourish their bodies and spirits. Charlotte raised her glass, her heart swelling with love and gratitude for the family surrounding her. They toasted to the memory of their loved ones, a tradition that had become especially significant after Mari's passing, and the moment felt both bittersweet and uplifting.

"Before we begin, let's remember those who aren't with us," Charlotte's dad said as he raised his glass. "To Mari, to Kaya, and to all those we love. May their spirits live on in our hearts this holiday season."

The conversations flowed easily, laughter punctuating the air as they shared stories and recalled memories. The Adkins children, wide-eyed with excitement, eagerly awaited the moment they could open their presents, their joy infectious.

As the clock struck midnight, they raised their glasses to toast to Christmas Day, a celebration of love, hope, and the enduring spirit of family. After the toast, Charlotte's dad quickly dashed away to dress up as Santa, while everyone else rushed the kids outside to look for him. They returned moments later, laughter filling the room, only to find Charlotte's dad, still placing gifts under the tree. The children's eyes widened in amazement as they realized they had just seen Santa. He handed out gifts, each one met with squeals of delight, before giving a hearty laugh and making his exit.

As Christmas Day dawned, Charlotte awoke to the soft glow of early morning light filtering through her bedroom window. The ringing of laughter and chatter from the adjoining guest house—where the Adkins family had spent the night—filled the air with excitement.

However, as she lay in bed, Charlotte's mind drifted back to the trial. The connections between Kaya's tragedy and Mari's were too significant to ignore. Determined to uncover the truth, whatever that might look like, she felt convinced she had secured true justice for Kaya, but the unsettling thought of potential new suspects in Mari's case clouded Reynolds's guilt in Kaya's case. The more she considered the implications, the more anxious she became, knowing that any revelation could shift the narrative and impact the pursuit of justice for both girls.

Pushing those thoughts aside for the moment, Charlotte wanted to embrace the joy of Christmas with her family. She slipped out of bed and dressed in a cozy red sweater adorned with snowflakes, paired with dark leggings that kept her warm. The festive outfit wrapped around her like a comforting hug, a reminder of the love that filled the home.

As she made her way downstairs, the aroma of freshly brewed coffee and cinnamon rolls wafted through the air, drawing her into the kitchen. Her mom was bustling around, preparing breakfast with cheerful energy. Grandma Ann and Mrs. Adkins were helping, while Mr. Adkins and the kids sat in the den. In addition to the cinnamon rolls, her mom was making an eggs Benedict casserole, layering rich hollandaise sauce over fluffy English muffins, smoked ham, and perfectly cooked eggs. The scene was cheerful, with the sounds of clinking pots and laughter echoing in the background.

"Good morning, dear!" her mom said, her smile brightening the room. She wore a festive green apron over her plaid shirt, the colors reflecting the holiday spirit.

"Morning, Mom! Smells amazing in here!"

Grandma Ann, dressed in a cozy cream sweater that contrasted beautifully with her olive-green pants, turned to Charlotte, her eyes sparkling. "We're just about ready to take the cinnamon rolls out of the oven. You'll want to enjoy them hot and fresh!"

As they all worked together in the kitchen, the chatter and laughter flowed. The excitement of the day ahead filled the air, and Charlotte felt a renewed sense of hope as they prepared to celebrate Christmas Day together.

Just as the delicious smells filled the house, Charlotte's dad made his entrance, always late to help with breakfast but just in time to partake in the feast. With the table beautifully set and the inviting spread of cinnamon rolls and eggs Benedict casserole, Charlotte couldn't help but feel a flicker of joy amidst the storm of thoughts swirling in her mind. Today would be about family, love, and remembrance, and she intended to embrace it fully.

As the family and the Adkins gathered around the table, conversation flowed, but beneath the surface, Charlotte's mind was still racing with thoughts of the trial and the connections between her sister's case and Kaya's.

After breakfast, once the plates had been cleared, Charlotte excused herself and moved to a quiet corner of the living room, where the soft glow of the Christmas tree lights illuminated her face.

It was then that she recalled the conversation with Mr. Adkins at the Underwoods' farm—the cryptic information he had shared about his suspicions and the strange occurrences surrounding Kaya's death. His words stayed with her, and she realized she could no longer delay her investigation. The urge to honor Mari's memory and seek the truth about what had happened to her surged within her.

With a sigh, Charlotte resolved that as soon as the holiday festivities were over, she would delve into the information Mr. Adkins had shared. She needed to sift through the details to understand whether there were connections that could lead her closer to the truth.

Yet a small voice in her head reminded her to stay grounded. *The judge in Kaya's case had denied the defense's motion for a new trial, and rightfully so*, she thought. After all, there were few details about the new victim that had been found. Yes, there seemed to be some similarities to Kaya's case, and the new victim would appear to have been abducted while Reynolds was in prison. But that only meant Reynolds might not have been responsible for the new victim; it had nothing to do with Kaya's case—at least based on what they knew—and they didn't know much at this point.

Charlotte was grateful that the judge had denied the new trial, allowing the investigation into the new victim to continue. If that investigation uncovered any new information that could exonerate Reynolds, they could deal with that later. For now, however, she wanted to concentrate on what she could uncover about Mari's case and ensure that justice was served for both girls.

CHAPTER XVII

Charlotte knew she needed to find a way to talk to Emmanuel Salazar. Mr. Adkins had mentioned that he might be living in the nearby town. Floyd, Virginia, was a small town nestled in the foothills of the breathtaking Blue Ridge Mountains. It was a quaint, rural town that had retained much of its charm since the sixties. In the eighties, it was known for its intimate community and picturesque landscapes, with a population that barely breached a few thousand, making it a friendly atmosphere where everyone seemed to know each other.

As Charlotte drove through the winding roads leading into Floyd, she admired the rustic beauty of the area. The landscape was blanketed in a soft layer of frost, with the skeletal branches of deciduous trees glistening like silver against the crisp winter sky. The town was characterized by its charming wooden storefronts, many of which dated back to the early 1900s, their facades painted in muted pastels and adorned with handcrafted signs that swung gently in the cold breeze. The main street was lined with small shops—antique stores brimming with dusty treasures, their windows showcasing vintage trinkets and faded photographs; a family-run hardware store with creaky wooden floors that seemed to whisper stories of generations; and a cozy café, The Floyd Grind, which had been a staple of the community since before she was born. The smell of freshly baked goods wafted through the air from the bakery, famous for its rich apple pies, their sweet aroma mingling with the scent of freshly roasted coffee, drawing in visitors from nearby towns seeking warmth and comfort.

In stark contrast, she remembered how the town had changed over the decades. In the sixties, it had been even quieter, a simple, sleepy hamlet where the sounds of laughter and gossip echoed through the streets, traveling faster than the occasional car that passed by. Back then, the few shops that existed were mainly general stores, catering to the basic needs of the community, their shelves stocked with canned goods and household necessities. But now, with the emergence of artists and musicians drawn to the scenic beauty of the mountains, Floyd had developed a more vibrant culture, hosting occasional festivals that celebrated local crafts, bluegrass music, and the rich heritage of the area.

Charlotte parked her car beside the small police station, a modest building with a faded blue sign that read "Floyd

County Sheriff's Office." The structure, with its brick facade and white trim, looked like it belonged to a different era, standing as a guardian over the town's history. She stepped out and walked toward the station, adjusting her stylish navy blazer over a crisp white blouse, paired with tailored black trousers that accentuated her polished appearance. Her blonde hair was pulled back into a neat bun, and she wore minimal makeup, allowing her natural beauty to shine through.

Inside, she was greeted by Sheriff Thom Samuels, an old acquaintance from her high school days. The walls of the station were adorned with photographs of community events and commendations, a testament to the camaraderie between the officers and the townspeople. Sheriff Samuels was still the same friendly face she remembered, his dark hair slightly grayer now, and his smile warm and welcoming. "Charlotte! Haven't seen you in ages! What brings you back to Floyd?"

"Hi, Sheriff Samuels!" she replied. "I'm actually looking for Emmanuel Salazar. I heard he might be living around here."

"Emmanuel? Yeah, I think I heard he's been hanging around here lately. Might be living alone out by the old Thompson farm," he said, scratching his chin thoughtfully. "Last I heard, his wife left him a while back, and he's been getting by doing seasonal work at the farms. Not an easy life, that's for sure."

Charlotte felt a twinge of sympathy at the thought of Emmanuel's struggles—she could only imagine the toll it took on him. "Thanks, Sheriff. I appreciate it. Do you know if he has any of his kids or anyone else with him?"

"Just him, as far as I know. Not much family left around here," Sheriff Samuels replied. "You might want to be careful, though. He's had a rough time, and folks say he's not quite the same since... well, you know."

Nodding, Charlotte thanked him and stepped outside, her thoughts swirling. The pressure of her investigation pressed heavily on her, but she felt a sense of purpose propelling her forward. She needed to speak with Emmanuel soon.

As she walked down the main street, the familiar sights and sounds of Floyd surrounded her. The air was crisp and biting, and she spotted a familiar face at the café. It was Maya, an old friend from her Monacan community, who had always been a steadfast presence in Charlotte's life. Maya was wearing a vibrant red scarf that framed her dark curls beautifully, her warm brown skin glowing in the pale winter sunlight. She waved enthusiastically, her eyes lighting up as Charlotte approached.

"Charlotte! It's been too long!" Maya exclaimed, pulling her into a warm hug. The café was adorned with festive decorations, remnants of the holiday spirit still lingering in the air. "How are you? Come, sit down with me. I've heard some things... What's going on with you?"

"I've been all right, just busy with some things," Charlotte replied as she reluctantly took a seat, offering a soft smile. She was in a rush but didn't want to seem rude. "I'm actually investigating Mari's case. Just trying to piece some things together."

Maya's expression shifted. "I can't imagine how hard that must be for you to revisit the past. Have you found anything that could provide clarity?"

Charlotte hesitated, then decided to share a bit of what Mr. Adkins had told her about Emmanuel Salazar and her possible connection with Reynolds. After quickly summarizing her conversation with Mr. Adkins and the description of the parties involved, Charlotte paused, with some skepticism. "Mr. Adkins mentioned Salazar might know something about Reynolds and the people who worked at my grandfather's farm around Mari's death. I need to talk to him. In fact, I was on my way to find him when I ran into you."

Maya listened intently, sipping her coffee, the steam rising between them like a comforting veil. "You know, I've heard whispers about Jack Henry. People say he was around back then. Do you think he could be involved in any of this?" she asked.

Charlotte felt a shiver of unease at the mention of Jack Henry. "Yes, I know he was around. He spent a lot of time with me at the farm and with the crews that worked there," she admitted, her voice trailing off as memories of their shared past flooded her mind. She pictured Jack Henry helping her saddle her horse, as he often did back then.

She shrugged, brushing off the comment. "I don't know, Maya. Jack Henry's always been a bit of a mystery, but I don't think he's involved in anything nefarious. Especially nothing that involves human trafficking. We grew up together. He's not that kind of person."

"But you have to admit, it's strange, right? The way he just vanished for a while? And now with everything that's happening..." Maya pressed. "I heard from a friend at the local diner that he was seen hanging around the old Thompson farm recently. That's not a good sign, Charlotte."

Charlotte felt a chill throughout her entire body at the suggestion but quickly shook her head. "I doubt it. Floyd is a small and friendly community. I don't think anything like that could happen here."

Maya leaned in closer. "Still, you should keep your eyes open. After everything, we need to be careful of who we trust. Just be careful with Jack Henry and Emmanuel Salazar."

Charlotte nodded, as she thought of her complicated past with Jack Henry. Memories of their relationship flooded her mind, leaving her feeling torn. "I will. I promise, Maya."

As they chatted about old times and caught up on each other's lives, Charlotte felt a sense of warmth. Despite the weight of the investigation, reconnecting with Maya reminded her of the strength of their shared history and the bonds that held them together.

After saying goodbye to Maya, Charlotte slid into her car, her heart heavy with the memories stirred by their conversation. The warm buzz of nostalgia quickly faded as the urgency of her mission took hold. She turned the key in the ignition, and the engine purred to life, a comforting sound that grounded her amidst the swirling thoughts in her mind.

As she drove through the quaint streets of Floyd, the picturesque scenery blurred past her—charming wooden storefronts, frost-kissed trees, and the distant outline of the Blue Ridge Mountains. Each turn felt familiar yet distant, a reminder of a past that seemed both comforting and haunting. Her thoughts raced ahead, navigating through the tangled web of connections she had begun to uncover.

What if the abduction in broad daylight of this new victim was somehow related to Kaya's case? The chilling similarities stirred a fear deep within her. Kaya's case shared several connections with her own past. Could it be that the same monster who had taken Mari was behind this new tragedy? Or was there something darker at play—an insidious network that preyed on innocent children, with Reynolds at the center?

Charlotte's grip tightened on the steering wheel as she contemplated the disturbing possibility of child trafficking. The idea felt as foreign as it was horrifying, yet the recent discoveries weighed heavily on her. It was hard to shake the feeling that the threads of these cases were intertwined, a dark web woven from the memories of lost lives.

She recalled the reports of kidnappings, rapes, and trafficking of young girls that had emerged between the fifties and eighties—not just in Virginia but across the United States. Most recently, the case of Adam Walsh, a six-year-old boy from Hollywood, Florida, had dominated the news. Adam had been abducted from a mall, and his dismembered remains had been found by two fishermen two weeks later in a drainage canal in rural Indian River County, Florida. The post-World War II era saw a chilling rise in violent crimes against women and children, with increased media coverage awakening society to the horrors that lurked in the shadows. High-profile cases had dominated the headlines, each one a grim reminder of the vulnerabilities faced by young boys and girls. The nation was beginning to recognize the pervasive threat, and as the feminist movement gained momentum, discussions about sexual violence and exploitation began to break through the silence.

Yet here she was, in the heart of Floyd, facing the possibility that her own sister's kidnapping could be part of this horrifying legacy. The thought sent chills down her spine. *What if Emmanuel, with his connection to the farm, had been involved in something far more sinister than anyone had ever imagined? What if he had ties to a network of predators, exploiting children in the shadows?*

The road ahead twisted and turned, mirroring the confusion in her heart. She had dedicated her life to seeking justice, yet the complexity of these cases threatened to unravel everything she had worked for. Could she truly navigate this treacherous terrain without losing herself in the process?

As she approached Emmanuel Salazar's house, the reality of her mission sank in. She needed answers—answers that could link the past to the present and perhaps even illuminate the path forward. The possibility of child trafficking weighed heavily in her mind, and she knew that speaking with Emmanuel could either provide clarity or plunge her deeper into uncertainty.

Charlotte parked her car outside the modest home, the chill of the winter air creeping in as she stepped outside and tightened her jacket closer around her. The questions that plagued her—about Kaya, about Mari, and about the sinister patterns that seemed to emerge from the shadows—demanded answers.

As she strode toward the front door, the shadows cast by the setting sun lengthened ominously, and an unsettling feeling crept over her. The air felt thick, charged with an energy she couldn't quite place. Was it merely the chill of the evening? Or was something more sinister lurking just out of sight?

What had she truly uncovered? She felt as if she were stepping into a dark corner of her family's past, one that had long been hidden from view. The chilling thought that she might be on the brink of unearthing something dangerous sent a shiver down her spine.

With reinvigorated purpose, Charlotte smoothed her hair and knocked on the door, ready to confront the ghosts of the past and seek the truth that had eluded her for too long. No one answered. She raised her hand once more and knocked harder, the sound echoing through the stillness of the evening. Straining to hear any signs of life from within, she was met only with the soft rustle of leaves in the chilly breeze. A knot of anxiety formed in her stomach, tightening with every passing moment. She knocked again, each knock against the wood growing more desperate.

"Mr. Salazar?" she called out. No answer. The silence that enveloped the house felt oppressive. The setting sun cast long shadows across the yard, creating a foreboding atmosphere that only heightened her senses.

She stepped back from the door and glanced around the property, her gaze sweeping over the old wooden structure before her. The house appeared worn and dilapidated, its paint peeling and faded, revealing the weathered wood beneath. The windows were clouded with grime as if they hadn't felt the touch of a cleaning cloth in years. She moved cautiously along the side of the house, hoping to catch a glimpse of any movement inside.

Peering through the grimy glass, Charlotte squinted, trying to discern any signs of movement. The interior was dimly lit, shadows of the trees outside dancing across the walls, but she could make out the outlines of furniture lurking within. Dust motes floated in the air, illuminated by the fading light, giving the room an eerie quality. Was anyone really home?

Unable to dismiss the growing sense of foreboding, she decided to check the back door. The air was thick with tension as she cautiously made her way around the house, her footsteps muffled by the overgrown grass, which had emerged after some of the snow had melted. The backyard was untended, weeds creeping up in thick patches, and the remnants of a faded garden were barely visible under the tangled vines. Everything felt abandoned, as if time had frozen in this secluded corner of the world.

As she approached the back door, she felt a slight chill. The wood was weathered and cracked, the paint peeling like old skin. She reached for the handle, half-expecting it to be locked, but to her surprise, it turned easily in her grip. The door creaked open, revealing a darkened interior that felt like a gaping mouth, waiting to swallow her whole.

"Mr. Salazar?" Charlotte called again, as she peered into the murky depths of the house. The darkness seemed to swallow her words, and a shiver coursed through her as she stepped inside. The dim light filtering through the grimy windows barely illuminated the space, casting elongated shadows along the yellowed walls.

The air inside was stale and cold, thick with the scent of neglect. Dust clung to every surface, and cobwebs decorated the corners and window frames like ghostly curtains. Charlotte felt a wave of unease as she took in the disheveled state of the home. The living room was cluttered, filled with old furniture that looked as if it had been there for decades. An overstuffed armchair sagged in the corner, the fabric worn and faded, while a battered coffee table lay strewn with yellowed newspapers and empty takeout containers.

The remnants of a life once lived lingered in the air—an old television set sat silently in the background, its screen dark and lifeless. A layer of dust covered everything, as if the house had been frozen in time, untouched by human hands for years. The oppressive silence weighed heavily upon her, each creak of the floorboards beneath her feet echoing like a warning.

As she ventured farther into the house, Charlotte's senses heightened, her heart pounding in her chest. She moved slowly, scanning the dimly lit rooms. The atmosphere felt oppressive, heavy with the burden of secrets long buried. She turned her gaze toward the next room, her instincts screaming that something wasn't right.

As she stepped cautiously through the threshold, her breath caught in her throat. The sight before her sent a chill racing down her spine. The floor was littered with discarded food wrappers and a scattering of small roaches scuttling away from her intrusion. A stained blanket lay crumpled in the corner, its fabric frayed and dirty, as if someone had been sleeping there. The disarray of the room painted a vivid picture of neglect and desperation, and Charlotte's heart sank as she realized someone had been living in this squalor.

Her mind raced, piecing together the implications of what she had discovered. The sheriff had described Emmanuel Salazar's lifestyle as one of hardship and struggle, but this was something else entirely. *Where was he? Was he still here, or had he left?* The unsettling thought gnawed at her, urging her to uncover the truth.

Stepping back into the hallway, Charlotte's heart raced as she felt the weight of the silence surround her. The shadows loomed large, and the air grew heavier, thick with an eerie feeling. She turned back toward the rear entrance, considering her next move. Perhaps she should check the shed in the backyard; it might hold more clues.

As she stepped outside, the chill of the evening air hit her, but she pressed forward, her resolve guiding her through the tall grass and weeds that made the path to the shed challenging to navigate. The shed loomed ahead, its wooden door slightly ajar, swaying gently in the breeze. An eerie stillness surrounded the area, and the darkness within felt almost alive, beckoning her closer as the sun was quickly setting.

Just as she reached for the shed door handle, a sound caught her attention. It was faint at first—like the rustling of leaves—but it quickly escalated into the unmistakable sound of footsteps. Someone was outside, approaching quickly. Charlotte's heart pounded as the footsteps grew louder, echoing in the stillness of the evening.

She instinctively backed away from the shed and toward the back of the house, her breath quickening as she glanced toward the noise. It felt wrong, like an ominous presence creeping closer. Her instincts screamed at her to move, to hide. Every fiber of her being urged her to flee, but curiosity held her in place.

Charlotte quickly moved back toward the house, her heart pounding in her chest as she navigated the overgrown grass. The footsteps were louder now, echoing through the quiet evening, and she realized they were no longer just a distant noise—they were right outside. She ducked behind a nearby tree, pressing her back against the rough bark as she strained to listen.

The world around her faded into silence. *Who is out there? Is it Emmanuel? Or someone else entirely? What if it was someone dangerous?* The thought of being caught off guard sent a rush of adrenaline coursing through her veins.

Then, without warning, a figure sprinted past between Salazar's house and the neighbor's, racing toward the driveway that led to the street. Charlotte caught a glimpse of a large silhouette, the figure moving with urgency, their footsteps pounding against the ground. Instinct kicked in; she felt trapped in that moment, a deer in the headlights, her muscles tensed and ready to spring into action.

With her pulse racing, Charlotte emerged from behind the tree to follow, her instincts screaming at her to stay hidden. But as she rounded the corner of the house, her heart dropped. She collided with a solid form, the impact knocking her to the ground.

CHAPTER XVIII

Charlotte awoke slowly, the world around her a disorienting blur. As her senses sharpened, she became aware she was lying on a soft but unfamiliar bed. The sheets were a stark contrast to the chill that clung to her skin. The air was thick. She could smell a hint of cinnamon mixed with an unfamiliar scent that tugged at her memory. Shadows flickered around her like ghostly figures, and confusion washed over her.

She blinked, trying to gather her thoughts, but dizziness swept over her. Panic set in as she realized she wasn't wearing any pants. Only her briefs and an oversized shirt that hung loosely around her. The fabric slipped down her shoulder as she moved, exposing her skin to the cool air. It was a man's shirt, carrying the faint scent of cologne mixed with something earthy—something she couldn't quite place.

Charlotte's heart raced as she struggled to piece together the last thing she remembered—running into a tall, dark figure. *Where was she?* The question echoed in her mind.

Before she could sit up and look around, a weight settled over her hips, pinning her down. A large hand gripped both of her wrists, forcing them above her head, and her heart lurched. His grip was unyielding. A cold hand covered her mouth, its rough texture against her lips, sending a jolt of fear through her.

"Don't scream," a low voice whispered, almost soothing yet edged with a threat. The hand over her mouth stifled her panic, and she felt the warm breath of the man close to her face, his scent of cigarettes and sweat thick in the air.

Instinctively, Charlotte tensed, struggling against his hold. She could barely make out his form in the dim light, but the weight of him on top of her felt heavy and oppressive. Her heart pounded in her chest, each beat echoing her desperation to escape.

Slowly, the man shifted, his hand moving deliberately from her mouth to her chin and then down her neck. The touch was unexpectedly gentle, igniting a shiver down her spine. His face brushed against hers. His lips just grazed her ear. "Easy now," he murmured, his voice a blend of calmness and authority that both intrigued and terrified her. "Just relax."

As his hand traced down her neck, she felt the roughness of his fingers against her, reminding her of her vulnerability. She felt helpless. Her breath quickened, and her stomach churned with unease. She wanted to push him away, but the weight of his presence paralyzed her.

"Do not move," he whispered, his voice low and menacing, laced with a hint of something she couldn't quite place. *Excitement?* The thought made her stomach twist as he continued to run his hand down her chest, slow, steady, and deliberate, igniting a conflict within her: fear mingled with a strange familiarity.

Charlotte's mind raced, considering every possible escape route. She thought of the strength she had learned from her family, of resilience. But here, in this moment, she felt trapped. As his hand inched lower, tracing the curve of her stomach, panic surged within her.

Who are you? she thought, dread pooling in her stomach as his hand reached her hip, gently and slowly running lower and lower. His thumb grazed the lower part of her abdomen, then grabbed her thigh with a tight grip, then loosening as he began to spread her legs.

As he began to pull at her briefs, Charlotte's mind raced. *Please stop*, she thought to herself. She was desperate to get away but could not move. Just then something clicked—the familiar scent of his cologne, a mix of earthiness and pine that flooded her with memories. "Jack Henry?" she muttered, confusion washing over her like a wave.

The silence stretched between them, as if time had come to a standstill. The man stopped, his grip loosening. "Finally," he said with a soft calmness filling his voice, adding a hint of playful teasing. "You've been out for three hours. I was starting to wonder whether you'd ever wake up."

A surge of fury ignited within Charlotte, fueled by the violation of her space and the fear that clawed at her insides. How dare he think he could control her? The realization that her body was not his to command sent a wave of heat through her veins. A fierce determination replaced her paralysis—she would not be a victim.

Her heart raced, relief mingling with confusion. "Jack Henry?" she whispered again. "What am I doing here? What were you doing?" she demanded.

He smiled as he released her wrists and rolled off her, standing beside the bed. The light from a lamp flickered on to illuminate the room, revealing his old, rustic furniture that told stories of a life once lived.

Charlotte blinked against the brightness, her eyes adjusting to the scene before her. "Seriously, what were you doing?" she demanded angrily. Her tone was sharp as she pushed herself up to sit on the edge of the bed, self-consciously tugging the shirt down to conceal her undergarments.

"I was getting tired of waiting for you to wake up," Jack Henry replied. "You ran into me; your face hit my shoulder, and then you fell. You passed out and hit the ground."

"No, I don't believe that," Charlotte said, still confused. "What were you really doing there?"

Jack Henry looked at her, his expression shifting to one of genuine concern. "I ran into Sheriff Samuels at the coffee shop. He mentioned you had just stopped by his office and were asking questions about Emmanuel Salazar."

"You were worried about me?" Her voice softened. She searched his eyes, trying to detect sincerity behind his words. The tension in her chest eased slightly, but doubt lingered.

Jack Henry nodded, his gaze steadfast as he noticed the color rising in her cheeks. "Of course. Salazar is a strange man. You shouldn't have gone looking for him by yourself."

Her initial relief began to fade. "I didn't need your help," she replied defiantly, pursing her lips, but the warmth of gratitude simmered beneath her surface.

"You do need to be careful," he insisted. "I don't want you to get hurt. I know you are brave, but you must know when to tread lightly."

As they stared at each other, the atmosphere shifted, a blend of tension and unresolved feelings swirling between them.

Jack Henry stood tall, his presence commanding. He was a striking figure, embodying the strength of his Monacan ancestry. His dark skin glowed under the warm light, and his long black hair fell in loose waves just past his shoulders, framing a strong face with sharp, defined features. His square jaw was a testament to his rugged masculinity, and when he smiled, his white teeth gleamed, illuminating his face with a broad, infectious grin that could quickly disarm anyone.

His brown eyes held a kindness that seemed especially warm when directed at Charlotte, a softness that contrasted with the intensity of the moment. Those eyes had always conveyed a deep understanding, making her feel seen and cherished even in the most chaotic times. Though the years had passed, he looked every bit the same as he did twenty-two years ago, perhaps even more confident, his presence exuding an aura of self-assuredness that made her heart race.

Jack Henry was wearing blue jeans that hugged his muscular legs, a brown leather belt cinching his waist, showcasing a sizeable oval-shaped silver western buckle—a cherished gift from his grandfather when he was a teenager. The green and blue plaid shirt he wore was unbuttoned down to the lower line of his muscular chest, revealing the contours of his physique. He had always said undershirts were uncomfortable, a quirk Charlotte had found endearing and sexy, and it was clear that he wore his clothes with an effortless ease that suited him perfectly. His western cowboy boots, polished to a shine, added to his rugged charm, grounding him in the essence of his hardworking nature.

As Charlotte stared at him, taking in the familiar details of the man standing beside her, she felt a mix of nostalgia and a renewed sense of connection.

"Honestly, I was worried about you," he replied earnestly, stepping closer. "The last thing I want is for you to get hurt. I'll always protect you, whether you like it or not."

Charlotte opened her mouth to argue but forced herself to stop, drawn to the warmth in his gaze. "Seriously, what was that all about?" she asked, her voice softer now.

"I told you. I was getting tired of waiting for you to wake up," Jack Henry replied, a playful smirk tugging at the corners of his mouth. "So, I tried waking you up, the same way I always do. You know, just like back in your fancy apartment in D.C."

Charlotte felt a twinge of embarrassment at his words, a blush creeping up her cheeks. The connection between them hung unspoken.

As she gazed into his eyes, gratitude surged within her. "I appreciate it, Jack Henry," she admitted. "But I can take care of myself," she added, attempting to steer the conversation in a different direction.

Jack Henry smiled, genuine warmth radiating from him. "I know you can."

As they sat in the dim light of the room, the weight of unspoken truths hung heavy. Charlotte couldn't help but reflect on how much had changed since she and Jack Henry had reconnected after he separated from his ex-wife the year before. He had moved back to Floyd from D.C., yet their paths had crossed again months before that, in the most unexpected way. Their romantic rendezvous had taken place in her apartment in D.C., a haven where they could escape the scrutiny of friends, colleagues, and family. Despite the thrill of their clandestine meetings, Charlotte felt a nagging sense of guilt creeping in.

Her feelings for Jack Henry were complicated. On one hand, she was drawn to him. The chemistry between them was undeniable. On the other hand, she couldn't ignore her suspicions regarding his potential involvement in the troubling events surrounding Kaya's kidnapping and murder, as well as the disappearances of other victims—and even Mari's tragic fate. Each time she looked into his warm brown eyes, she felt both embarrassed and hypocritical. How could she harbor such doubts about the man she cared for, even as she craved his presence? Yet she hoped that keeping Jack Henry close could help shed light on the questions that haunted her.

They had spent countless hours together confiding in one another and enjoying private, intimate moments, but their conversations had never delved into the recent developments concerning Mr. Adkins, Reynolds, and Salazar. The fact that all their paths seemed to converge at her grandparents' farm— where Jack Henry had spent so much time—was a connection she couldn't ignore.

"Jack Henry," she began, her voice steady as she summoned the courage to shift the conversation to the serious matters at hand. "Mr. Adkins told me about the activists stealing horses, how they're trying to get back at Welsh descendants. Do you know anything about this? Are you involved in any way?"

Jack Henry's expression shifted. "I knew about it," he admitted. "But I couldn't betray my family or my people. I didn't say anything." He paused, his gaze drifting momentarily as he searched for the right words. "That's why I didn't show up at the campsite the night Mari died. I couldn't find a way to explain that situation to you."

Charlotte felt a knot tighten in her stomach. "What do you mean?" she pressed, her heart beginning to race as she leaned in closer, desperate for clarity.

Jack Henry looked pained, his features tense. "I had a huge fight with my brother that day. He was trying to convince me to stay true to my roots, to engage with our ancestors and the legacy they left behind. He believed that embracing our history was a way to honor those who came before us. But I wasn't ready to dive back into that world, especially with everything happening around us. When everything went down with Mari, I was torn. I couldn't face you and explain that I was stuck between my loyalty to my family and my feelings for you. I didn't want you to think for a second that I could be involved with people who wanted to harm your family or steal from them."

His honesty struck a chord within her. "But you were close to my grandfather," Charlotte said, her voice barely a whisper. "Didn't you think he deserved to know?"

Jack Henry shook his head, frustration etched across his face. "I didn't want to drag you into it. I always hated Reynolds and Salazar, especially the way Salazar spoke about you and stared at you and Mari. I'd heard rumors about their involvement with something bigger and darker. There were whispers of links to kidnappings related to sex trafficking, but I could never confirm those rumors. I knew some of my own people were involved with Reynolds and Salazar, but I thought it was related only to stealing horses around the area and selling them in other states to members of other tribes."

Charlotte felt a mix of relief and turmoil wash over her as Jack Henry's words sank in. "So, you're saying you had no part in any of this? You've never been involved with them at all?"

Jack Henry met her gaze. "I swear. I've never been involved with Reynolds or Salazar, other than the work we did at the farm. I despise what they represent. But I can't deny that I've heard troubling things about them. The way they operate, the threats they pose to our community… it's all wrong."

Charlotte nodded slowly. "I just wish I had more answers. This whole situation doesn't make much sense, and I can't dismiss the thought that we're all connected in ways we don't even understand yet."

Jack Henry reached for her hand, intertwining their fingers. "We'll figure it out together, I promise. I'll do everything I can to protect you and find the truth."

As Charlotte looked into Jack Henry's eyes, she felt the warmth of his assurance and the weight of their shared history. Despite the shadows of doubt that lingered, she knew that their bond was stronger than the secrets that threatened to tear them apart.

Charlotte felt the tension in the room shift as she mulled over Jack Henry's revelations. "Jack Henry," she said, "can you tell me more about your fight with your brother the day Mari died? It sounds like it was a significant moment for both of you."

Jack Henry's expression darkened, and he looked away for a moment, gathering his thoughts. "It was tough," he admitted. "My brother had become deeply involved in a lot of the tribe's activities, especially the ones retaliating against Welsh farmers in the area. He was consumed by anger over how our people had been treated, and it was changing him. He was no longer the fun, joyful kid I grew up with; instead, he was angry, constantly getting into trouble, and even dabbling in drugs."

"I can't imagine how difficult that must have been for you," she said softly. "What did you say to him?"

"I confronted him about it," Jack Henry replied. "I told him he needed to stop. His actions were becoming more reckless, and I was worried about what it was doing to him and how it was affecting our family and community. He and his friends would come to farms to steal horses and sometimes even sheep. They'd take what they could, claiming it was a form of resistance against the farmers who they believed had wronged our ancestors. Sometimes, they'd sell the horses or gift them to other tribes in the area as a way to build alliances.

My brother was instrumental in that movement, and I feared he was losing sight of what it meant to honor our ancestors."

As Jack Henry spoke, Charlotte could sense the weight of history pressing down on him. The Monacan Indian Nation had faced numerous challenges over the decades, struggling for social recognition and grappling with issues of identity and land rights. The civil rights movement had inspired many in the community to assert their identity as a Native American tribe, yet skepticism and resistance from the outside world had often met their efforts.

"My brother resented your family too," Jack Henry continued. "He didn't like that I was dating you. He was vocal about it, saying I was betraying our people by getting involved with someone from a family that had historically benefited from the very injustices we were fighting against. It was like he saw our relationship as a personal betrayal."

Charlotte felt a pang of guilt and sadness at his words. "I never wanted to be a source of division between you two," she said. "But you know, while I recognize that some of the Welsh in the region have had their differences with the Monacans, we generally got along very well. My family, in particular, has always appreciated the Monacans for helping us learn how to cultivate the land and the farming techniques we still use today. We've never had any issues with the Monacans or any tribe, for that matter. Our position has always been to treat everyone with respect and kindness, just as we want to be treated. But I understand how complex these feelings can be."

Jack Henry nodded. "That's true, and it means a lot to me. But my brother didn't see it that way. He resented your family and others for what he viewed as a betrayal of our people's struggles. He believed that I should be focused on our community's issues instead of pursuing a relationship with someone he viewed as part of the problem. That day, we fought about everything—about our family, about our future, and about how we were supposed to navigate the legacy of our people. It hurt, knowing that my brother was spiraling while I felt so helpless to pull him back."

Charlotte reached for Jack Henry's hand. "I can see why it was so hard for you to join us at the campsite that day," she said softly. "I had always wondered why you couldn't explain this to me in the past. You were always elusive and vague. But I understand now. You were caught between wanting to protect your brother and your feelings for me, all while dealing with the weight of your family's history and the challenges facing the Monacan community."

Jack Henry nodded. "It was a lot to carry, especially with everything else going on. I just wish I could have been there for you and Mari, but my brother's anger had me twisted in knots. I didn't want to be involved in any of it."

Charlotte hesitated for a moment, then asked, "Do you think your brother could have been involved in anything more sinister, like the disappearances and murders of young girls around that time? It's… it's a frightening thought."

Jack Henry shook his head firmly, dismissing the idea. "No, I don't think so. Despite everything, he loved our community and would never have hurt anyone like that. He was misguided, for sure, and lost in his anger, but he wasn't capable of something so horrific. I believe he was trying to fight for our people, even if he was going about it the wrong way."

As they sat in the dim light, the history of the Monacan Indian Nation echoed in their minds, a reminder of the struggles and resilience that shaped their identities. In that moment, Charlotte understood that the path forward would not be easy, but together, they would confront the shadows of the past and seek the truth that lay ahead. The promise of a new dawn began to break outside, hinting at the stories that lay ahead in the rolling hills of the Blue Ridge Mountains—the home that shaped Jack Henry's identity.

CHAPTER XIX

Located in the rolling hills of Virginia's Blue Ridge Mountains, the Monacan Indian community thrived in a landscape rich with history and natural beauty. The air was crisp and fragrant with the scent of pine and wildflowers, the vibrant greens contrasting beautifully against the deep blue sky. Jack Henry's family lived in a modest wooden home they had built themselves—a testament to their resilience and self-sufficient nature. The structure, while simple, was filled with warmth and love, adorned with handmade crafts that reflected their heritage and the stories of their ancestors.

The exterior of the home was a weathered yet sturdy log cabin, its wooden beams darkened by time but still strong against the elements. A small porch wrapped around the front, inviting visitors to sit and enjoy the view of the sprawling fields and nearby woods. The roof, covered in rustic shingles, sloped gently down, and a small chimney rose from one side, often puffing wisps of smoke when Tayanita prepared meals. Flower boxes clung to the windows frame, bursting with vibrant wildflowers that Nanyehi tended to lovingly, adding a splash of color to the earthy tones of the cabin.

Stepping through the front door, one was enveloped by a cozy, inviting atmosphere. The entrance opened into a spacious living area, where the scent of cedar and a hint of herbs lingered in the air. The room was anchored by a large stone fireplace that dominated the far wall, its hearth filled with firewood ready to provide the evening's warmth. Above the mantle hung an assortment of handcrafted items: dreamcatchers woven with colorful threads, traditional Monacan symbols, and family photographs in simple wooden frames that chronicled joyful moments over the years.

The living area was furnished with a large, well-worn couch covered in a handwoven blanket, its colors reflecting the rich earth tones of their land. A pair of comfortable armchairs, upholstered in soft, faded fabric, flanked the fireplace, creating a cozy nook perfect for reading or sharing stories. A wooden coffee table, scarred and polished from years of use, held an assortment of items: a bowl of fresh fruit, a few dog-eared books, and a small collection of stones and feathers that Jack Henry and his brothers had gathered during their adventures outdoors.

To the left of the living room was the kitchen, an inviting and bustling space where Nanyehi and Tayanita spent hours preparing meals. The kitchen was equipped with a simple wooden table, its surface polished from years of family gatherings around hearty meals. Surrounding the table were mismatched chairs, each one telling its own story of wear and tear. The walls were adorned with pots and pans hanging from hooks, as well as shelves lined with jars of dried herbs, preserved fruits, and vegetables, showcasing their dedication to sustainable living. A large, hand-carved wooden cabinet housed their dishes—intricate pottery that Nanyehi had crafted herself, often decorated with traditional patterns.

Adjacent to the kitchen was a small pantry, where the family stored grains and dried goods. The cool, dark space was filled with the earthy scent of corn and beans, staples of their diet. A handmade basket sat in the corner, filled with freshly harvested herbs that Nanyehi would use in her cooking, and a wooden crate held a selection of seasonal fruits picked from their garden and small orchard.

Moving through the living area toward the back of the house, one would find a hallway leading to the family's bedrooms. The first door on the right opened to Kweku's room. It was a sanctuary of sorts, decorated with posters of local wildlife and maps of the surrounding area. A sturdy wooden bed, covered in a patchwork quilt, occupied one corner, while a desk piled high with books and papers stood against the wall, reflecting his dedication to learning. A small bookshelf held a collection of stories passed down through generations, along with nature guides that Kweku often used during his explorations.

Next door was Atohi's room, which felt like an extension of the outdoors. His walls were adorned with sketches of the animals he admired, and a homemade wooden shelf was filled with various artifacts gathered from the forest—animal bones, colorful stones, and feathers. A cozy hammock hung between two posts, where Atohi often spent his afternoons reading or daydreaming, swaying gently as he listened to the sounds of nature.

At the end of the hallway was Jack Henry's room, a blend of his interests and aspirations. The wooden walls were decorated with images of Monacan history and symbols of his culture. A well-used desk filled with art supplies and notebooks showcased his creativity, while a bed covered in a vibrant handwoven blanket provided comfort and warmth. A small window offered a view of the mountains, allowing the sunlight to stream in and illuminate the room, filling it with a sense of possibility.

Across from the bedrooms was a shared bathroom, simple in design but functional. It featured a wooden vanity with a mirror framed by hand-carved wood above it, and a small tub where the family would wash after long days spent in the fields. The walls were adorned with woven baskets, storing toiletries and handmade soaps that Nanyehi crafted using herbs from their garden and milk from their goats.

The final room in the house was a small den, a place for family meetings and storytelling sessions. The walls of this room were covered in colorful textiles, each piece telling a story of their heritage. Cushions were strewn about the floor, inviting family members to sit together, share stories, and pass down traditions. A small altar stood at one end, adorned with sacred items, photographs of ancestors, and offerings of gratitude, reminding the family of their connection to their past.

The home was not just a structure; it was a living testament to the Monacan way of life, filled with love, laughter, and a deep respect for their heritage. It was a place where stories were shared, traditions were honored, and bonds were strengthened.

Jack Henry was the middle child among three brothers, each carrying a piece of their family's legacy in their own unique way. His eldest brother, Kweku, was known for his keen sense of justice and unwavering commitment to the Monacan cause, often spending his days organizing community meetings and educating younger members about their history. The youngest, Atohi, was a free spirit, always exploring the woods that surrounded their home, seeking adventure and solace in the embrace of nature.

Their parents, Nanyehi and Tayanita, were the backbone of their family, embodying the strength and resilience that defined the Monacan people. Nanyehi was a skilled weaver, creating intricate textiles that told stories of her culture and traditions, while Tayanita worked the land, cultivating crops that sustained his family and contributed to the community. Their home was often filled with the sounds of laughter, storytelling, and the rhythmic beat of drums during gatherings, where Monacan traditions came to life through dance and song.

Charlotte, a regular visitor to their community, had developed a strong interest in their culture and way of living. Her curiosity and inquisitive nature had been evident since she was a little girl, when she would wander into their yard, wide-eyed and eager to learn. The Monacan family welcomed her with open arms, delighted by her fascination with their traditions. Charlotte often joined them in the kitchen, helping Nanyehi prepare meals, her laughter mingling with the warmth of the hearth. She would listen intently as Tayanita recounted stories of their ancestors, her eyes sparkling with wonder as she absorbed every word.

One particularly poignant story that echoed throughout the family was how Jack Henry came into the world. His mother, Nanyehi, had been traveling with Tayanita when they found themselves stranded in the middle of nowhere, their old truck breaking down on a desolate stretch of road. As the hours passed, Nanyehi began to feel the first pangs of labor. Panic set in as they realized they were far from any hospital or help, the isolation pressing in on them like the thick summer air.

Just when despair threatened to overwhelm them, a friendly farmer happened upon their stranded vehicle. Sensing their distress, he quickly offered assistance, helping them into his truck and rushing to his farmhouse nearby. With his wife's help, the farmer tended to Nanyehi as she labored, providing comfort and support during those tense moments. It was there, in the warmth of that humble home surrounded by fields of golden wheat, that Jack Henry was born.

In gratitude for the farmer's kindness, Tayanita and Nanyehi decided to name their son after him—Jack Henry. The name became a symbol of not only their appreciation but also the community spirit that defined the Monacan way of life. Jack Henry grew up hearing the story of his birth, instilling in him a deep sense of connection to both his family and the broader community.

As he reflected on his family home, he thought of Charlotte's ongoing involvement in their lives. She often participated in community events, learning traditional dances and songs, and sharing her own stories in return. Her presence brought a sense of connection and understanding, bridging the gap between two cultures and fostering a mutual respect that had deepened over time.

The Monacans, descendants of a rich and vibrant culture, have long been Jakes of the land. Their history dates back thousands of years, well before the arrival of European settlers. Their people had faced numerous challenges throughout their history, long before most recorded history, starting in the early seventeenth century when European settlers began to arrive in the area. Displacement and conflict were generally common as the settlers sought to claim the fertile lands of Virginia for their own. But the Monacans had to navigate many more pressures that were unrelated to the newcomers. The complex dynamics with neighboring tribes, such as the Powhatan Confederacy and the Shawnee, were present long before the European settlers. Disputes over hunting grounds, fishing areas, and other natural resources often led to tensions and skirmishes, forcing the Monacans to fight to protect their way of life and the land they held sacred.

Despite these historical struggles, the community remained resilient, drawing strength from their deep connection to the earth and their ancestors. They practiced sustainable farming, planting corn, beans, and squash—known as the "Three Sisters"—in harmony with the cycles of nature. This connection to the land was woven into their way of life, a reflection of their respect for the environment and the generations that came before them.

The memories of his childhood flooded back—running through the woods with Kweku and Atohi, the laughter shared over meals, and the lessons learned from his parents about courage and respect for their heritage. Yet as the challenges of adolescence loomed large, Jack Henry felt a growing conflict between his loyalty to his family and the world beyond their community. He grappled with the expectations placed upon him, particularly in the wake of Mari's death and the tumultuous changes facing the Monacan Nation.

The Monacans had a rich cultural heritage, marked by traditions that celebrated their identity and resilience. Their gatherings often included storytelling sessions where elders recounted tales of bravery, survival, and the connection to their ancestors. These stories served not only as entertainment but also as a means of passing down knowledge and instilling pride in their heritage. Jack Henry cherished these moments, feeling a profound connection to the past and a responsibility to carry it forward.

Yet as he navigated the complexities of his relationships, his heart was heavy with the weight of his brother's struggles and the fear of losing the very essence of what it meant to be Monacan. The land, the traditions, and the stories were not just part of his identity; they were the foundation upon which he would build his future. And as the world around him continued to change, Jack Henry knew he would have to confront both his family's legacy and the challenges it presented.

As the sun rose in the horizon, casting a warm glow over the landscape, Jack Henry settled into the cozy guest house that his parents had offered him after his divorce. The guest house stood a stone's throw away from the main cabin, a charming structure crafted from the same weathered logs of the family home. Nestled among towering pines and blanketed with fresh snow, it provided a sense of tranquility, a respite where he could gather his thoughts and heal.

The exterior of the guest house mirrored the main cabin, with rustic shingles adorning the roof and sturdy wooden boxes beneath the windows, filled with evergreen sprigs that added a touch of life against the winder backdrop. A small porch wrapped around the front, where a pair of rocking chairs invited quiet contemplation as the world awakened or drifted into slumber. Inside, the atmosphere was warm and inviting, the air filled with the comforting scent of cedar and fresh linens.

Upon entering, one was greeted by a small yet functional living area, furnished with a plush armchair and a simple wooden coffee table. A handwoven blanket lay draped over the armrest, a reminder of his mother's nurturing touch. The walls were adorned with photographs of family gatherings and nature scenes, capturing moments of joy and connection. A compact kitchenette, equipped with a small stove and a sink, offered the essentials for preparing light meals, while shelves held an array of mugs, plates, and a few of his favorite books— each a cherished escape.

The bedroom, just beyond the living area, was a sanctuary filled with rich hues and natural light. The bed, covered with a vibrant quilt that echoed the colors of the Monacan landscape—deep greens, rich browns, and warm golds—provided a comforting embrace at the end of the day. A nightstand, crafted from reclaimed wood with a rustic charm, held a small lamp that cast a gentle glow and a journal where Jack Henry often poured out his thoughts and reflections, its pages filled with sketches and dreams yet to unfold. The window framed a picturesque view of the mountains, their peaks kissed by the first light of dawn, a daily reminder of the beauty surrounding him and the strength of his heritage.

On this particular morning, Jack Henry found himself gazing out the window, lost in thought. His mind drifted to the memories of his childhood—the laughter, the traditions, and the bond he shared with his family. He felt a profound sense of longing for the stability he once knew, a longing that deepened whenever he thought of Charlotte, who was still asleep in the bed. Her presence brought a flicker of warmth to the otherwise quiet guest house, a beacon of comfort during this tumultuous time in his life.

As he looked at her, Jack Henry admired how peaceful she appeared, her chest rising and falling gently with each breath. The soft glow of the morning sun illuminated her features, casting delicate shadows that highlighted the contours of her face. He felt a rush of gratitude for her companionship, especially in the wake of his divorce. She had become an anchor, a reminder of the beauty that still existed in the world, even amidst the chaos of his emotions.

Lost in his thoughts, Jack Henry reflected on the connections that bound them all—their shared experiences, the intertwining of their lives against the backdrop of Monacan traditions, and the way Charlotte embraced their culture with open arms. He felt a deep sense of pride in his heritage and a renewed desire to share it with her.

Morning light began to filter through the window, gradually brightening the room. The soft chirping of birds outside heralded the arrival of a new day, their cheerful songs weaving through the open window like a gentle invitation. As the sun climbed higher, Charlotte stirred, her eyelids fluttering open. Blinking against the light, she smiled sleepily, her eyes meeting Jack Henry's.

"Good morning," he said softly, a smile spreading across his face. "Did you sleep well?"

She stretched, a contented sigh escaping her lips, and Jack Henry noticed the way her hair fell, tousled and beautiful around her shoulders. "Better than I have in a long time," she replied, her voice still thick with sleep.

Jack Henry's heart swelled at her words. "I'm glad to hear that. I spoke to my mom earlier this morning. She said we were welcome to join them for breakfast in the main house. Would you like to join us?"

Charlotte's face brightened at the suggestion, a spark of excitement lighting up her eyes. "I would love to! I can't wait to try one of Nanyehi's famous pancakes," she said, her enthusiasm evident as she swung her legs over the side of the bed and stood, stretching her arms above her head.

Jack Henry chuckled, recalling how his mother's pancakes were legendary in their community, fluffy and warm, often served with fresh berries and honey. "Trust me, you won't be disappointed," he assured her, rising from his chair and moving toward the door.

As they stepped outside, the morning air greeted them with a refreshing chill, invigorating and crisp. The sun bathed the landscape in a warm glow, illuminating the bare branches of trees dusted with frost and the occasional evergreen standing tall against the soft white blanket of snow. Jack Henry and Charlotte walked side by side, the familiar path leading them to the main house, where the inviting scent of breakfast wafted through the open windows.

As they approached the cabin, laughter and the sounds of pots clanging greeted them, a warm welcome that reminded Jack Henry of the love and unity that defined his family. The sun continued to rise, casting a radiant light over them, while the air was crisp and clear, creating a serene backdrop for their walk.

As they rounded a bend in the path, Jack Henry noticed something unusual. A familiar vehicle was parked near the main house—a pickup truck with a weathered exterior and a bright blue stripe along the side. Jack Henry's heart skipped a beat as he recognized it immediately: it was Charlotte's father's truck.

"Charlotte," he said, his tone shifting slightly, "look over there." He gestured toward the vehicle.

Charlotte's expression changed as she spotted the truck. "Oh no, that's my dad's truck," she murmured. "He must be looking for me."

Jack Henry felt a wave of apprehension wash over him. He knew how protective Charlotte's parents were. The realization hit him—they must have grown concerned when she hadn't returned home the night before.

"Do you think they're worried?" Jack Henry asked, glancing back at Charlotte as he noticed the gears turning in her mind.

"I can't believe I didn't think about them," she said. "They probably thought something was wrong when I didn't go back home last night. I did mention to them that I was trying to find Salazar."

As they approached the main house, Charlotte's thoughts raced back to the previous evening. After she had decided to stay with Jack Henry, her parents had likely panicked when they noticed her absence. They must have spoken to the sheriff, who could have mentioned her stopping by the sheriff's office asking questions about Salazar's address. Jack Henry had left his pickup truck parked near Salazar's house and driven home in Charlotte's car after she had passed out. Charlotte's parents must have connected the dots when they saw his pickup truck.

"If they called Sheriff Samuels, I am sure he mentioned I had stopped by his office. He knew where I was going. I assume my parents went to Salazar's place to look for me," Charlotte said, as she pieced together the timeline. "They must have seen your truck parked outside and put two and two together."

Jack Henry nodded. "Let's go inside and reassure them. I'm sure they just want to know you're safe."

As they crossed the threshold into the main house, the delicious aroma of breakfast enveloped them. The sounds of laughter and chatter filled the space, and as they stepped into the kitchen, they were greeted by the sight of Jack Henry's parents, Nanyehi and Tayanita, bustling around the stove. At the table, Charlotte's parents, along with her grandmother Ann, were already seated, their faces lighting up as they caught sight of the two of them.

"Charlotte!" her mother exclaimed. "We were worried sick about you!"

Charlotte rushed forward, her cheeks flushing with embarrassment. "I'm so sorry. I didn't mean to worry you!" Charlotte said, wrapped in a warm embrace by her parents. Their concern was apparent, but the relief in their eyes softened the moment.

Jack Henry stood back, observing the scene. He could see the love and tenderness etched on the faces of Charlotte's parents, the way they hugged her, their tension melting away. At the table, Grandma Ann beamed at the sight of her granddaughter.

"Come, sit! We've made plenty of food," Tayanita called over her shoulder, effortlessly flipping a pancake onto a plate with a practiced motion. "You need to eat."

As they settled into their seats, Jack Henry felt a sense of belonging. The room buzzed with conversation, the clinking of utensils against plates, and the laughter shared among family and friends. The kitchen was a vibrant tapestry of colors, aromas, and sounds, the warm glow from the morning sun illuminating the faces of those gathered around the table.

"So, you two have some explaining to do," teased Grandma Ann. "Are you together again?" Her gaze danced between Charlotte and Jack Henry, her smile encouraging, knowing well the unspoken feelings that had simmered between them for years.

Charlotte's cheeks turned a deeper shade of red. "I didn't know how to tell you or what you all would think," she stammered, glancing at Jack Henry for support. "So, we just thought keeping it quiet was best for now."

Jack Henry felt his heart race, warmth flooding his chest as he exchanged a glance with Charlotte. There was a sense of vulnerability in sharing this part of their lives, yet also a thrill in the acceptance they found in the company of loved ones. It was a moment of connection, not just between them but with their families—a bridge between their worlds that felt more solid than ever.

As the laughter and chatter settled around the table, Grandma Ann leaned in slightly. "So, Charlotte, what happened with Salazar? Were you able to talk to him?"

Charlotte paused, glancing at Jack Henry for a moment. "Well, I went to the address I found, and it was... strange," she began. "The place looked empty, almost abandoned. It had this eerie feeling, like no one had lived there for a long time."

Jack Henry listened intently, as he recalled the events of the previous night.

Charlotte continued, goose bumps forming on her skin at the memory. "I noticed a single blanket on the floor. It looked like someone had been there not too long ago, and it was strange. I walked around, trying to find any clues—anything that might tell me where Salazar could be. There was a shed outside, so I walked toward it. As I approached the door, I heard someone's footsteps in the distance. The sound became louder and louder, so I turned and decided to walk back to the back of the house."

She took a moment, reflecting on the rush of adrenaline that had surged through her during the search. "I felt so determined to figure it out, when I ..."

A slight smile crept onto her face as she recalled the unexpected turn of events. "I was so caught up in my thoughts that I didn't pay attention to where I was going. I turned around too quickly and—bam! I ran headfirst into Jack Henry's shoulder." She chuckled softly at the memory. "And then everything went black."

The room filled with a mix of gasps and laughter as Charlotte recounted the moment, but Jack Henry's expression turned serious as he leaned closer, fully engaged in her story.

"When I finally woke up," she continued, "I found myself in the guest house. I had no idea how I got there." She met the concerned gazes of her parents and others around the table. "It was a little disorienting."

Charlotte's father turned toward Jack Henry. "And what were you doing there? Were you following her?"

Jack Henry cleared his throat, ready to explain. "I ran into Sheriff Samuels earlier that day. He had told me about Charlotte and that she was asking about Salazar. I was worried and decided to go find her. I wanted to make sure she was okay. Then, well... as Charlotte said, she ran into me and passed out. I drove her home and stayed with her until she woke up, to make sure she didn't have a concussion." He glanced at Charlotte, hoping his sincerity came through.

Charlotte's father nodded slowly, his expression softening. "I appreciate that, Jack Henry. I just... I didn't know what to think when I saw your truck parked close to Salazar's house. It's good to know you were looking out for our girl."

Grandma Ann chimed in. "Well, it sounds like you both had quite an eventful night. I'm just so glad you're here with us now. Charlotte, you really need to take care of yourself. You should never have gone out there alone."

Charlotte smiled, feeling the compassion of family embrace her as the anxiety from recounting the previous night began to dissipate. "I promise I'll be more careful next time. I just got caught up in the moment."

Jack Henry reached for Charlotte's hand under the table, a silent promise that they would face whatever came next, together.

As the morning sun rose higher, illuminating the rich wooden surfaces and the vibrant family photos lining the walls, Charlotte couldn't help but feel a sense of comfort. This was a space filled with love and unity, a stark contrast to the turmoil and uncertainty that had consumed her thoughts in recent days. Jack Henry's family buzzed around her, their warmth surrounding her like a protective cocoon.

Just as Charlotte began to relax, a sharp knock on the door cut through the chatter. The door creaked open, and Sheriff Samuels stepped into the kitchen, his expression serious and preoccupied.

"Morning, everyone," he said. "I need to speak with you, Tayanita, privately for a moment."

Jack Henry's parents and the Joneses exchanged concerned glances. Charlotte's heart raced as she sensed something was wrong. "What's going on?" she asked.

"Please, just give us a moment," Sheriff Samuels replied, gesturing for Tayanita to step outside. The air felt heavy with unspoken worries as they exited the kitchen, leaving everyone else at the table.

"What do you think this is about?" Jack Henry asked.

"I don't know," Charlotte admitted. "But it can't be good."

Minutes stretched into what felt like hours as they waited for the sheriff and Jack Henry's father to return. The lively banter that had filled the room faded, replaced by an unsettling silence. Charlotte felt a knot tighten in her stomach, anxiety creeping in as she glanced around the kitchen, trying to focus on the present rather than the unknown.

When Tayanita and the sheriff finally reentered the kitchen, their expressions were grave, and Charlotte's heart dropped further. "Charlotte," Tayanita began, "it's about Emmanuel Salazar. He was found dead by the riverbank, close to the area where Mari was discovered."

The weight of those words crashed over Charlotte, leaving her momentarily speechless. Memories of her sister flooded back, a haunting echo of loss and pain that twisted in her gut.

"What? How? What happened?" Charlotte stammered.

"Investigators are still piecing together the details, but it appears he was murdered," Sheriff Samuels continued. "He was found near the river, but investigators believe he was killed somewhere else before being dumped there. We also found a blanket at Salazar's home that matches the description of one belonging to a nine-year-old girl who has been missing for several months. She was taken from her home in broad daylight, and her family has been searching for her ever since."

Charlotte's pulse quickened at the mention of the missing girl, the implications of Salazar's death sending a chill through her. *What does this mean?* she thought, her mind racing with the possibilities.

"You and Jack Henry were the last known people to be at Emmanuel Salazar's place last night. I need you both to come to the station to provide information and answer some questions so we can rule you out as suspects," the sheriff explained.

Charlotte's breath hitched at the accusatory words. "Suspects?" she protested with indignation. The thought of being linked to a murder made no sense.

"I know," Sheriff Samuels replied softly. "But this is the situation we're in right now. I just want to ensure that everything is handled properly."

Jack Henry's expression hardened. "We'll go," he said. "We need to clear this up. We'll follow you in Charlotte's car, if that is okay?"

The sheriff nodded, acknowledging their willingness. "I'll come with you," Charlotte's dad firmly stated, his protective instincts kicking in.

As they prepared to leave, Sheriff Samuels turned to Jack Henry. "By the way, have you heard from your younger brother lately?"

Jack Henry's brow furrowed at the unexpected question, and he slowly shook his head before he responded. "No. I haven't spoken to him in several weeks. I don't know where he is," he replied. The question hung in the air like an unanswered riddle, a sense of foreboding settling over them. *Why would the sheriff bring up my brother now?*

Sheriff Samuels nodded, his expression shifting to one of mild concern.

As they stepped outside, Jack Henry leaned closer to Charlotte, whispering, "Please, don't mention anything about what I told you last night." His breath was warm against her ear, and his hand rested lightly on her hip.

"What?" Charlotte replied, confusion knitting her brow. "You mean about you and your brother fighting that night? His involvement with the activists stealing horses...?" Her voice dropped to a whisper.

"Yes. Please, not yet. We don't know who we can trust."

Charlotte looked at him intently for a moment, searching his eyes for reassurance, then nodded in understanding. With that, they climbed into Charlotte's Mercedes, the gravity of the situation pressing heavily on their minds as they followed the sheriff toward the station. With the windows down, the morning air felt crisp and biting as they drove, each passing moment thick with anxiety. Questions swirled in Charlotte's mind ... *What had truly happened to Emmanuel Salazar? And how did it connect to the darkness that has haunted my family for so long?*

Upon arriving at the station, Sheriff Samuels led them through a set of double doors and into a small conference room. The stark walls were adorned with a few photographs of the town, and a large table dominated the center of the room, surrounded by office chairs. A coffee maker hummed softly in the corner, and the scent of freshly brewed coffee hung in the air, mingling with the unease that filled the room.

"Please, make yourselves comfortable," Sheriff Samuels said, gesturing toward the chairs. He poured three cups of coffee, passing one to Charlotte and another to Jack Henry, before taking a seat across from them. Charlotte's father remained standing near the door, his presence a quiet reassurance.

"Thank you," Charlotte murmured, taking a small sip. The warmth spread through her, giving her a fleeting feeling of normalcy in this strange situation in which she now found herself.

"Now, since we all know each other, I want to make this as easy as possible. I'd like to hear about last evening," the sheriff began. He had spoken with both Jack Henry and Charlotte before they went to Salazar's house, and he was well aware of their intentions.

"Charlotte," he prompted as he crossed an ankle over his knee, "can you detail what you did or saw at the house?"

Charlotte gathered her thoughts. "Sure. When I arrived at Salazar's place, I knocked on the front door a few times and called out, but no one came. So, I walked around the house and went to the back. There, I noticed the back door was unlocked, slightly ajar. I pushed it open and stepped inside. The house was filthy—dust and grime coated everything in sight, and it looked like no one had lived there for years," she recounted, her voice steady but laced with some anxiety about being questioned by the sheriff. "It was eerie, like a ghost town."

She paused, recalling the unsettling atmosphere. "As I walked through the house, I entered the room closest to the front door. In the corner, I saw a blanket. It looked like someone had been there recently, which struck me as odd compared to the condition of rest of the house. It made me uneasy; I thought that it could have been Salazar's. Sheriff, you had already warned me he was living through a rough time, so I figured that might have been his living condition—sleeping on the floor."

The sheriff nodded, encouraging her to continue as he leaned forward slightly.

"I noticed some takeout food containers littered around the kitchen, which reinforced the thought that someone had been there recently, but I didn't dwell on it. I felt like I was intruding, so I decided to head outside. There was a shed in the back, so I walked toward it to look inside. That's when I heard footsteps in the distance. As the sound grew closer, I froze. Without thinking, I turned and hurried back towards the house, around the corner—"

Charlotte's voice faltered as she recalled the moment. "I didn't even know it was Jack Henry. I just… ran straight into him and was knocked out cold."

Jack Henry interjected. "Yeah, I heard Charlotte's footsteps. When I turned around, she came barreling towards me. I didn't have time to react." He glanced at Charlotte. "She was unconscious, so I picked her up, put her in her car, and drove her to my place to make sure she was going to be okay."

Charlotte's father listened attentively, his expression a mix of concern and care for his daughter. The sheriff leaned back in his chair, processing their words.

After a brief silence, Charlotte asked, "What about the nine-year-old girl? Who is she? What can you tell us about her and what happened to her?"

Sheriff Samuels looked at her. "I'm afraid I can't give you many details beyond what's already publicly known. Her family reported her missing a few months ago. They haven't had any leads since."

Charlotte's heart raced as she connected the dots in her mind, unease settling deep within her. "This is too coincidental. Another young girl disappears, and then Salazar is killed—his body found right after I come looking for him? And it's discovered near the area where my sister's body was found many years ago?"

The implications of her thoughts felt suffocating. "What on earth is going on here?"

Jack Henry reached across the table, placing his hand over hers. "We'll figure this out, Charlotte. We have to. I'm sure the sheriff and his department will get to the bottom of it."

Sheriff Samuels leaned forward. "I understand this is overwhelming, but we need to keep our focus. Right now, you need to tell me everything you can. Your accounts will help piece together what happened, not just with Salazar but possibly with the missing girl as well."

Charlotte nodded. She knew she had to keep digging, not only for herself but for the young girl who was still missing and might still have a chance. The connections were too strong to ignore, and the unsettling feeling in her gut urged her to uncover the truth.

"Thank you for listening, Sheriff," she said softly. "I just want to make sure that whatever happened, it doesn't happen again."

Sheriff Samuels regarded her thoughtfully before shifting the conversation. "Charlotte, is there anything else you've uncovered? I know you've been talking to people. Any other information that might be relevant to the investigation?"

Charlotte hesitated for a moment, considering how much to share. She thought of Jack Henry's earlier words, asking her not to share details about his revelations the night before, about her conversation with Mr. Adkins, and the unsettling connections he had hinted at. "Actually, I spoke to Mr. Adkins the other day," she began. "He mentioned some troubling things about the activists he used to work with. He talked about horse and sheep thefts back in the sixties, and there were rumors of young girls going missing around the same time. He suggested that those incidents might be tied to a larger operation."

Jack Henry's grip on her hand tightened as she spoke, and she noticed Sheriff Samuels's interest piquing as he raised an eyebrow.

"Did he give you any specific names or connections to this so-called operation?" the sheriff asked, leaning forward, his pen poised over a notepad and his foot bouncing under the table.

"No," Charlotte replied, shaking her head. "He was vague about it, but he seemed genuinely concerned. I didn't want to push him too hard given the recent circumstance with his daughter, but I got the feeling there was more to the story. He confirmed that he and Salazar had known each other, and that he had worked with Reynolds in the past as well. All three of them had worked at my grandfather's farm in the sixties." Charlotte thought about her grandpa's records and the names of all the workers that had been at his farm throughout the years, but she thought it was best not to mention it right now.

Sheriff Samuels scribbled notes rapidly. "This could be significant. Any information about connections between those individuals might help us piece together the bigger picture here."

Charlotte felt a growing sense of alarm as she spoke. "I just can't ignore the fact that all of this seems connected. Another girl missing, Salazar's death, and the history of disappearances in this town and across the state... It's like we're standing at the edge of something much darker than we realize."

Sheriff Samuels nodded in agreement. "You're right to be concerned, Charlotte. This isn't just about one case anymore. We need to keep digging and see where these leads take us."

Charlotte's heart pounded at the sheriff's words. She was ready to confront whatever shadows lingered in the town's past, not only for herself but for the young girl who deserved to be found. As the sheriff continued to ask questions, Charlotte felt a sense of purpose solidifying within her—a resolve to uncover the truth, no matter how dark it might be.

"Tell me more about your conversation with Mr. Adkins," Sheriff Samuels suggested. "What else did he say about him and his connection to Reynolds and Emmanuel Salazar?"

Charlotte took a moment to gather her thoughts. "Mr. Adkins worked at my grandfather's farm years ago. He mentioned that Salazar and Reynolds may have been involved in some questionable activities while he was there—things so bad that he wasn't sure if they were true or not."

Sheriff Samuels nodded. "We need to explore those connections further. I wasn't aware they were all involved with each other. The previous sheriff never mentioned it. If Emmanuel Salazar was involved in something illegal, it could shed light on the entire situation surrounding both cases."

"What about Reynolds?" the sheriff asked.

Charlotte felt her resolve strengthen. "Reynolds is in prison in Washington D.C. I just prosecuted him for the kidnapping and murder of Mr. Adkins's daughter. The jury convicted him only a few weeks ago." The sheriff's expression shifted to one of shock as he processed the details of events that had unfolded just a few hundred miles away. "Reynolds killed Mr. Adkins's daughter?"

"He did," Charlotte confirmed. "Mr. Adkins thinks Reynolds could have done that in retaliation for something that happened between the two back then, when they worked at the farm. Mr. Adkins didn't say much more."

"I'll reach out to Mr. Adkins and see if he is willing to provide more information," Sheriff Samuels replied. "Keep me updated on anything else you find. This could be the key to unraveling the web of connections we're dealing with."

As they wrapped up their meeting, Charlotte, Jack Henry, and William prepared to leave the station. Just as they were about to step out, Sheriff Samuels called out with a softer tone. "Charlotte," he said, pausing for a moment as if weighing his words. "Be careful."

"I will," Charlotte said quietly, then walked away.

CHAPTER XX

As they stepped out of the station, the cool December air greeted their skin like a refreshing wave, invigorating yet laced with the bite of winter. The overcast sky hung low, casting a muted light over the afternoon, and the ground was slick with remnants of the recent rain.

Charlotte turned to Jack Henry. "Jack Henry," she said, lowering her voice so her father wouldn't overhear. "We need to talk. Would you please come with my dad and me to my grandparents' farm?"

Jack Henry met her gaze, sensing the weight behind her words. "All right," he replied. "Let's go get my truck first. It's still by Salazar's house."

"There is no time for that," Charlotte urged. "Please, come with us. I promise I will drive you to your truck later."

With a nod, Jack Henry complied and climbed into the back seat of Charlotte's Mercedes. Charlotte's father sat on the passenger's seat, unaware of the tension simmering between them. The drive back to the farm felt longer than usual, the silence heavy with unspoken thoughts.

When they finally arrived at her grandparents' farm, Charlotte felt a rush of nostalgia wash over her. The open fields stretched before her, rolling hills dotted with patches of frost that glimmered in the weak winter sunlight. She could see the barn close to the farmhouse, a sturdy structure that had stood the test of time, its weathered wooden planks whispering stories of generations past. It had served many purposes over the years: a shelter for sheep and a place where shearing crews not only sheared the sheep but also found refuge for the night. The barn had been filled with wool bales during shearing season and hay bales in the winter months. It had also functioned as stables for the horses and, in her younger days, a playground where she loved to climb to the top of the hay bales, reliving the joy of those carefree moments. The faint smell of hay and the distant sound of rustling leaves brought those memories rushing back.

"Let's hurry," Charlotte urged, stepping out of the Mercedes and leading Jack Henry toward the barn. The cold air nipped at her cheeks, and she pulled her scarf tighter around her neck.

The barn loomed ahead, its presence both imposing and comforting, a symbol of her childhood and family legacy. As they entered, the rich scent of hay and earth engulfed them, grounding Charlotte in the moment. The interior was spacious, with high ceilings supported by wooden beams that had weathered countless storms. Sunlight filtered through the gaps in the walls, casting warm shafts of light that danced across the straw-strewn floor.

Charlotte moved with purpose, her heart racing as she thought about the conversation she wanted to have with Jack Henry. As she approached Blaze's stall, the mustang stood tall and proud, his chestnut coat gleaming even in the dim light of the barn. Blaze was a living embodiment of the wild spirit that had run through Charlotte's family for generations. She reached out to stroke his neck, feeling the warmth of his body beneath her fingertips.

"Hey, buddy," she murmured, her voice softening as she connected with the horse that had always been her steadfast companion. Blaze neighed softly, leaning into her touch as if sensing her need for reassurance.

"Let's get him tacked up," Charlotte said, her focus shifting to the task at hand. She secured a saddle pad first, then moved to the saddle rack, carefully selecting her favorite saddle—the rich brown leather gleaming softly in the light. As she lifted it, the familiar scent of the leather filled her senses, reminiscent of the first day it was given to her as a birthday present. It was intricately tooled with floral designs, a testament to the craftsmanship that went into creating it. The stirrups hung gracefully at the sides, while the cinch straps were thick and robust, ensuring a secure fit against Blaze's powerful body.

Beside her, Charlotte's rifle rested in its holster, a constant companion on her rides, ready for any unforeseen danger. As she worked, Charlotte could hear Jack Henry in the background, as he readied his tack. He had chosen a striking black mare named Rhiannon, a perfect companion for Jack Henry on their ride. Rhiannon was known for her gentle temperament and strength, her sleek coat glinting in the light as Jack Henry led her out of her stall.

"Ready to ride?" Jack Henry asked, a playful smile crossing his face as he secured the saddle onto Rhiannon's back. The contrast between Blaze's fiery chestnut coat and Rhiannon's deep black created a striking visual, a sign of diverse beauty and unique personalities.

"Just about," Charlotte answered, her mind still racing with thoughts of the conversation they needed to have.

As they finished saddling and bridling the horses, Charlotte felt a mix of excitement and apprehension. The barn felt alive with the sounds of horses shifting in their stalls, the gentle whinny of Blaze, and the soft rustling of hay. The familiar rhythm of preparing for a ride brought a sense of comfort, but the weight of her questions loomed large in her mind, a silent acknowledgment of the difficult conversation that awaited them.

"Do you remember the last time we rode together?" Charlotte asked, her voice steady despite the unease that filled the air. She glanced at Jack Henry, knowing they were on the brink of discussing something he had long kept to himself. "It was right before... everything that happened with Mari."

"Yeah, I remember," Jack Henry replied, his tone turning somber. A distant look crossed his face as he recalled the memory. "We rode through the meadows, the sun setting behind the mountains, painting the sky in shades of gold and crimson. It felt like nothing could touch us that day, just the two of us and the world fading away." He paused, his gaze lingering on Charlotte. "I can still feel the way the wind danced around us, like it was carrying our laughter. I wish we could find that moment again."

Charlotte nodded, her heart aching at the memory. "I miss those days, Jack Henry. Before everything changed."

He paused. "We can make new memories, Charlotte."

With their horses ready, Charlotte mounted Blaze, the familiar sensation of being atop her trusted steed grounding her. Jack Henry climbed onto Rhiannon, the horse's powerful frame shifting beneath him. As they prepared to set off, Charlotte felt the adrenaline surging through her veins, a mix of excitement and trepidation at the thought of the adventure ahead.

"Let's head toward the back trails," Charlotte suggested. The trails wound through the woods, offering a chance for them to talk privately away from prying eyes.

As they rode side by side, the cool winter air whipped against their faces, and the sound of hooves crunching against the frost-covered ground filled the silence. The trees stood tall, their bare branches reaching toward the sky like skeletal fingers, a reminder of the harshness of the season. The landscape seemed painted in muted tones of brown and gray, the earth blanketed in a soft layer of frost that sparkled in the sunlight.

Charlotte felt a mix of exhilaration and anxiety as they rode deeper into the woods. The tranquility of the surroundings contrasted sharply with the tension building between her and Jack Henry. She could sense that he was holding something back, just as he often had in the past when difficult topics arose. His recent story about his fight with his brother had felt incomplete, as if he had glossed over crucial details. Now, it was time to confront him.

"Jack Henry," she began, her tone serious as they slowed their horses to a gentle trot. "I've been thinking about everything, and I feel like you're hiding something from me."

He glanced at her, surprise flickering in his eyes. "Hiding something? What do you mean?"

"I mean about what you know," Charlotte pressed. "You mentioned your brother's involvement with the activists and your fight with him that day. I also remember you worked at the farm that summer, at the same time Mr. Adkins, Reynolds, and Emmanuel Salazar did, and you know more than you're letting on. It's time to talk, Jack Henry."

The weight of her words hit him hard, and Charlotte could see the conflict in his expression. "I... I just don't want to drag you into this," he said, his voice low and his gaze downcast. "It's complicated."

Charlotte felt a surge of frustration. "Complicated or not, I deserve to know the truth. We're in this together, remember? I'm fighting for justice, and I need you to be honest with me."

Jack Henry hesitated. The forest around them felt alive, the rustle of leaves and the distant call of birds carrying a quiet warning. "All right, but we need to keep our voices down," he replied. "There's more to this than you realize."

As they continued to ride, Charlotte felt a quiet resolve settling over her, intertwining with the weight of their conversation. The path ahead was uncertain, but she was determined to face whatever truths lay ahead—together.

They soon reached a secluded clearing that was a cherished destination in many memories from their childhoods. It was here that Charlotte and Mari had spent countless afternoons. The clearing was framed by a circle of tall pines, their needles gently swaying in the breeze, creating a serene atmosphere that invited reflection.

Dismounting, Charlotte led Blaze to a fallen tree, its massive trunk providing a natural bench where they could sit. The ground was blanketed with a soft layer of frost, the chill seeping through Charlotte's boots as she settled down. Jack Henry followed suit, easing himself onto the log beside her, his presence grounding and familiar.

"Tell me," Charlotte asked, her voice softer now, inviting him to share his thoughts.

"I only know what I heard people talking about when I was around that summer," Jack Henry began, his gaze distant as he recalled the past. "So, I don't really know exactly what's true or what's not. But some of it was related to what my brother was doing with the Monacans trying to get back at the Welsh, stealing horses, sheep, and anything else the Welsh farmers had going on at their farms. As I mentioned before, I couldn't betray our people by snitching or anything. I could have gotten in worse trouble if I did, but I did draw the line when things started getting serious about harming your family in any way. I said I didn't want any part of it, and that cost me. But I couldn't betray you or your family. You've always mattered the most to me."

Charlotte's heart ached at his words, the sincerity in his voice resonating deeply within her as she placed a hand on his knee. She could see the pain etched on his face, and it tugged at her own heartstrings. "What else do you know?" she pressed, eager for more details.

"Around the farm, the sheep shearers were usually the ones that would talk about what was going on. After a long day of work, they would all get together for dinner. Alcohol and other substances were involved, and people would overshare things they would not typically talk about otherwise. Fights would also frequently erupt, and clearly, the supervisor shearer held a grudge with Reynolds. I can't remember his name. Some white guy name. If you have the names of all the crews, I can probably recognize it. Anyway, those two would constantly start fights, and many times they had to be separated by the rest of the crew."

Charlotte nodded slowly, her mind racing as she processed this information. "What about the rumors you heard?" she asked. "The rumors about Reynolds."

"The rumor was that Reynolds had some shady business dealings with the activists, and so did the supervisor shearer. Reynolds was mostly involved with the activists stealing horses and sheep, but this other guy, the supervisor shearer, had some business around stealing the very wool he and his crew would shear and pack. Generally, all that wool would be packed and pressed into big bales and then transported to be sold. These people had some way of intercepting the wool bales and stealing a few here and there. Since they were involved in the shearing and packing, they always knew where the bales would go, the routes, dates, etc. So, they had a way to steal from the trucks without being noticed."

Jack Henry paused for a moment. "I am not too sure about the details on that or how they are related to Reynolds's business. There was also some talk about them being involved in darker business, you know... kidnapping and selling young girls. But I had always thought that was crazy talk and not something that could be real. My younger brother, Atohi, was involved with some of those activities, but I could never believe he would ever be involved in anything related to human trafficking. That's just crazy to think about. But now, with everything we've learned recently, I simply don't know what to think anymore. I can't believe Atohi could be involved with anything that sinister. But it sounds like at least those rumors I heard from the shearing crews may have been true. I swear, that's all I know or have heard. I couldn't say anything because of my brother and what that would have done to my family in our community. When Mari died, I was torn. I didn't know what to do or what to say because I couldn't help but think that maybe the whole thing could have been related to Reynolds and the activists' actions trying to get back at the Welsh farmers, including my own brother. Mr. Adkins too. But I never even considered the rumors about human... or sex trafficking being a real thing or having anything to do with Mari's death."

Charlotte sat there, contemplating his words, her mind rushing with thoughts and mixed feelings about Jack Henry and everything he just divulged. She had always trusted him, but now doubt crept in just as it had so long ago, whispering uncertainties that threatened to unravel the bond they had slowly and carefully rebuilt.

Just then, the atmosphere shifted. The wind picked up, rustling the dry leaves and sending a chill breeze through the clearing. An eerie silence descended, the once vibrant sounds of nature fading into an unsettling quiet. Charlotte turned to Jack Henry, her heart beat picking up as she sensed the sudden change.

"Do you feel that?" she whispered, her voice barely audible.

He nodded. "Yeah, something doesn't feel right."

With a shared glance, they stood up, instinctively moving closer together as they scanned the surroundings. The trees loomed tall and silent, their branches swaying gently in the cool breeze, but an unsettling feeling of being watched clung to the air like a heavy fog. The clearing that had once felt like a safe haven now seemed shrouded in uncertainty, the tranquility of nature replaced by an ominous silence that made Charlotte's skin crawl.

"Let's get back to the horses," Charlotte suggested, her voice feigning calmness despite the unease growing within her. The urgency of the moment propelled them forward as they quickly mounted Blaze and Rhiannon, the familiar sensation of being atop their trusted steeds grounding them somewhat. The rhythmic sound of hooves against the frost-covered ground offered a brief comfort, but Charlotte's heart raced with the foreboding sense that something was amiss.

As they began to ride back toward the farmhouse, the path wound through the dense trees, sunlight filtering through the branches and casting dappled shadows on the ground. The stillness of the forest was abruptly broken when Charlotte heard a sudden rustle—an unexpected sound in front of them, far too close for comfort.

"Jack Henry, wait!" she called, turning back to see him looking over his shoulder, confusion etched across his features.

Before they could react further, a sharp twang pierced the air—a sound that sent a jolt of fear coursing through Charlotte's veins. In an instant, an arrow barely missed Rhiannon's head and struck Jack Henry in the side of his abdomen.

"Ah!" Jack Henry howled in agony, the pain radiating through him like fire as Rhiannon bucked in response, rearing up in shock. Charlotte felt her heart drop as she instinctively leaned forward and tried to steady Rhiannon.

"Hold on!" she shouted, panic rising in her chest. She could see the arrow jutting from his side when a second arrow grazed his thigh, stopped by the saddle beneath him. Blood seeped through his jeans, staining the leather. Thankfully, the thick leather of the saddle and the woolen saddle pad had prevented the arrow from penetrating deeper, sparing Rhiannon from a grievous injury. The horse's movements were erratic as her rider bellowed in pain, and Charlotte's breath quickened as she feared for all of their lives, Blaze and Rhiannon's included.

Just as she reached for Jack Henry, a third arrow whizzed past her head, narrowly missing her and grazing her ear. A sharp sting erupted as she felt the piercing pain, and she instinctively reached up to touch the wound, feeling the warmth of blood trickling down her cheek.

"Charlotte!" Jack Henry cried, his voice filled with anguish, but she couldn't focus on the pain. In a moment of instinct, she grabbed her rifle from its holster, aiming into the shadows where the arrows had come from, her heart pounding in her chest like a war drum.

Without knowing who she was aiming at, she pulled the trigger, the sound echoing through the trees like a cannon blast as the bullet raced into the woods. "We need to get back to the house!" she shouted, adrenaline surging through her veins, propelling her forward.

With fierce resolve, they urged their horses into a gallop, racing back toward the farmhouse. Jack Henry gripped the reins tightly, his expression a mix of pain and fierce determination, while Charlotte fought to maintain her internal balance amidst the chaos surrounding them.

As they approached the house, the warm glow of lights illuminated the scene against the backdrop of the encroaching evening, casting a false sense of safety over the turmoil. A sudden wave of dread washed over Charlotte as she spotted smoke rising from the direction of the barn. "No! The barn!" she gasped, fear coursing through her veins.

The barn, once a sanctuary filled with the comforting smells of hay and earth, was now engulfed in flames, the fire licking at the wooden beams with a ferocity that sent a shiver down her spine. Her heart raced as she realized two more horses were kept inside, their lives hanging in the balance, trapped in a hellish inferno.

"Help!" she shouted, as Jack Henry struggled to dismount, the arrow still lodged in his side. He winced in pain, beads of sweat forming on his forehead and upper lip, but she urged him on. "We have to help the horses!"

Charlotte jumped off Blaze, her heart pounding as she ran toward the barn, adrenaline fueling her every step. She could see her parents and grandmother rushing toward the flames, their faces etched with determination as they fought against the encroaching blaze. The heat radiated toward her, a fierce reminder of the danger they faced, and the acrid smell of smoke filled her nostrils, choking her resolve.

"Charlotte! Help!" her mom cried, as she strained against the onslaught of fire. Irma and her son, David, had arrived, their faces filled with fear and resolve as they joined the effort to save what they could.

"Jack Henry!" Charlotte shouted, glancing back at him. "Get yourself and the horses to safety! I'll handle this!"

Jack Henry shook his head, despite the pain in his leg. "No way! I'm not leaving you!"

Charlotte dashed toward the barn, her heart pounding as she fought against the overwhelming heat to get to the horse stalls. The flames danced and crackled, consuming the wood with a terrifying intensity. She could see the encroaching darkness inside, the frantic grunts and distressed squeals of the trapped horses echoing in her ears, their cries filled with fear and confusion. The sight of their silhouettes against the flames tore at her heart. She had to save them.

As she approached the entrance, the heat intensified, and she could hear the frantic neighing of the horses inside. Just then, she spotted her parents pushing against the heavy door, desperately trying to pry it open. "We need to get them out!" she shouted, rushing forward to assist.

Together, they struggled against the heat and the weight of the door, finally forcing it open with a loud creak. The smoke poured out like a living entity, wrapping around them in a suffocating embrace. Charlotte's lungs burned as she inhaled the sulfurous and smoky air, but she pushed through the discomfort, fueled by the need to save the horses.

"Go! Get the horses!" Charlotte's mom shouted, her voice rising above the chaos. The tone ignited a fire within Charlotte, spurring her into action.

Charlotte dashed into the barn, the flames licking at her clothes as she made her way toward the stalls. The panicked neighing of the horses filled her ears, their eyes wide with fear, reflecting the flickering light of the flames. The sight of their silhouettes against the blaze tugged at her heart, urging her forward.

"Come on guys, we're getting you out of here!" she urged, reaching for the two horses. The mustangs seemed to sense her urgency and moved toward her, their powerful frames steady amidst the chaos.

As Charlotte quickly unlatched the stall doors, she felt the heat intensify, the inferno roaring around her. Sweat dripped down her brow, mixing with the soot that clung to her skin. She grabbed the horses' halters, coaxing them toward the exit as the flames closed in.

"Keep moving, don't stop!" she urged, pushing through the suffocating smoke. The horses responded, their powerful frames carrying them through the inferno.

Once outside, the cool night air hit Charlotte like a balm, offering a brief reprieve from the blistering heat. She led the horses to safety, her heart pounding with relief as she saw her family and neighbors working together to control the blaze by throwing buckets of water and spraying garden hoses to douse the flames that threatened to spread.

"Charlotte! I think I am going to pass out!" Jack Henry's voice broke through her focus, and she glanced back to see him leaning unsteadily against Rhiannon, his face pale with pain from the arrow embedded in his side.

"Just hold on!" she called back, rushing to him. She slipped his arm around her shoulder, supporting him as she tried to help him walk. The urgency in her heart swelled as she realized they were racing against time.

"We need to get you inside!" she urged, as the flames roared behind them, the heat intensifying with each passing second.

With a grimace, Jack Henry leaned heavily on her, his expression strained. "We have to get out of here!" he gasped, as they moved forward together.

As they made their way back toward the house, Charlotte felt the heat of the flames at her back, the fire consuming everything in its path. She could see her parents already on the porch. Her mom was shouting orders to Irma and her son, directing them to grab buckets and form a line from the nearby well to douse the flames before they could reach the home.

"Charlotte! What happened to him?" her grandma cried, spotting them as they staggered onto the porch. "We need to get him inside and see what we can do with that arrow!"

Charlotte nodded, fear heavy in her chest. "Jack Henry, let's get you inside!" she repeated.

With her support, Jack Henry managed to step onto the porch, his legs giving way beneath him as he collapsed against the wooden railing. "I can't …" he gasped, anguish written all over his features.

"I know, I know," Charlotte said soothingly, her heart breaking at the sight of him in pain. "You are going to be okay. We'll figure this out. Fire department is on the way."

With her grandmother's help, they eased Jack Henry into the house, the cool air inside contrasting sharply with the heat of the flames outside. The living room was dimly lit, but it felt like a sanctuary amid the chaos. Charlotte hurried to grab supplies while Grandma Ann tended to Jack Henry. Having served as a nurse during World War I, she had seen injuries far worse than this, and her steady hands were a comfort in the turmoil.

"What happened?" she asked again, eyeing Jack Henry's side with a practiced gaze. "We need to get a look at that arrow wound."

"Open the first aid kit, please!" Grandma Ann instructed, as she assessed the situation. "And we need some liquor."

"I'm fine, I'm fine," Jack Henry insisted through gritted teeth, but the pallor of his skin told a different story.

"Sit still!" Grandma Ann ordered, kneeling beside him with the aid kit as she ripped Jack Henry's shirt open. She reached for the arrow, examining the wound with a nurse's precision. "This is going to hurt, but we need to get this out before it causes any more damage." She then poured some bourbon over the wound, the liquid stinging as it made contact. "I don't have anything else, and this should help prevent infection," she explained, her voice firm as she prepared to remove the arrow.

Jack Henry nodded, his jaw clenched, and Charlotte felt her stomach twist with anxiety as she watched her grandmother work. As Grandma Ann took care of Jack Henry, Charlotte felt a wave of helplessness wash over her. "I'm so sorry, Jack Henry. I didn't mean for any of this to happen," she whispered, her voice thick with emotion. Here, drink this! She added, handing him the bottle of bourbon. Jack Henry did not complain and took a long gulp, hoping it would help with the pain and steady his nerves. As the warmth spread through him, he braced himself for what was to come.

"None of this is your fault," he replied, his eyes meeting hers in agony.

Before she could respond, a loud crash erupted from outside, and the house shook momentarily. The flames had spread, and the sound of timber snapping filled the air. "We need to hurry!" Charlotte urged, her voice rising in desperation.

With swift movements, Grandma Ann grasped the arrow's shaft and prepared to pull it out. "On the count of three," she said, her tone steady and calm. "One... two..."

Jack Henry wailed in pain as the arrow came free, but Charlotte was right there beside him, gripping his hand tightly. "You're okay, you're okay," she murmured, trying to keep him centered amidst the chaos before he completely passed out from the pain.

As the arrow fell to the floor, Charlotte's stomach dropped. The wound was deep, blood oozing from the puncture in Jack Henry's side, next to his abdomen. "We need to clean it!" she shouted, panic creeping into her voice.

"We need more cloths!" Grandma Ann shouted, as Charlotte rushed searching for more cloths in the kitchen. "I need more clean cloths and maybe some more liquor!"

Charlotte's mind raced as she searched for anything that could help. She felt helpless as the fire crackled and roared outside, but she focused on Jack Henry. They were in this together, and she would do everything she could to keep him safe.

As they worked to tend to Jack Henry's injury, the noise from outside grew louder, and the fear of losing everything they held dear threatened to consume her. But deep down, Charlotte knew they had to stay strong. With every heartbeat, she felt time slipping away, the fire threatening to take more than just their home.

As the chaos settled and the fire began to diminish, the sounds of heavy footsteps and hurried voices echoed through the yard. Two neighboring farmers, along with their crews, had seen the fire and rushed to help. They arrived with buckets and more hoses, ready to assist in any way they could. Together, they formed a line, working tirelessly to douse the flames that still flickered defiantly at the edges of the house.

For hours, the battle against the fire raged on. The night wore on, heavy with stress, the air thick with the acrid smell of smoke and charred wood. Charlotte and her family fought alongside their neighbors, their faces streaked with soot and sweat, hearts pounding with the fear of losing everything. As the first hints of dawn began to creep over the horizon, the morning sun slowly broke through the darkness, casting a golden glow over the smoldering remains of the barn.

Finally, the last embers were extinguished. The barn, once a robust structure filled with life, lay in ruins, its wooden beams blackened and crumbled. It would have to be rebuilt from the ground up, but amidst the devastation, there was a sense of relief that washed over them—the horses and their home had been saved.

They gathered in a weary circle, surveying the damage. The house had suffered substantial damage, but miraculously, most of the bedroom areas had withstood the flames. Only one guest bedroom had been significantly affected, its walls charred and its contents reduced to ash, while the others remained intact, albeit singed around the edges.

Jack Henry was still passed out from the pain, his earlier bravado having faded into unconsciousness. Charlotte glanced at him, concern etched across her face feeling grateful that her Grandma had worked tirelessly through the night to keep him stable until they could get him proper medical attention. In her heart, she knew that they had narrowly escaped a greater tragedy.

As they stood together, taking in the devastation, the smoke still gently wafting from the burned-down barn, her father William turned to Charlotte. His expression was serious, yet there was a flicker of respect in his eyes. "I guess you have been asking the right questions... you may be closer to the truth than we have ever been," he said. "Someone is certainly trying to send a message."

Charlotte nodded slowly. She felt a mix of gratitude for the support of her neighbors and sorrow for what had been lost. As she sat quietly, gazing into the horizon where the sun began to rise, the warm rays slowly illuminating the world around her, she contemplated the challenges ahead.

CHAPTER XXI

As morning broke, the exhaustion of the previous day weighed heavily on everyone. Grandma Ann and Charlotte's mom had prepared a hearty breakfast, the aroma of toasted bread and freshly brewed tea filling the air. The kitchen, with its wooden cabinets and worn linoleum floor, was filled with the comforting scents of home—Irma's freshly baked pies cooling on the counter mingled with the lingering smell of smoke from the fire that had ravaged the barn. The soft sounds of clinking dishes and low murmurs created a sense of normalcy, though it felt fragile, like a thin veil over the remnants of turmoil from the night before. Jack Henry was still asleep in the guest room, his body recovering from the ordeal of the previous night. The paramedics had finally arrived late last night, finding him still unconscious but stable. They decided to let him rest and asked to be called back to take him to the hospital once he woke up.

Charlotte sat beside her dad, who wore a faded plaid shirt and jeans, nursing a cup of tea with a pensive expression. His brow furrowed, a testament to what they had endured as he glanced around the kitchen, taking in the remnants of their family's shared history. Irma, their close family friend, was helping out, slicing various pies to add to their breakfast. Her apron, flour-dusted and colorful, contrasted with the somber mood of the morning. Her son, David, had gone back home after the fire, but Irma had insisted on staying to lend a hand, her unwavering support a comforting presence amidst the aftermath of the chaos.

Charlotte felt disheveled, her hair a tangled mess and dark circles under her eyes betraying her exhaustion. Guilt gnawed at her for what had happened to Jack Henry, and she wrestled with the burden of the night's events, feeling as if she had failed her family.

"Looks like we've got a long day ahead of us," Charlotte's dad said, rubbing his temples as if trying to shake off the weariness. "But we can't rest yet. There's too much to do."

"Yeah, I know," Charlotte replied, the memory of the previous night's terror flooding her mind. "I can't believe someone actually tried to kill Jack Henry and me. We could have been…" She paused, her voice trembling as the reality of the situation sank in. "And the barn? Why did they have to burn the barn? All of you were at risk too! It's clear this is a message directed at us, especially me. Someone definitely knows I'm getting closer to the truth about what happened in the sixties with Mari's death, not to mention the recent victims, including Kaya. And then there's Salazar's body washed up on the riverbank where Mari drowned. It all feels connected."

Her dad's expression darkened. "We need to be careful, Charlotte. Whoever is behind this won't hesitate to escalate their actions if they feel threatened."

"I know," she replied. "But I can't just sit back and do nothing. We have to keep pushing forward."

"What happened? Where were you and Jack Henry when you got attacked?" her dad asked, the worry in his voice evident.

Charlotte tried to steady herself as she recounted the frightening experience. "We were at the clearing I like to go to. You know, where Grandpa taught me how to shoot a rifle?" Her dad nodded, his eyes narrowing as he listened intently. "So, we were just sitting there, talking, when everything felt too quiet."

She hesitated, the memory flooding back with vivid clarity. They had just started riding back to the farmhouse when this happened. "Then, suddenly, Jack Henry was struck by an arrow. I can still hear the whoosh of it slicing through the air." Her heart raced as she relived the moment, remembering the adrenaline surging through her veins. "When I turned to see what was going on, another arrow grazed his thigh and a third arrow almost hit me too." She turned her head slightly, revealing the small cut on her ear, the pain a stark reminder of how close the danger had been. "I shot my rifle toward where I thought the arrows had come from, but I couldn't see anyone. It felt like we were being hunted. In that moment, I thought it was best to run, but then... then we saw everything in flames. The barn was burning, and I knew we had to get back to help."

As she spoke, her dad listened closely, his jaw tightening with concern. "It has to have been the same person. Or maybe more than one?"

Charlotte nodded, her voice trembling. "Yes. It seems like someone wants to silence me before I uncover the truth."

Her dad sighed, running a hand through his hair in disbelief. "This is serious, Charlotte. We need to take this threat with the utmost concern."

"I understand," she said. "But I can't let fear control me. There's something else I need to tell you. Jack Henry mentioned something interesting yesterday—about the shearing crews back in the day."

Her dad raised an eyebrow, intrigued. "What about them?"

"They had a supervisor, but Jack Henry couldn't remember the name. I think we should check the records I brought from your house to see if we can find out more about those crews—especially the name of the supervisor Jack Henry couldn't remember," she suggested. "It seems like there may be some connection between them and Reynolds's illegal activities."

"Odd… But, all right, then let's go grab them," her dad replied, his tone shifting to one of agreement, sensing the importance of her request.

Charlotte's anxiety levels rose as she headed back to her room, where she had stored the records. The hallway felt unusually stark, heightening her sense of unease, and contrasting sharply with the warmth of the kitchen. As she opened her bedroom door, the familiar scent of old paper mixed with smoke from the night before wrapped around her.

Once inside, she quickly grabbed the large binder filled with records from her grandfather's time. As she made her way back to the kitchen table, she felt a mixture of excitement and anxiety building within her. What would they find?

Her father and the others were deep in conversation about the events from the day before, their voices low and serious. Sunlight filtered through the lace curtains, casting soft patterns on the floor, creating a stark contrast to the weighty atmosphere. "I've got the records!" she announced, setting the binder down on the table with a soft thud.

"Great!" her dad said. "Let's take a look" he added as he put on his reading glasses.

As Charlotte began to flip through the pages, she felt a surge of impatience. The records were meticulously organized, detailing the names, dates, and roles of everyone who had worked at the farm over the years. "Here are the shearing crews," she said, her voice rising with enthusiasm. She began scanning the pages, her heart beating harder as she searched for any mention of the supervisor.

Just then, Grandma Ann joined them, peering over Charlotte's shoulder. She wore a cozy cardigan that had seen better days, but her eyes sparkled with warmth and wisdom. "What are you two up to?" she asked.

"We're looking for information about the shearing crews from the past," Charlotte replied. "Jack Henry mentioned a supervisor he couldn't quite remember, and I thought these records might help."

"Oh, I remember those days," Grandma Ann said, a hint of nostalgia in her eyes. "Your grandfather always made sure to hire the best crews. It was hard to find good workers, though. We relied on recommendations from neighboring farms, and sometimes we even had to combine our sheep with those from other farms so that multiple farmers could share the same shearing crews, making the work more efficient."

Charlotte's dad nodded, a smile creeping onto his face as he recalled the memories. "That's right. The shearing season was always a busy time for us. We would have the crews stay in one of the barns for a few days, and they'd work tirelessly until the job was done. It was a good system, and once we found a reliable crew, we tried to keep them year after year."

"What were the crews like?" Charlotte asked. "Did you ever have any problems with them?"

"Most of them were hard workers, at least the ones we hired," her dad replied, his tone reflective. "But there were always a few rotten apples. Some had histories with the law— public disturbances or fights in town. We made sure to hire only those without any records related to theft or worse. If they had a bad reputation, we steered clear."

Grandma Ann chimed in. "There was always some gossip behind the scenes too. Some crew members would try to get your grandfather's attention, hoping to be chosen as the crew supervisors. They would negotiate for better pay, and sometimes it would lead to tension among them."

Charlotte couldn't help but smile at the memories. "I remember those times… it was a different world back then."

Her dad continued, "The crews would spend long hours working. They would start at sunrise, sharpening and oiling the shears to ensure they were ready for the day. By the sixties, mechanical shearing machines had become increasingly popular among sheep farmers in Virginia due to their efficiency compared to hand shears. Keeping the shears sharp was crucial for a clean cut, as dull blades could hurt the sheep and slow down the process. Oiling the shears helped them operate smoothly and prevented overheating during long hours of use. After that, they would work until the evening, breaking for lunch and maybe a short nap here and there."

"That's right." Grandma Ann added. "The crews would often come from nearby towns, and it was always a challenge to find the right mix of people. Some of them would even travel from as far away as West Virginia, Tennessee, and North Carolina for the shearing season. We would typically hear only about the best ones through word-of-mouth."

Charlotte felt a sense of connection to the history of her family's farm, the stories weaving together. But as she scanned the list of names, a spark of curiosity ignited within her. She was eager to find the name of the supervisor, a key detail that could link everything together.

Just then, Jack Henry slowly stepped into the kitchen, each movement deliberate, clearly battling against the pain that radiated from his injuries. He was wearing a clean shirt Charlotte had borrowed from her grandfather's closet, along with some loose-fitting jeans that reminded her of her grandfather's long legs. The sight of Jack Henry, with his injured body and determined expression, gave her a sense of comfort and solidarity, but it also stirred a pang of guilt within her. She felt a little guilty for focusing on her own quest for information when he was enduring such pain. "Mind if I take a look at those records?" he asked, his expression serious as he approached the table.

"Jack Henry, you shouldn't be here. You need to rest." Charlotte argued softly.

"I know, but I can help," he insisted.

Charlotte hesitated for a moment, then nodded. "Alright, just be careful," she said, stepping aside to give him room. She felt her curiosity deepen as he began to scan the pages.

After a few moments, Jack Henry's gaze landed on a name. "Here it is," he said, pointing to the page. "John

Samuels. That was the supervisor of the shearing's crew that year."

Charlotte froze at the revelation. "Samuels?" she echoed. "As in, Sheriff Samuels?"

Jack Henry nodded, the gravity of the connection settling in. "Yeah, I remember now. John Samuels was Sheriff Samuels's uncle. Back then, Sheriff Samuels was around our age. He was in some of our high school classes, Charlotte. Remember? John Samuels must have been in his thirties or forties back then."

This connection felt crucial; if John Samuels had ties to both the past and the sheriff, then any secrets he kept could potentially link back to Charlotte's investigation into the suspicious events surrounding Mari's death and the recent attacks.

"He was well-respected in the community," Charlotte's dad, William, interrupted. "He worked hard and had a very good reputation as a shearer. Based on these records, it looks like he spent several seasons at our farm. I didn't realize it was him."

"I remember him," Irma interjected. "John Samuels took his nephew in after his brother—Sheriff Samuels's father— passed away years ago. He raised him alongside his other two boys and encouraged Sheriff Samuels to pursue a career in law enforcement. I can't say for sure why he did that; maybe he wanted something different for his nephew since his own boys were always getting into trouble. Sheriff Samuels was the opposite of that when he was a teenager. There's no way he would have been involved in anything sinister. This can't be right."

"Maybe Jack Henry misheard something," Charlotte suggested, glancing at Jack Henry with uncertainty. "But his name keeps coming up. We should be cautious and not jump to conclusions."

Jack Henry hesitated, his expression pained, thinking he was sure about what he had heard, but he didn't want to argue. "Maybe," he said. "What else do you remember about John Samuels and the rest of the shearing crews?" he asked, almost ignoring the implication. "Where did they come from? What were they like?"

William looked at Charlotte, his expression serious as he considered the question. "Well, as I was saying just a moment ago," he said, directing his attention to Jack Henry, "it was always a challenge to find good crews. Farmers would often rely on word-of-mouth recommendations or previous experience. In the sixties, many of the shearers were local men who had grown up in the area. They knew the land, the animals, and the rhythms of farm life. But there were always some who came from farther away, especially during the peak shearing season. They came in groups, ready to work for a few days and then move on to the next farm. It was a tough life, but it was what they knew." He glanced back at Charlotte, a hint of exasperation flickering in his eyes, as if wishing Jack Henry had caught the earlier discussion.

"Did you ever have to deal with complaints or situations where you and your father had to handle theft or fights?" Jack Henry inquired.

Charlotte's dad shook his head slowly. "Not really. We heard whispers here and there, but nothing that ever escalated to a serious issue. There were some evenings we had been called after a big fight had just been broken up, but nothing that caused major problems. A night of drinking almost always resulted in some minor altercations."

Charlotte listened intently, absorbing the details. The stories of the past were starting to form a clearer picture, and she was determined to uncover how they all connected. She felt a deep connection to the history of her family's farm, the narratives intertwining in her mind.

"We need a plan," Charlotte suggested. "We need to go through these records again and see if we can find anything more about John Samuels. If he is the sheriff's uncle, we can't simply confront the sheriff and start asking questions. We need more than that."

Her dad nodded thoughtfully. "Speaking with Mr. Underwood could help. He's been around for years and might have heard something about the shearing crews or any potential thefts. He often hired the same crews we did, so it's worth a try."

Charlotte paused for a minute, looking down thinking about their last visit to the Underwoods' farm, her mind processing every detail she had just heard. "Okay. Let's go," she said, standing up quickly.

"Now?" her dad asked, pushing back slightly. "No, we all need to rest. It can wait until this afternoon. At least take a shower and get some sleep. Everyone is exhausted, and Jack Henry needs to go to the hospital."

"But you said there's no time to rest—there's too much to do, remember?" Charlotte replied.

"That was before all this new information about John Samuels came to light," he explained. "If we're going to proceed with our plan, we need to get some rest now."

"Yes, you are right," Charlotte agreed with some hesitation. "I guess we can wait a few more hours."

As she settled back into her chair, Charlotte felt a flicker of hope igniting within her. They would uncover the truth, no matter the cost.

CHAPTER XXII

John Samuels was a man of many talents, respected in the community for his skill as a sheep shearer and his passion for carpentry. He was known around town for his ability to repair and refurbish canoes, particularly the traditional Monacan canoes that held a special place in the hearts of the local community. His workshop, located in the back of his modest two-story home at the edge of town, was a testament to his craftsmanship and dedication.

The house itself was unassuming yet inviting, with weathered wooden siding and a front porch adorned with potted plants that added a touch of color to the otherwise muted exterior. The porch swing creaked in the gentle breeze, a comforting sound that spoke of lazy summer afternoons and quiet contemplation. The windows were framed by dark green shutters, and the roof, though showing signs of age, stood strong against the elements.

Inside, the home was a reflection of John Samuels's orderly nature. Despite being inhabited by three men, it was remarkably clean and organized. The living room, with its worn but comfortable furniture, was a welcoming space where family gatherings often took place. The walls were adorned with photographs that chronicled the passage of time—the smiling faces of family members, moments of celebration, and the occasional candid shot that captured the essence of everyday life.

The kitchen was a functional hub, centered around a large wooden table that served as the heart of the home. It was here that John Samuels would gather his family for meals, insisting on the importance of sitting down together to share the events of the day. The wooden cabinets were filled with neatly arranged dishes, and the countertops, though worn, gleamed from regular cleaning. The aroma of freshly baked bread often lingered in the air, a testament to the simple pleasures that filled their lives.

John Samuels's two sons, Derek and Jake, were roughly the same age as their cousin, Sheriff Thom Samuels, who had come to live with them after the untimely death of his father. John had taken the young Thom under his wing, raising him alongside his own sons with a firm but caring hand. Despite the challenges of raising three boys alone after the passing of his wife, John had managed to instill a sense of discipline and responsibility in them.

Derek and Jake, were lazy and had a mischievous streak that often got them into trouble. They were known for their boisterous laughter and playful antics, but they also had a tendency to bully their cousin Thom, making his life difficult at times. One particular incident stood out in Thom's memory—a day after baseball practice when the adults had left, and Derek, Jake, and a few other kids began throwing rocks at him. The memory of ducking and weaving to avoid the barrage of stones, only to be struck on the hand, remained vivid in his mind. It was swollen for a week, making it difficult for him to complete his homework, a painful reminder of the challenges he faced growing up.

John Samuels, while a kind man, had a temper that could flare up unexpectedly. His short fuse was well-known, and his sons had learned to tread carefully around him. Despite this, he was a dedicated father who worked tirelessly to provide for his family. When he wasn't shearing sheep during the peak season, he could be found in his workshop, indulging in his true passion—carpentry.

The workshop was a spacious, high-ceilinged structure filled with the scent of sawdust and varnish. It was a haven for John, a place where he could lose himself in the rhythm of his work. The walls were lined with tools, each with its designated place, and the large workbench was often cluttered with projects in various stages of completion. The centerpiece of the workshop was a collection of canoes, each one meticulously restored to its former glory. The Monacan canoes, in particular, held a special place in John's heart, their graceful lines and rich history a source of inspiration.

John's sons occasionally joined him in the workshop, their own interest in carpentry sparked by their father's passion. Though they lacked the discipline and dedication that John possessed, they enjoyed the time spent working alongside him, learning the intricacies of the craft. It was one of the few interests that had managed to bridge the gap between them, fostering a sense of connection that transcended their differences.

As Sheriff Thom Samuels grew older, he came to appreciate the lessons imparted by his uncle. Despite the challenges of his upbringing, he had developed a strong work ethic and a sense of duty that guided him in his career. The memories of his time in the Samuels household, though marked by moments of strife, were also filled with warmth and love—a testament to the resilience of family bonds in the face of adversity.

CHAPTER XXIII

The late afternoon light bathed the Virginia hills in a warm glow as Charlotte and her dad prepared for their drive to the Underwoods' farm. After a brief shower and a few hours of restless sleep, they gathered their thoughts and fortified their resolve to uncover the truth. The air was crisp, filled with the earthy aroma of damp leaves and the promise of snow. Charlotte climbed into her dad's truck, the engine purring to life and the familiar hum of the tires on the gravel road creating a comforting rhythm.

"Are you sure you're ready for this?" her dad asked, casting a sidelong glance her way. But Charlotte could see the unwavering support in his eyes.

"I need to do this, Dad," Charlotte replied. "There's something about John Samuels that I can't get past. We need to know what he might have been up to before we can connect all the dots."

As they drove, the landscape changed, shifting from rolling hills to dense thickets of trees lining the narrow road. The shadows grew longer as twilight approached. Each mile felt heavier. The Underwoods' farm was just a few miles away, but the uncertainty of what awaited them sent a shiver of apprehension through her.

The last time Charlotte had been to the Underwoods' farm was a few weeks back, to talk with Mr. Adkins, shortly after she had discovered her grandfather's employee records. Now, the thought of returning under such grim circumstances sent a wave of dread through her. As they approached the familiar turnoff, her heart raced with anxiety. The stakes had never felt higher.

When they arrived, the sun had dipped below the horizon, leaving behind a palette of deep blues and purples that painted the sky. The farm appeared eerily quiet, the only sound the gentle rustling of leaves in the cool evening breeze. Charlotte surveyed the scene before her. The barn stood steadfast against the backdrop of the twilight sky, but the air felt thick, as if the very land were expecting them.

"Something doesn't feel right. Stay close," her dad instructed as they both grabbed their rifles and stepped out of the car. The cold air bit at their skin, causing Charlotte to pull her jacket tighter around her. Together, they made their way toward the main house, the wooden steps creaking beneath their feet as they approached the front door.

"Mr. Underwood?" Charlotte called, her voice echoing in the stillness. "It's Charlotte and my dad, William. We're here to ask you a few questions if you don't mind."

Silence greeted them, and a knot tightened in Charlotte's stomach. "Maybe they're out in the barn?" her dad suggested, glancing around the property. The dim light spilling from the windows of the house cast an inviting glow, but the absence of movement sent a wave of unease coursing through her veins.

"Let's check," Charlotte replied. They made their way toward the barn, the familiar scent of hay mingling with the cool evening air.

As they approached, an unsettling feeling washed over Charlotte. The barn doors hung slightly ajar, swaying gently in the breeze—a sight that deepened her unease. "You are right. Something doesn't feel right," she whispered, glancing at her dad, who nodded in agreement.

"Be careful," he said, his voice low as they pushed the doors open. The sound of creaking wood echoed in the silence, and the interior of the barn welcomed them with a suffocating stillness. Shadows lingered along the walls, illuminated only by the faint twilight filtering through the gaps in the wood.

"Mr. Underwood?" Charlotte called again, her voice feigning calmness. The silence felt oppressive, and she felt the knot in her stomach tighten. "Are you in here? Mr. Adkins?"

They stepped farther inside, the air thick with dust and the scent of hay. The familiar sounds of the barn—horses whinnying, the rustle of straw—were absent, replaced instead by an eerie quiet that made Charlotte's skin crawl. She felt exposed, as if the shadows themselves were watching, hiding secrets just beyond her reach.

"Let's check the tack room and stalls," her dad suggested, moving cautiously toward the first row of stalls. Charlotte followed closely, as they peered into the dimly lit stalls. The horses were gone, their absence amplifying the sense of unease that settled over them, tack room unnaturally still.

"Where could they be?" Charlotte murmured. "They never leave without someone around. Why have a caretaker otherwise?"

As they moved deeper into the barn, they noticed overturned buckets and scattered hay—evidence of a struggle that had taken place. The ground was marked with deep hoof prints, and a long, dark trail in the dust suggested something had been dragged across the floor. Panic surged through Charlotte as realization struck her. "Dad, what if something happened?"

Her dad's expression darkened. "We need to find them. Stay with me," he instructed, as he moved farther down the row of stalls.

Charlotte nodded, tightening her grip around the rifle. They reached the end of the barn, but still, there was no sign of the Underwoods. "Maybe they're in the house?" she suggested with desperation in her voice.

"Let's check," he replied, leading the way back toward the entrance. The barn felt oppressive, the shadows stretching as if trying to ensnare them. Charlotte's instincts screamed for her to escape this place, but she pushed through the unease, knowing they had to uncover the truth. To do that, she needed to locate the Underwoods.

As they stepped back outside, the cool night air washed over them, a stark contrast to the tense atmosphere inside the barn. They hurried toward the house, their footsteps crunching on the gravel path. The shadows seemed to loom larger, a reminder of the danger that lurked in the darkness.

Charlotte reached for the doorknob on the front door of the house, her palms clammy as she pushed the door open.

"Mr. Underwood?" she called again, her voice echoing through the empty rooms. "Mrs. Underwood? Is anyone in here?" The stillness that followed felt unnervingly profound.

The absence of response sent a jolt of fear through her. Charlotte exchanged a worried glance with her dad, who stepped cautiously into the hallway, his expression tense as he held his rifle at the ready. "We need to look around," he said, his voice low as he moved toward the living room.

Charlotte followed closely, taking each step with hesitation as they entered the dimly lit space. The living room was a tableau of stillness, the flickering light from the dying embers in the fireplace casting elongated shadows across the walls. The furniture was impeccably arranged, but an unsettling quiet hung in the air.

"Maybe they're just in the back," Charlotte suggested, her voice barely a whisper. The growing dread twisted in her chest, coiling tighter with each passing moment.

"Let's check the kitchen," her dad replied, moving toward the doorway that led to the back of the house. Charlotte followed closely, her senses heightened as they entered the kitchen, the familiar scents of home-cooked meals lingering in the air. The table was set for dinner, but the absence of movement left an unsettling silence hanging around them.

"Where are they?" Charlotte murmured as she scanned the room. The kitchen felt too quiet, too still. She could hear the faint ticking of the clock on the wall, each tick amplified in the empty room.

Her dad moved to the back door, peering outside into the gathering darkness. "I don't see anyone," he said, his voice barely above a whisper, tinged with worry. "We should check the bedrooms."

"Right," Charlotte agreed. They moved toward the hallway, the wooden floors creaking beneath their feet as they approached the first door on the left.

Her dad opened the door slowly, revealing a guest bedroom neatly made up with a cozy quilt, but it was empty. The bed was perfectly made, the pillows fluffed, but it felt eerie in its stillness. "No one here," he said quietly, moving to the next door.

Charlotte felt a deepening sense of dread as they went from room to room, each door revealing nothing but emptiness. The master bedroom was similarly vacant, the bed neatly made and the curtains drawn.

Finally, they moved to the last room—the office. As her dad opened the door, Charlotte followed, her rifle held low but ready for action if necessary. The room was dimly lit by a small desk lamp, casting long shadows along the walls. The desk was cluttered with papers and books, but the atmosphere felt unsettling, as if something were amiss.

"What on earth are they up to?" Charlotte whispered. She stepped farther into the room, scanning the shelves lined with books and family photographs. Suddenly, something caught her eye—a flicker of movement in the corner of the room near the floor.

"Charlotte, be careful!" her dad warned, his voice low as he stepped forward. But she was already moving, drawn to the figure that had emerged from the shadows.

As she approached, her breath caught in her throat. It was a body—a figure lying on the floor, motionless. Time seemed to stand still as reality crashed down around her. "No... no... no!" she gasped, her voice trembling as her dad knelt beside the figure and automatically felt for a pulse in her neck, tears beginning to well in her eyes.

It was Mrs. Underwood. Her lifeless eyes stared blankly at the ceiling, a look of terror etched on her face. A wave of nausea washed over Charlotte as the harsh reality of the situation sank in. "Oh my God," she whispered, the world around her beginning to spin.

She felt a haze of disbelief engulf her as she stared at the body, tears flowing down her cheeks. The air in the room felt thick, suffocating, and Charlotte struggled to breathe.

Just then, Charlotte's gaze flickered to the door of the room, and an instinctive dread pushed her to her feet. "We need to get out of here," she said, her voice shaky. Danger loomed in the air, and she sensed that they weren't alone after all.

"Charlotte, stay put," her dad urged, as he moved to check the other rooms. "I'll be right back."

"No! We can't split up," Charlotte insisted, panic rising in her throat as she wiped her tears. "What if there's someone still here?"

Her dad hesitated for a moment, as he considered her words. "All right, let's stick together," he agreed, as he moved back toward her.

As they lingered in the office, the oppressive reality pressed down on them like a dark cloud and Charlotte struggled to process the horror before her. "What happened here?" she whispered, her voice trembling.

"I am not sure," her dad admitted, as he surveyed the room. "But we need to get out of here and call for help." Where was Mr. Underwood?

Suddenly, a noise echoed from the back of the house—a sound that sent terror coursing through Charlotte's veins. It was a low, guttural growl. "What was that?" she gasped, her eyes wide with fear.

Her dad's expression shifted. They exchanged a glance, the unspoken understanding passing between them. They needed to get out of the house—now. "Let's move!" her dad urged, tightening his grip on his rifle as he quickly checked the chamber. Charlotte instinctively adjusted her own rifle, as she followed his lead. As they turned to leave the office, the growl echoed again, closer this time, amplifying Charlotte's panic.

"Go, go, go!" she urged, as they hurried down the hallway, the sound of their footsteps pounding against the wooden floors. The house felt alive with tension, every creak and groan of the old structure heightening the sense of horror surrounding them.

As they reached the front door, Charlotte's dad swung it open, and they stepped outside into the night's cool air. But the sense of safety was short-lived as they spotted something in the yard—a figure standing in the shadows, just beyond the reach of the porch light.

"Who's there?" her dad called, rifle pointing in the same direction, his voice steady and commanding. The figure shifted, their silhouette obscured by the darkness. "Show yourself!"

The figure moved closer, still in the shadows barely revealing a face that sent a jolt of unease through Charlotte. She could not believe it. It was … Mark Reynolds? But that wasn't possible. Mark Reynolds was in prison miles away.

Charlotte stood frozen in disbelief. "You shouldn't have come back here," Reynolds sneered, a twisted smile emerging from the darkness.

"What have you done?" Charlotte shouted, as she pointed her rifle toward Reynolds. But before she could react, Reynolds lunged toward the forest, a flash of metal glinting in the light.

"Run, let's follow him!" her dad shouted at Charlotte. "Don't let him escape!" The adrenaline surged through her veins as they turned to flee, the sound of Reynolds's footsteps pounding ahead of them.

The night was clear, the full moon shining brightly, illuminating their path as they sprinted toward the forest, leaving the farmhouse behind. Charlotte's breath quickening as she tried to process what had just happened. The world around her felt suspended in time, and the shadows seemed to stretch and twist, hinting at the unknown lurking just beyond the light.

In that moment, doubt gnawed at her, but she pushed the fear aside, focusing on the task at hand. They had to catch Reynolds and uncover the truth that had eluded them for far too long.

The trees stood tall and silent, their branches swaying gently in the breeze as they forged ahead. Charlotte felt the adrenaline coursing through her, propelling her forward, a reminder that they were not alone in this fight. The shadows thickened around them, and the air grew colder as they ventured farther into the forest. Charlotte's instincts were on high alert as they navigated the winding path.

Suddenly, a rustle in the underbrush caught her attention, and Charlotte froze, her breath hitching in her throat. The sound was close, too close. She turned to her dad, their eyes wide. "Did you hear that?" she whispered, her voice barely audible over the pounding of her heart.

"I did," her dad replied, as he stepped in front of Charlotte as a shield, ready to react.

After a moment, the stillness returned, but unease lingered in the air. "We should be cautious," Charlotte said, her voice low as they moved deeper into the woods, searching for any signs of Reynolds in the moonlight.

As they ventured farther, shadows danced among the trees, and the sense of danger loomed larger. Charlotte struggled to steady her breath as she scanned the area, her instincts on high alert.

"Come closer to me," her dad urged, as they navigated the winding path.

Charlotte nodded, her breath quickening as they pushed forward, the darkness closing in around them as the vegetation became more dense. The woods felt alive, the shadows shifting like specters in the night, and she felt they were being watched.

A figure darted between the trees, a flash of movement that sent a jolt of energy coursing through Charlotte. "Get down!" her dad demanded, instinctively crouching low as he pulled her close into the underbrush.

Charlotte instinctively raised her rifle, scanning the darkness for further signs of danger. "What was that?" she gasped, her voice quivering with apprehension.

"I don't know, but we need to keep moving," her dad replied as they pressed forward.

As they navigated through the dense forest, Charlotte's mind raced with possibilities. Who had just run past them? Was it Reynolds, or someone else entirely? An unsettling doubt loomed over her, and a fierce resolve ignited within her.

The moon hung high in the sky, casting a silvery glow over the landscape, illuminating the path ahead. They moved quickly, hearts racing as they made their way through the woods, the sound of their footsteps muffled by the soft earth beneath them.

Unexpectedly, another rustle in the foliage caught her attention, and Charlotte stopped in her tracks. The sound seemed close, but she couldn't be sure exactly where it came from.

"Stay alert," her dad urged, his hand instinctively moving toward the rifle slung across his back. Charlotte raised her weapon, scanning the area cautiously, her instincts kicking into high gear.

The rustling grew louder, and Charlotte sensed an oppressive stillness settle around them, tightening its grip. Dark shapes flickered among the trees, and though she could barely distinguish the outlines of leaves and branches, the threat felt tangible and urgent.

With a sudden burst, a figure emerged from the foliage—
a flash of movement that ignited a surge of energy within
Charlotte. "Get down!" her dad shouted, his voice
commanding as he crouched low, ready to react.

But as the figure stepped into the moonlight, Charlotte's
heart sank. It was not a threat, but rather a small deer, startled
by their presence. The creature stood frozen, wide-eyed and
trembling, before darting away into the darkness. The stiffness
in Charlotte's shoulders slowly eased, but the shock of what
could have been lingered.

"False alarm," her dad breathed, a hint of relief in his
voice as he lowered his rifle. "Let's keep going. We can't
linger here."

Charlotte nodded, the importance of their mission
pushing her forward. They pressed on through the dense
woods, the underbrush crunching beneath their feet as they
navigated the winding path. The shadows cast by the trees
loomed ominously, but the moonlight filtered through the
branches, guiding them toward safety.

The deeper they ventured into the forest, the more
Charlotte felt the gravity of the situation settle over her.
Silence pressed in around them, broken only by the distant
sounds of rustling leaves and the occasional hoot of an owl

echoing in the night. The air was cool and crisp, and Charlotte continued to feel like they were being watched.

"We should not be too far from that old hunting cabin," Charlotte's dad suggested. "If he knows the area, he may be headed that way. It's partially sunken into the ground, obscured by the dense trees and thick vegetation, making it notoriously hard to spot. It would be a great hiding place—if you knew how to get there."

"Lead the way," Charlotte said, determination etched across her features as she matched his pace.

They moved quickly, a tight knot of apprehension clutching at them as they navigated through the shadows. Yet for the first time that night, Charlotte felt a sense of comfort as they walked along the familiar trails.

Finally, they arrived at the hunting cabin. The dense trees shrouded it in shadow, creating an air of mystery that surrounded the structure. Its rustic exterior, weathered and worn, stood out against the darkness, evoking memories of simpler times that now felt distant. The door was securely locked, but a faint sound from within stirred a mix of nostalgia and trepidation as they hesitated at the threshold, aware that something unknown awaited them inside.

As they stood there with uncertainty and caution, Charlotte's dad stepped forward, determined to see what was inside. He grasped the old, rusted handle and gave it a firm tug, but the door wouldn't budge. A chain with a surprisingly well-preserved lock, contrasting sharply with the rest of the cabin's weathered hardware, held it firmly in place. With a resolute expression, he retrieved his rifle and used the butt of it to strike the lock with precision. The metal shattered under the force, and with a final push, he swung the door open, revealing the shadowy interior.

The interior was dark, save for the faint moonlight filtering through the cracks in the wooden walls. Charlotte cupped one ear as she leaned in closer, her eyes wide with apprehension. "Do you hear that?" she asked, her voice barely above a whisper, straining to catch the faint sound that broke through the oppressive atmosphere around them.

Her dad nodded. "Yeah, I do. It sounds like someone's crying."

Charlotte and William moved cautiously toward the source of the distress, their rifles held tightly in their hands, poised for action. The shadows cast by the meager moonlight filtering through the walls loomed larger, morphing into dark shapes —a reminder of the danger that seemed to lurk in every corner. Each creak of the floorboards beneath their feet echoed ominously, heightening their sense of awareness as they ventured deeper into the cabin.

As they walked down the narrow hallway, they caught sight of a figure huddled against the wooden wall—a young girl, no older than nine, her face streaked with tears that glinted in the dim moonlight. Her tangled hair framed her frightened expression, and she clutched her knees tightly to her chest. She was dressed in a tattered shirt and a pair of dirty wool socks that barely protected her small feet from the chill of the floor. "Help!" she cried, her voice choked with fear. "Please!"

Charlotte's heart sank as she rushed forward, her dad right behind her. "It's okay! We're here to help!" Charlotte called out, her voice steady despite the torrent of emotions surging within her.

The girl looked up, her eyes wide and shimmering with terror. "They took me!" she sobbed, trembling. "I don't know where I am! I want to go home!"

Charlotte felt a rush of empathy flood through her as she comforted the girl, wrapping her in her own jacket. "You're safe now," she assured, glancing at her dad, whose expression reflected a mix of concern and haste. "We need to get you out of here. Can you tell us your name?"

"Lily," the girl sniffled, wiping her eyes with dirt-streaked hands. "They said I was a bad girl, but I didn't do anything! I want my momma!" her voice trembled as she clung to the hope that her mother was out there, searching for her.

"Lily, listen to me," Charlotte said, kneeling down to the girl's level. "I promise we're going to help you. But you have to be brave for just a little longer. Can you do that for me?" She looked at her dad, who nodded, his gaze steady.

"Do you know who took you?" her dad asked, his tone gentle yet firm.

Lily shook her head, her hair falling into her eyes. "I don't know. I just remember they had a big truck and they took me into the woods first, and then into some dark place."

The impact of Lily's words resonated deeply within Charlotte. "We need to get you out of here," she said. "Can you walk?"

Lily nodded, though her small frame was shaking. But as Charlotte looked down, she noticed the girl's bare feet, protected only by the dirty wool socks. "Oh, sweetie, you're not wearing any shoes," she said softly. "You must be freezing. Dad, can you carry her?"

Without hesitation, William knelt down, carefully placing Lily on his back, one hand protecting the rifle while securing her with the other. "Follow me," her dad instructed, stepping out first to survey the area as the moonlight cast long shadows across the ground.

As they stepped outside, a cold gust swept through the clearing, making Lily and Charlotte shiver. The air felt charged, heavy with the anticipation of danger. "We need to move quickly," her dad urged, glancing around as if expecting someone—or something—to emerge from the darkness.

They made their way toward the path, Charlotte maintaining a firm grip on Lily's hand. The shadows seemed to stretch and bend around them, the branches overhead whispering like voices just out of reach.

"Do you think they're looking for her?" Charlotte whispered to her dad, concern tightening her voice.

"Maybe they are," he replied, his eyes scanning the tree line. "But we can't take any chances. We need to get to the truck and go find help."

As they pressed on, Charlotte felt the forest close in around them. The farther they moved from the cabin, the more the oppressive silence wrapped around them.

Suddenly, a loud crack echoed from behind them, followed by hurried footsteps. Charlotte felt her pulse quicken as she turned to her dad. "What was that?" she hissed.

"If they are looking for Lily, it could be one of them," he replied. "We need to hurry!"

They quickened their pace, moving deeper into the forest. Charlotte's breath came in short gasps as she pushed herself to continue running. The sound of the footsteps grew louder, echoing in the stillness, and she could feel the weight of unseen eyes upon them.

"Keep going!" her dad urged, glancing back over his shoulder. "Don't look back!" But Charlotte's instincts screamed at her to turn around. Something—or someone— was pursuing them, and the knowledge sent a jolt of fear coursing through her. "We can't let them catch us!" she thought desperately.

As they ran, the underbrush snagged at Charlotte's legs, causing her to stumble slightly, but she quickly regained her footing, driven by a primal instinct to survive. Lily clung tightly to William, who adjusted his hold on her every so often to help her stay secure.

"Almost there!" her dad shouted. They were nearing the edge of the woods, where the truck waited just beyond the tree line.

As they approached the edge of the forest, they all stopped abruptly as a dark figure emerged in front of them. Charlotte instinctively reached for her rifle, quickly stepping in front of her dad and Lily like a protective shield.

Not entirely sure who the figure was, she called out, "Who's there?" Her voice steady despite the surprise.

"Charlotte," a low voice replied. "It's just me." As the figure stepped into the light, Charlotte couldn't believe her eyes. It was a familiar face, but one she hadn't expected to see.

"Sheriff Samuels?" she whispered in disbelief. "What are you doing here?" Charlotte demanded, her voice trembling with anger. She and Jack Henry had evaluated the possibility of Sheriff Samuels being involved in, or at least having knowledge of, his uncle's potential illegal activities. No one would believe them, and no one else knew that she and her dad were at the Underwoods' farm, aside from her mom and grandmother. The realization hit her like a punch to the gut as she took a step back, her instincts screaming at her to flee.

"Calm down, Charlotte," Sheriff Samuels said, his tone smooth and disarming. "I just came to help."

"To help?" Charlotte echoed. "How did you know we were here?"

Samuels smiled. "I heard about the fire last night, so I stopped by your grandparents' farm. Your Grandma told me where to find you. Jack Henry had already been taken to the hospital, so I drove here."

The implications of his words struck Charlotte, twisting her gut with uncertainty. Was he truly there to help, or did he have a more sinister motive? She exchanged a worried glance with her dad, who stood tense and watchful, rifle ready as he guided Lily behind him.

"Listen, I don't trust you," Charlotte said, her voice firm. "Not after everything that's happened. We found Mrs. Underwood dead in the house, and Mr. Underwood is missing. Then we thought we saw Reynolds, which seems implausible if he's still in prison. How do we know you're not involved?"

Samuels's expression shifted slightly, a flicker of annoyance crossing his features. "I'm here to assist you, Charlotte. We need to focus on getting that girl to safety," he gestured toward Lily, who stood trembling behind William, eyes wide with fear.

"Safety?" Charlotte shot back incredulously. "How do we know you're not the one who put her in danger? You're supposed to be the sheriff, but you've been nowhere to be found when we needed you! After the attack on Jack Henry and me, and with the fire raging all night, we didn't see you at all. It's almost been a full day, and now you show up?"

Her dad stepped forward. "Charlotte, we need to think clearly. Right now, Lily is our priority. We can't leave her here." He turned to Samuels. "If you truly want to help, then you'll escort us as we get her to the hospital. We need to make sure she's okay."

Samuels nodded slowly, but Charlotte sensed an underlying unease in his demeanor. She could see the flicker of something in his eyes—was it irritation or something darker? They had come too far and seen too much to let their guard down now.

"All right," Charlotte said. "But if anything happens, I swear—"

"Nothing will happen," Samuels interrupted, his tone sharp with his hands up in mock surrender. "I'm here to ensure you all get home safely. Or, to the hospital, in this case. Let's go."

Charlotte nodded with frustration. They had to get Lily to the hospital, and whatever else was happening could wait. "Let's move," she said, leading the way as they made their way toward the truck.

As they climbed into the truck, Charlotte made sure Lily was settled comfortably between her and her dad, offering a reassuring squeeze across the long seat on the old single-cab truck. "It's going to be okay, sweetie," Charlotte whispered, wrapping her arm around Lily gently while simultaneously thinking about the image of Mrs. Underwood's lifeless body.

The absence of Mr. Underwood created a dark cloud of uncertainty hanging over them. What had happened in that house? And why did it feel like they were being drawn into something much larger than themselves?

"Charlotte," her dad said softly, breaking through her spiraling thoughts. "We'll figure this out. We'll get Lily the help she needs, and then we can talk about what we saw."

"Do you think she's the girl Samuels said they've been looking for?" Charlotte asked, glancing at Lily, who was curled up against Charlotte, her small frame shivering with fear.

"Maybe," her dad replied. "She could be. We need to make sure she's examined thoroughly. If she was taken... we need to find out who did this."

Charlotte nodded. They had to uncover the truth behind the Underwoods and the sinister secrets lurking just beneath the surface of their quiet town. With every passing moment, she knew they were on the brink of something much darker than any of them had anticipated.

As they navigated the winding roads, the moonlight bathed the surroundings in a ghostly glow, illuminating their way to the hospital. Yet despite the brightness ahead, an unsettling feeling lingered, a stark reminder that the night's threats were far from behind them.

"Hold on, Lily," Charlotte said, her voice gentle as she squeezed the frightened girl even tighter against herself. "We're going to get you help. You'll be with your mommy and daddy very soon." The little girl nodded, her eyes welling with tears, and Charlotte felt a surge of protectiveness wash over her.

Pulling into the hospital parking lot, Charlotte knew they had uncovered a horrifying reality, but they were determined to find answers.

***

The sterile smell of antiseptic filled the air as they rushed Lily into the E.R. "Stay strong, Lily," Charlotte whispered, gently squeezing the girl's hand before they were separated. As nurses swiftly ushered Lily into a small examination room, their voices blended into a calm efficiency that contrasted sharply with the chaos of the emergency room. Charlotte and her dad remained just outside the doorway, a storm of concern brewing inside her as she watched them spring into action.

"Is she going to be okay?" Charlotte asked a nearby nurse, worry creasing her forehead.

"We're doing everything we can," the nurse replied, offering a reassuring smile before joining the other nurses in the examination room.

Minutes stretched endlessly as they waited, each second amplifying their unease. Finally, Sheriff Samuels entered the hallway, his expression serious yet strangely composed. He caught Charlotte's eye and nodded, conveying the unspoken message: *She's the girl who has been missing.* He then entered the examination room, where Lily was receiving care. Turning his attention to her, he pulled up a chair and sat down to her eye level and said, "Your parents are on their way over. Is it okay if I ask you some questions while we wait? Can you tell me what happened?"

Before Lily could respond, Charlotte stepped inside, her eyes pleading with the sheriff to let her stay. After a brief moment of consideration, he nodded slightly, acknowledging her need to be there.

Lily nodded slowly, her small frame trembling. "I remember… they put me in a big truck," she began, her voice barely above a whisper. "Everything was dark. I couldn't see anything. I was scared."

"What else, Lily?" Samuels encouraged, his voice soothing.

"There were sounds... like water dripping and... whispers, too," Lily continued, trying to concentrate. "I think I heard someone talking, but I couldn't understand what they were saying. It was dark, and I felt cold. I couldn't see anything except shadows."

"You are doing great, Lily. Do you recall anything else?" Samuels pressed. "Can you tell me more about the place where they took you?"

Lily hesitated, her small hands twisting nervously in her lap. "It felt... tight, like I was in a small space," she said, her eyes wide with fear. "There was a smell, like wet earth and something... rotten. I heard water, like a stream or something, but it was far away. And there were... voices. They were angry voices."

As Lily spoke, Charlotte experienced a flutter of dread in her gut. The descriptions were eerily familiar, mirroring the cavern where she and Mari had been taken. Terror gripped her as she recalled the dark, damp space—the fear that she had experienced when she realized they were trapped in a cavern. Her face went pale as the connection was undeniable, and the memories surged forward, unbidden. The whispers, the darkness, the overpowering fear—it all came flooding back, overwhelming her with its intensity.

"Charlotte?" Her dad's voice broke through her spiraling thoughts, concern on his face as he noticed her pale complexion. "Are you okay?" He had quietly entered the room, slipping in without anyone else noticing.

She shook her head, tears brimming in her eyes. "No, it's just... it sounds like—" Her voice faltered, a lump forming in her throat. "It sounds like what happened to us."

Samuels glanced at Charlotte, a flicker of understanding crossing his features. "What do you mean?" he asked, his tone now more urgent.

"Lily seems to be describing the cavern where Mari and I were taken," Charlotte explained, her voice trembling. "There were whispers, darkness... it sounds just like it! I—I truly believed we were going to be stuck in there forever."

"Lily, do you remember anything else about this place?" Samuels pressed, his intensity growing as he focused on the little girl.

Lily looked up at Charlotte, her wide eyes filled with fear and uncertainty. "I remember... I was really scared, and then I saw a light. It was small, in the distance. I thought it was coming from the outside."

Charlotte's recollection stirred within her. "The light…" she whispered, the memory of her own desperate search for safety flooding her thoughts. "I wanted to find a way out too."

"How long were you there?" Samuels asked gently. "Did you see who took you or where they went?"

Lily's gaze dropped to her lap, her small shoulders trembling. "No," she admitted, her voice barely audible. "I just remember being scared and wanting to go home."

"That is okay. I have one more question and then we can let you rest, okay? Can you remember how you got to the cabin where they found you?" Sheriff Samuels asked softly, as his gaze turned to Charlotte and William at the foot of the bed.

"I don't know. I was there when I woke up… I want my mommy!" Lily exclaimed, her voice rising with distress.

Charlotte felt a surge of protectiveness for Lily, a fierce resolve igniting within her. "We'll find out who did this," she promised Lily with conviction. "We won't let anyone hurt you again."

As the weight of their shared experiences settled over them, Charlotte realized the connections were deeper than she had anticipated. The resolve to uncover the truth burned brightly within her, igniting a fire of determination that would guide her through the shadows.

Samuels looked at Lily again. "Lily, we're going to step outside for a moment while the nurse takes care of you, okay? Your parents are on their way, and they'll be here soon. I promise you're in good hands," he said, his voice calm and reassuring.

Lily nodded slowly, her small face still etched with fear, but there was a flicker of trust in her eyes. "Okay," she whispered.

"Just focus on the nurse. She'll make sure you're comfortable," Samuels said before standing up and motioning for Charlotte and her dad to follow him outside.

As they stepped into the cool night air, the fluorescent lights of the hospital illuminated the parking lot, stark against the darkness surrounding them. But even in the comfort of the hospital, the impact of their conversation loomed heavy.

Samuels turned to Charlotte, who seemed to have forgotten about her skepticism about the sheriff. "I need to know more about the place you and Mari were taken. You mentioned it before, but I want to understand everything you can remember."

Charlotte's memories flooded back as she recalled the terror of that night so long ago. "It was a cavern, but it felt different than any cavern I've ever seen. It was dark and damp, with rocks that felt like they were closing in on us. I remember the sounds—water dripping, echoes of whispers… it felt like someone was always there, watching."

Samuels listened intently, nodding as she spoke. "I've spent years trying to figure out where that place was," Charlotte continued, her voice tinged with frustration. "I've researched everything I could find about caverns in Virginia. I thought I could find it, or at least understand what happened to us. There are famous caverns like Luray Caverns and Natural Bridge Caverns, but they're all at least two hours away from Floyd or from the lake where we were camping that night. It just doesn't make sense. None of those places could have been where we were trapped."

Her dad chimed in, with some hesitation. "It's almost impossible that someone could have taken you that far without being seen. Even back then, with tourists around. You were found not too far from our farm and the Underwoods too. It just doesn't fit."

Charlotte nodded, her frustration bubbling to the surface. "Exactly! Those caverns are popular tourist spots, and they were back then as well. People would have noticed if someone went missing or if there were strange sounds coming from the caverns. But no one ever reported anything like that."

Charlotte paused, trying to gather her thoughts. "It can't be that far. But no one had ever been able to find anything resembling that dark cavern near their farm. And what was Lily doing alone in the hunting cabin? It had to be connected to what had happened to the Underwoods. Wouldn't it?" The haunting image of Mrs. Underwood's lifeless body flashed through her mind, and a cold wave of dread crashed over her.

The Underwoods! Charlotte thought, panic surging as realization struck. *Has anyone found Mr. Underwood? We haven't seen him anywhere since everything spiraled into chaos.*

"Sheriff," she said breathlessly, desperation in her voice, "what about Mr. Underwood? Has he been found?"

Samuels's expression darkened. "Yes," he replied, his voice heavy with gravity. "My crew found him... he was in a terrible state."

"What do you mean?" she pressed, gripping her father's arm for support.

"He was found with a noose around his neck, tied to a horse," Samuels continued. "He was hidden in the dark, just to the side of the house. That's why you didn't see him before. It seems like they were trying to torture him. He was unresponsive. Possibly in a coma. But he survived, and he's on his way here now."

The image of Mr. Underwood, helpless and tormented, made her feel noxious. "Oh God," she whispered, her eyes wide in horror. "What did they do to him?"

"What I was told is that when my crew found him, he was unconscious, bruised and battered. There were signs of struggle, and his hands were raw from fighting against the ropes. He looked like he had been through hell. I can't imagine what he must have endured."

As Samuels spoke, Charlotte's mind painted a vivid picture of the scene. She envisioned the darkened area beside the house, the moonlight casting eerie shadows over the ground. Mr. Underwood, once a proud figure, now reduced to a broken man, gasping for breath, his face smeared with dirt and blood. The noose would have dug into his skin, leaving angry red marks, his eyes wide with fear and desperation as he fought against the restraints. It was a nightmare she struggled to comprehend. Her only hope was that he didn't have to witness what happened to his wife.

"Just thinking about him tied up like that..." her father said, shaking his head, his voice thick with emotion. "It's unimaginable. How could someone do that?"

"I don't know," Charlotte replied, her voice laced with anger and sorrow. "It has to be related to what happened to Lily. There's something more sinister at play here. I just know it!"

"Exactly," Samuels agreed. "We need to connect the dots. The fact that Lily was alone in the hunting cabin means something, and we can't overlook it. We need to figure out what they were after."

The cool night air wrapped around them like a shroud. This was bigger than they thought. The mystery deepened with each revelation, the shadows of the past intertwining with their present.

Charlotte's heart raced again, not just with fear, but a burning desire for justice. "We have to find out who did this," she said. "We can't let them get away with it."

Samuels nodded, a fierce glint in his eyes. "We won't," he promised, his voice loud and clear.

CHAPTER XXIV

The sterile scent of cleaning products and medical supplies filled the air as Charlotte followed her dad down the dimly lit corridor of the hospital. The walls were painted a pale green, their color muted in the shadows, which cast an eerie ambiance that seemed to cling to her. The atmosphere felt cold—a stark contrast to the warmth of the holiday season outside, where carolers sang and twinkling lights adorned every window. Charlotte could hear the faint echo of their footsteps, each step amplifying the silence that surrounded them, as they approached Jack Henry's room.

"Are you okay?" her dad asked with a hint of concern.

"Yeah," Charlotte sighed, her voice steady, though her insides churned with unease. "I just want to see how he's doing, and we need to talk about everything that's happened."

They stopped in front of Jack Henry's room, the door slightly ajar. She pushed the door open, the hinges creaking softly, echoing her trepidation.

The room was small, but it was filled with the scent of flowers, a stark reminder of life amidst pain. The soft hum of medical equipment created a rhythmic backdrop, almost soothing, yet it underscored the fragility of the moment. Jack Henry lay in the hospital bed, a bandage wrapped around his abdomen, evidence of the pain he had endured. The pale blue curtains around the bed offered a semblance of privacy but did little to shield her from the harsh reality of his condition. The flickering lights of the machines monitoring his vitals pulsed like a heartbeat—steady yet fragile.

As Charlotte and William stepped inside, a wave of sorrow and guilt washed over her. Seeing him like this—vulnerable and hurt—made her heart ache, and she fought back tears, wishing she could erase the pain he had to endure, a pain she felt responsible for.

Just as they entered, Charlotte caught sight of Atohi sitting in a chair beside Jack Henry, his tall frame hunched slightly as he leaned in, deeply engaged in a serious conversation. The dim light in the room cast shadows on their faces, creating an intimate atmosphere that made Charlotte feel like an intruder. She paused, her breath catching at the unexpected sight of him. It had been years since she had seen Jack Henry's younger brother, and she had never anticipated running into him in this hospital room, especially since she wasn't sure how the brothers were getting along these days.

Atohi was a striking thirty-nine-year-old man, tall with dark skin that reflected his Monacan heritage. He favored their mother, with high cheekbones and a strong jawline, his features a mix of youthful charm and mature sophistication. His hair was styled in tight curls, framing his face and accentuating the warmth in his deep brown eyes. But today, there was an edge to his demeanor—a strain that suggested he was grappling with something beneath the surface.

As Charlotte moved closer to the bedside, leaving her father in the doorway, she overheard Jack Henry's voice, low and earnest, unaware of her presence. "You need to tell her what you know, Atohi."

Charlotte felt a jolt of surprise at his words, as she processed the implication. Atohi looked taken aback, his expression shifting to one of uncertainty. "What do you mean? I… I don't know if I should."

"Listen, you have to speak up. It's important," Jack Henry insisted, his tone firm yet encouraging. "She needs to hear what you know."

"Tell me about what?" Charlotte said, stepping fully into the room and positioning herself at the foot of the bed, eager to be brought up to speed on their conversation.

Atohi turned, surprise flickering across his face as he registered Charlotte's presence. "Charlotte! I didn't see you there," he said. "Are you and Jack Henry back together? Since when?"

"For a while, yes," she replied, as she took in the familiar yet distant figure of Atohi. "But what are you talking about? What does Jack Henry want you to tell me?"

Jack Henry sighed, glancing between his brother and Charlotte, the shock of the moment settling heavily upon him. The atmosphere in the room thickened, and Charlotte could feel it in the pit of her stomach. "It's not what you think. We were just discussing some things about the past—things that might be important," he admitted, his tone serious, almost grave.

Atohi's expression shifted, guessing what Charlotte might be thinking. "Charlotte, I've changed since those days. I'm no longer involved with the people I was back then. I regret those decisions. I want to help in any way I can."

Charlotte felt a flicker of skepticism. "You were involved with those people? The ones stealing sheep and horses from the Welsh farmers?" she asked, pretending she didn't know a thing about it, her pulse quickening with each word.

Atohi nodded. "Yeah. I've distanced myself from that life. I can't change the past, but I want to make amends."

"What do you know about John Samuels and his activities?" Charlotte pressed, her curiosity driving her forward. "I heard he was involved in stealing wool bales back then. Do you think he had any connection to Reynolds?"

Atohi's brow furrowed as he recalled the past. "Yes, I know Samuels was involved in stealing wool bales, but I don't know the details. Just that he was smart about it. He never stole more than one or two bales, to avoid drawing attention. After the initial thefts, he would find trucks loaded with bales destined for the ports and swap one of the bales on the truck with one of his own. Technically, nothing seemed missing. I think he got paid for this, but I'm unsure what the swap was for or who paid him. One of my old friends helped him once or twice, and they talked in hushed tones. I thought it was just about the wool, but now..." His voice trailed off, uncertainty creeping in. "He dealt with Reynolds. Reynolds's involvement with the Monacan movement against the Welsh farmers was a cover. He didn't care about sheep or horses; it was likely a cover for something else, something related to what Samuels was doing."

Charlotte felt her breath catch at Atohi's recounting, the implications of his words wrapping around her like a cold shroud. "What do you think they were hiding? Why would he swap the wool bales? Was something else in the bales Samuels was replacing the wool bales with?"

"I heard rumors," Atohi said slowly, his voice barely above a whisper, as if uttering the words aloud might summon the darkness they suggested. "Some said the wool bales were used to cover up something else. They'd load them onto shipping trucks bound for the ports in Virginia Beach and Baltimore, but no one knew for sure what it was. All I know is that it didn't sit right with me. I didn't want to be involved, but I was too scared to speak up back then."

Atohi hesitated, then continued. "You know, wool bales are large and heavy, often tightly packed to maintain their shape. They're usually wrapped in burlap or similar materials that are sturdy yet breathable. If someone removed some of the wool and created a hollow space, it could be possible to conceal a child or a small person inside. The burlap would allow for some airflow, making it feasible for someone to breathe, at least for a while. It wouldn't draw much attention, especially if the bales were stacked with others in a truck, looking just like any other load headed for the ports."

He paused, his eyes darkening as memories of fear and complicity flickered across his face. "Knowing what I know

now, I think it may make sense to consider that they were using that to hide people—children."

Charlotte's heart raced. "We need to find out more," she said, her voice steady despite the turmoil inside. "If there's any chance that what happened to Mari and other girls is connected to this, we have to dig deeper."

Atohi nodded, his expression shifting to one of resolve, but the flicker of doubt in his eyes told Charlotte there were still shadows lurking beneath the surface. "I'll help in any way I can. I want to make things right."

The gravity of their discussion created an almost suffocating atmosphere, growing more pronounced with every moment. Charlotte turned to Atohi. "What do you think about Sheriff Samuels? Do you think he knows anything about his uncle, John Samuels's dealings?"

Atohi shook his head. "I don't think Sheriff Samuels knows anything about his uncle's illegal activities. He's always been a straight-up guy, more focused on upholding the law than playing games. If anything, I'd look at John's two sons, Sheriff Samuels's cousins." He paused, his lips pressing into a thin line. "They've had their fair share of problems with the law, and there have been rumors about their involvement with some shady business. They never really learned what it means to work hard. They could have taken on their father's profession of shearing sheep, but they have always been too lazy to do that. Instead, they live off him, hanging around the house all day doing nothing. They're like parasites."

John Samuels's sons, both in their upper thirties, were a study in contrast to their father's once-respected stature. The older son, Derek, was a hefty man with a receding hairline that only accentuated the greasy strands of hair clinging to his scalp. His round face was perpetually flushed, as if he had just finished an unhealthy meal, and his beady eyes darted around with a blend of suspicion and disdain. He always wore a stained t-shirt that clung to his bulging belly, the fabric stretched to its limits, revealing a tattoo of a skull that seemed almost comical against the backdrop of his flesh. His hands were large and often dirty, with long, ungroomed nails that showed little care or attention. Instead of bearing the marks of hard labor, they were frequently found clutching a remote control or a half-empty soda can.

His younger brother, Jake, was similarly unkempt but slightly taller, with a thick neck that seemed to disappear into his shoulders. His unshaven face was dotted with the remnants of old acne scars, giving him a permanent look of juvenile recklessness. He would generally dress in ill-fitting cargo shorts that barely contained his girth, the pockets bulging with crumpled fast-food wrappers and receipts. His size contributed to a lethargy that suggested he preferred to lounge on the couch rather than engage in any form of activity. Both brothers had an aura of neglect about them, as if personal hygiene and responsibility were concepts just out of their reach.

Neither of them had ever married, though Derek had two kids from a brief relationship that ended in bitter breakup, leaving him buried beneath child support payments that made him even more resentful. The brothers were known for their crude jokes and loud laughter, which often rang hollow in the ears of those forced to endure it. They were the kind of men that no one liked or wanted to be around—consumed by their own self-interest, their lives a testament to the decay of ambition and decency. To many, they represented the worst of their father's legacy, embodying a life of ease built on the backs of others, leaving a trail of disdain wherever they went.

Charlotte absorbed Atohi's words, noting the stark contrast between the sheriff and his cousins. "That's alarming," she mused out loud, her mind spinning. "There's a significant difference between the values of the sheriff and those of his cousins."

"Exactly," Atohi agreed. "They were always looking for shortcuts, and that's how they ended up in trouble."

Charlotte felt things beginning to click into place. "It makes you wonder if their upbringing played a role."

"What about Mr. Adkins?" she asked. "He was also around when John Samuels and Reynolds were working at my grandfather's farm, and he was involved in some of the crimes against the Welsh farmers as well. Do you think he has any connections to them?"

Atohi nodded slowly. "Adkins did work with John Samuels in the past. They kept in touch, especially since Adkins has been the caretaker at the Underwoods' farm."

Charlotte's dad, who had been quietly observing from his position near the door, interrupted: "Charlotte, we didn't see Adkins at the farm last night. Unless... could it be that the person you thought was Reynolds was actually Adkins? They are similar in stature and build, and it was dark, so it's certainly possible."

Charlotte's fingers twisted the edges of the bed sheets she had been playing with throughout the conversation, as her thoughts spun. "That's a chilling possibility," she whispered, her voice barely above a murmur. "But ... I also remember Sheriff Samuels asking Jack Henry about Atohi the other day," she said, locking eyes with Atohi. "What could that been all about? The question came completely out of the blue."

Atohi looked taken aback. "I don't know for sure, but it could be related to Adkins," he replied carefully. "Sheriff Samuels knows that he and I are close, and he might have had questions about our connections, especially now that things seem to be escalating. If he suspects Adkins might know something, it makes sense that he'd want to ask."

Charlotte nodded. "Have you talked to him recently? I mean, to Sheriff Samuels?"

"No, I haven't," Atohi said, shaking his head. "But I can if you think that could be helpful. Why do you ask?"

Charlotte paused, thinking about the tangled web of relationships and secrets. "Let's think this through. You've been friends with Adkins since you were teenagers, and he was involved with your movement to get back at the Welsh farmers. During the summer when Mari died, John Samuels, Mark Reynolds, and Emmanuel Salazar all worked at our family's farm. They were involved in illegal activities, some of which included you and Adkins, and some, if you're telling the truth, were only between the three of them. We know Mark Reynolds was recently convicted for the kidnapping, sexual abuse, and killing of Mr. Adkins's daughter. Salazar may have been involved as well, but now he's dead. What we don't know is where John Samuels's sons fit in, if anywhere, and whether Adkins, John Samuels, and Mark Reynolds were working together. Aside from that, John Samuels and the friend you mentioned stole wool bales, allegedly in connection with the human trafficking as well. Is your friend still around?" Charlotte asked Atohi.

"No," he responded. "He passed a few years ago."

"Okay, then," Charlotte continued. "That leaves us with John Samuels, Adkins, and potentially John Samuels's kids. Were John Samuels's kids involved at all with the wool bale thefts?" she asked, her tone sharp, almost like she was interrogating a witness.

"Not that I know of. They're low-life people, but I don't think I've ever heard about them being involved. They're probably not smart enough for their father to trust them with any of that, but I don't know for sure."

"Fine," Charlotte replied, frustration bubbling just below the surface. "Then we need to figure out Adkins's involvement. I can't believe we had Mr. Adkins and his family at our home for Christmas just a few days ago!"

Could Adkins and John Samuels be responsible for Mrs. Underwood's murder? Charlotte thought to herself. She looked at Atohi, her voice firm as she challenged him. "How confident are you that Sheriff Samuels is not involved at all with any of this?"

"Confident enough to discuss all this with him," Atohi responded, a mix of confidence and defiance shining in his eyes.

"He should probably still be here at the hospital. He was waiting for Lily's parents to get here. Let's go find him," Charlotte said.

"Who's Lily?" Atohi asked.

"Come. I'll explain as we walk," Charlotte said, her voice steady as she turned to lead the way. Looking back at her dad and Jack Henry, she said, "Are you two okay to stay here?"

"I don't have much of a choice," Jack Henry replied, a sarcastic smile creeping onto his face.

"I'll come with you," her dad said. "Let's find Sheriff Samuels and see what he knows."

"Okay, let's go, then," Charlotte said as she opened the door and stepped into the hallway.

CHAPTER XXV

The soft glow of the kitchen lights illuminated the cozy space, casting a warm hue against the wooden walls and contrasting with the cool December night outside. The kitchen was alive with the sounds of tinkling utensils and the rhythmic chopping of vegetables on a cutting board. Charlotte's mother, Victoria, stood at the counter, her gaze focused in concentration as she finely chopped onions, the sharp scent filling the air and mingling with the warmth of the stove. Beside her, Grandma Ann worked on boiling a few eggs, counting the minutes to ensure they reached the perfect boiling point.

"Have you heard anything yet?" Victoria asked, glancing at the clock that ticked steadily on the wall, each passing minute heightening their concern. Hours had slipped by since Charlotte and her dad left for the Underwoods' farm, and the outside silence that surrounded the house felt deafening, amplifying the unease that had settled in Victoria's and Ann's minds.

"No, not a word," Grandma Ann replied. "I'm sure they're fine, but it's just not like them to be gone this long without checking in." The concern in her tone was unmistakable.

Irma, the family friend from the neighboring farm, was there to help. "Let's focus on getting dinner ready," she suggested, glancing at Victoria with a reassuring smile. "It'll do you both good to keep busy." The savory aroma wafted through the kitchen, mingling with the scent of onions, creating a comforting atmosphere that temporarily eased their worries. Irma took on the task of peeling the potatoes, her hands moving quickly as she tossed the skins into a bowl.

Victoria nodded, grateful for Irma's presence. Cooking was her way of coping, a familiar ritual that helped ground her amidst the daily stresses and the rising anxiety. "Charlotte loves shepherd's pie," she said to Irma, her voice softening at the thought of her daughter. "I adapted the recipe from Ann's original. I believe mine is simpler than hers but just as comforting. Not to brag, but I think Charlotte and William prefer mine," Victoria added with a hint of humor to lighten the mood.

As Victoria continued to chop the onions, she recalled the flavors of her daughters' childhood—the warmth of home-cooked meals shared around the table, laughter echoing off the walls. She was determined to create that same atmosphere tonight. "We'll make it just right," she murmured to herself, stirring the onions into the pan with the ground beef. The sizzling sound was music to her ears, a reminder of the warmth that filled their home.

Grandma Ann was supervising the eggs, still counting the minutes since the water started boiling to ensure they cooked to the perfect point. "You know, I still think your recipe is a bit too unorthodox," she teased. "Very far from my traditional Welsh recipe. And no salt? What's wrong with you!"

"Ann, you know Charlotte hates anything too salty," Victoria replied with a smile, her heartwarming at the playful banter. "Besides, the green olives bring enough flavor. Just wait until you taste it!"

It was a simple yet delicious recipe that only included a few ingredients. Yellow potatoes for the mashed potatoes that would sit on top of the ground beef in a glass dish. The ground beef was slightly cooked with the chopped onions, to which Victoria would add a few chopped boiled eggs, green olives, and spices. She kept it simple, with only cumin, paprika, pepper, garlic, and a few sprinkles of crushed peppers. The saltiness of the olives was enough for the perfect taste. Once the mix was ready, they would place it in the glass dish with the mashed potatoes on top. Victoria liked to add a design to the mashed potatoes with a fork, drawing lines around the edges following the shape of the dish and then some straight lines in both directions forming perfect squares across the dish. She would then sprinkle a little ground cinnamon on top and put the dish in the oven for about ten to fifteen minutes to finish cooking the ground beef, mix the flavors with the mashed potatoes, and add some crispiness on top.

The kitchen was a whirlwind of activity as they worked together. Irma had begun to set the table, carefully placing plates and cutlery with an eye for detail. The wooden table, polished to a warm sheen, was adorned with a simple, festive tablecloth featuring green and red patterns that still echoed the holiday spirit. A flickering candle stood in the center, casting dancing shadows on the walls that felt both intimate and comforting.

Outside, the cool December night wrapped around the farmhouse like a shroud. The moon, high in the sky, illuminated the remnants of the barn that had burned to the ground the night before, its charred remains dark and cold in the moonlight. The sight sent a shiver through Victoria as she looked out the window, a stark reminder of the turmoil that had engulfed their family just hours earlier. She could almost hear the echoes of the previous night—the crackling flames, the frantic shouting—memories that would linger long after the physical scars had faded.

"Dinner will be ready soon," Grandma Ann announced, her voice breaking the silence as she expertly removed the shells from the boiled eggs she had set aside. Each egg was placed carefully on the counter, their smooth surfaces gleaming under the kitchen lights. "We'll have plenty for everyone, and we'll save some for Charlotte and William when they get back."

Victoria forced a smile, but worry gnawed at her insides. "I just wish they'd call," she admitted, glancing at the clock again. "What if something has happened?"

"Don't think like that," Irma said. "They're probably just caught up in conversation. You know how much they like to talk."

As the minutes dragged on, the kitchen filled with the rich aroma of the shepherd's pie coming together. Once the potatoes were peeled and boiled, Victoria began mashing them with a few tablespoons of butter, creating a fluffy, golden topping. She hummed softly to herself, a song from her childhood, trying to drown out the growing anxiety. Irma helped by mixing the cooked ground beef with the chopped olives and eggs, the vibrant colors and scents bringing life to the dish.

With the mixture ready, Victoria layered the ground beef into a glass dish, smoothing it out before adding the mashed potatoes on top. She took extra care to create the design with a fork, drawing lines around the edges and forming perfect squares across the surface. It was a simple act, but it made her feel connected to her family traditions, the repetition of the task grounding her amidst the uncertainty of the evening.

"The oven is ready," Irma confirmed, glancing at the clock. "You said set the timer for fifteen minutes?" She reached for the familiar wind-up kitchen timer, the kind that would ring with a cheerful ding when the time was up.

As the dish baked, their nerves about Charlotte and William's unknown whereabouts gradually eased, replaced by the anticipation of a warm meal. The soft glow of the moon filtered through the window, while outside, the wind howled gently, a reminder of the chill that lingered beyond their cozy walls.

"Let's turn the radio on," Grandma Ann suggested, reaching for the dial. "We can listen to some music."

The sound of old holiday tunes filled the kitchen, blending with the comforting aromas of shepherd's pie. Yet despite the warmth that surrounded them, an undercurrent of worry remained—an anxiety that settled like fog in their minds. Would Charlotte and her dad return before the night grew darker?

As they gathered around the table, the quiet seemed to stretch, a heavy silence filled with unspoken fears. They exchanged glances, each woman lost in her thoughts, all acutely aware of the ominous shadows lurking just outside their warm haven.

"Victoria, dear," Grandma Ann finally said, breaking the silence. "What do you think is taking them so long? They should've been back by now." There was a hint of worry in her voice, a shared concern that echoed in the room.

"I don't know," Victoria replied, as she glanced toward the window. The darkness outside felt oppressive. "Maybe they got caught up with the Underwoods, or something may have delayed them."

"Or worse," Irma said, her voice dropping to a whisper. "What if something happened to them? What if they ran into trouble?"

Victoria's expression hardened at Irma's suggestion. "Let's not jump to conclusions," she urged, trying to maintain a sense of calm. But deep down, the fear lingered—a nagging worry that had settled in her gut, twisting and coiling like a serpent. The comforting aroma of shepherd's pie mingled with the scent of freshly baked bread, but the warmth of the kitchen did little to alleviate the growing unease.

"I'll go check on them," Irma offered, as she moved toward the door. "I'll drive over to the Underwoods' farm and see if they're still there."

"No, I don't want you to go alone," Victoria replied quickly, fear rising in her chest at the thought of Irma venturing out into the night. "What if something happened to them? What if the same person who shot Charlotte and Jack Henry came back?"

"Then I'll be there to help," Irma said. "I'm not afraid. If something happened, they'll need all the help they can get."

Victoria felt a surge of gratitude for Irma's offer, but the worry gnawed at her insides. "I can't just sit here and wait," she admitted, her voice shaky. "I keep feeling that something is wrong."

"Let's give them a few more minutes," Irma suggested, placing a hand on Victoria's shoulder in a comforting gesture. "I'm sure they'll be back soon."

But as the minutes dragged on, the uncertainty in the air grew thicker. Victoria glanced out the window again, the darkness outside feeling more suffocating than before. The remnants of the barn that had burned to the ground loomed in the distance, a chilling reminder of the dangers that surrounded them.

"Maybe I should call the sheriff," Victoria said. "Something is off."

Irma nodded in agreement. "It might be a good idea. Better to be cautious than to regret not acting sooner."

Victoria moved to the phone, her hands trembling slightly as she dialed the sheriff's office. The line rang, each tone deepening her anxiety until finally, a voice answered. "Sheriff Samuels's office. How can I assist you?"

"It's Victoria Jones," she said. "I'm calling because my husband and daughter left to head to the Underwoods' farm hours ago and haven't returned yet. We're starting to worry. Is the sheriff around?"

"No, he's not. Last I heard was that he was also headed to the Underwoods' farm," the sheriff's assistant said in a calm tone. "That was hours ago. I can check on him on the radio."

"Yes, please," Victoria replied. "I know it seems like I'm overreacting, but I can't ignore the feeling that something is not right."

"I'll let you know. Just hang tight, okay?" the sheriff's assistant assured her.

Victoria hung up the phone, knowing there wasn't much more she could do other than wait for the sheriff's assistant to call back. "The sheriff went to the Underwoods' farm too. Now I really am worried," she informed Irma, who nodded.

As they returned to the kitchen, an uneasy silence settled among them, each woman lost in her own thoughts. The shepherd's pie was nearly ready, its aroma wafting through the air, but even the smell of comfort food did little to ease the concern that clung to them.

CHAPTER XXVI

Charlotte, William, and Atohi made their way through the bustling hospital lobby, the sterile scent of rubbing alcohol lingering in the air like an unwelcome guest. The fluorescent lights buzzed overhead softly, casting a harsh glow over the scene. Their footsteps echoed against the polished tile floor, a rhythmic percussion that mingled with the distant sounds of nurses and doctors attending to their duties. The atmosphere was charged with a sense of impending crisis—an unspoken acknowledgment that lives hung in the balance.

The corridor stretched before them, a maze of uncertainty as Charlotte felt a whirlwind of emotions swirling within her—fear, determination, and a flicker of hope—as they searched for Sheriff Samuels and navigated through the hospital's sterile environment. The soft murmur of conversations buzzed around them, but her focus was singular, zeroed in on their goal.

As they approached the waiting area, Charlotte spotted Sheriff Samuels standing with Lily's father, a tall man with a rugged appearance. His face was etched with grief, shadows beneath his eyes betraying the sleepless nights he had endured since his daughter's abduction. He leaned heavily against the reception desk, his posture tense, as he spoke in hushed tones to the sheriff, the weight of recent events clearly pressing down on both of them.

When the sheriff caught sight of Charlotte and her group approaching, he stood up straight, his expression shifting to one of concern. He quickly walked over to them, trying to create a barrier between them and Lily's father, whose relief at having found his daughter alive was evident. "Atohi, I've been looking for you," he said, the gravity of the situation apparent in his voice.

"I'm here now. Can you talk?" Atohi replied.

"Let's go somewhere private," the sheriff suggested, glancing back at Lily's father. He didn't want to draw attention to their conversation, recognizing the delicate emotional landscape they were navigating.

Nearby, the receptionist—a striking young woman with Native American heritage—had been listening intently. She wore light green scrubs that complemented her warm brown skin. Her long, dark hair cascaded down her back in loose waves, framing a face that was both delicate and strong. High cheekbones and expressive eyes sparkled with intelligence and compassion, making her a comforting presence in the otherwise sterile environment. As the sheriff turned to her, she offered a warm smile, her voice soft yet confident. "The second room to the right down the hall is empty. You can go there if you'd like."

"Thanks," the sheriff replied, motioning for Charlotte, her dad, and Atohi to follow him down the corridor. The atmosphere grew heavier as they walked. Each step felt like they were moving deeper into a web of secrets, the fluorescent lights flickering overhead.

"Make it quick," the sheriff said as they entered the small examination room, his voice weary, the strain of the night evident in his tone. "I'm exhausted. I want to finish here and go home."

Charlotte bristled at his words, irritation welling up inside her. "Go home? Mrs. Underwood was just murdered. Mr. Underwood barely made it out of there alive. Jack Henry and I were shot less than forty-eight hours ago. Someone is clearly trying to kill us! And you want to go home?" Her voice trembled with emotion, fueled by the urgency of their situation that felt too pressing to brush aside.

"Aren't you being a little dramatic?" the sheriff replied. "Look, I understand. But there's nothing we can do right now. It's late and we all need to rest. Whoever is behind this is not going to go away. We can start looking tomorrow, with fresh minds."

Charlotte's dad, who had been quietly observing, interjected, "I agree with the sheriff, Charlotte. We should go home too. We've had a long day, and we need to take care of ourselves too."

The anger surged through Charlotte, disbelief mingling with frustration. "Dad, you don't understand. This is about our family and innocent children! We can't just sit back and let this go!" Her voice quivered, emotions threatening to spill over. She turned to the sheriff, searching for support, but he seemed reluctant to interject on family matters.

The sheriff looked at Atohi, sensing the need to redirect the conversation. "What did you want to talk about?" he asked, his tone shifting to a more serious note, his eyes narrowing slightly.

Atohi cleared his throat, a flicker of hesitation crossing his mind as he prepared to speak. "I just had a conversation with Charlotte and her dad in Jack Henry's room. We discussed some things about the past—about Mark Reynolds, Emmanuel Salazar, and also your uncle." Atohi then described the details of their conversation and the connections they had made. "I think there are connections you need to explore."

The sheriff's expression darkened slightly. "That's not possible. Those rumors about my uncle are not true. He's an honest man."

Charlotte felt a wave of disbelief. "Sheriff, with all due respect, have you really looked into it? You can't just ignore these connections." She knew the weight of her words and challenged him to acknowledge the truth.

Samuels shook his head, frustration creeping into his voice. "I'm not saying I dismiss them, but I've known my Uncle John my entire life. He's a good man. He would never be involved in something so sinister."

"But what if he was?" Charlotte pressed, rising her voice. "You have to at least consider the possibility that he might be connected in some way."

The sheriff sighed, clearly agitated. "The prior sheriff investigated him when Mari died because of those unfounded rumors, and he was clean. There's no reason for me to start snooping around my own uncle. As I said, he's a good man."

Charlotte shook her head, disbelief flooding her. "The fact that you won't even investigate is exactly why I'm worried. We need to look into everything—everyone who could be connected!"

Samuels's gaze turned serious as he redirected the conversation. "I think our focus should be on Adkins. Have you seen him recently?"

Atohi nodded. "It's been a couple of days since I last saw him. He mentioned that he was planning to take his family back to their home in D.C. on Christmas Day, after spending Christmas Eve with the Joneses."

"I'm not sure when he was supposed to go back to work at the Underwoods after the holidays," Atohi added.

"Let me know if you hear anything, then," the sheriff instructed. "I'll need to find him tomorrow so we can bring him to the station for questioning. I sense he may be connected to all this somehow."

As the conversation wound down, Charlotte felt frustrated and helpless. After the sheriff left, she just wanted to go to Jack Henry's room and stay by his side, but Atohi assured her he would stay with him overnight. "You need to go home, Charlotte," he said gently, concern etched on his face.

Charlotte looked at Atohi, anger rising within her. "I can't just leave him alone."

"He won't be alone, Charlotte. I am telling you I will stay with him," Atohi reassured her.

"Charlotte, it's for the best," her dad chimed in, his voice steady. "We'll all go home. We need to take care of ourselves too."

With a heavy heart, Charlotte nodded, knowing they were right but feeling the weight of disappointment settle in her stomach. "Fine," she sighed, her voice barely above a whisper. "But I'm coming back first thing in the morning. Maybe Mr. Underwood will be conscious by then, and we can ask who did that to him."

After saying goodbye to Jack Henry, her dad walked with her outside to his truck. The chill of the evening air hit her as they stepped outside, the shadows of trees looming large at the edge of the parking lot. "You could have taken my side back there," Charlotte said, her voice laced with frustration as she opened the truck door.

William turned to her, his expression softening. "I am not taking anyone's side, Charlotte. Sheriff Samuels was right in saying you need to rest, and your mom and grandmother are probably worried," he explained gently. "It's very late. We have to get back home."

Charlotte's emotions felt like they were boiling just beneath the surface. "You think I'm just going to sit back and do nothing while someone is out there trying to kill us and hurting young girls? We're all in danger, Dad! We can't just go home!" Her voice trembled with the weight of her frustration.

"Look, I get it. I want to help, too," William replied. "But you need to consider that you're not seeing the bigger picture right now. We need to ensure we're safe, too. And right now, we all need to rest and recover. We'll come back tomorrow, and we can figure this out together."

Charlotte stared at him in disbelief. "You want me to just go home and pretend everything is fine? What if something happens while we're just sitting around?"

"I'm not saying that, Charlotte," William said. "But we can't rush into danger without a plan. We need to think things through."

Charlotte's anger flared, her emotions surging as she met her dad's gaze. "How can you be okay with this?"

"Because it's the right thing to do. You're not alone in this. We'll find a way to tackle this. But for now, we need to prioritize your safety and everyone's well-being."

"I just think we are running out of time," she whispered, her voice trembling. "I think we are very close to finding the answers we've been searching for, and after what happened at the Underwoods, it is clear whoever did that is not afraid to kill."

As they sat in the truck, surrounded by the shadows of the trees, Charlotte felt a sense of defeat building within her. The drive back to the farm felt oppressive, a cloud of uncertainty hanging over her. The night deepened around them, and the stars twinkled overhead as if holding secrets of their own.

CHAPTER XXVII

The next morning, Charlotte awoke before everyone else, the early light of dawn creeping through the window and casting a soft glow across the room. She grabbed a cup of coffee, its warmth a comforting embrace in her hands, and was ready to go, but her grandmother stopped her at the kitchen door.

Grandma Ann stood there, clad in a thick, pink robe that wrapped around her like a protective cocoon. The fabric was a soft wool, faded from years of wear, with frayed edges that showcased its enduring comfort. She wore fluffy wool slippers, their texture worn but still cozy, keeping her feet warm against the chilly floor. Her dark hair, streaked with gray, was pulled back into a loose bun, a few wisps escaping to frame her face. The lines of age and wisdom etched on her skin told stories of resilience and love, and her warm brown eyes sparkled with kindness, reflecting the depth of her years and experiences.

"You can't leave without eating anything, Charlotte," she said gently. "You'll need your energy. Here, I'll make you some toast." Before Charlotte could respond, Grandma grabbed the long, serrated bread knife from the knife block and sliced two thin pieces of her homemade German beer bread loaf on the cutting board.

"Have a seat, dear. I'll take care of you. Please," she insisted, her smile unwavering.

Without saying a word, Charlotte sat at the kitchen table, the familiar scent of toasted bread mingling with the aroma of fresh coffee. The kitchen table was slightly smaller than the dining room table, but it held its own charm. It was made of warm, polished wood, its surface covered with a thin sheet of glass. Underneath, photographs of the family from various gatherings—birthdays, holidays, and cherished moments— were displayed like a tapestry of memories. Charlotte's gaze landed on her favorite: a snapshot of her, Mari, and Grandma at a family gathering, with Grandpa Louis in the background roasting a full lamb over an open fire. The laughter, warmth, and joy of that day flooded her mind, reminding her of the importance of family.

As Grandma placed a plate with two perfectly toasted slices of bread in front of her, she offered a butter knife along with a block of creamy butter and a jar of homemade elderberry jam, Charlotte's favorite. "Eat!" Grandma urged. "Tell me, what's your plan for today? Do you think Mr. Underwood will be awake by now?"

"I hope so," Charlotte replied. "If he was able to see who attacked him or even hear their voices, that could give us the answers we've been searching for. This has to be related to what happened to Mari and me back then. There's no other reasonable explanation."

Grandma nodded in agreement, her expression serious as she leaned closer. "But I don't know," Charlotte continued. "Sheriff Samuels said he was in very bad shape when they found him. It's a blessing he was found alive."

"Poor Mrs. Underwood," Charlotte murmured, thinking back to the moment she had discovered Mrs. Underwood lying lifeless on the floor of their home. "It's so sad. I don't understand why anyone would do that to her. It doesn't make any sense."

As they discussed the events of the previous evening and Charlotte's theories about what could have happened, it became increasingly clear that whatever transpired at the Underwoods' farm had to be connected to the events of her own past. Charlotte shifted in her seat as the realization sank in. She glanced away, biting her lip, the atmosphere charged with an unsettling feeling that made it hard to breathe.

After finishing her toast, Charlotte thanked her grandma, who offered her some tea as well. "I have to go," Charlotte said, grabbing her coat and keys. "I need to try to speak with Mr. Underwood and check on Jack Henry."

"Go easy on him, honey. He's been through enough," her grandma replied with some concern. Charlotte nodded, knowing the truth in her words.

She stepped outside into the brisk morning air, feeling a rush of cold against her cheeks. The landscape was quiet, the snow glistening under the soft light of the rising sun. As she climbed into her Mercedes, the interior enveloped her in a comforting feeling, a welcome refuge from the chill outside.

The drive to the hospital was a familiar route, but today felt different. A sense of unease was clouding her thoughts. She navigated through the winding roads, the trees lining the path dusted with new snow, the sunlight sparkling off their branches like diamonds. The landscape unfolded before her, a breathtaking tapestry of white and gold, yet the beauty felt muted against the backdrop of her worries.

With each passing mile, her mind raced, thoughts swirling like the snowflakes dancing through the air. The recent revelations about Reynolds and the connections to her sister's death tugged at her heart, intertwining with memories of Mari that felt both comforting and painful.

What if Mr. Underwood had seen something? What if he had heard the voices of those who attacked him? Each question weighed heavily on her mind, and she couldn't shake the sense that time was running out. The sun climbed higher, casting a warm glow over the landscape, but the shadows of uncertainty lingered in her heart.

Arriving at the hospital, Charlotte parked her car and rushed inside, her heart pounding. The hospital scent filled the air as she made her way through the bustling lobby, the sounds of nurses and doctors mingling with the soft murmur of anxious families. She approached the reception desk, her heart racing as she inquired about Mr. Underwood's condition.

"Still in a coma," the nurse replied. "We're monitoring him closely, but there's been no change."

Charlotte felt a rush of disappointment. "Thank you," she said softly, considering her next steps. With a shift in her plans, she made her way to Jack Henry's room, hoping Atohi was still there so he could help him think thorough some of the questions that haunted her mind.

As she entered, the soft light of the room enveloped her, and she spotted Jack Henry propped up in bed. He had been awake, though uncomfortable throughout the night, his leg still throbbing with pain from the arrow wound. The bandages wrapped tightly around his thigh were stained with blood, a stark reminder of the violence they had both endured.

"Atohi is still asleep," Jack Henry whispered, trying to sound nonchalant, but the strain in his voice betrayed him.

"No I'm not," Atohi responded, stirring awake at the sound of their voices from the arm chair reclined in the corner.

Charlotte approached Jack Henry's bedside, her heart aching at the sight of him. "How are you feeling?" she asked, her voice gentle as she settled into the chair beside him and took his hand in hers.

"Like I got hit by a horse," he admitted, a faint smile tugging at his lips. "But at least the bleeding has stopped, thanks to your grandma. She really worked her magic."

"Yeah, she always knows what to do," Charlotte replied, grateful for her grandmother's nursing skills. "But I heard the doctors may need to perform surgery to fix the damage properly?"

Jack Henry nodded. "I'll be okay. This isn't going to slow me down." But even as he spoke, Charlotte could see the pain etched across his face, the struggle to remain strong evident in his eyes.

A pregnant silence filled the room, heavy with unspoken thoughts and emotions.

"Atohi, how did you know about the farms back then? I mean, how to steal the animals without being noticed?" Charlotte asked, eager to continue the conversation and draw out more information.

Atohi sat up slowly, rubbing the sleep from his eyes. "We had maps from the entire region and had marked which farms we wanted to target," he explained, his voice steadying as he recalled the details. "The maps included information about their roads, fences, where the gates were located, and even the geography of the land. We knew where the forests were in relation to the areas where the animals were kept, and we also knew which farms had rivers running through them. That's how we were able to come and go without being noticed."

Charlotte listened intently, absorbing every word. "Do you still have those maps?" she asked, her voice tinged with urgency. "Do you think there is a map showing my family's farm and the Underwoods' farm?"

"Probably," Atohi responded thoughtfully. "I'm sure they're still at my place. I can go find them now if you'd like. I could use the time to take a shower as well."

"Sure," said Charlotte, considering the possibility of uncovering more connections. "I'll stay here. But please, don't take too long."

"I won't," Atohi assured her, rising from the chair and moving toward the door.

"What was all that about?" Jack Henry asked with a hint of confusion. "Why do you need those maps?"

Charlotte looked at him, debating whether to share her thoughts. After a moment's hesitation, she decided to explain. "After everything that happened last night, and your brother's revelations about all the different people involved, along with the possible shady dealings, I started thinking. I believe the Underwoods' farm may be the key to finding out what's going on now *and* what happened to Mari and me back then. But I need to be sure."

Jack Henry's expression softened. "I'm not really following," he admitted. "But I trust you. I always have."

Charlotte's heart swelled at his words. "Thank you, Jack Henry."

Just then, Jack Henry shifted his weight slightly, wincing as discomfort shot through his abdomen. "So, have you heard anything about Mr. Underwood?" he asked, changing the subject, his gaze searching hers.

Charlotte shook her head. "No, I haven't seen him yet. The nurse told me he's still in a coma."

Jack Henry leaned back farther against the pillows, a thoughtful expression crossing his face. "And Sheriff Samuels? Have you seen him around?" he inquired.

"I have not seen him yet," Charlotte replied. "But I want to resume our conversation about his uncle and cousins. There may be something there. I'm not sure."

Jack Henry nodded, a look of understanding crossing his face as he recognized the gravity of her words.

As they waited for Atohi to arrive with the maps, Charlotte and Jack Henry, exhausted from the emotional toll of the previous days, gradually succumbed to sleep, their bodies seeking refuge from the chaos of the world outside. The quiet hum of the hospital room enveloped them, a lullaby of machines and distant voices that faded into a hazy dreamscape.

A couple of hours passed. The familiar sound of nurses bustling in the hallway faded into the background, leaving only the rhythmic beeping of the heart monitor to punctuate the silence.

Suddenly, the door creaked open, and Atohi slipped inside, his presence a welcome interruption to the stillness. He stood for a moment, taking in the sight of Charlotte and Jack Henry asleep, their faces relaxed in the temporary peace of slumber. With a determined expression, he approached them, gently shaking Charlotte's shoulder.

"Charlotte," Atohi whispered urgently, his voice barely rising above a breath. "Wake up. I have the map."

Charlotte stirred, her eyelids fluttering open as she grasped the reality of the moment. She sat up quickly, adrenaline surging through her veins. "What? You found it?" she asked, her voice still thick with sleep.

"Yeah, it's right here," Atohi replied, rolling out an old map—a large, weathered piece of paper that had seen better days. The edges were tattered, and the ink was faded in places, but it held the promise of answers. He handed it to Charlotte, who accepted it with anxious hands, her heart racing as the significance of the moment settled in.

She unfurled the map, the rustling sound breaking through the lingering silence. The paper was thick and coarse, the creases deep from years of storage. As Charlotte examined the intricate details, her breath quickened. The familiar shapes of the landscape began to emerge, and she traced her fingers over the landmarks, her heart pounding with recognition.

"Here's Grandma's farmhouse," she said, excitement bubbling in her voice as she pointed to the marking on the map. "And here's the Underwoods'. There's the wire fence that separates the two farms." She continued to scan the map, her eyes darting across the contours and lines. "Here's the river, and up here is the lake where Mari and I were camping back then. And here... here's where I was able to get out of the river, and here's where Mari's body was found after she drowned."

A feeling of immediacy coursed through her as she pointed to the markings, but then her brow furrowed as she searched for something specific. "I don't see the hunting cabin on this map, but it has to be around here," she said, pointing to an area close to the river. "That's where we found Lily. I don't know. I keep thinking about this... The Underwoods' farm, the hunting cabin, the river—they all seem awfully close, if you think about it." Atohi leaned in closer, studying the map with her.

"You said the farm caretakers used to help your cause with the Monacans back then, by keeping gates open, correct?" she asked.

"Yes, but I don't remember who the Underwoods' caretaker was back then, if that's where you are going with this," Atohi admitted. "I know it wasn't Adkins. He was a teenager back then and was working at your grandparents' farm during the summers."

Charlotte felt a wave of frustration. "Yes, I know," she replied, her eyes clouded with disappointment. "Still, there's something about this area that I think is important. We found Lily in the hunting cabin, and when the sheriff was asking her questions, she described the cavern Mari and I were in. I'm sure about that. That cavern was never found, but Lily was definitely there. The way she described it—the details… it has to have been the same cavern, and it has to be close to the hunting cabin."

As Charlotte spoke, the atmosphere in the room shifted, filled with an unspoken intensity. The gravity of their words lingered between them, and Charlotte could feel the moment closing in around them like a tangible force. They were on the brink of uncovering something much darker, and the uncertainty loomed like a shadow in the corners of her mind.

As they studied the map further, Charlotte felt a pulse of adrenaline surge within her, the thrill of the chase igniting a fire in her heart. They were on the cusp of something significant, and the importance of their mission loomed over them.

Suddenly, a loud noise echoed from the hallway, breaking their concentration and startling all three of them. Charlotte glanced toward the door, her instincts urging her to remain vigilant. "What was that?" she whispered, her voice barely audible.

"I don't know" Atohi replied, as he moved closer to the door, peering out into the dimly lit corridor.

Charlotte's pulse quickened as she exchanged glances with Jack Henry. The silence stretched around them, heavy with the weight of everything they had endured over the past few days. They listened intently, their hearts racing as they strained to hear any sounds beyond the door, aware that their recent encounters had heightened their senses and made them acutely alert to any potential danger.

Just then, footsteps echoed down the hallway, heavy and deliberate. The sound drew closer, and Charlotte's breath hitched in her throat. The door creaked open slowly, and the figure that stepped into the room sent a wave of relief washing over Charlotte. It was Sheriff Samuels, his expression serious as he surveyed the room.

"Sorry to interrupt," he said. "We need to talk."

Charlotte felt a mix of relief and apprehension as she met his gaze. "What's going on?" she asked, quickly standing.

"There's been a development in the investigation," Sheriff Samuels said, his eyes narrowing as he stepped farther into the room. "This could change everything."

"I spoke to Lily again this morning," Sheriff Samuels said, his voice low. "She told me that before she was put in the place she described last night—the cavern—a man had placed her on some sort of boat. Her head was covered, so she couldn't see anything, but from her description, it sounds like she was floating on a river for quite some time." He paused, collecting his thoughts. "From everything I've learned, I believe she was first taken to Emmanuel Salazar's house. That's where we found her blanket, remember? Her parents confirmed it was hers. Then they took her to that cavern, and when you found her, I think they were planning to move her somewhere else…"

Charlotte's pulse quickened at the implications of his words, each syllable striking her like a thunderclap. She leaned closer, a gasp escaping her lips. "A boat? Floating on a river?" A chill crept down her spine, gripping her with the horrifying thought of what Lily might have endured.

The sheriff continued. "On the night you found her in that cabin, she said she could hear two men arguing. Apparently, one of them wanted to 'cancel the plan,' and the other one didn't."

"Cancel the *plan?*" Charlotte echoed. "What plan?"

"I don't know," the sheriff admitted, shaking his head. "But like I said, it sounds like they were taking her somewhere. One of the men wanted to put her back in the cavern."

A weighty silence settled over them, thick with implications. Charlotte felt the dark truth starting to take shape, each revelation chilling her to the bone.

"And then what?" she pressed, as dread pooled in her stomach. "Did Lily say anything else?"

The sheriff hesitated. "She mentioned that she heard one of them say someone had died. I think what she heard was probably about Mrs. Underwood." The gravity of his statement hung heavily in the air, a stark reminder of the tragedy that had unfolded, a wound that had barely begun to heal.

A surge of anger and despair welled up inside Charlotte, a tempest brewing beneath her composed exterior. "It sounds like there may have been more," the sheriff continued. "She thinks there were other girls in that cavern. She couldn't see any, but she says she could hear them crying sometimes."

A knot formed in Charlotte's stomach as she processed this harrowing information. "Whoever did this to her was on the move to take her somewhere, but something happened that prevented that."

"They must have been discovered," Charlotte continued, her gaze intense as she locked eyes with the sheriff. "Maybe that's what happened to Mr. and Mrs. Underwood. They must have seen something they weren't supposed to."

The sheriff nodded. "It looks like that could have been the case—yes. The pieces are beginning to fit together, but we need to act quickly. If there are other girls involved, we can't afford to waste time."

As the reality of their situation pressed down on them, Charlotte felt a rush of adrenaline course through her veins, sharp and electric. The significance of their mission intensified, and she could sense the looming threat like a storm gathering on the horizon, dark clouds swirling ominously above.

"We have to find that cavern. If Lily heard other girls, we must save them before it's too late."

An intense focus filled the room as they exchanged determined looks, each aware of the risks ahead. They prepared themselves to confront the darkness that lay before them, readying their resolve for what was to come.

"I have an arrest warrant for Mr. Adkins," Sheriff Samuels announced. "I have reason to believe he is one of the two men Lily heard arguing."

Charlotte's heart seemed to stop. The sheriff leaned in closer. "Do you know who the Underwoods' caretaker was in the sixties?" he asked, holding her gaze with an intensity that made her stomach twist.

"Who?" Charlotte asked.

"Adkins's father, Ned Adkins," the sheriff revealed. "Khali Adkins took over after his father passed."

Charlotte felt the connections falling into place, but a sense of dread began to unfurl in her chest. "I came here to warn you, Charlotte," the sheriff continued. "I think Adkins and whoever the other person is are dangerous. I don't want you near them. Please, stop looking for them and let me do my job."

Charlotte opened her mouth to protest, to argue that she couldn't just sit back and let others handle it, but the words caught in her throat. Instead, she nodded silently, almost hesitantly.

With a final, lingering look, Sheriff Samuels turned to leave, the door clicking shut behind him and leaving Charlotte, Atohi, and Jack Henry alone with their swirling thoughts.

CHAPTER XXVIII

A cold wind swept through the bare trees, carrying with it the promise of more snow as the search for Adkins began late in the afternoon. Sheriff Samuels and his team scoured the area. Each rustle of leaves and snap of twigs heightened their senses, the looming threat of what they might uncover sending an electric current through the group.

"Keep your eyes peeled," Sheriff Samuels instructed, his voice low but commanding, reverberating with a gravity that echoed through the assembled teams. Each officer nodded, their expressions a mix of determination and anxiety as they prepared for the search ahead. A heavy silence enveloped them, the significance of their task looming like a storm cloud ready to burst.

The sheriff had organized multiple teams to scour the town of Floyd, each unit assigned to a specific area. One group focused on the dense woods that surrounded the Underwoods' farm, known for its tangled underbrush and hidden paths. Another team was stationed at key checkpoints along the roads leading in and out of town, ensuring no one could slip away unnoticed. Officers checked vehicles, their expressions serious as they interrogated drivers and searched trunks for any signs of Adkins or unusual activity.

As they ventured into the woods, Sheriff Samuels felt a surge of adrenaline that matched the gravity of the moment. The trees loomed overhead, their bare branches clawing at the sky, casting long, skeletal shadows on the frozen ground. The scent of damp earth mixed with the crispness of the air, invigorating yet filled with foreboding. Each crunch of the leaves underfoot felt like a drumbeat, echoing the pulse of their search.

The teams moved methodically, their breaths visible in the cold air as they fanned out, scanning the ground for any signs of disturbance. The sheriff led his group toward the banks of the river, its icy waters rushing past like a relentless tide. The sound of the water filled the silence, a constant reminder of the danger that lurked beneath its surface.

"Split into pairs," he instructed, gesturing for his deputies to cover more ground. "Stay within earshot, and report anything unusual." The officers nodded, their eyes sharp as they moved deeper into the underbrush, branches scratching against their jackets and uniformed legs as they maneuvered through the thicket.

After a few hours, the search felt like an eternity as they combed through the dense foliage, their breaths coming in heavy puffs. Night had fallen, and the sheriff couldn't shake the gnawing feeling inside him—a primal fear that time was slipping away. Every moment wasted could mean the difference between catching Adkins and losing him forever.

As they scoured the banks of the river, the sheriff's thoughts raced. He replayed the details of the case in his mind, piecing together the fragments of evidence that had led them to this moment. Adkins was a key player in a game that had far-reaching consequences, and the stakes had never been higher.

Suddenly, a shout pierced the air, cutting through like a knife. "Over here!" one of the deputies called out, his voice echoing through the trees. The sheriff's heart leaped in his chest as he sprinted toward the sound, adrenaline surging through him.

"What did you find?" he barked, his breath coming in sharp gasps as he reached the scene. The deputy stood at the edge of the river, pointing excitedly toward the water. The sheriff followed his gaze, and there it was—a Monacan canoe bobbing gently in the current, seemingly empty, drifting several miles down from the Underwoods' farm.

The sight sent a jolt through the sheriff's body. "Get a team down to the riverbank!" he commanded, his voice cutting through the commotion. "We need to secure the area and check for any signs of Adkins around here!"

As officers hurried to follow his orders, the sheriff's mind raced with possibilities. The canoe could hold vital clues—perhaps it was where Adkins had been hiding, or maybe it had been used to transport him away from the area. The current was swift, but the sheriff knew they had to act quickly before any evidence was lost to the relentless flow of the river.

The team quickly assembled along the bank, their flashlights sweeping over the water's surface, searching for any signs of disturbance. They formed a human chain, ready to wade into the icy water if necessary, each deputy aware that their actions could mean the difference between life and death.

"Keep your guard up!" the sheriff called out, his voice firm as he scanned the surrounding area. "Adkins may not be alone. We can't rule out the possibility of accomplices."

The deputies nodded, their expressions resolute as they prepared for whatever might come next. The intensity of the moment hung in the air, charged with a sense of impending confrontation. They were on the cusp of uncovering something significant, and the stakes had never felt higher.

The sheriff's gaze remained fixed on the canoe, his heart pounding in his chest. Time was against them, and they could not afford to lose the trail now. Each second felt like an eternity as they worked tirelessly, the weight of their mission pressing down on them like the frozen earth beneath their feet.

"Is that...?" Sheriff Samuels's voice trailed off as they drew the canoe closer, the figure slumped inside the canoe slowly coming into focus. It was Adkins, his face pale and drawn, an expression of resignation etched into his features as he floated downstream, oblivious to the chaos surrounding him. The sheriff could see the weariness in Adkins's eyes, a man worn down by fear and guilt, his shoulders slumped under an invisible weight.

"Get him!" Sheriff Samuels commanded, urgency lacing his voice, as they maneuvered the canoe toward the riverbank. The deputies sprang into action, their movements swift and practiced. They secured the canoe, their hands gripping the cold, damp wood as they carefully pulled Adkins from the canoe, ensuring he wouldn't slip away.

As Adkins was hoisted from the canoe, he looked around, his expression a mix of confusion and defeat. The sheriff stepped forward, his heart pounding as he reached for the handcuffs hanging from his belt. With a practiced hand, he clicked them around Adkins's wrists, the metallic sound echoing ominously in the still air. "You're under arrest, Adkins," he said. The sheriff paused, steeling himself for the task at hand, as he prepared to recite the words that would underscore the gravity of the situation. His voice was steady, yet there was an undercurrent of intensity that reflected the weight of what lay ahead. "You have the right to remain silent. Anything you say can and will be used against you in a court of law. You have the right to an attorney. If you cannot afford an attorney, one will be provided for you. Do you understand these rights as I have read them to you?"

As he recited this crucial statement, the sheriff was acutely aware of the significance of each word. He knew how imperative it was to ensure that every action taken in this moment adhered strictly to the law. The *Miranda* rights, originating from the landmark Supreme Court case *Miranda v. Arizona* in 1966, served as a critical safeguard for individuals in police custody. This ruling established that anyone taken into custody must be informed of their rights prior to any interrogation, ensuring that they are aware of their ability to remain silent and to seek legal counsel. The importance of this ruling could not be overstated; it was designed to protect defendants from self-incrimination and to guarantee their right to fair legal representation. The sheriff understood that any misstep—any deviation from these established protocols—could jeopardize the entire prosecution case against Adkins, potentially allowing a guilty man to escape justice. In this high-stakes moment, the sheriff's resolve strengthened; he was determined to uphold the law and seek the truth, no matter how hidden or painful it might be.

Adkins didn't resist; he simply nodded slightly, as if acknowledging his fate. As they started walking up the slope from the riverbank to where the patrol car was parked, the chatter of his deputies faded into the background, replaced by the sound of crunching gravel underfoot.

The silence between them was heavy, laden with unspoken words. Adkins shuffled along, his eyes focused on the ground, shame radiating from him. The sheriff couldn't help but feel a pang of sympathy. They had shared moments in the past—holiday dinners, laughter over cups of coffee—but now, those memories felt like distant echoes in a world that had turned dark.

Once they reached the patrol car, Sheriff Samuels opened the back door and physically guided Adkins inside, ducking his head to avoid the frame. The interior was stark, the harsh light from the overhead bulb illuminating the tension etched in the sheriff's features. Adkins slid into the seat, the weight of his body pressing against the cold plastic. The sheriff closed the door with a soft thud, sealing Adkins inside the confines of the vehicle, as if trapping him in his own guilt.

As the sheriff climbed into the front seat, he could feel the quiet settle around them, thick and suffocating. He turned on the ignition, the engine rumbling to life, a sound that felt like a roar in the otherwise silent air. The ride to the station was marked by an unyielding quiet, the atmosphere heavy with the weight of what was to come. Adkins sat in the back, his posture hunched, staring out the window as the landscape blurred past—trees, houses, and the familiar streets of Floyd transformed into a haunting backdrop to the unfolding drama.

The sheriff stole glances in the rearview mirror, studying Adkins's reflection. He could see the shame etched across his features, the way his eyes darted away from any semblance of connection. The silence was deafening, filled only with the sound of the tires rolling over the asphalt. Each mile felt like a journey deeper into the chasm of uncertainty, a path leading them toward the truth that lay shrouded in darkness.

Finally, they arrived at the station, the building looming ahead like a fortress of justice. Sheriff Samuels stepped out and walked around to the back, opening the door to let Adkins out. "Let's go," he said, his tone brokering no argument.

Adkins shuffled out, his feet dragging as they made their way inside. The fluorescent lights overhead were bright, casting a harsh glare that felt unforgiving. The sheriff led him down the corridor to the interrogation room, eager to start questioning him. Each step echoed ominously, a reminder of the intensity of the situation.

Once inside, the atmosphere shifted. The room was small, stark, and claustrophobic, with peeling paint and a single flickering fluorescent light casting an unflattering glow on everything. A metal table dominated the center, flanked by two chairs, one of which held Adkins, handcuffed and slumped forward, his eyes downcast. The other chair awaited the sheriff, a silent witness to the confrontation that was about to unfold.

As the sheriff took his seat, Adkins remained silent, his gaze fixed on the table, lost in a world of his own making. The sheriff knew that breaking through the wall of shame and fear that surrounded him would take skill and patience—qualities that had served him well in his years on the force.

But as he looked at Adkins, he felt that whatever lay ahead would change everything. The truth was waiting in the shadows, and he was determined to bring it into the light.

Meanwhile, Charlotte was still at the hospital, a whirlwind of emotions swirling within her as she absorbed the news of Adkins's arrest. The moment she heard, an out-of-body impulse propelled her to leave the hospital behind and rush to the station. She had to be there—to question Adkins herself, to find out if he held the key to unraveling the darkness that had plagued her family.

When Charlotte arrived at the station, she found Sheriff Samuels in the interrogation room, still attempting to extract information from Adkins, who sat unyielding, his silence a fortress against the questions hurled at him. Through the large, one-way window in the wall, Charlotte could see the sheriff's frustration mounting. Time seemed to stretch infinitely, each second an echo of frustration as Sheriff Samuels worked tirelessly to break through Adkins's defenses, but the man remained resolute, his expression unreadable.

After what felt like an eternity, the sheriff finally emerged from the room, his shoulders heavy with the weight of failure. "Let me talk to him," she urged, her voice steady yet urgent. "I just prosecuted Adkins's daughter's killer. I've spoken to him many times before. He may respond to me."

The sheriff's gaze hardened, a flicker of hesitation crossing his features. "No, Charlotte. He's not going to want to talk," he replied firmly, his tone leaving little room for negotiation. He could see the resolve in her eyes but was acutely aware of the potential consequences of allowing her to step into that room. Adkins hadn't even asked for a defense attorney, which could potentially complicate matters further.

Charlotte refused to back down. "Please, Sheriff. I know how to reach him. This isn't just about this case; I've waited for this moment for years! He might open up to me in a way that he won't to you."

Samuels studied her for a moment, weighing the risks against the desperation in her voice. He knew how deeply personal this was for her, how the past few weeks had taken their toll. Allowing Charlotte to interrogate Adkins was fraught with potential legal implications; as someone not directly involved in the prosecution of his case, her presence could complicate matters if anything she learned was later deemed inadmissible in court. There was also the chance that Adkins might say something that could jeopardize the integrity of the investigation related to the attack on Mr. and Mrs. Underwood, Lily's kidnapping, any other potential victims— or even eventually lead to a mistrial. The sheriff hesitated, the weight of his responsibilities pressing heavily on him.

After several moments of awkward silence and Charlotte's persistent pleas, he finally relented, albeit reluctantly. "Fine," he said. "But you need to understand—if he starts to shut down, I'll pull you out of there. No arguments. We can't afford any legal complications right now."

Charlotte nodded. She moved past him and toward the door, steadying herself for the confrontation that lay ahead. She felt a wave of empathy wash over her, ready to confront Adkins about the truth that had eluded them for so long.

Charlotte stepped into the interrogation room, the door closing behind her with a soft click that felt final. She paused, steadying herself before sitting down across from Adkins. His eyes remained fixed on the floor, the weight of guilt and shame hanging heavily between them.

"Adkins," she began softly, her voice low. "You lied to me." His gaze remained downcast, a deep frown etched on his features. "After everything I've done to help you and your family get justice for Kaya," she continued, her heart tightening with emotion. "Why?"

Silence stretched between them like a chasm. Adkins didn't respond, merely shifting uncomfortably in his seat, his hands clenched into fists.

Charlotte pressed on, her voice steady but filled with desperation. "My family opened our home to you and your family. You spent Christmas with us. You know how much my family has suffered all these years."

"What do you know?" she pressed, leaning forward slightly. "Was it you who took Mari and me that day?"

Finally, Adkins looked up, his eyes filled with a mix of sorrow and regret. "No. That wasn't me. I would have never hurt you," he murmured, his voice barely a whisper.

"Then who was it?" Charlotte asked. "You know who it was, don't you?"

Adkins looked away, his silence deafening.

"Tell me," she urged, desperation creeping into her voice. "Who was it? After everything I've done for you, you at least owe me this."

The seconds stretched as she waited. Just when it seemed like nothing else could be done to make him speak, Adkins broke. "That man... the man that showed up at your campsite that night with Mari ... was my father."

A shocking wave of silence swept through the room, freezing Charlotte in place. The implications of his words crashed over her like a tidal wave, leaving her breathless. She stared at him, her mind racing to comprehend the gravity of what he'd just revealed. Adkins looked away, his shoulders trembling slightly as the reality of his confession settled in. The weight of guilt and shame hung heavily between them, and he seemed to fight against the emotions threatening to spill over. He swallowed hard, his expression a mix of regret and fear.

After the shocking revelation, neither one spoke. The atmosphere was electric, charged with the significance of the information Adkins had just shared. Adkins's hands shook, and Charlotte could see the conflict raging within him. After what felt like several hours, Adkins continued, his voice trembling.

"But the man you saw that day in the cavern... that man was John Samuels, Sheriff Samuels's uncle."

The room erupted with tension, an incredulous gasp echoing in the small space as she processed the incredible revelation. Charlotte's mind raced, the implications spinning wildly. The threads of their lives were becoming dangerously intertwined, a web of deception and darkness that threatened to ensnare them all. As the reality of his confession settled in, Charlotte felt a frigid sensation grip her, the unsettling truth falling into place in a way she had not expected. Charlotte knew that she was on the brink of uncovering the truth—a truth that could shatter everything they thought they knew.

Suddenly, the door swung open with a decisive thud, and Sheriff Samuels reentered the room, his presence commanding. "What do you mean that it was my uncle? You can't be serious! Answer me—now!" he demanded, his voice resonating with authority as he slammed his hands down on the table in front of Adkins. Adkins, visibly shaken, paused for a moment, uncertain about whether he should continue volunteering everything he knew without a defense attorney present.

She leaned forward, her eyes locked onto Adkins with fierce determination. "Please, just talk to us," she urged. "This is your chance to share your side, to tell your story. We need to understand."

After a long moment of silence, Adkins finally nodded, the resolve in his expression softening as he looked at Charlotte. The atmosphere shifted, as he prepared to unveil the layers of his story. Charlotte felt a wave of hope wash over her, knowing these revelations could change everything. As Adkins took a deep breath, she sensed his fear and hesitation— this was the beginning of an untold narrative that could unravel the very fabric of their intertwined lives.

Adkins' hands were trembling slightly as he prepared to share the harrowing story that had haunted him for so long. "The whole operation has been going on for decades," he began, his voice low and heavy with the weight of his confession. "I don't know exactly who is behind it, but I have my suspicions. There are powerful people involved—people with connections, even politicians." His gaze shifted from Charlotte to Sheriff Samuels, desperation etched across his face. "John Samuels and I did our part, yes, but before me, it was my father. He and Samuels had a long history together."

The words poured out of him like a dam bursting. Adkins paused, his breath hitching as he fought back tears, allowing Charlotte and the sheriff to absorb the magnitude of what was being shared. She exchanged a glance with Sheriff Samuels, who stood rigid, his expression a mixture of disbelief and disgust.

As Adkins continued, his voice broke, revealing the depth of his pain. "The whole business involved kidnapping young girls to sell them. I don't know who buys them. I just know that John Samuels is the main contact for that."

The sheriff's jaw clenched at the mention of his own uncle's name. Adkins pressed on, the words pouring out of him like a dam bursting. "My father and I were the caretakers of the farm, and we had access to the perfect spot to hide them—the cavern. No one knew the cavern existed. Not even the Underwoods, I think. Until Mr. Underwood discovered it, which is what got him in trouble." Charlotte's stomach churned at the thought, and she could see Sheriff Samuels visibly tense, his fists clenched at his sides.

Questions bubbled in Charlotte's mind, but she held her tongue, recognizing the importance of letting Adkins continue to share the bigger picture. "The process was always the same," he explained, his voice becoming more animated. "They'd kidnap the girls and keep them in the cave until they were ready to transport them. Samuels would handle the transportation because he had access to the wool bales we used to hide them. The cave was convenient; we could float down the river in canoes, never seen by anyone."

Adkins paused, his eyes darkening as he continued. "You see, there was already an old well on the property that hadn't been used in years. My father discovered it when he first started working for the Underwoods. It was crumbling and overgrown, but when he looked down into it, he realized it went deeper than anyone had thought. That's when he got the idea to start expanding underground."

Charlotte leaned in, captivated by his words. "He needed a way to get to the bottom of the well in order to start expanding. You know, a way that was not out in the open. It needed to be concealed. So, he dug into the earth, creating a network of tunnels that eventually formed a large cavern." "It took him years of hard work. He used basic tools to chip away at the stone, and I know he got help from some of the seasonal out of town workers who came to shear sheep. They were sworn to secrecy about what they were doing down there, and many of them were just grateful for the extra pay. Together, they expanded the cavern so that it extended all the way to the riverbank, creating an underground passage that was nearly impossible to detect from above."

He continued, his voice growing more serious as he described the cavern. "It was dark and damp, but it offered the perfect hiding place. The entrance was concealed, hidden behind some thick foliage and underbrush, and once you were inside, it opened up into a vast expanse. There were stalactites hanging from the ceiling, and the sound of dripping water echoed through the chambers. My father had even carved out a few small chambers for storage, where they could keep supplies and other stolen goods. It became a sort of prison for the girls they took, a place where they were hidden away from the world outside."

Charlotte could hardly believe her ears as she absorbed the details. "So, you're saying that this cavern was used not just for hiding, but as a hub for their operations?" she asked with horror.

"Exactly," Adkins said, his expression grim. "Over time, it became a well-guarded secret, a place where they could hold the girls until it was safe to move them. The river was convenient for transportation, as I said; they could float down in canoes, out of sight from prying eyes. There were even times when my father and I would help move the girls ourselves, using drugs to ensure they were quiet and compliant. I hated every moment of it, but I felt trapped. The fear of what would happen if I spoke out kept me silent."

Charlotte listened to Adkins's confession in disbelief. The cavern, once a place of confinement and fear for her and her sister, now loomed like a dark shadow over her family's history. As he spoke, she could almost feel the horrors that place must have witnessed over the years. She glanced at the sheriff, whose expression had turned grim as he absorbed every detail. Adkins continued. "Reynolds and Salazar were also involved with the kidnappings, but they created this side business with the Monacans to cover their tracks. It was never meant to kill any of the girls, but sometimes that happened accidentally during the transports if the wool bales weren't properly prepared." His voice broke slightly, the weight of the truth evident in his tone.

Adkins paused, his eyes glistening with unshed tears. "There were many times over the years when I wanted out. Once, I threatened to reveal all the secrets. That's when Samuels told Reynolds to do something to keep me quiet. I don't know how, but they learned I had told my wife about it. So, they punished us by kidnapping and killing Kaya." His voice cracked, the pain evident as he recounted the horror. "They said if we spoke, they would do the same to the rest of our children. I had no choice."

Charlotte felt her heart ache for him for a moment. "Back then, my dad was also part of the movement against the Welsh farmers," he added, his gaze dropping to the floor. "That's why my father kidnapped you and Mari," he said, looking directly at Charlotte.

At that moment, the weight of his guilt became too much for him to bear, and Adkins broke down in tears. "I am sorry. I never meant to hurt you or anyone in your family. That was my father's doing—not me." His sobs filled the room, a haunting sound that echoed off the walls, leaving Charlotte and the sheriff in stunned silence.

Charlotte's heart twisted with conflicting emotions— anger, sorrow, and compassion mingled within her as she watched the man before her unravel. Her hands gripped the edge of the chair as she fought to process the enormity of the situation, and sensed the sheriff's discomfort as he absorbed the implications of Adkins's confession.

Charlotte leaned forward, her voice steady but laced with softness. "Why did you attack Mr. and Mrs. Underwood?" she asked, her eyes locked onto Adkins.

Adkins hesitated for a moment, his gaze dropping to the table. "That wasn't me," he said, his voice trembling slightly. "That was John Samuels."

Charlotte shivered at the mention of Samuels, the man who had haunted her nightmares. "Samuels? Why?"

Adkins' eyes clouded with regret. "Samuels was discovered with Lily near the hunting cabin by Mr. Underwood. He had to leave Lily in the cabin and ran to get Mr. Underwood. I wasn't there, so I'm not sure why he killed Mrs. Underwood. She must have gotten in the way or something."

Charlotte's heart ached at the thought of Mrs. Underwood's life cut short by senseless violence. "And Mr. Underwood?"

"Samuels wanted to know how much Mr. Underwood had seen," Adkins continued, his voice heavy with sorrow. "He was angry, so he decided to shut him up by killing him. I know you won't believe me, but I am glad he survived. He's a kind man."

The sincerity in Adkins's voice took Charlotte by surprise, and for a moment, she saw the flicker of humanity in him, a man trapped by his own choices.

"What about the fire at my grandparents' farm?" Charlotte asked, her voice tinged with frustration. "Or the attack on me and Jack Henry?

Adkins shook his head vehemently, his eyes wide with earnestness. The attack on you and Jack Henry was Samuels as well. He was also the one who burned your family's barn."

Charlotte felt a surge of anger at the thought of Samuels targeting her family, putting their lives at risk. "Why would he want to burn my grandparents' barn?"

"Rumors had reached him that you had been asking questions, that you had spoken to me, and that you were trying to locate Salazar to question him as well," Adkins explained, his voice low and resigned. "Samuels wanted to stop you from that."

The room was silent once more. "Where is Samuels now?" Charlotte asked, her voice steady despite the turmoil swirling within her.

Adkins shook his head, his eyes filled with a mix of regret and fear. "I don't know where he is now."

Charlotte felt a flicker of doubt. "I don't know if I can believe that. But let's move on. Tell me, are there more girls in the cave?"

"No, there were four other girls in the cave the night you found Lily. Samuels moved them somewhere else. I'm not sure where."

The thought of more victims, more innocent lives torn apart by this darkness, made Charlotte tremble. "And Lily? Why was she left behind?"

"Lily had already been sold to someone who had already paid in full," Adkins explained, his voice tinged with desperation. "Since Lily was gone, he is probably trying to find a similar girl to sell. The other girls are older, and this buyer didn't want that."

Charlotte's heart ached for Lily, for all the victims who had been caught in this web of deceit and violence. "If I had to guess," Adkins continued, his voice barely above a whisper, "I would imagine Samuels is trying to kidnap another nine-year-old as we speak."

The thought of Samuels on the loose, hunting for another victim, sent a wave of unease through Charlotte. She had to stop him before he could claim another innocent life. She knew that time was running out. That every second counted in the race to stop Samuels and bring justice to those who had suffered.

Charlotte met Sheriff Samuels's gaze, seeing the same resolve mirrored in his eyes. They were united in their mission, bound by a shared determination to confront the darkness and bring it to light.

Sheriff Samuels looked out through the mirrored window, his expression resolute as he addressed his team. "We need to start the search for my uncle immediately," he ordered. "We can't afford to waste any time."

He turned to Charlotte, his expression softening slightly. "You need to stay out of this, Charlotte. Go to your grandma's farm and stay there until we find Samuels. I can't risk anything happening to you."

Charlotte opened her mouth to protest, but the sheriff's firm gaze silenced her. She knew he was right—her presence in the investigation could complicate matters further.

Sheriff Samuels then walked outside of the interrogation room and addressed his staff, his tone grave. "I don't want anyone to divulge what Adkins has confessed. We need to keep this quiet. The public needs to believe that Adkins isn't cooperating. We can't afford to scare Samuels off."

As the sheriff began organizing the search efforts, Charlotte felt helpless. But she also knew that she had to trust in the sheriff's plan. That their combined efforts would bring Samuels to justice and protect the innocent.

CHAPTER XXIX

The search for John Samuels started early the following morning—before dawn. Sheriff Samuels wasted no time in mobilizing his team, every second ticking away like a countdown to an unknown catastrophe. The stakes were unimaginably high; the life of several innocent children could hang in the balance.

The sheriff's department was a flurry of activity, officers huddled around maps, radios crackling with updates and directives. Every available resource was called upon—canine units, helicopters scanning from above, officers combing through the dense forests and open fields that surrounded the town.

Sheriff Samuels stood at the center of it all, his presence a steadying force for his team. Yet he still could not fully believe that his own blood was capable of such a heinous crime. His mind raced with possibilities, each more dire than the last. He knew his uncle well enough to understand the depths of his cunning and the lengths he might go to evade capture. As the chaos unfolded, one thought remained clear: the first place he needed to check was his uncle's home.

The search extended to every corner of the county. Roadblocks were set up on the major highways, and neighboring towns were alerted to be on the lookout for John Samuels. Flyers with his photograph were ordered to be printed and distributed, and the local news stations broadcasted his image, urging the public to report any sightings.

As the search expanded, Sheriff Samuels knew he had to confront the part of his uncle's life that intersected with his own. He drove to his uncle's house, a modest two-story building that stood at the edge of town, its appearance unassuming yet somehow foreboding in the context of their mission.

The driveway was lined with overgrown shrubs, and the porch light, still on before sunrise, flickered intermittently. Sheriff Samuels approached the front door, his heart pounding with a mix of dread and determination. He knocked firmly, the sound echoing in the stillness of the early morning.

The door creaked open, revealing Derek and Jake—his cousins. Derek stood tall, his expression one of curiosity tinged with apprehension. Jake, shorter and stockier, hovered behind his brother, his eyes darting nervously between the sheriff and the interior of the house.

"Derek, Jake," Sheriff Samuels greeted. "Is your father home?"

Derek shook his head, a flicker of something unreadable passing across his face. "Haven't seen him since yesterday," he replied, his tone guarded.

Jake shifted uncomfortably, his gaze fixed on the floor. "He said he had business to take care of," he added, his voice barely above a whisper.

Sheriff Samuels studied his cousins, searching for any hint of complicity or hidden knowledge. Their eyes were restless, their postures tense, as though they were trying to conceal something. "Has he mentioned anything unusual lately? Anything you think I should know?"

The brothers exchanged a look, a silent conversation passing between them. Derek hesitated, his brows furrowing with indecision. "There's been... talk," he admitted finally, his voice low and cautious. "But we don't know much. Dad's always been secretive about his dealings."

Jake nodded in agreement, his expression troubled. "We thought it was just his usual work. But then things started getting weird. He was more on edge."

Sheriff Samuels felt a knot tighten in his stomach. The ambiguity of their responses only added to the growing sense of unease. He decided he needed to take a closer look. "Mind if I come in and look around?" he asked, trying to keep his tone casual despite the urgency simmering beneath the surface.

Derek and Jake exchanged another glance, with hesitation. "Uh, sure, I guess," Derek replied reluctantly, stepping aside to allow the sheriff and one of his officers to enter.

The interior of the house was as he remembered—modest yet surprisingly clean. The unusually tidy state of the home sent a jolt of suspicion through him, an indication that something was amiss. The living room was organized, with a worn sofa and a coffee table adorned with neatly stacked magazines. Family photos lined the walls, capturing moments of joy and camaraderie that felt at odds with the current climate. The air inside was still, almost expectant, as if the walls themselves were holding their breath.

Sheriff Samuels moved deliberately, his eyes scanning every corner as he walked through the house. The kitchen was clean, the countertops bare except for a few dishes drying on the rack. The scent of freshly brewed coffee lingered in the air, a comforting aroma that seemed out of place amidst the underlying tension.

He continued his inspection, moving down the hallway to the bedrooms. Each room told a story—Derek's was cluttered with clothes and sports memorabilia, while Jake's was neat and sparsely decorated, the bed made with military precision. Sheriff Samuels paused in front of his old room, memories flooding back as he glanced inside. It was unchanged, a time capsule of his youth, filled with relics of his childhood— books, trophies, and a model ship he had painstakingly assembled.

Satisfied that the house held no immediate answers, Sheriff Samuels returned to the living room, where Derek and Jake waited, their expressions a mix of curiosity and apprehension. "Thanks for letting me look around," he said. "But I'd like to check out the workshop in the back, if you don't mind."

The brothers hesitated, exchanging another glance that spoke volumes. "What are you looking for?" Jake asked, his voice tinged with reluctance.

"It's important," Sheriff Samuels replied, his tone leaving no room for argument. "I need to be thorough."

With a resigned nod, Derek led the way to the back door. The workshop loomed ahead, its presence both familiar and foreboding, a place of craftsmanship and secrecy.

As they approached, Sheriff Samuels felt a surge of anticipation mixed with dread. The workshop was a spacious structure, the scent of sawdust and varnish filling the air, evoking memories of his uncle's meticulous craftsmanship. The walls were lined with tools, each with its designated place, and the large workbench was cluttered with projects in various stages of completion.

The officer accompanying him took long strides, their flashlights cutting through the darkness, illuminating the corners hidden in shadow as the sun had yet to rise. Sheriff Samuels felt his heart race as he quickened his pace, each hurried step echoing his mounting anxiety as he searched for any sign of his uncle's activities.

Amidst the unease, a strange silence settled over the workshop, the only sound the soft hum of the fluorescent lights overhead. As they moved deeper into the space, Sheriff Samuels's attention was drawn to a small, adjoining room, its door slightly ajar. A sense of foreboding washed over him, and he motioned for the officer to follow as he cautiously approached.

The air felt heavier as they stepped inside, the dim light revealing what appeared to be a storage area. The room was cluttered with various items—old furniture, boxes of tools—but something in the corner caught his eye. A pile of animal skins lay haphazardly, as if hastily arranged to conceal something beneath.

With a sinking feeling in his stomach, Sheriff Samuels approached the pile, his heart pounding in his chest. The officer stood beside him, flashlight trained on the skins as the sheriff reached out, slowly removing the top layer.

The sight that greeted him shocked every sense of his body—four cages, each one containing a young girl. They looked dirty, their clothes ripped and soiled, but somehow warm enough to avoid freezing in the chill of the room. Their eyes were wide, reflecting a mixture of fear and confusion, yet there was an unsettling stillness about them, as if they had been drugged. They showed no reaction to being found, their expressions vacant, trapped in a haze that rendered them unable to comprehend their dire situation.

Sheriff Samuels felt a wave of horror crash over him, the reality of the situation settling in like a lead weight. In that moment, everything shifted within him—his uncle was not just a family member but a monster who had preyed upon the most innocent. The anger bubbled up inside him, mingling with the guilt of their suffering. His thoughts raced, churning with a desperate resolve. *How could he have missed the signs?*

How could blood tie him to such evil? He thought. The name John Samuels would forever be intertwined with this atrocity, and he knew he had to stop him at all costs.

The officer sprang into action, radioing for backup as they worked to free the girls, their movements swift and practiced. Every second mattered, their hearts pounding in sync with the rapid clicks of their tools.

As the girls were carried out of the workshop, their faces still bearing the marks of fear and confusion, Sheriff Samuels felt a surge of relief tempered by the gravity of the situation. He turned to see other officers arriving on the scene, having apprehended Derek and Jake as they attempted to escape. The two men were being escorted to meet the sheriff outside the barn, their expressions a mix of shock and disbelief.

"You're under arrest," he said, his voice firm but tinged with sadness. The brothers offered no resistance, their shoulders slumping in resignation as they were handcuffed and led away.

Suddenly, the sharp crackle of his radio broke through the charged air. "Sheriff! We have reports of suspicious activity near the old mill—possible sightings of John Samuels!"

The weight of their discovery lingered in the air, but the reality of the ongoing search pressed down on him with renewed intensity. He felt the adrenaline surge again as he knew they couldn't afford to let their guard down now. As the officers rushed the girls to the hospital, Sheriff Samuels stood in the workshop, the magnitude of what they had uncovered washing over him.

The search for John Samuels continued throughout the day and into the night, the darkness adding another layer of complexity to their efforts. Officers scoured the woods with flashlights, their beams cutting through the dense foliage like searchlights in the void.

Helicopters circled above, their searchlights sweeping across the landscape, illuminating the ground for brief moments before moving on. The radio crackled with updates—sightings that turned out to be false alarms, leads that led to dead ends.

In the midst of it all, Charlotte had spent all day at her grandmother's farm. Sheriff Samuels had asked her not to get involved, and for once, she had complied. Still, the weight of helplessness, the knowledge that she could do nothing but wait and hope for news. Her heart ached for the victims, for the lives hanging in the balance, and she clung to the hope that the search would yield results before it was too late.

The night wore on, the tension mounting with each passing hour. The search for John Samuels was relentless, a race against time and the shadows that threatened to swallow them whole. But despite their efforts, he remained elusive, a ghost in the night, leaving only questions and uncertainty in his wake.

CHAPTER XXX

After arriving at the station, Sheriff Samuels had locked his cousins, Derek and Jake, in a jail cell to buy himself some time to think about how to approach them. He suspected they held crucial information about their father's whereabouts, but he knew that any misstep could lead them to shut down and conceal the truth from him. He briefly considered sending one of his units to search the cave that Mr. Adkins had described, but he feared that any hint of police presence could scare his uncle away. He needed to tread carefully and strategize his next move.

Should I use Mr. Adkins's information to set a trap? But why would my uncle return to a place where he might suspect the police were already circling? It had been more than twenty-four hours since they had arrested Mr. Adkins and nearly half a day since the arrest of John Samuels's sons.

Although Sheriff Samuels had ordered that no information about the arrests be shared with the media, the lack of contact with Mr. Adkins alone should have raised alarm bells in his uncle's mind. Sheriff Samuels knew how intuitive his uncle could be.

His mind was flooded with unanswered questions. By early afternoon, a storm was brewing. The town, usually a haven of tranquility, had transformed into a cauldron of whispers and rumors. The events of the past weeks had cast a long shadow over the community, and beneath the surface of everyday life, fear and suspicion simmered like a pot on the verge of boiling over.

At the heart of this turmoil stood the sheriff, a man who had dedicated his life to upholding the law and protecting the people of Floyd. But now, with the revelation of his uncle's involvement in a trafficking ring, the very foundation of his world had been shaken. As the search for John Samuels intensified, Sheriff Samuels found himself caught between his duty and the tangled web of family ties that threatened to unravel everything he held dear.

As darkness deepened from the night falling and the storm brewing, Sheriff Samuels sat at his desk, his mind a maelstrom of conflicting emotions. The room was filled with the scent of strong coffee, the bitter aroma mingling with the faint smell of old paper and wood polish. The walls were adorned with photographs and commendations, reminders of a career spent in service to his community. But now, those reminders felt hollow, overshadowed by the unimaginable secrets he had uncovered.

The sheriff's thoughts were interrupted by a soft knock on the door. "Come in," he called.

The door creaked open, and Deputy Charly Monroe stepped inside. Although she was new to the sheriff's team, her confidence was evident. Standing at a commanding height, Charly was a no-nonsense woman in her early thirties, with eyes as sharp as a hawk's and a mind that was always two steps ahead. Her auburn hair was pulled back in a practical ponytail, revealing a face that was both youthful and marked by experience. Her uniform was immaculate, the badge polished to a high shine—a testament to her dedication and pride in her role.

Charly's presence was a steadying force in the midst of chaos, her calm demeanor and unwavering resolve a balm to the sheriff's frayed nerves. She had an innate ability to cut through the noise, to see the heart of a problem and tackle it head-on. Her sharp intellect and keen intuition made her an invaluable ally, and the sheriff was grateful for her unwavering support.

"Thom," she began. "We've got a problem."

The sheriff looked up, his expression tightening with unease. "What is it?"

Charly hesitated, glancing around the office as if ensuring they were alone. Her gaze was piercing, taking in every detail, every nuance that might be out of place. "There's been another disappearance," she said finally. "A young girl, just like the others."

The sheriff's heart sank, a cold knot of dread forming in his stomach. "What? Where?" he asked.

"Just outside of town," Charly replied, her expression grim. Her eyes, usually so full of determination, held a shadow of worry that mirrored the sheriff's own fears. "Her parents just reported her. They said she went out to play and never came back."

The sheriff could not believe what he was hearing. "Do we have any leads?"

Charly shook her head, her eyes filled with frustration. "Not yet. But we're working on it. I have a team canvassing the area, talking to neighbors, looking for anything that might give us a clue." Her tone was strong, a reflection of her determination to leave no stone unturned.

The sheriff nodded, his mind already formulating a plan. "What about the highway patrol? Have they set up roadblocks?"

"Yes," Charly replied. "We're coordinating with them to cover as much ground as possible. But if Samuels is involved, he knows how to avoid detection." Her words were laced with the weight of their shared history, the knowledge of how cunning and elusive John Samuels could be.

The sheriff's jaw tightened, a surge of anger coursing through him. "We can't let him get away with this," he said. "We have to find him before it's too late."

Charly nodded, her expression mirroring his strong demeanor. "We will, Thom," she said softly. "We'll find him. And we'll bring him to justice."

As Charly left the office, the sheriff sat back in his chair, his thoughts mingled with fear of losing another child. He knew that time was running out, that every second counted in the race to find the missing girl and stop John Samuels once and for all. He couldn't afford to falter, not now. The lives of yet another innocent child was at stake, and he had to do everything in his power to protect her.

With renewed urgency, the sheriff picked up the phone, dialing the number for the state police. As he waited for the call to connect, he glanced out the window, the darkening sky a reminder of the storm that loomed on the horizon.

The town of Floyd was a small community bound together by shared history and mutual respect. But now, with the revelation of the trafficking ring and the involvement of one of their own, that bond was being tested in ways its citizens had never imagined.

Rumors spread like wildfire, whispers and half-truths weaving their way through the streets and into the hearts of the townspeople. Fear and suspicion took root, casting a pall over the once-peaceful community. Neighbors who once greeted each other with friendly waves and warm smiles now exchanged worried glances, their trust eroded by the insidious presence of doubt and fear.

The sheriff knew that trust was fragile, that it could be shattered by the slightest hint of betrayal. And as the investigation into John Samuels continued, he found himself questioning everything he thought he knew about his family and his community. The specter of his uncle's betrayal loomed large, casting long shadows over the memories of shared meals and laughter that had once filled their lives.

The line connected, and the sheriff spoke with the state police, coordinating their efforts and sharing information. Each conversation was a step forward, as they worked together to close in on Samuels. The tone in their voices mirrored the urgency in his heart, a relentless drive to bring justice to those who had been wronged.

But even as they made progress, the sheriff knew they were running out of time. The thought of another child falling victim to the trafficking ring filled him with a fire that burned in his chest. He knew that they had to be vigilant, to leave no stone unturned in their search for Samuels. The stakes were too high, the consequences too dire to allow any room for error.

His thoughts drifted to Charlotte, the young woman whose determination and courage had brought the truth to light. He admired her strength, her unwavering resolve in the face of danger. She had risked everything to uncover the truth, and he knew that she would continue to fight for justice, no matter the cost. Her bravery was a source of inspiration, a reminder of the resilience that lay within each of them.

As night fell, the sheriff left the office, the cool air a welcome relief against his weary body. He knew that the road ahead would be long and difficult, but he was determined to see it through. The town of Floyd lay shrouded in darkness, the stars above a reminder of the hope that still shone amidst the shadows. He knew it was time to face his cousins. Every moment counted in their quest to bring John Samuels to justice and put an end to the trafficking ring that had plagued their community. Right now, however, he needed some air. The storm was holding up and a short stroll would help him mentally prepare for what his was about to face.

With renewed resolve, the sheriff set out into the night, ready to face whatever challenges lay ahead. The path was fraught with danger, but he was determined to see it through, to bring justice to those who had been wronged and ensure that the town of Floyd could once again find peace.

CHAPTER XXXI

While Sheriff Samuels was deep in his investigation, Charlotte remained at her grandmother's farm, consumed by worry. As dawn began to break on the horizon, the search continued, the determination of Sheriff Samuels and his team undiminished. They knew the task before them was monumental, but they also knew they could not rest until John Samuels was found and brought to justice.

When the sun crept over the horizon, casting a pale glow across the farmland, Charlotte sat by the window of her grandmother's house, having been unable to sleep through the night. Her mind was a whirlpool of thoughts and emotions, and the search for John Samuels weighed heavily on her, the uncertainty gnawing at her piece of mind.

The radio crackled in the background, its steady stream of updates a lifeline to the outside world. Charlotte clutched her mug of coffee, the warmth seeping into her hands, grounding her as she listened intently to the broadcast.

Suddenly, a chilling report interrupted the regular news cycle. "Breaking news: authorities have received a report that another young girl has gone missing from a nearby town. The circumstances are eerily similar to previous cases linked to the ongoing investigation. Officials urge vigilance and caution as the search for John Samuels continues."

Charlotte's heart dropped, the news confirming her worst fears. She knew, deep in her soul, that this had to be Samuels. The pattern was unmistakable, the timing too perfect to be mere coincidence.

As the sky lightened, the truth crystallized in her mind. She knew where Samuels would have taken the girl. The realization felt like a jolt of electricity coursing through her veins—an old, abandoned hunting cabin, deep in the woods, hidden away from prying eyes.

Charlotte's thoughts raced, each one sharper than the last. She felt the pull of the cabin, a magnetic force drawing her toward the truth, despite the danger it promised. Her instincts roared within her, compelling her to act, to take the risk and confront the darkness head-on.

She knew it would be dangerous. The cabin was isolated, the perfect place for someone like Samuels to operate without fear of detection. It had been the scene of horrific events in recent days, and the missing girls had been found there. So, Sheriff Samuels was probably still at the station, tirelessly interrogating his cousins for clues about his uncle's whereabouts. *It made sense that the sheriff wouldn't think to go back there to investigate*, Charlotte thought. But there was no time to waste. Another girl's life was at stake. Charlotte couldn't bear the thought of standing idly by, waiting for the official search to catch up.

Her heart pounded with adrenaline, her mind racing to quickly evaluate the risks. But she knew, with every fiber of her being, that she had to do it. She had to follow her instincts, to take the chance before it was too late.

CHAPTER XXXII

Charlotte stood in the dim light of the barn at Irma's farm, her fingers tracing the rich leather of her saddle, a gift from her grandfather. The warmth of the material brought back memories of his proud smile and the adventures they had shared. She felt a rush of gratitude that she had used it the day of the fire; otherwise, it would have been lost forever, consumed by the flames. A shiver ran through her, intertwining sorrow with the warmth of remembrance.

The barn itself felt like a sanctuary, the air thick with the comforting scents of hay and the faint musk of horses. Sunlight streamed through the slats of the old wooden walls, illuminating dust motes that danced lazily in the air, as if celebrating the stillness of the moment. Each beam of light felt like a memory, fragile yet vibrant, and Charlotte could almost hear her grandfather's laughter echoing in the corners, mingling with the soft whinnies of the horses. She ran her fingers over the saddle's surface, tracing the embossed patterns—each line and swirl telling stories of rides past, adventures shared, and the bond between them that had transcended time and tragedy.

Turning her gaze to Blaze, the magnificent mustang stood patiently in his stall, his chestnut coat glimmering in the sunlight like polished copper. His kind eyes met hers, filled with a gentle understanding that made her heart swell with affection. Blaze was more than a horse; he was a confidant, a partner in her quest for truth, a steadfast companion on the path ahead.

With a determined breath, Charlotte mounted Blaze, feeling the familiar rush of excitement and purpose surge within her. She knew where she had to go—the back of her grandparents' farm, a place where memories intertwined with secrets long buried. She heeled Blaze to gallop out of the barn, the powerful surge of speed igniting her resolve. The rhythmic sound of hooves against the dirt felt like a heartbeat, steady and reassuring, echoing her resolve.

The path led her to the wire fences separating her family's land from the Underwoods' farm. She dismounted and maneuvered the gate open, the familiar creak echoing in the stillness, a reminder of her childhood —her dad had always teased her about handling these gates, the unsteady wires often stubborn and uncooperative.

Once through the last gate, she mounted Blaze again, guiding him quickly toward the riverbank, her pulse quickening with anticipation. The landscape shifted, the air thickening with the scent of damp earth and the distant promise of water. Not far from the riverbank stood the hunting cabin, its presence shrouded by trees and tangled vegetation, a secretive silhouette against the vibrant backdrop of the woods.

As she approached, her heart raced, a mix of anxiety and dread coursing through her veins. Between the cabin and the riverbank, she spotted an old well, half-hidden by the underbrush. Memories of childhood adventures flashed through her mind, intertwining with the shadows that now seemed to taint them. She led Blaze carefully through the thick greenery, aware of the echoes of laughter that lingered in this place, now overshadowed by a sense of foreboding.

Reaching the well, Charlotte peered down into the darkness, her view being swallowed by the shadowy depths. It was a void, and as she looked around, the silence pressed in around her, heavy and suffocating. After a few minutes of fruitless searching, unease settled in her gut, a knot tightening in her chest. She turned back toward the cabin, the weight of her thoughts becoming almost unbearable.

The cabin stood hidden among the trees and wild vegetation, its weathered wood blending seamlessly with nature, as if it were an extension of the earth itself. As she stepped inside, the air thickened with the musty scent of mildew and old wood. Sunlight struggled through grimy windows, illuminating the sparse furnishings, remnants of a lifelong abandoned. It was small, with one bedroom, a narrow hallway, and a bathroom barely big enough for a shower.

The kitchen was simple, dominated by a rusty gas burner and an old pot that seemed to have collected years of dust, a ghost of meals long past. It looked as if it hadn't been used in ages, and the silence within the cabin felt almost oppressive, pressing against her as she inspected every corner. She moved slowly, deliberately, her senses heightened as she took in the details—the peeling logs, the creaking floorboards, the cobwebs that hung like curtains in the corners, each thread a reminder of neglect. Nothing of importance revealed itself, and after a thorough search, a sense of unease settled deeper into her bones.

As Charlotte made her way back toward the riverbank, she grabbed Blaze's reins, leading him carefully through the dense brush, the undergrowth clawing at her legs. Once past the thickest part of the forest, she mounted Blaze again, guiding him toward the river, the tranquility of the moment a deceptive veneer over the storm of thoughts swirling in her mind.

But then she noticed something—a subtle change in the vegetation, a trail barely discernible among the grass and fallen leaves. It wasn't well marked, but the difference in the ground texture was undeniable. Curiosity piqued, she dismounted again, pulling Blaze along as she investigated further. The trail led to nowhere, but just as she was about to mount Blaze again, a sound caught her attention.

Was that water? She frowned, puzzled by the distant noise. It didn't make sense; she was far from the river. But the sound intensified, clear and flowing, beckoning her closer, urging her to uncover its source. As she approached, she began to circle the area, searching for its origin, but then, without warning, the ground gave way beneath her foot. She plunged knee-deep into mud, the cold muck sucking at her boot as she steadied herself against a nearby tree.

Pushing herself up, she looked around, her eyes narrowing on a small man-made canal that ran nearby, obscured by the overgrown vegetation. It was no more than half a foot wide, and as she stepped back to regain her composure, she tied Blaze to a tree, the reins secure and steady. Walking cautiously along the canal, she noticed the water trickling quietly, leading in the direction of the cabin, while the other end seemed to lead toward the river—a hidden route that pulsed with secrets.

As she followed the canal, something glinted in the sunlight, drawing her attention back to the trail she had seen earlier. She knelt down, brushing aside leaves and vines, and gasped as she uncovered a trap door, its surface worn and weathered, as if it had been waiting for her all along. Heart racing, she slowly opened it, revealing a set of steep stairs that descended into an uncertain darkness.

Charlotte hesitated for a moment, the shadows at the bottom beckoning her with an unknown promise that sent a shiver of both fear and excitement through her. Gathering her courage, she grabbed the rifle from the holster on Blaze's saddle. It felt like an extension of her will, a protective charm against the unknown.

The air was damp as she stepped down the narrow passage, the slick walls adding to her unease. The passage opened into a cavern thick with the scent of decay, an unsettling familiarity that formed goose bumps on her arms and neck. Gripping her rifle tightly, she moved cautiously, every sound amplified in the oppressive silence.

With each step, the unease within her grew. The walls felt alive, a damp embrace that pulsed with hidden secrets. She reached a larger area and gasped, her heart racing as the realization hit her: she had been here before, over twenty years ago, disoriented and frightened. The round shape of the wall of the well loomed before her, its stone walls slick with moisture, and she could feel the echo of her past resounding in her mind, a chilling reminder of what had transpired in this very spot.

Suddenly, a sensation washed over her—a feeling of being watched, as though unseen eyes lurked in the shadows, tracking her every move. Charlotte's heart quickened, her pulse thundering in her ears as she paused, scanning the shadows that clung to the cavern's edges. But the darkness revealed nothing, offering only silence and the oppressive weight of her own breathing, quick and shallow, the sound echoing ominously off the damp walls she was holding onto for support.

As she resumed her cautious steps, the sensation intensified. The air grew thick, each footfall sounding louder than the last, a drumbeat in the quiet stillness. She moved deeper into the shadows, the passageway stretching endlessly before her, offering no escape, no relief from the growing unease that coiled within her.

The walls seemed to close in around her, the darkness becoming a living entity, breathing softly, rhythmically, as if whispering danger into her ear. With each step, the urge to turn and confront the unseen watcher grew stronger, but she resisted, her instincts guiding her forward, deeper into the unknown.

Time seemed to slow, the seconds stretching into eternity as she pressed on, her senses heightened, every nerve tingling with anticipation. She hoped to find a corner to turn, a place to hide, but the passage offered no such reprieve, only an unending tunnel of shadows and uncertainty.

Finally, she reached a bend in the passage. Her heart leaped with hope, but she knew she couldn't let her guard down. She knelt low, making herself small, her rifle aimed back in the direction she had come. The silence was deafening, the weight of the unknown pressing heavily on her chest as she waited, breath held in anticipation.

She waited, and waited more, her finger hovering near the trigger, muscles tense and ready to spring into action. But no one came. The darkness remained undisturbed, the unseen presence lingering just beyond her sight. She stayed on the floor, just in case, her senses alert, the rifle a comforting weight in her hands.

As the moments dragged on, her mind drifted to a memory—a haunting echo of the past. She remembered finding Mari, still alive, in that very spot, the terror and heartbreak of that day etched into her soul, a scar that time could never truly heal.

A sound from outside the cavern jolted her back to the present, voices carried on the wind, too far away to discern. She strained to listen, her heart pounding with the effort, but the words eluded her, a tantalizing whisper of danger that danced just out of reach.

She remained on guard, her breath shallow, her rifle aimed toward the entrance.

The flicker of light grew brighter. Her heart raced, adrenaline surging through her veins as the light was suddenly blocked by a dark, tall figure. The silhouette loomed large, casting an ominous shadow that seemed to stretch toward her, reaching with unseen hands.

Charlotte's stomach twisted in knots as the figure walked into the cavern, the light revealing its form—a man, carrying something in his arms. Her mind raced, fear and determination intertwining as she wondered if the figure could see her, hidden in her alcove. She convinced herself that he couldn't, that she was safe for the moment. But what was he carrying? The question gnawed at her. "Be confident," Grandpa Louis had said. "Trust in yourself. You are brave."

She repeated the mantra in her mind, a lifeline in the storm of uncertainty as she tightened her grip on the very rifle her grandpa had gifted her. She couldn't tell what the figure was carrying, the shadows obscuring the details, but she knew she had to act.

Time stretched, each second a lifetime as she watched, waiting for the right moment. Her heart thundered in her chest, the anticipation building like a storm, until finally, she saw it—a child, her legs dangling to the side, limp and vulnerable in the man's grasp.

In that moment, everything crystallized. She held her breath, her resolve hardening into steel. With a steady hand and an impeccable aim, she squeezed the trigger, the gunshot ringing out in the cavern like thunder, reverberating off the walls as if the very earth had felt the impact.

The bullet struck the man between the eyes, the force sending him crashing to the ground, lifeless, a finality that echoed through her soul. The cavern fell silent, the drip of water from the walls the only sound, a haunting reminder of the life that pulsed outside.

Charlotte stood frozen, the reality of what she had done crashing over her like a tidal wave, as she realized the man laying lifeless right in front of her was John Samuels. She had confronted her demons; yet even in this moment of victory, she knew that the shadows of the past would always be a part of her, echoes of the pain that would never completely fade.

As she remained there, rifle still raised, she understood that this was not just about vengeance; it was about reclaiming her life, about protecting the innocent, about honoring the memory of those she had loved and lost. And in that moment, she felt a sense of peace begin to settle in her heart, knowing that she had finally taken a stand against the darkness that had threatened to consume her.

With a steady hand, she picked up the child. She seemed unconscious. "You are safe now," Charlotte said with tenderness in her voice, as she turned and made her way back through the cavern.

***

Almost two years had passed. As Charlotte made her way to the courthouse, she was surrounded by a city alive with the vibrant tapestry of the holiday season. It was 9 a.m., December 8, 1986. The streets were bustling with activity, a mix of hurried footsteps and the rhythmic hum of traffic creating a symphony of urban life. The air was crisp and invigorating, carrying with it the faint scent of pine and fir trees from the Christmas trees lining the sidewalks and the enticing aroma of roasted chestnuts from street vendors.

The architecture of the city stood as a testament to its rich history and grandeur. Majestic federal buildings loomed with their neoclassical facades, their columns and porticos reminiscent of ancient Rome and Greece, lending an air of dignity and permanence to the capital. The Washington Monument pierced the sky, its marble surface gleaming in the winter sun, a silent guardian overlooking the nation's heart.

Along Pennsylvania Avenue, the majestic Capitol Building sat in regal splendor, its iconic dome framed against the clear blue sky. The National Mall stretched out like a green carpet, its vast expanse dotted with leafless trees that stood stark against the wintry landscape. The Smithsonian museums flanked the mall, their grand entrances inviting visitors to explore the treasures within.

The city was adorned with festive decorations, twinkling lights woven through the branches of trees, casting a warm and inviting glow. Wreaths hung from lampposts, and garlands draped elegantly over doorways, infusing the air with a sense of celebration and anticipation. The storefronts were a riot of color, their windows filled with elaborate displays that captured the whimsy and wonder of the season.

As Charlotte walked, the rhythmic clatter of her heels on the cobblestone sidewalks mingled with the distant sound of carolers singing beloved holiday tunes, their voices rising and falling in harmonious waves. The people around her moved with urgency, bundled in coats and scarves, their breath visible in the chilly air, creating small clouds that dissipated into the ether.

The vibrancy of the city was a striking contrast to the solemnity of her thoughts, yet it offered a comforting reminder of the life and energy that pulsed through the streets. As she approached the courthouse, its imposing stone facade loomed before her, a symbol of justice and order amidst the bustling chaos. Given the extensive nature of the federal crimes spanning Virginia and D.C., the prosecution and the defense had agreed to consolidate all cases in this very court, making it a pivotal location for the proceedings.

Charlotte paused for a moment, taking in the scene around her—the kaleidoscope of lights, the tapestry of sounds, the mosaic of people—and felt a strong conviction settling in her heart. The path she had walked was fraught with challenges, but the city, with its resilience and beauty, mirrored her own journey of strength and determination.

The federal courtroom was a hive of activity when Charlotte made her entrance. The scent of polished wood mingled with the faint aroma of leather-bound law books, creating an ambiance that was both stately and charged with expectation. The walls were adorned with dark mahogany paneling, their rich tones absorbing the soft, golden light streaming in through the high, arched windows. The light cast a warm glow over the room, accentuating the deep burgundy of the carpet that muffled the footsteps of those present.

The gallery was packed with spectators, their whispered conversations creating a gentle murmur that filled the space. Faces turned eagerly toward Charlotte as she walked down the aisle, her heart swelling with pride as she caught sight of her family. Her mother, father, and grandmother sat together, their expressions a mixture of relief and joy, while Jack Henry's supportive smile bolstered her confidence. Their presence was a beacon of encouragement, a testament to the journey they had all shared.

As Charlotte's gaze met Jack Henry's, a flood of memories washed over her. They had grown up together, attending the same schools and sharing countless adventures. Jack Henry had always been her protector, stepping in whenever someone tried to bully her, his unwavering loyalty a constant throughout their youth. They had spent endless summer afternoons fly-fishing and horse riding, their laughter echoing through the fields like a melody of innocence and joy. Their relationship had blossomed in high school, turning from friendship into something deeper, until the tides of life pulled them in different directions when she left for college.

Yet despite the years and the miles, Jack Henry had remained steadfast, reentering her life after his own marriage ended. He treated Charlotte like a princess, always ensuring her safety and comfort. He cooked for her, supported her in every endeavor, and was her sounding board for every opening statement, closing argument, and witness interrogation she rehearsed. They had weathered many storms together, and his presence in the courtroom was yet another testament to his unwavering support.

Just then, Charlotte paused for a brief moment, glancing down at her engagement ring. The light caught the facets of the stone, and she felt a swell of emotion. There had been moments of doubt, times when Charlotte wondered if their paths would ever cross again. But seeing him here, now, she felt a pang of guilt for ever questioning his loyalty. With a deep breath, she looked back at Jack Henry, their eyes locking once more. In that instant, she felt a renewed sense of certainty and gratitude for the unwavering love he had always shown her.

Charlotte moved with an air of assuredness, her attire a testament to her sharp intellect and refined elegance. Her tailored navy blazer hugged her figure perfectly, the fabric soft yet structured, creating a silhouette that exuded professionalism and grace. The blazer's deep hue complemented her complexion, the subtle sheen of the material catching the light with each step. Beneath the blazer, a crisp white blouse peeked out, its collar perfectly pressed and framing her face with an air of sophistication. The blouse's fabric was smooth and cool against her skin, a reminder of the meticulous preparation that had brought her to this moment.

Her tailored pencil skirt fell just below the knee, its sleek lines accentuating her poised posture as she walked. The skirt's fabric moved fluidly with her, a testament to its impeccable tailoring. Her legs were encased in sheer tights, their subtle shimmer adding a touch of elegance to her ensemble. On her feet, polished black heels clicked rhythmically against the wooden floor, their sound a steady beat that matched the cadence of her determined stride.

Charlotte's hair was styled in a sleek bun, a few soft tendrils artfully framing her face and enhancing her features. The style was both practical and elegant, a nod to her unwavering focus. Minimalist silver jewelry adorned her ears and wrist, the pieces catching the light with each movement, subtle yet striking. Her ensemble was a carefully curated reflection of her strength and grace, each element chosen to convey her readiness to make her mark in the realm of justice.

As she approached the small gate that separated the public from the lawyers, memories flooded her mind. She recalled her first day of law school, the judge's words ringing in her ears: "That is one of the great feelings of being a lawyer. Opening that small gate and closing it behind you is what separates the general public from a trial lawyer. Trust me when I say, that is an amazing feeling. A feeling that will never ever go away."

In that moment, standing before the gate, Charlotte felt a familiar exhilaration course through her veins. The anticipation of stepping into the sacred space of the courtroom, of crossing the threshold into the realm where justice was served, was as thrilling now as it had been then. She stopped for a moment, savoring the moment, before opening the gate and stepping into the well of the court.

She placed her coat and briefcase on a chair by the prosecution's desk, settling into the chair next to it, her nerves sharpening into focus. The room was a symphony of muted colors and hushed tones, the dark wood of the judge's bench contrasting with the soft beige of the walls. The ceiling soared overhead, its intricate moldings a testament to the grandeur of the space. The gallery sat in expectant silence, the air thick with the shared anticipation of the verdict.

Moments later, the judge entered, his presence commanding and authoritative, ready to hear the jury's verdict. A respectful silence fell over the courtroom as the bailiff announced the judge's arrival. All eyes turned toward the bench, anticipation hanging in the air as everyone awaited the jury's decision.

Charlotte stood, her heart pounding in her chest as she took in the significance of the moment. The world outside faded into oblivion, leaving only the solemnity of the proceedings. The judge's gaze swept over the courtroom, his expression inscrutable as he surveyed the assembled gathering. He then turned to the defendant.

"Mr. Adkins, please stand," he commanded, the weight of his words echoing in the stillness. Charlotte's breath caught in her throat as Mr. Adkins rose.

The judge began to read the verdict, each word striking like a hammer against an anvil. ""On the charges of Transportation of minors with intent to engage in criminal sexual activity ... guilty. On the charges of conspiracy to commit trafficking... guilty."" The pronouncement reverberated throughout the courtroom, a finality that resonated in the hearts of all present.

As the judge continued, Charlotte's mind began to drift, a wave of emotion washing over her. She closed her eyes for a brief moment, allowing the memories of Mari to envelop her—her smile, the warmth of her embrace beneath a starlit sky, the laughter shared around their last campfire together.

In that instant, Charlotte felt an overwhelming sense of closure, a bittersweet reminder of the journey that had brought her here. Justice was being served, and she was ready to embrace the future, knowing that Mari's spirit would forever be a part of her.

As the verdict echoed through the courtroom, Charlotte stood tall. She had found closure for her sister, Mari, and for herself. She felt a profound peace settle within her. In that moment, she was ready to face whatever came next.